BITTEN BY DESTINY

TRUE IMMORTALITY
BOOK 4

S. YOUNG

BITTEN BY DESTINY

A True Immortality Novel

By S. Young
Copyright © 2025 Samantha Young

Without limiting the rights under copyright reserved above, no part of this publication may be reproduced, stored in or introduced into a retrieval system, or transmitted, in any form, or by any means (electronic, mechanical, photocopying, recording or otherwise) without prior written permission of the above author of this book.
This is a work of fiction. Names, characters, places, and incidents are either the product of the author's imagination or are used fictitiously. Any resemblance to actual events, locales, or persons, living or dead, is coincidental.
This work is registered with and protected by Copyright House.

Edited by Jennifer Sommersby Young
Proofread by Julie Deaton
Cover Design by Hang Le
Couple Cover Photography by Wander Aguiar

OTHER TITLES BY S. YOUNG

War of Hearts (A True Immortality Novel)

Kiss of Vengeance (A True Immortality Novel)

Kiss of Eternity (A True Immortality Short Story)

Hunted (War of the Covens 1)

Destined (War of the Covens 2)

Ascended (War of the Covens 3)

The Seven Kings of Jinn (Seven Kings of Jinn 1)

Of Wish and Fury (Seven Kings of Jinn 2)

Queen of Shadow and Ash (Seven Kings of Jinn 3)

The Law of Stars and Sultans (Seven Kings of Jinn 4)

Fear of Fire and Shadow

PRONUNCIATIONS

Niamh – Neev
Kiyo – Kee-yo

Irish Gaelic (Connacht dialect)
Fionn – Fee-on
Aine – Awn-ya
An Breitheamh – Un Bre-huv
An Caoimhnóir – Un Keev-neer
Mo Chroí – Muh Kree
Mo Ghrá – Muh Graw
Aoibhinn – Ay-veen
Caoimhe – Kee-va
Diarmuid – Dear-mid
Samhradh – Sow-ruh
Solas – Sol-as
Geimhreadh – Geev-ru
Réalta – Rail-tuh
Earrach – Err-ack
Fómhar – Foe-var

Éireann – Air-un

Scottish Slang

'nae' on the end of a word is the equivalent of ''nt', the contraction of 'not'.
Didnae – Didn't
Dinnae – Don't

Scottish Gaelic

Ceannsaichidh an Fhìrinn – Cyown-seech-ee in yeer-in
Mhairi – Var-ee

*For my readers, who patiently waited until I could find the right words to bring Thea, Conall, Rose, Fionn, Niamh, Kiyo, Elijah, and Echo's story to a conclusion I hope is worthy of them.
With love and gratitude.
Sam xo*

PROLOGUE

Something infiltrated her dreams, an annoying buzzing.

Echo grunted into her pillow, squeezing it around her face to drown out the noise. Even with the silk pillowcase smothering her nose, the dark, coppery tang of blood and peaty whisky filled her nostrils.

She stiffened.

I don't own silk pillowcases.

The hair rising on the back of her neck, Echo lifted her head slowly and opened her eyes to the dimly lit room. When she was still human, she and the girls from her boarding school snuck out one night and got drunk in the woods. The next day, her mouth felt filled with cotton wool, her body weighted with rocks, her stomach weak, and an invisible person had taken up residence in her head with a large drum they wouldn't stop beating.

Fragile.

She'd felt fragile.

Echo hadn't experienced fragility since the ritual that turned her into a vampire when she was twenty years old.

Until now.

Which could only mean one thing.

There was blood on the cream silk pillowcase that didn't belong to her. The blood or the silk. Glancing to the side, she saw her phone on a nightstand next to a half-empty glass of whisky.

A little moan at her back filled her with dread.

Pushing herself onto her knees, horror filled her to see blood splattered all over the sheets. And lying beside her was the worst bed partner imaginable.

Roark Bakker.

Born with a silver spoon in his mouth seventy years ago, he was entitled, spoiled, and ambitious. Echo genuinely hated the son of a bitch. To get closer to William, he'd been hounding Echo for six years to become his mate.

Revulsion filled her as she looked at the sleeping vampire. He was handsome in slumber. Or he might have been if she didn't loathe him so much. Plus, he was covered in blood, dried around his mouth and chin.

The owners of the blood that decorated Roark and the bedding were curled up on his other side. Twin humans. Barely legal from the look of them.

Echo suddenly remembered the events of the last few nights.

Her investigations had only confirmed the files Niamh Farren had given her three weeks ago. Destroyed by the realization her father was truly a monster, Echo was feeling particularly destructive when Roark came to visit. She'd let him take her to his favorite club.

Their nights together since had been filled with nothing but getting drunk on human blood, chasing it with whisky, and fucking until dawn. She looked down at her naked body and saw the dried blood splattered across her breasts and in her hair.

Her stomach turned.

"Cream silk sheets? Really?"

"I like to see the blood. I buy new sheets every week."

She remembered sneering at Roark even in her drunken state as they stumbled into his bedroom with the redheaded twins they'd met at the club ... and two young men.

Echo's eyes darted around the room. Naked, blood on their necks where their now-healed puncture wounds would have been, were the two men she'd picked up. They were wrapped around each other in sleep. Last night, she'd let them devour her before she'd literally devoured them.

Seeing the steady rise and fall of their chests, Echo could only be glad she'd had enough control to not cause them any permanent damage.

Self-recrimination filled her. Automatically, her first thought was what would her father think of her reckless behavior? Then she remembered what had led her to her bender in the first place. What did it matter? Nothing mattered now. Everything she'd been raised to believe was a fucking lie.

The annoying noise that had woken her earlier chirped again.

It was her cell phone ringing.

She reached for it, swaying with her hangover, and almost dropped the damn thing at the realization it might be her father calling. But then she saw Odette's name on the screen.

Odette.

How could she have forgotten Odette in all this? *Stupid, stupid!* She answered, turning from the wretched sight of Roark. Echo shuddered. "Hey, little darling." Her voice sounded croaky even to her ears.

Her sister's voice was not only a balm to her pain, but a big reality check. "Where have you been? I've been calling for two days!"

Remorse filled her.

How could she forget Odette?

So selfish. "I'm sorry. I've been working on something for ... Father." It was difficult to call him that now. Although she'd always known she was adopted by William "the Bloody" Payne, she'd thought his actions benevolent. He was her hero. She hadn't realized the reason she'd needed adoption in the first place was because he was a cruel psychopath.

How many people in The Garm knew what he'd done to her?

"Oh. Well ... okay, then." Odette sighed. "I just really needed to talk about something."

"I'm sorry." The hair on Echo's nape rose again, and she turned her head slowly. Her eyes met the black of Roark's. He smirked and reached out to draw his finger across her nipple.

Enraged, Echo swatted his hand away, and he burst out laughing.

"Who is that?" Odette asked, having heard.

"No one." Echo glowered at Roark in warning. "Can I call you back? I won't be long, I promise."

Her sister heaved another heavy sigh. "Okay."

Echo hung up and moved to get off the bed.

Roark wrapped a hand around her wrist to stop her.

Despite the fact she'd only been a vampire for six years and he for forty, Echo broke his hold with ease. She was strong for a young vampire. This had pleased her fath—William—very much.

Disgusted with William, with herself, and always with Roark, Echo got off the bed and searched the room for her clothes.

"You can't leave," Roark said, his voice husky. "The sun hasn't set yet."

Echo's back straightened at the reminder, and she glared at the window. It was fitted with state-of-the-art blackout blinds, much like the ones in her own apartment. For six years, she'd told herself William loved her, that turning her was a gift she should be grateful for. Echo had buried her grief over losing the daylight. At knowing she'd never watch a sunrise again or close her eyes and turn her face toward the sun to feel its warmth on her skin.

Now she knew the truth.

William had stolen *everything* from her.

He'd trapped her in this hellish, eternal night.

And she was going to make him pay for it.

But first ... she needed to make sure he never got the chance to do what he'd done to her, to Odette.

Odette.

She was the bucket of ice-cold water Echo needed to pull herself out of her pity spiral.

Though he made no sound, she sensed Roark cross the room seconds before his arms slid around her waist. He jerked her against his hard, naked body and pulled her hair aside so he could glide his tongue up her neck.

Echo's stomach turned. "If you don't release me this second, I'm going to cut off that thing prodding my ass."

Roark chuckled and gave her a squeeze. "You know, you only make me want you more when you resist."

"That's because you're sick." She broke away from him, turning to glare into his pretty-boy face. "Does William know about your hedonism? Is this why you can't quite make your way into the inner circle?"

His eyes narrowed. "I *am* the inner circle."

She taunted, "No, sweetheart, *I'm* the inner circle. And as someone definitely *in* the inner circle, I know when someone *isn't*."

"You think your father hasn't fucked and sucked his way through a million orgies?" Roark snapped. "I've witnessed him do it! Wake up, princess! This is the real world." He gestured behind him to the four humans sprawled across his bedroom. "All that bullshit Payne feeds you about control and respect and feeding for necessity, not for pleasure, is just his fucked-up way of keeping you on his leash."

Well trained by William, Echo didn't flinch, even though she felt Roark's words score through her like the tip of a wooden stake.

He was right. She had no doubt William lied about feeding from humans for mere necessity. It would all have been part of the image he wanted to present to Echo.

An honorable vampire. A supernatural with a mission. Hard, but fair.

He was none of those things.

For twenty-six years, she'd been raised to believe that he and his now-dead boss Eirik led their organization, The Garm, with altruistic purpose. To find the prophesied fae-borne and kill them before they could open the gates to Faerie. Eirik had been to Faerie. Had lived when the fae walked among humans freely. It was a dark age, he'd told her.

The fae were to be hated, spurned, killed.

And yet, she'd discovered only days after her appearance in Echo's apartment that Niamh Farren wasn't a witch like she'd suspected. William had finally entrusted Echo with their game plan and shown her the files The Garm had on those they knew were definitely fae. He'd shown her images of the ones The Garm had hunted and killed. Three of the seven were dead. Of those who were left, they'd identified two, plus an extra fae who had nothing to do with the prophecy.

A petite brunette named Rose Kelly.

A hulking, ancient Celtic king, Fionn Mór, not fae-borne but made fae by the Faerie Queen herself, and now mated to Rose Kelly. *A dangerous mating*, William had said.

And a tall, willowy blond Echo had recognized immediately.

Niamh Farren.

She'd kept her expression clear of any recognition as William explained who Niamh was—a particularly powerful Irish fae with psychic abilities.

Three weeks ago, Niamh Farren broke into Echo's apartment undetected by William's men who watched her place. She disabled the bugs Echo knew William had planted. And then

Niamh dropped files at Echo's feet filled with information that blew her world apart. At the time, Echo had sensed her magic and thought her a witch.

Now she knew Niamh was a fae. And psychic. It would explain how she knew about Echo's mother and father. And why she'd brought the files to her in the first place. To undermine William. To drive a wedge between him and his daughter.

Mission accomplished.

Taking the information William shared, Echo had done her own digging. Not just on her parents, but on Niamh.

Everywhere the psychic had been spotted in the last year, Echo found news articles on miracle events. Human accidents and crimes that had been averted. Niamh Farren had presumably been using her fae gifts to save people.

Not exactly the monster William had painted the fae to be.

But more than that ... Echo remembered the feeling she'd gotten from Niamh as the blond stood in her apartment.

She couldn't explain it, other than it was almost spiritual. Like she was standing before a being who was pure of heart. Sounded cheesy and trippy when she said it like that, but Echo didn't know how else to explain it.

And the truth was, she no longer knew what to believe about the prophecy, about The Garm. They'd killed innocent people in their mission, and she'd compartmentalized that. They were casualties of war.

Or were they?

Maybe they were casualties of Eirik's and William's madness, of their desperate desire to remain at the top of the food chain.

Glaring at Roark, who wanted to be one of them, Echo demanded, "Clothes. Now."

He rolled his eyes like a child. "For a moment there, I actually thought you were loosening up. But you're still wound tighter than a fucking nun."

"That's a contradiction," she muttered under her breath as she searched the bedroom for her clothing.

"What?" he snapped at her back.

"Nothing. Clothes."

Suddenly, Roark grabbed at her again, and all the rage simmering deep inside Echo threatened to escape. She spun in his arms, pressed her palms to his chest, and flew them across the room at vamp speed, slamming him so hard into his wall, the plasterwork crumbled around him.

"Touch me again without my permission, and I'll cut off your cock and make you watch as I cook it for William's wolves."

Roark shoved her off and she stumbled back, readying to fight.

Instead, he gestured at the damage behind him. "You owe me a wall."

"You owe me two nights of my life I'd like to throw up and forget, so I guess we're even."

Finally spotting her jeans and shirt, Echo whipped them from the floor and threw them over her shoulder. "I'm using your shower. Follow me and die."

"One day, you'll be mine again," Roark taunted.

"Again." Echo looked back at him pitilessly. "We fucked, Roark. If that was all it took, there would be a football team of men out there calling me theirs. But that's *not* what it takes. So get this through that thick skull of yours now ... I will never, *ever* belong to you."

As she stepped into his luxurious shower, unable to relax for fear he would ignore her and follow her in, Echo washed the dried blood from her body as realization settled over her.

She would never, ever belong to anyone.

She wouldn't live long enough to.

Not after she executed the plan forming in her mind.

It was a vampire's supernatural sixth sense to know when the sun had risen and set. As Echo rinsed the last of the blood from her hair, she perceived the sun had disappeared behind the horizon. Relieved, she dried and clothed herself and stalked out of the bathroom. Roark was again in bed with the still-sleeping twins.

"Your cell rang." He tossed it at her and smirked. "It was Daddy Dearest. I hope you don't mind that I answered."

Shaking her head at his childish antics, Echo checked the call list. It didn't matter if Roark answered. Echo was fully aware William had her under surveillance since her move to Munich. The Garm's headquarters were here. She wasn't constantly tailed, but her apartment was bugged, and now and then, she sensed she was being followed.

William would already know about Roark.

She let herself believe William's measures were put in place because of his position and his fear that someone would use Echo against him. Now she knew differently. It wasn't about love. It was about control.

She was nothing more than a tool of revenge.

Without another word to the asshole, Echo strode out of his apartment, hurrying down the stairwell and into the open night air. She took in a lungful of oxygen. Vampires weren't dead like the myths suggested. They breathed, their hearts beat, and they ate and drank human food. But they needed blood so they wouldn't starve. Unless they were decapitated, staked in the heart with wood, or had their heart ripped from their chest, a vampire, like the fae, would live forever. Despite breathing, a vampire's supernatural healing powers meant they'd never die of oxygen deprivation.

And yet, maybe because she knew that, Echo had never really experienced the joy of her lungs filling with crisp, fresh air since she'd turned. So many little things, so many big things she missed about being human.

That grief crawled across her, and she shoved it back.

No time for that.

Hitting speed dial on her cell, she called William.

"She lives," he answered coldly.

"I fucked up. Got drunk. Hated it. I'm currently disgusted with myself and would appreciate a distraction." She said all the words she knew William needed to hear.

"You do realize this will only make him hunt you for longer, and his financial resources are too important for me to kill him for touching you."

Hearing the true anger in William's words, Echo strode down the street toward her apartment. She was William's possession. His to give to whomever he wanted. How was she only starting to see this now? "I can deal with Roark. Is that why you called? Or is there business I need to attend to?"

"Headquarters. Now." He hung up.

Roark owned the entire apartment building he lived in, an art nouveau residence in the heart of Maxvorstadt. It was an impressive investment, his penthouse the height of luxury. But even it didn't compare to The Garm headquarters, only several blocks from Echo's apartment in Seeligerstraße. Pulling shadows around her body to hide her unnatural speed from the humans, Echo sped across the city, covering the hour walk in just ten minutes.

William had turned his €8 million townhouse and four of the neighboring houses worth millions of euros into The Garm headquarters after Eirik was killed. William's was a modern house with Scandinavian influence, inspired by William's friendship with Eirik. It was not at all what anyone would expect of a supernatural intelligence operation. Which was the point. William hired powerful witches and warlocks to spell the headquarters from attention from the human world.

Several vampires guarded the houses at night, while werewolves guarded them during the day. The two vampires guarding the main entrance to William's recognized her and nodded as she moved past them and into the house. The place was always buzzing with supes. Nodding at folks as she moved, Echo could thank William for his training, at least. Without it, she'd never be able to face these people. She'd never be able to face him.

"He's in his office," Orla, a two-hundred-year-old vampire, promoted to second-in-command after Eirik died and William took over, gestured to the office as Echo approached. "He wants to see you alone."

Trying not to worry about what that meant, Echo kept her expression placid and strode in, closing the door behind her. Bright lights illuminated the Scandi-designed space. Sleek, minimal, a hidden place for everything so it never looked cluttered.

William sat on the edge of his desk, staring at her expressionlessly. At just over five hundred years old, William was one of the most powerful supernaturals in the world. The son of a wealthy London merchant, William had wanted for nothing and thus grown into an industrious and handsome man. When he was thirty years old, married, a father himself, he'd gone on one of his many work trips to France to buy French wares to sell back in England. It was there he caught the eye of a French aristocrat who'd turned him.

He was tall, broad of shoulder, had thick dark hair, and ice-blue eyes.

Cold, emotionless eyes.

My God, I've been so blind.

"F-father," she forced out in greeting.

He looked away, the muscle in his jaw twitching. "Am I to brush off the last two nights of debauchery as youthful impetus that is never to be repeated? Or should I be concerned?"

"Youthful impetus. Believe me, no one is kicking my ass more than I am right now."

His blue eyes seared right through her. "Why?"

Knowing what he asked, Echo shrugged. She'd already

thought of an excuse that could be verified as truth. "Do you remember my friend Cassandra from boarding school?"

"The one who got you drunk on vodka when you were but sixteen?"

Echo shrugged again. "I bumped into her at a restaurant here in Munich." She didn't lie. She had, in fact, bumped into Cassandra a few evenings ago and spent much of the encounter evading questions about her life. "Here, of all places." Their boarding school had been in Canada. "I … I faltered briefly. Forgot to be grateful for the gift you've given me."

Understanding dawned. "You grieve your human life."

"I know it was ungrateful."

He sighed and shook his head. "I forget how young you are. Your physical strength and professionalism belie your years. It is quite normal to grieve for these things at your age. Know it will pass."

I hate you. I want to drive a wooden stake through your fucking black heart and watch the horror on your face, knowing it was me who ended you. "Thank you for your understanding, Father."

He nodded abruptly. "You are done with it now? You feel … strong again?"

"Absolutely."

"Good." William picked up the iPad on his desk and handed it to her. "Because you're going to Vienna."

Surprised, Echo looked at the screen and saw an image of a familiar man. She wasn't sure why he was so familiar until she read the information on the screen. Looking up at William, she frowned. "Why are we interested in a rock star?"

"Because word in the magical community is that he's a powerful warlock."

"Okay?"

William curled his lip in disgust. "But there are those who

suspect he is able to do magic without taking energy from the Earth and its occupants."

Echo's pulse began to race. "You suspect he's one of the fae-borne."

"I'm not sure. But, as always, we must investigate. I need someone young, beautiful, smart, and strong to infiltrate his life and uncover his origins."

Her eyes narrowed. "You want me to seduce it out of him?"

"If it comes to that."

"Why me?"

"Well, you are all the above … and it's time you made your mark here. If anything were to happen to me, I want *you* to take over, not Orla."

Shocked, Echo raised an eyebrow. "Does Orla know that?"

"She does. And she will accept it … if you prove yourself." He pointed to the iPad. "If Elijah Webb is one of the fae … you're going to kill him and cement your position as my second-in-command."

1

THE CROWD WAS ALREADY SINGING one of their songs, and they hadn't even taken to the stage.

Elijah looked over at his bandmates, and Phil grinned at him. "Never gets old, mate."

He shook his head, grinning back. No, it never got old.

"I still can't believe we're playing at Arena." Adam flipped a drumstick, feet bouncing, buzzing to play.

To be fair, Elijah was buzzing too. Arena in Vienna was one of the most iconic music venues in Europe. It was an old slaughterhouse, covered in graffiti, and within its walls was a courtyard where some of the best rock bands in the world had played. Now they were among them. And on this surprisingly warm May evening, the open-air venue was ideal.

His cell buzzed in the back pocket of his jeans—a text from his mum. He opened it.

Good luck, darling! Have another amazing gig! Love, Mum and Dad xx

Elijah's grin widened and he quickly texted back a thank-you and "I love you too."

"Mummy again?" his bass player Jamal teased.

"You're just jealous." Elijah winked.

Phil snorted. "If the fans knew you were such a mummy's boy, we'd never sell tickets."

"Good thing they'll never know then, huh?" He clapped Phil on the back just as the crowd's yells grew impatient. "Time to do this, boys."

As he led the band onto the stage, Elijah took hold of that golden hum of power within and let it gently exude out of him. He'd noticed years ago that it affected the boys in the best way, allowing them to play gig after gig without becoming as exhausted as they should. It meant they rarely, if ever, had an off gig.

The roar of the crowd blasted into the four of them as they took their positions. A rush of adrenaline flooded Elijah, and he grinned wickedly at a group of young women at the front. They screamed hysterically, and Elijah turned to catch Jamal's eye. "Mummy's boy?" he mouthed, gesturing to himself.

Jamal laughed. "Just fucking start, you vain prick."

Chuckling, Elijah looked back out at the hundreds of fans before them and raised a fist. That's all it took. They stamped their feet, the thundering noise flowing up toward the stage like a crashing wave.

"Hello, Vienna!" he yelled into the mic, and the screaming went beyond deafening. "We're the Strix."

He let the ensuing roar reach new heights, and then Phil, his guitarist, fed up with Elijah milking it, played the first notes of their latest hit, "Afterlife."

There was nothing like the buzz of being onstage, of having hundreds of people singing the Strix's songs back at them. They'd played much bigger venues, but there was something about the smaller, iconic places that added an extra touch of magic.

At one point, through the glare of the stage lights, Elijah started one of their slower, romantic songs (written by Phil for his fiancée Nicole) to one of the young women at the front. The pretty brunette and her friends grew more hysterical as he held eye contact with her. And then suddenly, the brunette's eyes rolled back in her head, and she crumpled between her friends.

They reached to grab the unconscious woman. It wasn't the first time he'd made a fan faint, but it never stopped being a little disconcerting. He liked driving them wild ... he didn't like driving them unconscious. Especially in a crowd this rough. They were pushing around the women, uncaring they might trample them.

"Back up!" he shouted at the people behind. His bandmates followed suit and stopped playing. "Give them room. Can we get a medic in the front row?" He directed toward stage left where the staff hovered.

Jamal caught his eye and said into his mic, "Making them faint again, Eli?"

He grimaced at his bandmate's teasing as the crowd laughed.

Once the paramedics had safely removed the brunette and her friends from the crowd, Elijah apologized to the fans, and they restarted the song. This time, he didn't sing it directly at anyone. Soon the incident was forgotten, and the two-hour set flew by.

Even after their encore, the crowd demanded more.

"It's never fucking enough," Phil griped, wiping a towel across his sweat-soaked forehead as the manager led them back to their dressing room, a place they wouldn't be staying long. At least Elijah wouldn't. He was still vibrating with unleashed energy.

"Be grateful, you grumpy fuck," Jamal said as they disappeared into the room. As soon as the door shut, they technically couldn't hear the crowd anymore, but for hours after a gig, Elijah still heard the roar in his ears.

"I am grateful. I'm also bloody knackered."

Elijah frowned. Maybe he hadn't poured enough energy into the guys tonight. Patting Phil on the shoulder, he leaked some of that energy into his friend. "Only a few more gigs. Belgium. Then home."

Yeah, their tour was almost over. As always, Elijah experienced a mixture of deflation and relief.

Phil's eyes brightened ever so slightly. "You're right. And you know what, I'm not actually that tired. Guess I'm just missing Nicole and Alex."

"Still can't believe you've got a two-year-old, mate." Jamal shook his head. "You're making me feel old."

"Why? I'm the one with the kid." His expression fell. "Who I haven't seen in weeks."

"We'll all be back in London before we know it," Adam said. "Let's enjoy being here. I read about this bar just five minutes away. Let's go get fucked."

"Not me." Phil stood. "You know Nicole doesn't like it."

"Pussy-whipped." Adam glared at him.

"Don't start. I wouldn't like it if she was out clubbing with her mates, and she's not a bloody famous musician with groupies trying to stick their hands down her fucking trousers all the time."

"Leave off him." Jamal shoved Adam playfully. "I'm not going either. I just want to read a bit."

Adam shook his head in amazement. "Read a bit? You're the hot bass player from the Strix. Besides pretty boy here"—he gestured to Elijah—"you're the one the fans want to see. And you're going to read a book?"

Smirking at Jamal's beleaguered expression, Elijah snorted. The members of the Strix hadn't started out as the rock stars they were now. Once upon a time, they were all geeks who schoolyard bullies got a kick out of abusing. The bookish, intelligent, reserved boy in Jamal had never really gone away, and Elijah wouldn't want it to. Adam was the only one who'd let their fame go to his head. Elijah liked to play into it, but he was careful not to allow his ego off its leash.

"Let him read his book, for Christ's sake." Elijah grinned at Adam. "I'll come with you."

"At least one of you isn't a pussy-whipped swot."

"Adam, I love you, mate, but you're such a prick sometimes." Elijah pushed him toward the door. "Night, lads," he called back to Jamal and Phil. "See you back at the hotel in the morning."

"Make sure he doesn't end up the cover story for an Austrian newspaper," Jamal warned.

Elijah nodded in promise and followed Adam out.

Their security met up to escort them, and all the time Elijah pretended to listen to his friend whine about their bandmates. Sensing his agitation growing, Elijah smacked Adam on the shoulder and filtered a little calming energy into him. Almost immediately, his attitude changed.

"I suppose I understand it with Phil. He's got his bird to think about. But what's Jamal's deal?"

Elijah couldn't answer as they left Arena, their security shoving them forcefully toward the SUV as screaming fans tried to push past to grab hold of them. It was weird how used to that he'd gotten. At first, it had been jarring as hell.

Once they were ensconced inside the vehicle and the driver had directions for their destination, Elijah answered Adam. "Before we were the Strix, you never gave Jamal shit for being who he is."

Adam frowned. "What do you mean?"

"Other than a great bass player, Jamal was always quiet, read a lot, and liked his own space. That didn't change because we got famous. And why should it? You giving him shit for it makes you a dick."

The drummer scowled. "A dick?"

"Yes, a dick."

"I'm not the one the fans care about. It's not me and Phil plastered across fan sites or the media. It's you and Jamal. It's always the best-looking ones who get all the attention."

"Do you hear yourself?" Elijah sighed. Maybe a break from the band was a good thing after all. "Are you ever without men and women throwing themselves on your cock?"

Adam frowned. "No."

"As a virile, bisexual man, do you not enjoy the sexual benefits of being the drummer in a famous rock band?"

Rolling his eyes, Adam sighed. "I get your point."

"Then stop complaining and worrying about what everyone else is doing, and just enjoy yourself."

"My point is that no one recognizes me unless I'm with one of you."

"I'm with you right now. Jesus, you're giving me a migraine." He sent out another calming wave of energy toward Adam.

"You're right." Adam gave him an apologetic, somewhat loopy smile. "I'm being a total prick. Let's just enjoy the rest of the night. I'll apologize to the boys in the morning."

Thank God for that.

Minutes later, the driver pulled up to the club Adam had picked. A long line to get in stretched down the block. One of their security team spoke quietly to the doorman as the waiting clubbers started to recognize him and Adam. Whispered excitement lit the night air, but thankfully their security ushered them inside. The doormen must have communicated to the management because a tall, gorgeous redhead appeared before them and introduced herself as the manager.

"There is a dance club in the basement," she said in perfect English as she sashayed ahead of them, leading the two men across the bar in her tight black dress. "For now, allow me to offer this complimentary VIP area for your use only." She stopped at a raised, roped-off area that held two large, blue velvet banquettes, a space big enough for them to host a small party.

"And will you be joining us?" Adam flirted with the gorgeous manager.

She lifted her left hand to smooth back an imaginary hair from her face. A large diamond glinted on her ring finger. "I'm afraid not."

"Too bad." He winked at her. "Dom Pérignon for the table, then."

"A pint of ale for me," Elijah interjected. "Something local."

The redhead nodded. "Of course." She gestured across the room and another beautiful young woman, this one a brunette, strode toward them. She wore a similar tight black dress and killer stiletto heels. "The VIP area comes with your own personal server. Gentlemen, this is Leoni, and she will be looking after you this evening."

Leoni beamed at them, her dark gaze locking on Elijah, hot with intent.

He grinned as he dragged his eyes down her supple body. If she was offering, he was taking.

"Lucky bastard," Adam muttered at his side.

Ignoring him, Elijah settled down on the plush banquette and repeated his order to Leoni. Their security hovered on the edges of the VIP area, always alert. And drawing attention from the club goers as the room filled.

"I think I might check out the dance club," Adam said loudly to be heard over the music. Elijah didn't need him to raise his voice. He'd realized at a very young age he had better hearing than the average person.

But before Adam could leave, a group of three women and a young man appeared before the ropes. "We're huge fans!" a blond yelled. "We'd love to buy you a drink!"

Elijah's bandmate welcomed the group onto the banquette, and Elijah turned on the charm for the blond who practically shoved her way past Adam to get to him. He tried not to laugh and gave her his entire attention. It cost him nothing, and it made her night.

A few pints of ale for him later, and the blond grew a little touchy-feely, her hand smoothing over his thigh as they chatted. He frowned, wondering how to react. He'd already decided he was leaving with Leoni tonight. He didn't want to get the little blond's hopes up.

Suddenly, the hair on the back of Elijah's nape rose, and shivers cascaded down his spine. A strange heat pooled in his groin, and instinct had him lifting his gaze out toward the club.

Like he was a magnet and she his opposite piece, Elijah's focus zeroed in on a beautiful woman sitting at the bar. The pendant lights made her face completely visible in the otherwise moodily lit club.

His heart thumped in his chest.

Fuck, she was stunning.

And she was watching him.

As if his feet had a mind of their own, Elijah was abruptly moving, ignoring the protests from his companions as he stepped over the rope with ease and strode across the room to the bar. A few hands touched him. People did that. It was strange. Like he was a god or something. Unnerving.

Ignoring it, he didn't stop until he was right before her.

She twisted on the bar stool to face him. Much like every other woman in the club, she wore a short, tight dress. Her legs were long, slender, shapely. Amazing fucking legs. Skin was pale, but silky smooth like ivory. Thick, gleaming blond hair cascaded down around her shoulders in waves. Mesmerizing jade eyes. Her features were refined, elegant. She was beautiful, but no more beautiful than many women he'd met. And yet she was. She was definitely the most beautiful bloody woman he'd ever seen, and he couldn't explain why.

And then she tilted her head in the light, and those jade eyes momentarily flashed silver, the color of mercury.

Elijah raised an eyebrow as he let his senses completely open.

This was no ordinary woman.

She was a vampire.

Did she sense his magic, his power? He knew he was a draw to supernatural beasties that went bump in the night. Apparently, more so than other warlocks. Something about his blood, perhaps. Maybe he smelled extra tasty.

Turning to the man who sat at the bar beside the vampire, Elijah asked politely, "May I have this seat?"

The man frowned at him, about to argue, and Elijah stared deeply into his eyes and sent out a mental suggestion toward him. "You want me to have this seat, don't you, mate?"

He nodded and slipped off the stool, disappearing into the dark of the club. Elijah took his place and turned to the vampire. They studied each other again, and he realized his pulse was still racing too fast. She excited him, and she hadn't even opened her mouth.

"I'm Elijah."

"I know who you are," she replied in an American accent. "I was at Arena tonight."

He was disappointed. Weirdly, he didn't want her to be a fan. "Ah, I see."

"Do you?" She smirked.

He frowned. "What does that mean?"

"I'm a journalist for a paper in Toronto." Not American, then. Canadian. "Not a music journalist, but my colleague who's been following your European tour got really sick. With only a few dates left, they asked me to fly out to cover. I don't know why. I don't know a lot about your music. Sorry."

Relieved, Elijah grinned. "Don't apologize. I prefer it."

She raised an eyebrow. "Really?"

"Believe it or not, yes." He frowned, realizing something. He leaned toward her. "Does being a vampire make your job difficult?"

Amusement sparked in her eyes, but it couldn't hide her sadness. Or was he just sensing sadness from her? And something else underlying. Something black, like rage.

Elijah pulled away from her.

How could he sense that?

Fuck, was he actually drunk for once?

Shaking his head at his own nonsense, he focused as she replied, "You know what I am. Good. Whatever you are drew me to this bar tonight."

Whatever *he* was? Didn't she know? Perhaps she was a newbie vamp. In human years, she didn't look much older than twenty, twenty-one. "I'm a warlock, love. Haven't you met one before?"

She tilted her head again, eyes flashing silver in the light once more. Her expression was unreadable, but Elijah had the feeling she was trying to read him. "A warlock? I have met witches and warlocks. You ... you must be more powerful than they were."

Dangerous ground.

He shrugged. "You know my name." He changed the subject. "But I don't know yours."

"Echo."

"Pardon?"

"My name. Echo."

It suited her perfectly. "A very unusual name. Wasn't Echo a nymph in Greek mythology who withered away from unrequited love until all that was left was her voice?"

Her smile died, her expression neutral. Annoyingly so. "You know your mythology. Impressive for a rock star."

"Contrary to popular belief, many of us do know how to read," he teased.

Echo's lips curled at the corners. What he wouldn't give to see her really smile. Or laugh. Elijah sensed she hadn't laughed in a while. For having only met the vampire, that didn't sit right with him at all. She should have many reasons to laugh.

"Apologies for presuming."

"No apology necessary. So … Echo." He leaned into her. "Can I buy you a drink?"

Her gaze fell to his neck, and she licked her lips.

The mere thought of her biting him sent a sharp blade of lust through his groin, surprising the hell out of him.

As if she could read his mind, her nostrils flared, shock lighting her gorgeous eyes. She swallowed hard and looked away. "Sure." She didn't speak loudly to be heard over the music, knowing he could hear her just fine. "House red."

"Was that innuendo?" he teased.

Her gaze flew back to him. "No, I didn't mean …" She trailed off at his laughing expression and rolled her eyes. "You're kidding. Right."

Laughing, Elijah tapped the bar top to get the server's attention and ordered a red wine and another ale.

He sensed her attention on him and liked it. Elijah turned to lock gazes again. "Tell me about yourself."

"Do you really want to know? Or do you think you're obliged to ask so I'll fuck you tonight?"

Chuckling at her bluntness, excitement flooded Elijah's veins. "You don't beat around the bush, do you?"

"I'm not really the kind of girl who likes to be a bush among many."

He grinned harder. "Is that how you think we rock stars work? Fucking our way across the world?"

"Absolutely. Would you deny it?"

"No," he replied honestly.

She lowered her eyes, hiding her expression from him, and he hated the loss of connection. Far more strongly than he should for having just met her. What was it about her? It couldn't be the vampire thing.

Since walking through the golden gates of the rich and famous to enter their elite world, he'd discovered he wasn't so different after all. Vampires and werewolves and witches and warlocks were real, as were other supernatural beasties. But the former were the ones at the top of the food chain, vampires at the very top since they were immortal. He'd partied with them before. Never had sex with one. His instincts, until now, had warned him not to. Same with werewolves. He'd steered clear despite their many attractions.

He had fucked a witch or two in the past, though.

"I saw that girl faint at the concert tonight," Echo continued. "Is that what you expect? For women ... and maybe men too ... to swoon at your feet?"

"Just women," he clarified. "And no, I don't expect that. Not at all."

"Oh dear. Is the poor little rock star growing weary of the adoration?"

Elijah found himself amused. "What if I am?"

"I don't believe you."

"You know ... it's weird, but until this very moment, I wasn't weary of it. But I find your utter lack of deference strangely erotic."

To his delight, Echo laughed. It was a low, husky sound that heated his blood. He had to stop himself from reaching for her. He wanted to wrap his hand around her nape and claim her with a kiss that would rock both their bloody worlds.

He'd been attracted to women upon meeting them, but never with such a visceral, electric desire to throw her on the nearest bed and fuck her until they were both wrung dry.

Holy hell. "Come back to my hotel with me," he blurted.

In answer, Echo studied him. Thoughtfully. So long, Elijah nearly opened his mouth to beg her. He didn't beg for anything.

Then suddenly, Echo hopped off her stool with the speed and lightness of a supernatural being. Flutters awoke in his gut as the vampire pressed in between his legs. And then she did what *he* had wanted to do.

Echo wrapped her hand around his nape, curled her fingers tight into his hair, and pulled him toward her. As soon as her lips brushed his, electricity sparked through him. She teased, whispering her mouth over his for a second or two before finally kissing him properly.

Possessiveness flooded him, and he gripped her waist tight to hold her to him, taking over her kiss, deepening it, forcing her lips open so he could slide his tongue against hers.

Echo's whimper made him instantly hard, and he chased her for more, devouring her.

Elijah completely forgot where they were as he tried to pull her closer.

But suddenly, his hands were holding air and his lips were missing hers.

Blinking rapidly, dazed, to his disappointment when he focused, he found Echo standing a foot away. Over the loud music, she spoke. "I'll be in Brussels for your gig. I'm staying at the Heritage. It's not far from the venue. I'll leave your name and an extra room card at the front desk. If you still want me when you're sober, come get me."

Frustrated and angry at being deprived of her, Elijah opened his mouth to argue that he wasn't fucking drunk, but she was already moving across the club away from him.

And then it occurred to him this was a game.

Echo wanted to control this thing.

Didn't want to be just another groupie who fell on his cock.

Annoyed, Elijah slid off the stool and willed his arousal to fade.

He shouldn't play her game.

Shouldn't chase her.

And yet, he could still taste her on his tongue, feel her supple body against his, and the heady scent of her, like vanilla and spice, clung to him.

He was definitely going to her hotel room when he arrived in Brussels.

Catching Leoni's eyes across the room, seeing the smirk and come-hither look on her face, Elijah was shocked and even more irritated to discover that the gorgeous Austrian now elicited no reaction from him whatsoever.

None.

His body had decided only one woman would do. A freaking vampire of all people! Where were his instincts now? Usually he'd be running for the hills.

But not only did he want to ruin Echo for any other man, there was a dark, secret part of him that wanted to know what it would be like to feel her teeth sink into him.

2

THE ROOM WAS PERFECT.

Echo pulled on the iron handcuffs William had given her to make sure they were locked securely to the bed frame. It had taken a while to find accommodation that used metal bed frames. It wasn't the best hotel, but Echo imagined that would only make her part as a journalist on assignment more realistic.

She slid her fingers over the silvery iron. Pure iron wasn't as tough as the iron used in most products these days. It was slightly more malleable. For instance, if it were Echo being locked into these things, she'd snap them off in a second.

William had warned her that fae sensed when iron was in the vicinity, but considering Elijah didn't know what he was, Echo reckoned he wouldn't understand if he suddenly experienced fatigue when he entered the room.

William thought she was still in the early stages of investigating Elijah. That she hadn't been able to learn much about him in Vienna but that she'd caught his attention, and they'd agreed to meet on the last leg of the band's tour. Garm soldiers had accompanied her but were staying in a different hotel to not arouse suspicion. Echo was to call on them if she discovered Elijah was in fact fae. And William had given her the handcuffs to test him.

She didn't need to test him.

Echo had known as soon as she got close to Elijah in that bar that he was fae. Not only did he emit incredible energy that pushed against her body like a wave but he smelled so similar to Niamh Farren. Sweet, heady, like hot caramel. And yet his scent was different too. It was also smoky and woodsy, almost like a werewolf's base scent but not quite. An intriguing combination. His scent had been hard to resist, as had the pulse in his neck.

In that bar, sitting across from him, she'd imagined sinking her teeth deep into him and drinking while he thrust inside her. That never happened to Echo. She always had her bloodlust and sexual desire under control.

Elijah Webb wasn't even her type.

Echo curled her lip in self-recrimination.

It had to be the fae thing.

And yet ... she hadn't felt drawn to Niamh Farren like this.

Maybe Niamh hadn't stuck around long enough for Echo to feel the draw.

Shaking off her ridiculous anxiety over being attracted to the damn fae, Echo launched up off the bed and smoothed her tight dress down her body. It was short but classy. Way more expensive than a journalist could probably afford, the designer navy cocktail dress molded to her figure. It had a modest high neckline but bare shoulders, and in the back was where all the fun was to be had—except for one strip of beaded fabric holding the dress together, Echo's back was bare.

Six-inch navy stilettos made her legs look like they went on forever.

She was dressed to seduce a fae so she could trap him in iron.

It should be easy enough.

Before arriving in Vienna, she'd used the file William gave her to research Elijah Webb thoroughly. Born in Carlisle but moved around England until approximately six years old. From there was settled and raised in East London by the Webbs—Nancy, a midwife, and Bill, a high school math teacher. In his youth, Elijah seemed to make no mark on the world at all, though his school records proved he was intelligent and industrious. He'd been accepted into five of the top schools in the UK and had gone to UCL with two of three friends he'd formed a band with at age sixteen. The Strix, named after a mythological bird of ill omen who (ironically) fed on human blood (Echo wondered if that wasn't a prophetic name to give his band considering her current plans), had gotten a record deal when Elijah was twenty. The Strix found fame with their second studio album two years later and had grown in popularity over the last four years.

Contrary to the lie she'd told Elijah, even Echo had listened to and enjoyed some of their music.

In all that time, there had been no news articles surrounding Webb, no incidents mentioned in the supernatural websites or online chat groups until the last eighteen months. Nothing in his medical records. No illnesses as a child, no fever, no flu or broken bones. Odd, but not something people would likely have picked up on. It made Echo question if his parents knew about his abilities.

Online mentions of Elijah only surfaced after supes who'd met him commented on the energy levels he exuded. This was the reason William had sent Echo after Elijah. And Elijah had no idea to mute himself because he didn't know he was in danger from The Garm.

Because he didn't know he was fae.

And Echo was one hundred percent positive he *was* fae ... because ... she sensed it. When she'd called him a warlock, she perceived no denial within him, only discomfort that someone might guess how powerful he was. How Echo could feel that, or any of his emotions, she didn't know. And she didn't care to understand. It was probably all in her head.

The handcuffs would prove her gut feeling right or wrong, anyway.

And if he was fae and had no idea, that would only work in her favor.

That he'd been attracted to her also worked in her favor. At least, she was sure he desired her. What she felt pressing against her skin was foreign and male and all-consuming. *How am I sensing these things?*

It didn't matter. She shook off her concerns. All that mattered was that he wanted her and that the lust she'd felt toward him was probably just an instinctual, animal reaction to his own uncontrolled desire.

Yeah, Echo was pretty confident Elijah would show at her hotel room this afternoon. It was five thirty. The band's flight landed earlier this afternoon. One of the werewolves working for William had informed her of the band's arrival at their hotel.

Two hours they'd been there, probably settling in, getting some rest. Not that Elijah needed much.

But he was coming.

The werewolf, Jacques, had texted to let her know Webb had left in a cab ten minutes ago.

She chewed on her lip and checked the room again. The sun didn't set for hours in Brussels. Echo used to like long days when she was human. Now she loathed them. The blinds and curtains were drawn, but still Echo stayed away from the vicinity of the window in case daylight shone through any cracks.

A bottle of champagne and a bowl of fresh strawberries sat on a room service tray. Not very original, but it set the tone. Music played from her cell as it charged. Nothing by the Strix, but a playlist comprised of angsty indie rock about sex and love.

Finally, Echo acknowledged the butterflies in her belly. She hadn't experienced butterflies since the first night she'd fed from a human. For months, William allowed her to drink nothing but blood from the donor bags he procured on the black market. Then about six months after her turning, he took her on a hunt to teach her control. Echo hadn't needed it. The thought of drinking from an innocent human had tormented her into nausea. She hadn't wanted to admit it to William. Didn't want him to think her weak.

Instead, he'd praised her control, admired it, even. But he'd also forced her on another hunt. This time they followed a male who had spiked a woman's drink at a nightclub in Munich. They'd switched the drinks on him so he was drugged instead, and then they'd manhandled him into the alley behind the club. From there, Echo had bitten a human for the first time.

The sensation was entirely different from drinking from a bag.

More intoxicating.

Not sexual with him. Just hunger.

But her control never slipped.

She took what she needed, released the would-be attacker, and licked his wound closed with the healing properties in her saliva. William had been blown away by her discipline. She'd glowed under his obvious pride. Said she was one of the most composed vampires he'd ever met. And she knew that's why he trusted her, most likely why he wanted her to become his second-in-command despite her youth.

Echo wasn't so sure about her control, even then. She had a vengeful streak. The next evening, she'd gone out to stalk the human she'd fed from, to take away his ability to attack women ... only to discover he was already dead.

Drained of his blood.

She'd never asked questions.

Assumed William had disposed of him for the same reasons.

Now she knew better.

He wasn't called William "the Bloody" Payne for nothing.

How could she have blinded herself all these years?

"Stop it," Echo muttered angrily. She threw back her shoulders. Odette was counting on her to get this right. To get Elijah Webb exactly where they needed him.

Odette, who was so human her biggest problem right now was a girl bullying her at the same boarding school in New Brunswick that Echo had attended. Twelve-year-old girls were the worst. Echo had given her sister some advice on how to handle her bully, hoping it would be enough until she could come for her herself.

"It's so unfair," Odette bemoaned. *"My dad and sister are these scary, badass vampires who could break her neck just looking at her, and yet I can't tell her that because—"*

"She'd have you committed," Echo said in a warning tone.

Just like Echo, Odette was raised with knowledge of the underworld that existed beneath most human awareness. Unlike Echo, Odette was far more eager for the promise of becoming a vampire than Echo ever was. She'd turned to please William. Odette, however, was filled with childish romantic notions about immortality.

If it was the last thing Echo ever did, she'd save her sister from the reality.

"Hold on a bit longer, little darling," Echo whispered.

A knock sounded on the hotel room door, drawing Echo out of her meanderings. Elijah Webb's golden energy pulsed from beyond it. The fool really needed to learn how to mute that. The door suddenly clicked open and in he stepped, holding the room card up that she'd left for him at reception.

His tight expression relaxed as his gaze dragged down her body and back up to her face.

"You're really here."

She tried and failed to ignore the shiver his deep voice elicited. He had an unusual East London accent. Not quite fully Cockney.

As if he'd sought to refine it over the years, but the Cockney slipped through.

"Did you expect to find someone else?"

"I wasn't sure. This is all very cloak-and-dagger." He closed the door behind him, and his eyes dropped to her legs and heated before they returned to meet hers again. "You look incredible."

Her heart raced, and she willed it to slow. If he was fae, he could probably hear it.

Come to think of it ... Echo could hear Elijah's.

Fast and pounding.

Huh.

His excitement? Nervousness?

A little surer now, Echo took a step toward him. "You look far too good for a man who's been on an exhaustive world tour for nine months."

He did look far too good.

Which made no sense to Echo.

He wasn't even her type.

Although she'd never been with a man for more than two nights, they all pretty much had one thing in common. They were reserved, sometimes even shy, and monosyllabic. Never too good-looking that they knew it. She didn't like cocky, arrogant, or pretty boys. Echo wanted to be the one controlling the situation, always.

However, Elijah Webb was none of the above. He was gorgeous and exuded sex, and he knew it. He was tall, but not too tall. Six feet according to the many fan sites dedicated to him. Broad-shouldered, lean, and muscular. Other than the chin-length, wavy dark blond hair he wore tied in a knot at the back of his head, the tattoos his shirt concealed, and his pierced ears, there was nothing rock star about Elijah's style. Not even onstage. He always wore some form of a suit. Sometimes a three-piece, or sometimes just a dress shirt and suit pants.

He wore that now. A blue dress shirt, too many buttons undone at the collar, with navy suit pants.

Together, they kind of matched.

Elijah's mouth, surrounded by a well-maintained, dark blond beard, curled at the ends.

His most attractive feature lit up. Mossy, golden-green irises, beautiful eyes she'd found almost impossible to look away from at the club in Vienna. And again now.

They both had green eyes. The rarest color. But his were warm while hers were icy.

"You're staring," he said in that rumbly, too-sexy voice that lent itself well to the growling vocals of a rock singer.

"So are you."

He smirked, and then his attention moved away from her to take in the champagne and strawberries. "For me?"

She nodded, her pulse increasing with her growing nervousness. It took all of her famed control to not glower at him for making her feel this way. "If you want." *Or we could just get straight to the point.*

Elijah chuckled and stepped forward. "I appreciate the effort, but you didn't need to go to the trouble, love. Even shitty hotels charge a fortune for this stuff." He frowned, his gaze dropping, and Echo sensed his energy change, like it was weighted with fatigue.

Bingo.

"Fine. Then let's get to it, shall we?" Before Elijah could respond, she sped across the room, grabbed him by the shirt front, and brought him down on the bed. Her dress refused to budge so she could straddle him. Echo held him down with one hand while she pulled her dress up her thighs so she could clamp them tight against his hips to hold him still.

All of this at vamp speed.

Elijah blinked up at her in shock, his features strained. "Love, I hate to tell you this because I am enjoying your aggressive seduction more than I thought possible ... but I suddenly feel bloody hellish."

Echo could feel his energy flicker, dimming. It wasn't significant. It wouldn't be significant until she snapped the iron around his wrists.

"Don't worry. You'll feel better once you understand."

He frowned up at her. "What?"

With a practiced move, Echo used her vamp speed to handcuff each of his wrists to the bed frame. He hissed in pain and bucked under her before she'd even snapped the first one closed. The strength of that buck almost threw her off the bed, but Echo kept her cool and handcuffed the other.

"What the fuck?" Elijah's face was contorted in agony as he slumped helplessly. He glared at her through narrowed eyes. "What the fuck ... ahh! What have you done?"

Echo winced, sensing his torment and hating every second of it. She hadn't known the iron would hurt him this much. "I'm sorry." Her cool facade cracked. "Let me explain everything to you quickly with no interruption, and I'll let you go."

"Why do I feel like I have rings of fucking ... fucking FIRE around my wrists?"

"Shh." She hurried back toward the bed. "Don't shout."

Sweat slid down his temple, surprising her. She hadn't known a fae could sweat. "Is this some kind of spell, you treacherous ... fuck!" Elijah yanked weakly on the handcuffs, trying to break them. "I have no strength. What the hell is this?"

"Elijah." Her expression strained with remorse, Echo knelt beside him on the bed. "Concentrate on my face."

His rage pulsed into her in waves as he stared up at her, eyes dazed with pain.

"You're not a warlock, Elijah. Warlocks and witches can only draw power from the things around them. Earth, trees, flowers, animals, people. In order to cast spells, they have to sacrifice something in nature—draw the energy out of it to use elsewhere. You don't need to do that."

"I know," he bit out. "I'm more powerful than most."

"No, it's not possible for a human with magical abilities to do that. Moreover, witches and warlocks aren't strong like you. They'd need to cast a powerful spell for that kind of strength, and even then, it would wear off. You've never been sick a day in your life, have you?"

He was weakening, his color turning alarmingly pale and pasty. "Where ... where are you leading with this?"

"You're immortal, Elijah."

He gave a guffaw of feeble laughter.

"I'm not kidding." Fear scored through Echo. The iron had a much greater effect on fae than she could ever have imagined. She didn't like it. She was essentially torturing him. "Elijah, if I uncuff you, will you promise to stay and listen to what I have to say?"

His eyes rolled in his head. "Fuck you," he whispered angrily.

Echo's will was crumbling, the control she was so well known for disappearing. She hated seeing him like this. Worse, that she was the reason.

Odette. Think of Odette.

Thinking fast, Echo turned the bedcovers, ripped strips from the sheet, and wrapped them around where the cuffs rested against Elijah's skin. Tears of self-directed rage filled her eyes when she saw the burn scars on his wrists. Those wouldn't fade. She'd scarred him for life.

The fae groaned in agony as she worked to create a barrier between the iron and his flesh. If she'd known, she would have padded the cuffs so that he was merely weakened.

Once she'd wrapped as much fabric around them as she could, Echo retreated and found Elijah watching her with more focus.

"It doesn't hurt nearly as much anymore," he said quietly. "But I still feel as weak as a lamb."

"I apologize," Echo replied stiffly. "I didn't realize how badly the iron would affect you."

"Iron?"

"Elijah ... you're not a warlock. You're an immortal fae."

Silence filled the room as he stared blankly at her.

Then, "Are you high on something?"

Angry, she leaned over him. "This isn't a joke."

"You're right," he snarled. "Being held captive in a hotel room by a psychotic fan is no joke."

"Get over yourself and pay attention. Do you know anything about the fae or Faerie?"

"Fairy?" He raised his eyebrows. "You believe in fairies?"

"Faerie. As in the place. As in there are countless multidimensions, and one of them definitely exists called Faerie where immortal, all-powerful beings reside. And two thousand years ago, the gate between our dimension and Faerie came down, allowing the fae to move freely in our world and us in theirs. Unfortunately, mating between species caused an evolution of humans into vampires and werewolves. Is any of this ringing a bell?"

Elijah stared aghast. "You believe in the origin stories?"

Relieved, she nodded. "You've heard of them. Good."

"I've heard bits and pieces. I don't know much," he said wearily. "Just that some ... some supernaturals believe vampires and werewolves were born from this supposed mix of fae and human."

"It's all true, Elijah."

He scoffed. "You really are crazy."

"I'm not crazy. The stories of Faerie are true. Do you know of the true-mate bond?"

"Why are you doing this to me?" Elijah growled. "What the fuck did I do to you?"

Ignoring her guilt, she pushed forward. "Do you know of the true-mate bond?"

"The ridiculous notion that some supernaturals are cosmically bound to one another as soulmates? Yes, I know of it. Now, let me go before I whittle a stake with my mind and drive it through your heart."

For a moment, he gave Echo pause. Could he do that? She eyed the handcuffs. No. He couldn't do that. Still, she edged away from him and pretended to not have heard his threat. "I'm going to tell you everything you need to know about Faerie."

"Because I'm fae?" He curled his upper lip.

"Yes, Elijah. Because you're fae."

He frowned at her. "God, you actually believe this. This isn't … fuck. You're mentally unwell."

Echo rolled her eyes. "Shut up and listen." From there Echo explained about the Fae. About the queen, Aine, and her royal subjects. How she lived in Samhradh Palace among the fae courtiers of the Samhradh Royal House. That this place was called the Day Lands because they lived in a part of Faerie that never grew dark and was in constant summer. That sunlight on Faerie didn't burn a vampire. One of the reasons there were vamps outside The Garm who would happily see the gates opened.

"Anyway, among them live princes, princesses, lords and ladies, their servants, and, once upon a time, their human slaves. On the other side of Faerie is Geimhreadh Palace, ruled over by a Geimhreadh prince of the Geimhreadh Royal House. It is known as the Night Lands as they live in constant darkness.

"Between these two are the countries ruled by the Earrach and Fómhar Royal Houses, called the Dawn and Dusk Lands. The royals are powerful fae who rule over a slightly less powerful aristocracy, and even less powerful middle and peasant classes.

"When the fae first invited humans to Faerie, the royal houses began to play games with them. This led to supernaturals. A new species first came to be when a courtier of the Geimhreadh House fought over a human woman called Isis with a member of the

Samhradh House. In their fight, the woman was killed, and the fae of Geimhreadh tried to heal her with his blood. This was forbidden because they discovered when they started invading our world that their blood healed humans. In *our* world.

"However, on Faerie, magic is less stable for humans. It changed Isis instead of healing her. She was the first vampire. She would live forever, like the fae, as long as she drank blood and no one killed her. Though someone did with a stake, centuries later." Echo studied Elijah carefully. "Are you following this?"

"I'm tied to a hotel bed with spelled handcuffs. I've nothing else to do at this point but follow you. Why are the beautiful ones always so fucking crazy?"

Echo ignored his last comment. "Not spelled. They're made of pure iron, which I'm getting to. But back to the story. Aine allowed it to stand, to let Isis live, despite the danger she posed. But the other houses were angry. Samhradh House cast a spell over Isis so a wooden stake, a weapon of nature, could kill her. And the greatest weapon they spelled against her was the earth's sun." Echo shuddered. "Fae can be impossibly cruel, but what they forgot was there's something bigger out there than all of us. Nature. And nature gave Isis a little gift. She had the ability to turn other humans into vampires. But as she did, the spell they'd cast over her transferred to those she'd turned. We're not dead like the myths would have people believe."

"I'm aware of that," he snapped impatiently and gave a limp tug at his handcuffs.

"Okay, moving on. When a shape-shifting fae, a rare species among the Day Lands, bit a human while wolf and accidentally transferred her gift to the human man, the werewolf was made. The Night Lands remembered what Day did to Isis, and they spelled the wolf. While vampires were controlled by the earth's sun, they made sure the full moon would control the werewolves.

"Moreover, the fae wore jewelry as symbols of their houses.

Geimhreadh House wore silver. Samhradh wore all precious metals and stones but usually fashioned to look like leaves and trees. Earrach wore gold, and Fómhar House, copper. Because Samhradh fashioned a weapon for the vampires from wood, Geimhreadh fashioned a weapon for the wolves out of silver. A werewolf can heal from almost any injury if he or she shifts. But if a wound is inflicted by silver, it'll leave a scar at best, kill at worst. So, that's how vamps and wolves came to be."

"Thank you for that fascinating bedtime story, but I'd like to get the fuck out of here now and away from your extremely deranged self."

"I'm not finished. And I'm not deranged. So ... back then on Earth, humans had discovered fae blood healed them. The thought of being immortal like the fae was too big a lure, and humans started to hunt the fae. They were on the brink of a war that would decimate the humans. Apparently, Aine's seer, a fae with psychic visions, had seen the destruction that lay ahead for both sides. Because of the mating bond."

"Ah, the true-mate bond. I really hope this isn't leading to 'Elijah, we're true mates and meant to be together and I'll keep you tied to this bed until you agree.'"

Echo glared at him. "Would you get over yourself, you arrogant prick?"

"I'm the prick?" He yanked angrily on the irons again. "I didn't handcuff you to a bed, you nutcase!"

Attempting to keep her cool, Echo took a deep breath. "On Faerie, a soulmate isn't some romantic notion. They are literally destined for one other fae. Not all meet their soulmate, but when they do, the bond that connects them is something that cannot be broken. Something beyond any fae, even the queen. Once they meet and know each other, they love forever.

"The mating bond began to forge between supernaturals and fae. Vampires and fae, werewolves and fae, druids and fae ... soulmates. The problem with that was there were supernaturals who still clung to their human past. Like a vampire I knew called Eirik."

"Okay, since I can't do anything else, I'll play along. Who ... who was Eirik?"

"He *was* the leader of The Garm. I'll get to that in a minute because it's pretty important. Eirik and Jerrik were made vampires millennia ago when the gate was open, and Jerrik loved the fae. He had a mating bond with a fae princess. Eirik, on the other hand, despised the fae for what they were doing to humans. So when Aine's seer foretold the coming war with humans and Aine decided to close the gate permanently, Eirik was pretty happy.

"But that's not all she did. Before she closed the gate, she sent back all the humans and supernaturals to Earth, even those who'd mated to the fae. They'd discovered a werewolf bite could kill a fae if they weren't mated. Another reason to dispel them from their world, considering they would end their true immortality. But being the twisted cow Aine was, she cast a spell that she knew would keep ambitious supernaturals warring with one another over the centuries, for a shot at true immortality. The spell brought to fruition seven children, born to human parents, but fae. Seven fae children with fae gifts and fae immortality ... and more importantly with the ability to open the gate.

"Whoever used the children's blood to open the gate would be welcomed into Faerie where they could live forever."

"And what fairy tale did you read this in, love?" Elijah drawled, sounding a little drunk with weakness.

"I didn't read about it. I was told the story from a primary source—Eirik himself. So adamant that the gate remained closed, Eirik formed a group over the centuries called The Garm. They purport to be protectors. Their sole purpose is to hunt down the fae children and kill them before they can be used to open the gate. Eirik so believed in this that he murdered his own brother

Jerrik, because Jerrik was determined to protect the children so he could use them to return to his love."

Elijah narrowed his eyes. "Why are you telling me all this?"

"The Garm have killed many innocents over the centuries. But now they know ... the children were born twenty-six years ago, all to human parents. They've killed three of the seven already. And I know this for a fact because my adoptive father, William Payne, was Eirik's second-in-command until Eirik was killed last year. Now William is the leader of The Garm, and I'm one of his soldiers."

She tasted the coppery tang of fear, and her stomach flipped as Elijah said hoarsely, "You think I'm fae, so you're going to kill me."

"No." Echo leaned over him, so close their faces almost touched, but she wanted him to see the sincerity in her eyes. "The fae cannot die on Faerie. But here on Earth, they can be injured or killed by pure iron. William gave me the handcuffs you're wearing and sent me here to uncover whether you are fae. The fact that the iron affects you proves it. But I'm not here to hand you over to William. I'm here to convince you to help me, and in exchange, I'll help keep you alive."

"You're crazy," he muttered.

"I recently discovered I am nothing but a tool of vengeance for William. That everything I've ever been told are lies. I need your help to protect someone from him, and then I need your help to bring him down. And in doing so bring down The Garm, which would keep you and the other fae-borne safe from them."

Elijah chuckled, shaking his head. "I can't believe this."

"In return, I will take you to a known fae-borne. She's a psychic. And rumor has it she knows everything about you all. She can give you the answers you need and teach you how to use and control your gifts."

"I don't need a mentor." He strained against the cuffs. "I need you to let me go. And if you do so of your own free will, I will forget about this and leave without meting out retribution. I think that's a fair deal, considering the circumstances, love. I'd take it."

Growing exponentially frustrated by his stubborn refusal to believe, Echo had to take a couple of deep breaths. "Elijah, you are in danger. Not just from The Garm. There are others. A coven, a powerful coven, who, if they discover you are fae, will take you away from everything you love and kill you to open the gate. They'll kill your friends, your family, if they stand in the way."

"It can't be that hard to whittle a stake," Elijah murmured. "And I'm good at everything. I could probably whittle ten stakes in ten seconds. That would be a gruesome end, but I can't say it would be an undeserving one. I wonder if there's a timber yard nearby ..."

"Fine." Enraged but not stupid, Echo reached over him and uncuffed one hand. His arm fell limply above his head. She reached for the other and unlatched it.

To her shock, there was a blur of movement, and she found herself pinned beneath Elijah. Panic suffused her, and she tried to move, but it was like having an entire apartment building sitting on top of her. Echo had never encountered this kind of strength before. And this was when he was weakened from iron.

Holy crap.

He straddled her, his face flushed, green eyes sparking with rage. He bent his head toward her, his lips almost brushing hers. "If I ever see you again, vampire, I will rip out your fucking heart with my bare hands. Understood?"

Echo glowered up at him but nodded.

His anger banked slightly as he eased from her, but then his attention caught on his wrists. Holding her down easily with one hand, he studied the inflamed wounds there. "What the bloody hell?"

"It's the iron. You react to it like a wolf to silver or a vampire to a stake."

Uncertainty flickered in his expression, and he swallowed hard.

"Elijah ... I'm not lying."

His eyes returned to hers. Denial hardened his features. "If this leaves a scar, you better hope I never see you again, love."

And then her hair whipped around her face as if a gust of wind had blown through the room. The weight holding her down was gone. Echo sat up.

Elijah was gone.

"Holy shit," she whispered, pressing a hand to her forehead.

Eirik hadn't lied.

The fae were stronger and faster than she could have ever imagined.

3

For the first time, Elijah cursed his inability to get truly bloody drunk. He needed a distraction. A numbing, blissful distraction from the fact that he'd been held hostage by a crazy vampire with crazy notions about what he was.

And scarred by the handcuffs she'd used on him.

He examined the healed burn around his left wrist. It had taken less than half an hour after he'd left Echo behind in that shitty hotel room for the wounds to heal. But he was left permanently marked by the iron.

"Fuck." Elijah lifted his other arm to stare at his right wrist and the matching scar.

"The fae cannot die on Faerie. But here on Earth, they can be injured or killed by pure iron. William gave me the handcuffs you're wearing and sent me here to uncover whether you are fae. The fact that the iron affects you proves it."

He sat up, ignoring the moan from the groupie lying naked beside him. A quick glance told him the brunette was asleep, as was the pink-haired friend curled around her. Elijah had hoped a fuck-a-thon with a couple of groupies might distract him from

Echo's voice in his head, but no such luck. Especially when they both asked where he'd gotten the scars. Hopefully, they'd never mention it to anyone else.

Swinging his legs off the bed, he reached for the wide leather cuffs sitting on the bedside table. Thankfully, he had several he often wore, usually one on each wrist and only when he wore his shirt sleeves rolled up. Buckling them on now to cover the unfortunate new marks, Elijah scowled. He'd worn them under his shirt in case the fabric slid up during their gig. He hadn't wanted the guys noticing and asking questions he couldn't answer.

For over a decade, Elijah had managed to keep his gifts hidden from his bandmates. The only two people in the world who knew about them were his parents.

"The spell brought to fruition seven children, born to human parents, but fae. Seven fae children with fae gifts and fae immortality ... and more importantly with the ability to open the gate.

"Whoever used the children's blood to open the gate would be welcomed into Faerie where they could live forever."

"Get out of my head," he muttered, pushing up off the bed to cross the room into the sitting area of the presidential suite. Uncaring of his nakedness, Elijah pulled back the curtains and stared out at the city. The hotel was in Old Town and his suite was just high enough to see across the top of the building adjacent. The city was abuzz with early-morning traffic. It was a sunny May morning.

No cloud cover.

Total daylight.

Suddenly, Elijah wanted nothing more than to get out of the hotel and onto the streets where a treacherous vamp couldn't get at him. Uncaring of the women still sleeping in his bed, Elijah showered quickly, threw on jeans and a T-shirt, tucked his phone in his back pocket, slipped on sunglasses, and departed the room. Phil and Jamal were happy to share a suite, but since Elijah and

Adam fucked around a lot, they always got their own rooms. The rest of their entourage stayed throughout the hotel.

Knowing the guys would still be asleep after their long gig last night, Elijah strode down the corridor and got on the lift.

Last night had been the worst gig of their careers.

All because Elijah's head wasn't in it.

And like the good guys they were, they'd just patted him on the shoulder and told him they understood. They were all tired. It was time to go home.

But it wasn't quite. They still had one more night to play in Antwerp.

And then Elijah could fuck off somewhere alone to deal with the mental fucking trauma Echo the deranged vampire had caused.

He didn't know what was worse: what she'd told him and believed about him, or the absolute disappointment of her turning out to be psychotic. Ever since their meeting in Vienna, Elijah hadn't been able to think about anyone else.

The anticipation he'd felt walking into her hotel room and seeing her looking so damn gorgeous was immense.

All for it to come crashing down.

What a bloody disappointment.

"And a mind fuck." *Fae? Him? Was she nuts?*

Clearly.

With a heavy exhalation, Elijah stepped off the lift and strolled across the lobby. Almost immediately, the hair on his nape rose, his pulse racing, and dread settled over him. Unnerved by the sudden sensation, one he'd experienced only a few times over the years, and always before something horrible happened, Elijah stopped. He glanced around at the hotel guests and staff, searching for anything untoward.

Nothing.

Not that he could see.

And Echo wouldn't chance coming here in the daylight.

Not that ...

He stiffened.

He'd never felt this way around her.

This particular feeling, he called his sixth sense. He'd experienced it a few times as a child, once before a bully pulled a prank that had injured him. He'd experienced it when he was seventeen, right before he and his dad got in an accident. Elijah had launched himself at his dad, grabbed him, and the next thing they were outside of their vehicle, a hundred yards away, watching as it was decimated by the drunk driver who'd lost control of his car.

That had been a difficult one to explain to the police.

In the end, they lied and said their car had been stolen that night.

No one could explain the lack of bodies in the vehicle.

It was the first time he and his parents realized he could move magically from one place to another.

His mum and dad had begged him not to do it again, terrified someone else would find out how different he was and take him away from them. He hadn't been able to do it again, anyway. He reckoned it was his fear for his father at that moment that had fueled the ability.

Elijah stared around the lobby again, searching, searching. Then a pulse of energy caught his attention, and he noted the man reading a newspaper in an armchair near the lobby bar. He paid no particular attention to Elijah, but there was something in the man's aura that reminded him of the warlocks he'd met.

Was he the reason Elijah sensed danger?

"Elijah, you are in danger. Not just from The Garm. There are others. A coven, a powerful coven, who, if they discover you are fae, will take you away from everything you love and kill you to open the gate. They'll kill your friends, your family, if they stand in the way."

Growling in frustration, Elijah stormed out of the hotel. Echo was making him paranoid.

However, as he marched aimlessly, Elijah's pulse refused to slow. It was like walking through electrically charged air, and the dread would not leave him. A few minutes from the hotel, he strolled onto a busy square in front of a theater built in the Greco-Roman style with Ionic columns.

The sensation of danger became too much to ignore. He stopped, staring around the square at the passing faces.

And then, like magic, they appeared.

Their power pulsed out at him.

One by one, Elijah spotted the witches and warlocks in the crowd.

The amount of energy they emitted suggested one thing: They were a coven.

And if his sixth sense was accurate, they weren't here for his autograph.

She can't be right about this.

Elijah lifted his wrists, glowering at the leather cuffs.

But what if she is?

Suddenly uncaring of who would see, Elijah drew on every ounce of power within and sped away from the square at full speed. Such a blur, the humans would conjure up some benign explanation for it.

Now and then, he'd stop to check Maps on his phone, but he still arrived in Antwerp in only twenty minutes. It took an hour to drive there, according to the app. Shooting a quick text to Jamal that he was already in Antwerp and he needed his buddy to make sure the team organized his luggage, Elijah checked into their hotel.

Once alone in the room, he took a minute.

His sixth sense for danger had dissipated.

However, the dread hadn't.

Because now Elijah was starting to worry Echo wasn't so crazy after all.

Reaching for the phone on his bedside table, he called down to reception and ordered room service and requested a computer.

Ten minutes later, his food arrived, along with an iPad.

Logging in and using the private browser, Elijah searched the supernatural sites and chatrooms he'd discovered over the years on the shadow web and did something he'd avoided doing. He typed in his name. Sure enough, he'd been the subject of much discussion over the past few years. Apparently, he gave off tremendous energy, and there were rumors he must be an incredibly powerful warlock.

Fuck.

He spent hours searching. Looking up this Eirik and Jerrik but not finding anything for ages because he'd spelled their names wrong. Finally, he found lots of information on them, all related to the origin myth, the myth that quite a few online supes seemed to believe in devoutly. They also believed in the prophecy about the seven fae born on Earth to human parents, children who had the ability to open the gate to Faerie. That led him to the Blackwood Coven, an immensely influential and powerful North American coven who were purported to be on the hunt for the fae children.

Elijah searched The Garm and grew increasingly concerned when he discovered everything Echo had told him about the organization was true. Including the fact that they were headed up by a five-hundred-year-old vampire called William "the Bloody" Payne. And that William had an adopted daughter named Echo.

A quick search on Echo found few mentions of her in the chats, though those that did noted she was physically strong and fast for one so young. Only twenty-six years old, a vampire for only the last six. So William had kept her human until she was twenty and then turned her?

Wasn't that a little fucked up?

Elijah threw the iPad on the bed and rubbed his weary eyes.

What if everything Echo told him *was* true?

What if today he'd just escaped the clutches of the Blackwood Coven?

That meant The Garm were onto him.

And no wonder! He was all over the shadow web.

What if they targeted his parents?

Panic rising, Elijah took a deep breath and exhaled slowly.

"Calm down. It could all be an elaborate hoax on Echo's part."

An extremely elaborate hoax.

Fumbling for his phone, he hit the speed dial for his mum.

She answered after three rings. "I didn't expect to hear from you until you got back. How are you, darling?"

Immediately, he relaxed.

His parents were fine.

Everything was fine.

It had to be.

But just in case, he needed to learn how to dim his energy. "I'm fine, Mum," he lied, and then he followed it with truth. "Just looking forward to coming home, seeing you and Dad for a bit."

"Well, be careful what you wish for. Your father just bought this shed and its flat pack, so he thought maybe you and the boys might be able to help him build it. I told him …"

Elijah sank into the bed cushions, letting his mother's familiar voice soothe him back to a place of normality where he was just a guy with strange abilities, a bit like the heroes in the comic books he'd read growing up.

Just a guy who was a little different.

A rock star with "gifts."

Not the fruit of a prophetic spell.

Not the conduit to the end of the fucking world.

4

"I TOLD you I have this under control."

"You're taking too long. Jack said that pretty boy was in the hotel room with you for thirty minutes. That was plenty of time to get the handcuffs on him."

"I was lulling him into a false sense of security." Echo sneered at Jack who stared back unrepentantly. Sajid, the other werewolf William had sent as her escort, stood at Jack's side. "It's not my fault the rock star likes to talk."

"And is it your fault he fled the room?" her father's voice commanded from the speaker on her cell.

"I told you, I don't know why he did that," Echo lied.

"I think it's fairly damning. He obviously sensed the iron in the room. You will take Jack and Sajid to Webb's concert in Antwerp tonight. No arguments. The three of you will restrain him with the cuffs, and if he's fae, you will kill him, Echo."

Right on cue, Jack stepped forward and revealed a long, narrow gift box. He lifted the lid, and nestled on a silk bed was a blade carved from pure iron.

Every inch of her rebelled at the idea of stabbing Elijah in the heart.

He'd be no good to her dead, after all.

Feigning awe, Echo reached for the dagger and lifted it from the box.

"Jack gave you the blade?" William asked.

"Yes. It's beautiful. Thank you."

"Tuck it somewhere safe. I'm almost certain you're going to need it." His voice was hard with grim satisfaction. "If Webb is fae … this will be a momentous night. It will leave only three, and we know who two of them are."

Echo's nerves were stretched taut with having to listen to William for so long. "We need to go. We'll check in soon." She hung up before he could answer, and she saw Sajid's raised eyebrows at her lack of deference.

She no longer cared.

Echo was stuck with Jack and Sajid. William had commanded them to stay with her, so there was no shaking them, for now. Unfortunately for them, William's order had signed their death warrants. There was no way she could escape them with Elijah and leave them alive to tell her father she'd betrayed him. Her plan only worked if William thought she was a victim of the fae for as long as possible.

The weight of the werewolves' lives sitting on her shoulders, Echo forced herself to meet their stare. "We go to Antwerp, we go to that concert, and we find a way to get backstage so we can take Webb."

Nodding, Jack wandered over to the bed and opened a black box. From inside, he removed three earpieces. "These are spelled to work like a three-way radio." He handed them out. "This way if we split up, we stay in contact."

It would be better if they split up, if she could shake them so they weren't there to witness her leave with Elijah. So ... she didn't have to kill them.

There were a lot of assholes in The Garm.

Why couldn't William have sent two of them with her instead of Jack and Sajid?

They were professional, never inappropriate with her, and offered her respect.

"If it comes to a fight, you leave it to me," Echo ordered.

The werewolves looked at each other and then Jack gave a negative swipe of his head. "We have orders to stay with you. If Webb is fae, it'll take all three of us. You should never have been in that hotel alone in the first place." The New York werewolf clamped his lips tight as he realized he'd inadvertently questioned William's decisions.

Dread nauseated Echo. She didn't want to murder these wolves, these wolves who clearly wanted to protect her.

Since meeting Elijah, she'd become weak.

The cool efficiency and cold compartmentalization she'd learned from William ... it had fled her.

Could she really blame Elijah, though?

She'd become weak from the moment she'd uncovered the truth about her adoptive father.

Throwing her shoulders back, she narrowed her eyes on Jack. "I'm faster and stronger than you. I can take care of myself. Now, if we get separated and I encounter Webb on my own, I will handle it. Is that understood?"

"Sure." Sajid shrugged in answer instead of Jack. "*If* we get separated."

In other words, they weren't going anywhere.

Fuck!

Odette. Think of Odette.

She was all that mattered.

And these two men weren't innocent. They had killed innocent people for William. She'd seen them do it. Echo needed to remember that.

"Bring the car around. We can't afford to wait for the sun to set."

Jack gave her a grim nod, and he and Sajid stalked out of her hotel room.

There was nothing worse than traveling in the trunk of a car, but there was no other option. They needed to get to Antwerp in time for the concert. It started before the sunset, which meant Echo needed a safe way inside the building.

Once they were in, she'd do whatever it took to convince Elijah to come with her. If she couldn't convince him, she'd kidnap him, and if that didn't convince him, she'd have his parents kidnapped.

Absolutely nothing else mattered but saving Odette and destroying William.

As soon as he stepped onstage, Elijah knew.

The hair on his nape rose, his heart raced, and dread filled him.

He slowed as the band moved into position. The roar of the crowd, thousands of fans this time, hammered him like a wave, but it didn't fill him with the usual euphoria.

The venue seated two thousand and was the last stop on their tour. Legends had played there. It should have been another special moment for the Strix.

Instead, Elijah could feel the pulsing energy of magic spread out across the ground floor and balconies above.

"What is with you, mate?" Adam yelled, slapping him on the shoulder and pushing him toward his mic at the same time.

Elijah blinked, trying to focus. The guys had been asking him for the last few hours why he'd fled to Antwerp without them and why he was acting so bloody weird. But he had no answers for them.

None that would make sense.

"Don't burn out just yet, Eli," Jamal had advised with sympathy. "We're almost finished. Just one more gig."

Yeah, one more gig.

His eyes scanned the screaming, singing, yelling crowd of fans, and just like in the market square in Brussels, the energy of the coven acted as a signature. Elijah spotted them, one after the other, standing militantly among the crowd.

Waiting for him.

Fuck.

Echo hadn't been lying.

But had she inadvertently brought the Blackwood Coven to him?

Elijah had an entire gig to figure out how to get away from them. Adam hit the drums, leading them into their first track. On autopilot, Elijah began to sing, but before he'd even hit the second chorus, a strange fatigue settled over him.

The dread he'd been filled with became this overwhelming weight on his chest.

That's when the first screams cut through the music, and he saw bodies start to drop in the crowd. Body after body.

What the fuck?

Horror filled him as his knees buckled and his lids grew heavy.

"*Warlocks and witches can only draw power from the things around them. Earth, trees, flowers, animals, people. In order to cast spells, they have to sacrifice something in nature—draw the energy out of it to use it elsewhere.*"

Oh my God ... were they killing their fans to disable him?

He dropped to his knees, his limbs like concrete.

"Eli!" Jamal was suddenly kneeling before him, face tight with anxiety. "We need to get out of here, mate. Must be a gas leak or something!"

Hands grabbed at him and he turned to see Phil and Adam.

His band carried him offstage, but even as they followed the venue staff out of an exit door, he couldn't find his strength.

There was an explosion of panicked conversations in a mix of Dutch and English as Elijah tried to gain some control of himself. They were in an alley at the back of the building. People were on their phones. Sirens wailed in the distance.

Jamal knelt beside him as their bandmates talked with the staff, trying to figure out what was going on.

Gradually, Elijah started to feel somewhat better. Stronger.

"Jesus, fuck." Phil strode over to him and Jamal, face pale, eyes haunted. "They're saying people are dead in there."

"Oh my God." Jamal slumped beside him. "What the hell happened?"

Elijah reeled. It was true, then. Those witches and warlocks had killed people to draw their energy to use against him.

Oh fuck. The band. His boys. He had to get away from them. He couldn't have them in the coven's line of fire.

"Can you find me some water?" he asked Jamal.

Dazed, his friend nodded. Phil clamped Jamal on the shoulder, and the two of them wandered off. Elijah slowly stood, knees still shaking from the earlier assault.

Glancing around to make sure no one was watching him in the chaos, he drew up all his energy and fled at hyper speed from the alley.

He ran, a blur, mindlessly heading east. An old, red-brick bridge appeared before him, and Elijah flew through its tunnel. A highway, busy even at this time of night, was ahead, but he kept running, feeling the brush of a car against his leg, barely missing him. Then suddenly, he was shrouded in darkness.

Elijah stopped.

Sweat dripped down his back.

From fear?

Horror?

Shock?

All the above?

Trees surrounded him, their leafy smell filling his nose. The sounds of speeding traffic hovered on the edges of the woodland on either side. He was hidden in a section of greenbelt in the middle of the large motorway that cut through the city.

Taking a breath, Elijah slumped against the nearest tree.

He still wasn't entirely sure what had just happened.

All he knew was that innocent people had died.

She was right, wasn't she?

Echo.

She'd told him the truth.

Seething with rage, Echo followed Elijah's energy on foot. Unfortunately, she couldn't rid herself of Jack and Sajid. They hurried at her back as they moved quickly toward Elijah's scent.

The wolves were skeptical that she could find Elijah like this, but Echo knew with a certainty she still didn't understand that she was on the right track.

Those bastard Blackwoods had killed around a hundred Strix fans tonight.

All to try to weaken Elijah.

She'd been skirting the crowds when she'd sensed their combined power rising. Jack and Sajid had felt it too. Elijah had fallen to his knees, and Echo was moving toward him when his band suddenly pulled him from the stage.

They'd lost visual, but Echo *felt* him.

"This way." She ran under the tunnel of a red-brick bridge and then stopped as a car sped past. A double carriageway, and beyond, a small patch of woodland in the middle of the motorway.

There.

"Don't get killed, boys." *Though it would make my life easier.*

Echo hit vamp speed. In less than ten seconds, she found herself inside the woodlands, staring at Elijah Webb. He was slumped against a tree trunk but jumped at her sudden appearance in the darkness.

He opened his mouth to say something but was stopped when Jack and Sajid burst through the trees to stand at her back.

"I'll be damned. She was right," Jack murmured.

And then before she could speak, they flew at Elijah. In the blink of an eye, he was bound in iron cuffs, knees buckling, face contorted in agony as he bit back his pain. He glared at her in betrayal.

"Fae," Jack announced with satisfaction. He smirked in triumph at her. "Your turn, Echo. Kill the scum."

Heart pounding, she walked slowly toward the three of them, Elijah on his knees, Sajid and Jack at either side of him.

"Nervous?" Sajid teased, grinning. "Or excited to make history?"

They could hear her pulse racing.

She didn't answer.

Couldn't speak.

Could barely look at them.

Remember who they are. The lives they've stolen. Who they work for.

Stopping above Elijah, she looked into his golden-green eyes as he tilted his head to meet her gaze. "I told you," she whispered. "Didn't I?"

He looked like he wanted to spit on her.

Drawing up her strength, Echo punched her arms out wide, and her fists broke through skin, muscle, and bone. She flexed her hands inside Jack's and Sajid's chests and covered their beating hearts, the slick, wet throb of them pulsing against her palms.

And then she clenched her fists around them and yanked her arms back, ripping their hearts from their chests.

The wolves collapsed with dull thuds, their eyes staring up at the ceiling of branches, shock still marring their faces.

Tears of remorse flooded Echo's eyes, but she forced them back.

"Remember what they did," she whispered to herself as their hearts rolled out of her hands.

"What the fuck?" Elijah wheezed in pain.

Echo reached down and snapped the iron cuffs off him with ease and threw them with so much heft, they soared through the sky, probably for miles. Elijah groaned and slumped onto his back while Echo reached down and gently closed Sajid's and Jack's eyes.

"You killed them."

She turned to see Elijah sitting up, confusion wrinkling his brow. "I did. They were The Garm."

"And tonight ... was that the Blackwood Coven?"

Surprised, she raised an eyebrow. "You've done some reading since yesterday."

He rubbed his wrists, face still etched with pain. "I really am fae, aren't I?"

"Yeah, you are."

"And you just killed your own people to save me?"

Echo reached into her ankle boot and pulled out the iron blade Jack had given her. Elijah hissed, jerking away from her. "No." She raised a hand in reassurance. "I'm not going to use it. I was supposed to, though, to kill you." She dropped it by Sajid's body. "We'll leave it here. Let The Garm think you've taken me."

"Why?"

"So they're not onto us. Or onto me. We'll need to travel a little more covertly than you have so far." She smirked.

"How can you joke when you just killed two men?"

Rage flickered through her, and she knew her eyes silvered by the way Elijah sucked in a breath. "I killed two werewolves who have tortured, maimed, and murdered innocent people in their hunt for you and others like you."

"Fine. But where do you get off thinking we're traveling together?"

"Nancy and Bill Webb, 133 Old Fenwick Road, Peckham, London."

He paled at the same time she sensed a dangerous wave of energy come off him. "Don't you fucking dare threaten my parents."

A shiver cascaded along her spine at his deep growl. Echo raised a palm. "Calm down. I'm not threatening them. I'm letting you know that if I know where they live, so do others. They won't come for them yet. It'll be the last resort because the Blackwoods know you won't cooperate if they kill your parents. But William will go after them if he has to. Your parents need protection. And there are people out there who can do that ... fae ... who can give you all the answers you seek."

"And you're going to lead me to them?"

"Not for free." Echo took a step toward him, ignoring the sparks of awareness across her skin that made the hair on her arms rise. "We'll go to your parents, hide them, and then you'll help me get past The Garm to my sister so we can hide her too. Then you and I will take down The Garm. I can't do it alone. I can't protect my sister alone. So, you'll help me. Then I'll lead you to the fae who can help you."

"As simple as that?" He crossed his arms over his chest. "And I'm supposed to trust you?"

Anger snapped through her again. "I've just betrayed everything I've ever known to save your life, fae. Out of the two of us, I am the most trustworthy."

Elijah flinched and turned around, running his hands through his hair. "This is so fucked up."

"If we're going, we need to go now, before the coven finds you again."

He sank to his haunches, his fingers tight in his hair. "My band. I can't leave the boys."

"They're more protected than anyone. Supes prefer to leave famous people alone for fear of attracting too much attention. You're only an exception to the rule because you're fae."

Foreign emotions of anger, despair, grief, and fear flooded her.

And Echo knew it was everything Elijah was feeling.

Butterflies flurried in her belly.

She really could sense his emotions.

What the hell was that?

Alarmed beyond measure, her fists tightened at her sides.

Elijah suddenly looked over his shoulder at her, eyes narrowed. "What? What is it? Do you hear something?"

Confused, she frowned. "What do you mean?"

"I ..." He stood now, hands falling to his sides. "I thought I felt ... you ... panic or fear or something. I don't even know what I'm saying."

Could he feel her emotions too?

What. The. Actual. Fuck?

Echo shrugged off the worry this knowledge elicited. They had no time for it. "Are you ready?"

The muscle in his jaw ticked. "I have no choice, do I?"

"Not really."

"So my parents first, and then your sister? Is she a vampire too? Where is she?"

"Canada. And ask questions later." She grabbed his arm, pulling him away from Sajid's and Jack's bodies and the well of guilt inside her. "We need to get to London, pronto."

5

ONE OF THE things Elijah had learned to do ages ago with his fae gifts—

Fuck, fae gifts.

Would that ever stop being weird?

He was fae.

Fae.

A fucking fairy.

It was ludicrous.

But it was true.

Shaking his head, Elijah followed Echo down the boarding bridge. He had to stop going around in circles and just accept it. He was fae, and he was using his fae gifts to cast an illusion that allowed him to walk in public without recognition.

"And you've done this a lot since becoming famous?" Echo had asked when he'd explained why his fame wasn't an issue for remaining circumspect.

He answered in the affirmative. Whenever he was in public solo, he'd use it so he could go about his business without being bothered. People's gazes just passed over him, as if he was barely there.

As they boarded and Echo took her seat, Elijah reluctantly sat beside her. His reluctance wasn't because they were in economy and Elijah hadn't flown economy since before he was famous. It was because he still didn't trust the vampire. And he'd witnessed her kill two of her own men without even blinking.

Watching Echo rip the hearts out of the wolves' chests was the goriest fucking thing he'd ever seen in his life, and he was trying not to think about it.

He was desperate to get to his parents. They'd already wasted two hours stealing a car and crossing the border into the Netherlands. Echo had said using an airport in Belgium was suicide as those airports were being watched. So they were using this small airport in a place called Limburg. The only issue was its last red-eye flight was only going to Barcelona.

Which, according to Echo, was for the best because The Garm and the Blackwoods wouldn't expect it and wouldn't be watching either of those airports. From Barcelona, they would fly into Heathrow.

"Once we land in Barcelona, we'll need to move fast because our flight to London leaves not long after our arrival," Echo informed him.

Elijah frowned. They'd fled Antwerp around nine o'clock, and it was now just past eleven. "We'll arrive in Barcelona after one in the morning. There are no flights at that time."

Echo glanced around them to make sure no one was listening and then leaned into him. His eyes, with a mind of their own, dipped to her mouth as she spoke. "I have contacts William doesn't know about. One of them is giving me the use of their private plane. That involves pre-security checks and you'll need to use your mind-warping to get us out of that. We'll land on the edges of Heathrow. We can't be seen in the airport. The Garm will be running face recognition on their system since they know your parents are in London."

"You've thought of everything."

"I've been planning for days. It came at a pretty cost too."

"Won't William track your spending?"

She seemed surprised that he'd thought of that. The vampire really did think he was just a pretty boy who sang, didn't she? "I have secret accounts. Perhaps in the back of my mind, I always knew what William really was and suspected this day would come."

He frowned, growing ever curiouser about how William had betrayed his daughter. But Elijah had a more important question to ask first. "If we arrive in London on time, it will be closing in on four in the morning."

"That's correct."

"The sun rises at around five in London at this time of year."

"I'm aware."

"Well, my parents' house is over an hour from the airport." He leaned into her, ignoring her attractive scent. "Doesn't that sound problematic to you?"

"Don't condescend to me." Her eyes flashed silver. "Believe me, I know without looking at a clock when the sun rises and sets." They were so close now, their noses almost touched. "I'll have to travel in the trunk of the car."

"So I'll need to steal another vehicle, then?"

"Got a problem with that?" Echo arched a perfect eyebrow. "Are you unable to sacrifice your morals to save your parents?"

Fury ripped through him, and he slammed back on his seat. "Of course bloody not."

"There will be a vehicle waiting for us, anyway. Now, are we done with the twenty questions?"

Not by half. "Why do you want revenge on William?"

"You don't need to know that."

"I think I do. What if you've fallen out with Dear Old Dad over a lover he doesn't approve of or some such nonsense, and as soon as he says sorry, you're happy to dagger me through the heart?"

Echo glanced angrily around the plane and then hissed at him, "Will you shut up?"

He raised a palm and made a fist. Just like that, the surrounding noise deadened. Sensing the hum of the bubble of energy he'd created around them, Echo reached out and touched the electrically charged air. Wonder softened her face, unfortunately reminding him how fucking beautiful she was. "What is this? What are you doing?"

"No one can listen in on us now. If they try, they'll hear us yammering about a party we went to in Rome."

Her eyes widened. "You can do that?"

He gave an abrupt nod. "Among other things."

"How did ... you taught yourself all these things?"

Deciding he liked her like this, awed and more human rather than cold and businesslike, Elijah nodded again. "Trial and error over the years."

Something dawned on her. "Your parents know about you, don't they?"

"Of course. My abilities started showing up before I could even speak. They taught me to control it, allowed me to practice what I needed to, and pleaded with me to keep it hidden from everyone else."

"They knew you'd be taken otherwise." That cool frown of hers had returned. "You know human governments are aware of the underworld, and they're not above using supernaturals for their own means. They don't push it too far because they don't want a war ... but someone like you ... they would absolutely have taken you from your parents."

Hearing the grim truth, Elijah was thankful he'd listened to his mum and dad. "That's what they thought."

"They were smart to hide it." She tilted her head, studying him. "Your parents must be unusual people ... to have accepted a child who was so different."

Thinking of his parents, vulnerable to threats, emotion thickened his throat. "They're the best parents in the world." Determination hardened his voice. "I won't let anything happen to them because of me."

Echo's features turned to granite. "Nothing will happen to your parents, Elijah. We made a deal, and whatever you might think of me, I honor my promises. I'll protect your parents with my life."

Sensing her sincerity, he found himself softening a little toward her. "And in return, I'll help you protect your sister—who's apparently in Canada?"

Understanding there was more to his question, Echo said, "Odette is human. Only twelve years old. She lives in an all-girls' boarding school in New Brunswick. Once we have her out of there and hidden in a safe place, we go after The Garm."

"Yes, I know all that. What I don't know is how you can have a human sister or how you came to be adopted by William."

"You don't need to know any of that. And you should get some rest. We have a long day ahead of us." Abruptly, Echo closed her lovely jade eyes.

Irritated by her aloofness, Elijah scowled.

Her lashes were long and thick. She had high, rounded cheekbones, a perfect, straight nose, and bow-shaped lips. Her chin jutted in defiance; it suited her to a tee.

A stunning, symmetrical face.

The kind of face that could make a woman famous.

So beautiful, Elijah could look at her all day and probably write a million songs about her.

Dangerous, dangerous thoughts, considering who she was and what she was capable of.

"Stop staring at me," she said without opening her eyes. "And go to fucking sleep."

That made him laugh.

Echo's eyes popped open, her gaze dropping to his mouth as he grinned at her. Before she could hide it, he saw the flash of heat in her eyes, and he had to admit it soothed his wounded ego. But then she frowned. "What is it?"

Chuckling at her snappish tone, he shook his head. "Nothing, love. You're just funny, is all."

"Oh yeah, I'm a barrel of laughs," she deadpanned, which only made Elijah laugh harder.

When he finally stopped chuckling, he found Echo's expression had turned wary. His lips twitched as he asked, "What now?"

"Nothing. You're just very odd. Sleep."

"Yes, ma'am." He saluted her and settled back against his seat. His knees banged against the row in front of him, and he sighed, instantly irritated by the claustrophobia of economy. "But next time, I'm booking the tickets."

A sense of foreign amusement hit him, and he turned sharply to look at Echo whose eyes might have been closed but her lips quirked up at the corners.

Elijah's pulse raced a little. Had he sensed her spark of humor?

He knew he couldn't fully trust the vampire, which meant getting this ridiculous attraction to her under bloody control.

A panic Echo couldn't rein in, the panic of an animal in survival mode, had begun to rise within her as the small plane descended onto a private airstrip on the edge of Heathrow Airport. The sun would dawn soon, and she needed to get somewhere safe.

Her contact, a wealthy London financier she'd found on the shadow web who wanted to be turned into a vampire, had arranged a vehicle for them upon landing. She'd paid for the flight, of course, but the real reason the billionaire helped her was because he assumed that she'd bite him soon.

Echo had no intention of turning anyone into a vampire, ever. But she'd find someone who'd do it for a price. Eventually. Until he was no longer useful.

They disembarked and followed the pilot's direction to the car. It was parked on a private road a five-minute walk from the strip. Elijah moved with fae speed to keep up.

Skidding to a halt at the sight of the Range Rover, Echo found the key on top of the rear left wheel and beeped open the back. It lifted automatically. There was a retractable security cargo cover.

Perfect.

And it was a big space. Thank God.

"You're sure about this?" Elijah frowned. "Stuck in the boot of a car for an hour can't be fun. And will it completely shade you?"

Echo grabbed the large blanket that had been left per her instructions in the back and wrapped it around her body and head.

The fae smirked. "You look like ET."

"Shut up." She slapped the keys into his palm. "And drive." She rolled into the SUV until she was pressed up against the passenger seats. "Pull the shade cover over."

Sighing, Elijah did just that and then the trunk closed.

Darkness surrounded her.

As she listened to Elijah get in and start the engine, Echo took calming breaths. Her body was in survival mode, her heart racing, her nerve endings snapping so she was jittery and too full of adrenaline. The sun was rising.

Before the plane had landed, she and Elijah had gone over their plan for arriving in Peckham at his parents' house. On the off chance that William, having lost contact with Echo and most likely having already tracked Jack's and Sajid's phones to their bodies, was watching the Webbs' home, they had to go in as discreetly as possible.

It was a test of Elijah's abilities. While he could make himself appear nondescript and unrecognizable with a hazy energy spell, he'd never tried affecting someone else before. He'd have to carry Echo in a wrapped-up bundle into the house and make it look like he was carrying a rucksack, not a vampire.

Echo couldn't say she was looking forward to it all that much. If the blanket slipped at any point, she'd be toast.

Elijah had assured her with his usual cocky confidence that he could get her safely inside.

Trying to distract herself from her concerns, she thought of Odette.

Odette who had no idea what William had done to her.

But Echo could prove it, if she had to.

It was then she allowed something to infiltrate her mind. Something she'd steadfastly ignored when she realized Elijah's parents would need to be protected before she could ask for his help.

She was in London.

Echo was now in the same city as Margaret Lancaster.

And she couldn't go anywhere near her because William had Margaret under constant surveillance.

Twisted, psychotic fuck! Enraged tears filled her eyes.

"Uh, are you all right back there, love?" Elijah called.

Echo stiffened. "I'm fine."

"Are you sure? I'm getting serious fury vibes from you right now."

"What do you mean? Can you ... can you sense my emotions?"

Like how she could feel his urgency to get to his parents?

"Uh ... yeah, I can a bit. It's new. But I suppose it's just another of my fae abilities kicking in, right?"

"Right," she answered, but her mind whirled with the possibilities.

"You don't sound so sure about that. Something I should know?"

"Oh, for Christ's sake, you're like a chatty cab driver. Just shut up and drive," she snapped.

"I think you might be the most beautiful woman I've ever disliked," he replied almost cheerfully.

"Could you sound like any more of a rock star prick?"

"Yes, actually, I could."

Echo's lips twitched, and she stifled a snort of laughter.

"Ah ... I felt a twinge of amusement there," he said smugly.

"Get out of my emotions," she huffed.

"Then stop advertising them so loudly. Also, you are a very complicated woman. You veer from one emotion to the next so swiftly, it's almost hard to keep up."

"Guess what emotion I'm experiencing now?" she growled.

The bastard chuckled. "All right. Shutting up."

The jittery feeling within her increased suddenly. It was almost sunrise. Taking a deep breath in and exhaling slowly, Echo did this over and over as Elijah drove them through the early-morning London traffic. Traffic she could only hear.

Past landmarks she'd visited as a human in the daylight.

William had allowed her to travel much while she was human, to see Europe, its culture and history, in the light of day before those experiences were stolen from her forever. He'd never used the word *stolen*, of course.

But Echo did now.

She would never see Buckingham Palace or the Queen's Guard in their bearskin hats in the daylight ever again. London would only ever be visible in the darkness by artificial light.

Her grief seemed to grow every day.

As did her bitterness and thirst for revenge.

"We're here," Elijah said, and the car slowed. "And as per bloody usual, there are hardly any fucking parking spaces. I've offered to buy them a new house so many times, but they stubbornly refuse to m—space!" The car braked harshly, and Echo slammed into the back seats. "Sorry about that."

She couldn't speak. Fear that she hated crept over her as the car maneuvered into the spot.

"Right, we're three doors down from my parents' place. Are you bundled up tightly?"

Echo exhaled slowly. "Doing it now." She tightened the blanket around her, the fabric suffocating over her face, so much so that she had to remind herself she couldn't die of suffocation anymore. "You'll need to make sure it's tight around my legs." Her words were muffled by the blanket, but thanks to his supernatural hearing, Elijah answered in the affirmative.

Only a few seconds later, she heard the rear of the car open and then his hands were on her legs. The blanket was pulled so tight, she felt like a mummy.

"Right, I don't sense any danger around us, love, so I'm going to lift you now."

Sense danger?

He could sense danger?

Something to ask him later.

Abruptly, she was pressed against the hard heat of him, his heady scent too close. Her incisors ached all of a sudden. If the heat of the sun through the fabric didn't make her feel so bloody weak, Echo was sure her incisors would have sliced out of her gums of their own accord.

The fae's blood was too much of a damn temptation.

The trunk clicked shut, followed by the beep of the car locking.

"Walking swiftly as I can without drawing attention," he murmured. "Though there's no bugger about at this time."

Then there was a crack, like the splintering of wood.

"I now owe my parents a new door." There was a slamming sound, and she was being laid on something soft. "Closing all the curtains before we take off that blanket."

"Bill, call the police." Echo heard the faint whisper from upstairs.

She sighed. "Elijah—"

"I heard ... MUM, DAD! It's me!"

From above, Echo could hear Elijah's parents' movements. The tug of fabric brought her attention back to her companion, and suddenly she was staring up at him from a sofa in the middle of a living room. The curtains were drawn, though cracks of sunlight still spilled through at the edges. He'd switched on a few lamps.

To her surprise, his brow was creased with concern. "Are you all right?"

She nodded, pushing up off the couch to untangle herself from the rest of the blanket.

"Elijah, what on earth ..." A petite woman with short auburn hair rushed into the living room in a bright blue dressing gown embroidered with peacocks. At her back was a man as tall as Elijah with gray hair and striking jade-green eyes. They halted at the sight of Echo.

"Not that we're not happy to see you, son, but this is a bit untoward," Bill Webb said.

"Come here, come here first." Nancy, Elijah's mother, rushed her son, and Echo watched with more than a twinge of envy as they hugged. Elijah closed his eyes, distress straining his features as he tightened his hold on the human.

Echo sensed his love and fear flowing out of him in waves.

Irritated with her envy, she waited impatiently as father and son shared a quick hug that came with a hard patting of hands on each other's backs.

"Why is it so gloomy in here?" Nancy said, striding toward the curtains. "Let me—"

"No!" Elijah and Echo yelled in unison.

His mother startled to a stop, her dark eyes huge.

"Sorry, Mum." Elijah raised his palms toward his parents. "You can't open the curtains."

"Are you in trouble?" Bill asked, frowning.

"In a sense, yes ... There's something I need to tell you, and I think you better sit down for it."

6

THE LAST THING Elijah had expected after he'd told his parents everything about being fae and the prophecy was for his mum to turn to his dad and say, "I told you so."

His dad nodded grimly. "You did. I didn't listen."

What the hell did that mean?

"You told him what?" Echo asked before Elijah could.

"I told Elijah's father"—his mum looked at him now—"I told your father I thought you were fae."

Shocked, he slumped on the sofa next to Echo. "How did you know about the fae?"

"Well, it was a few years ago. You came back from your first tour, and you were agitated because you'd discovered that other supernaturals were real." She gestured to Echo. "Vampires and such. You told us about them because you wanted us to be aware of the danger."

"You did? You didn't tell me they already knew about supes," Echo said, tone almost accusing.

He nodded, barely paying attention. He wanted to know the

fae stuff. "But how did you come to the conclusion I was fae, and why didn't you tell me?"

"Your mum and I had been looking for answers for years, but the resources we had couldn't provide much evidence or answers that the supernatural world was real," Elijah's dad continued. "But when you told us there were vampires and such, I called up an old school friend who is now a professor at Oxford. He got me into the Bodleian Library and gave me access to some very old books on the supernatural world."

"Why didn't you do that before?" Elijah asked, stunned his father had a connection like that.

"Because we were so unsure of tipping anyone off, and I think we genuinely believed you might be one of a kind. But then you found out for certain there were others like you. Witches, warlocks. Except what you described of their powers seemed different from yours ... So I went to Oxford. I took extensive notes and brought them back. The more your mum and I pored over them, the more we questioned whether you were a warlock like you thought."

"The research said witches and warlocks had to pull their energy from other things, things that were sacrificed. You don't have to do that." Elijah's mum leaned forward. "Then I came across a section in your father's notes that spoke about the fae. Their abilities seemed to match up to yours."

"But there was nothing concrete, and what was said was that if the fae did exist, they were no longer in this dimension and hadn't been for millennia," his dad said. "Your mum wanted to look deeper into it, but I was afraid to stir up trouble. I just didn't believe it could be true. I'm sorry, love." He pressed a kiss to her temple, and she patted his hand in reassurance.

"Why didn't you tell me any of this?" Elijah scowled.

His parents blanched, so in sync with each other after all these years. His dad replied, "We didn't see the point. Or I didn't see the point. I'm sorry, son."

Echo stood from the couch. "Let's look on the bright side ... it means we won't have to spend days convincing your parents of the truth." She looked at them with her cool jade eyes. "You're very adaptable for humans."

If Elijah wasn't mistaken, she sounded impressed.

"Thank you?" his dad said dryly.

Elijah's lips twitched as he and his dad shared an amused look.

"The point is, we can skip all the 'I can't believe there are vampires and werewolves and fae, oh my' hysterics and focus on what matters. Elijah is in deep shit. Therefore, you are too."

Any amusement he'd felt died. "A little compassion and diplomacy wouldn't go amiss, Echo."

"Echo. What an unusual name." His mum stood up to study his companion. "And you're a vampire. What's that like?"

"You're not like other people, are you?" Echo murmured, her expression curious.

"I like to think not."

The vampire nodded. "Yes, my name is unusual. And yes, I'm a vampire. It sucks, literally and figuratively."

A wave of grief rolled off her, and Elijah's brows knitted together. He'd never met a vampire who hated being a vampire. The ones he'd met had all turned willingly. Not that he'd met many. Had the "gift" been forced upon Echo? The thought made him furious.

She flicked him a look of surprise but then masked the emotion just as quickly. "The point is, I'm afraid your lives are no longer your own. Elijah has already been attacked twice. Once by a group who wants to kill him to stop the gate from opening, and another time by a large coven who will kill others to get to Elijah to use him to open the gate. They've already killed people—at his concert last night in Antwerp."

"Bloody hell, speaking of ..." He reached for his parents' laptop that sat on the coffee table. A quick Google search made him bite out a curse.

"What is it?" His dad rounded the table to peer over his son's shoulder. "Oh my God," he whispered hoarsely as he read the news.

"What's going on?" his mum asked, concerned.

Elijah handed the laptop to his dad and slumped back on the couch. He looked at Echo, the weight of all those deaths lying heavily on his shoulders. "Over a hundred dead. They've covered it up as a gas leak in the building. And I'm missing. The boys must be losing their minds. I need to tell them I'm all right."

"No." Echo shook her head. "You *want* to tell them you're all right. What they need is to be oblivious to this world and to what you are."

"I should have told them about me. They all thought the vamps we met were just role-playing. I should have told them it was real. I've put them in danger. They're probably worried sick."

"Let them worry. You saved their lives by not telling them about you, Elijah. Don't screw up now. The less they know, the less danger they're in. They're too visible for either side to take them out without consequences. As long as everyone believes the boys know nothing about you or your whereabouts, they won't be targets."

Realizing she was right, he scrubbed his palms over his face and growled in agitation.

His dad rested a hand on his shoulder. "None of this is your fault, son."

"Isn't it?"

"No, it's not."

He met his dad's stoic gaze and a little of his calm filtered into him. He patted his father's hand in thanks.

"So, what do we do?" Elijah's mum looked up from reading the news article on the laptop.

"As soon as the sun sets, we're leaving," Echo said.

"Going where?" his dad asked.

"I have a place," Elijah answered. "No one knows about it. No paper trail, nothing. It's off-grid. Filled with supplies."

"You have a doomsday place?" His mum raised an eyebrow.

"Maybe I knew a day like this might come." He shrugged. "Anyway, it's deep in the French countryside, so we'll need to get you to Calais."

"Get *us* to Calais? You're not coming with us?"

"No, I'm afraid not, Mum." He looked at Echo, who stared stonily back. "Echo has someone in trouble too. I agreed to help her in exchange for aid. She knows other fae who might be able to help me."

"Really?" His dad was visibly concerned. "And they can be trusted?"

"The fae I'm talking about uses her gifts to save human lives. She can be trusted," Echo assured him.

"Who do you have in trouble?" his mum asked Echo.

"My little sister."

"Oh dear. Oh, well, yes, of course, you must help if you can, Elijah." His mum looked frazzled for the first time since they'd appeared at her doorstep. "I don't know what we should tell our work." She looked at his dad. "Do we tell them anything?"

"Yes," Echo replied instead. "We don't want the human authorities looking into this. A rock star and his parents missing ... we don't need that kind of heat. You'll leave a message with your respective bosses that your son is missing and you've gone to stay with family during this difficult time. Do you have anyone else in your lives who will kick up a stink if they can't contact you?"

"A few friends."

"Family?"

"Not any we're particularly close to."

"When I was little, my parents moved a lot to protect me," Elijah explained.

"Right. I knew that." Echo nodded militantly. "Leave the same message with your friends. Pack only what you need. Traveling light is important. We leave at sunset."

Usually Echo would be asleep at this time, and her eyelids were heavy with the urge. But she had to stay alert. Being stuck in the Webbs' modest terraced house like sitting ducks made her antsy. So much so that when Nancy started tidying up, Echo helped as a distraction.

Elijah was in the sitting room with Bill going over how to get to the safe house. He didn't want to write it down for fear of it landing in the wrong hands, so Bill memorized the directions.

"I don't know if that's smart," Echo murmured as she dried the dishes Nancy washed. Surely, Elijah could have afforded to buy his parents a dishwasher. Then she remembered what he'd said in the car about his parents refusing his offer to buy them a new house. Clearly, Nancy and Bill Webb had a lot of pride not to even accept a time-saving kitchen appliance.

"Bill has an excellent memory," Nancy said. "Don't you worry."

"Right."

Hearing her disbelief, Elijah's mom smiled at her. "You're funny."

"I've been getting that a lot lately."

"And very beautiful."

"Oh. Thanks."

"So you were sent to hurt my boy, use your feminine wiles against him," Nancy said bluntly, but there was no malice or anger in her voice. She really was the most unusual human Echo had ever encountered.

"Something like that."

"Your father is the head of this Garm group?"

"Adopted father."

Nancy raised an eyebrow. "I detect more than a hint of resentment there."

"He's not a good person."

"I see." She patted Echo's arm. "I'm sorry to hear that."

Something about her genuine sympathy made Echo's heart race a little. "Thanks," she mumbled.

"I appreciate what you're doing for my son, I really do. I hope he can be just as helpful taking care of your little sister."

"Thanks. I hope so too."

"He's a good man," Nancy stated firmly. "Always has been. With powers like his, he could have so easily gone the other way."

"Not with parents like you," Echo said, knowing her words were true despite having only known the Webbs for a few hours.

Elijah's mother smiled. "What a lovely thing to say."

"It's the truth." Echo shrugged, uncomfortable with the warm feeling passing between her and Nancy. "Anyway, as soon as Elijah helps me, I'll direct him to the other fae who can help, and then you'll see each other again. None of that should take too long."

"We shall see, I suppose."

Recognizing the worry shimmering in Nancy's eyes, Echo found herself promising, "I'll protect him with my life."

Elijah's mom smiled softly. "I believe you. Thank you." She turned back to her dishes. "I've never met a vampire before. At least that I know of. But you're certainly not what I expected."

Echo stiffened. "What did you expect?"

"I suppose ... I suppose I didn't expect you to be so human." Nancy smiled at her again over her shoulder. "You're awfully human, dear. That's rather a miracle considering the shadows in your eyes."

Stunned, Echo didn't know what to say.

She rather doubted Nancy Webb would have said the same a week ago if she'd seen her lying in Roark's bed covered in blood.

"Echo!" Elijah shouted from the sitting room, fear clear in his voice.

Her pulse leapt, and on instinct, she grabbed Nancy and zoomed with her into the sitting room.

Elijah was pale, his eyes wide. "Danger," he whispered hoarsely. "I sense danger."

The words had barely left his mouth when the front door slammed open. Echo shoved Nancy behind her as Elijah did the same with Bill, and they turned as members of the Blackwood Coven filtered into the room.

7

Ten Blackwoods entered. Echo watched them spread out in a half circle in the sitting room, blocking the front exit. She calculated their weights and heights, those who held themselves like warriors. The Blackwoods trained a third of their coven in combat so they could tag-team their victims. The fighter kept the victim physically distracted while the rest of the coven used their magic to detain them. She'd have to take out the warriors first. Echo suspected there were three trained enemies in the room—two warlocks, one witch.

The rest were there to combine their magic.

Standing in the middle was a warlock Echo pegged as a fighter —he was built like one. Looked to be in his late forties and had an air of authority. His gray eyes moved from Echo to Nancy and Bill and finally settled on Elijah. The warlock bowed his head in respect. "Mr. Webb, I apologize for the unorthodox interruption, but we need to make haste."

"Who are you?" Elijah's expression was impressively blank, all the while keeping his dad behind him.

Echo glanced over her shoulder to see Nancy peering past her in fear and not a little curiosity.

"My name is Lincoln Blackwood. My brother is the head of the Blackwood Coven."

Oh, they'd sent out the big guns.

Word was that Layton Blackwood, the coven head's son, had been killed by Niamh Farren. What did they expect? They'd failed spectacularly to bring in a fae because they continually underestimated their power. Echo could only hope Elijah knew enough about his abilities to get them out of this situation.

"And what do you mean by breaking into this house?" Elijah demanded.

Lincoln held up his hand, palm outward. "We're not here to fight. We're here to protect you." His attention flickered to Echo. "Do you know there is a vampire in your midst?"

Echo could only hope he didn't recognize her.

"And not just any vampire. If I'm not mistaken, this is Echo Payne, daughter of the head of The Garm." He curled his lip in a sneer.

Fuck. She'd have to kill him now.

Echo couldn't let word get back to The Garm about her defection. Not until Odette was safe.

"The Garm is an organization whose sole purpose is to kill the fae. Did you know that, Mr. Webb?"

"I don't know what you're talking about." Elijah shrugged, insouciant. "But I would like you to leave."

"We're not your enemy. We want to ensure your survival."

"If you're not my enemy, then you'll do what I ask and show yourselves out."

Lincoln gave him a weary look. "I can't. It's for your own protection. Please don't make me do this."

The hair on Echo's arms stood on end seconds before Nancy

and Bill dropped to their knees, clutching their chests as they cried out in pain.

"Mum! Dad!" Elijah fell before them, horror on his face.

Echo glanced frantically around the coven, but the energy was being channeled out of the Webbs by them all.

So be it.

Fast, faster than even most vampires, Echo was a blur around the room.

Snap! Snap! Snap!

Three coven members' necks broken in an instant.

Pain ricocheted through her as they turned their magic on her, but Echo never dropped her speed. She was accustomed to pain. It was literally in her name. Lincoln dove out of her way, but she kept going.

Crack, crack, crack, crack!

Another four dead, and the pain lessened.

Then suddenly, she was yanked out of vamp speed and hauled against a hard body. Echo struggled, knowing she could break a human's hold in seconds, but abruptly stopped when she saw the wooden stake touch her chest over her heart.

"Not so cocky now," Lincoln snarled in her ear.

Elijah leaned over his parents, guarding them. They were pale but didn't seem to be in pain anymore. Seven coven members' bodies littered the carpet. Energy crackled in the air as Elijah stood and when he turned to face them, Echo sucked in a breath.

His eyes were bright gold, and the energy she sensed was coming from him.

Oh, they'd pissed him off good.

What a sight he made.

She even heard Lincoln's intake of breath.

Echo smirked. *Good luck with that, warlock.*

Elijah's strange but beautiful golden gaze took in the dead and then Lincoln, holding Echo captive with a stake. A witch stood at either side of Echo and the warlock.

"You tried to kill my parents." Elijah's deep voice rumbled coldly. He didn't sound like himself at all. A shiver skated down her spine.

"We're trying to protect you," Lincoln replied. "And if you don't come with us willingly, I will stake your vampire girlfriend right through the heart."

"I don't think so," Echo said coolly.

"Shut up, vampire. This is between us men," the warlock said.

So the wrong thing to say.

She was a blur, knocking the wooden stake from his hand, and turning in his arms. Her incisors lengthened as she lunged at his neck, his flesh popping beneath her sharp teeth as she aimed for his carotid. His blood burst into her mouth, and Lincoln Blackwood, who had at first tried unsuccessfully to dislodge her, slackened in shock. Major artery hit, lifeblood flowing into her, and within ten seconds, his pulse slowed ... and then stopped.

And Echo was no longer hungry.

Two birds, one stone.

She felt little remorse. The Blackwoods had destroyed so many lives over the centuries.

"No!" a female shrieked behind her, and suddenly Echo was yanked back at the same time the curtains over the window were pulled away. The fading glow of the sun as it set crackled across Echo's body, and she screamed in agony as her skin reddened and bubbled like it was boiling.

A whoosh of wind blew her hair around her face, and then her back slammed hard against something as the pain receded. Muffled shouts were followed by familiar cracking sounds.

She blinked, panting for breath as cognizance returned with the easing of her pain. Elijah.

He'd sped her across the room, crashing her into the wall out of the sun's path. Shivering as her skin healed itself, she took in the sight of Elijah closing the curtains. The two remaining witches were on the ground, their heads turned at sick angles.

Elijah had killed them.

She sensed his despair, grief, and shock roll into her from across the room.

Clearing her throat, unable to look at his parents, Echo said softly, "They would have killed your parents and me. You did what you had to."

A moan drew her attention, and Echo's heart broke as Bill pulled a sobbing Nancy into his arms. They looked stunned.

And no wonder.

In less than five minutes, their sitting room had turned into a battlefield, a mass murder scene.

Elijah watched his parents with a hellish look on his face. He looked remorseful and grief-stricken ... but then something flashed across his eyes. Something vengeful.

Good.

He'd need that fire to get through this.

He looked at her. His eyes drifted over her face, something she didn't quite understand in his expression. Then she realized her lips and chin were covered in Lincoln's blood.

What did he think of her now?

Did he see that she was part animal, part savage?

Did it disgust him?

And why did it matter?

Concern wrinkled Elijah's brow. "Are you all right?"

It wasn't the reaction she'd expected. Pushing away from the wall, Echo looked down at her hands and saw they were as good as new. "I'm fine. If the sun hadn't already been setting, I would have been a goner. Thanks." She nodded at him. "For pulling me out of the way."

"Thank you for saving my parents' lives." He crossed the room, not looking at the bodies. "If you hadn't moved so quickly, they'd be dead."

Echo watched as son and parents reached for one another, embracing tightly. Elijah kissed his mother's forehead, whispering apologies she said he didn't owe her.

Emotion clogged Echo's throat. She allowed them some time and disappeared into the kitchen to clean the blood off her face. When she returned, she stepped toward them. "The sun has set. We need to move before others come. But we need to deal with the bodies first. Or should I say, you do, Elijah."

"Me?" he asked warily as he stood to his full height.

Knowing he wouldn't like the next part, Echo nodded hesitantly. "My father believes the fae are capable of cremating the dead. Even the living, actually, but only the most powerful fae are able to do that. But you should be able to do the former."

The rock star looked vaguely ill. "Cremate them? How?"

She stepped toward one of the dead witches. "I don't know. Throw your energy at the body and think it? Do whatever you usually do to tap into your gifts."

"You're acting like this is an everyday occurrence for me," he snarled, striding toward the dead witch at Echo's feet. "How can you so callously stand over this woman's body and ask me to cremate her?"

Refusing to give in to the guilt or consequent rage she felt at his accusatory tone, Echo narrowed her eyes. "Because she just tried to kill your mom and dad, and I happen to like them."

He squeezed his eyes closed, seeming in pain, but nodded. Then he lowered to his haunches and placed his hands palm down in the air above the witch. Unsure it was dangerous to be near Elijah when he used this type of magic, Echo strode over to the Webbs and shielded them. Elijah raised his eyebrow, stared at her for a moment too long, and then turned back to the witch.

Concentration strained his expression.

And then seconds later, the witch's body cracked and crumbled.

"Holy shit." Elijah almost fell on his ass, his eyes probably as wide as Echo's as she stepped closer in morbid curiosity.

With a whoosh and a puff of ash in the air, the witch disintegrated.

"Oh. My. God." Nancy looked shell-shocked and sounded it as she commented, "That's definitely going to clog my Hoover."

"Definitely," Bill agreed, dumbfounded.

Elijah turned to Echo. "What the fuck?"

She shrugged a little apologetically. "Told you."

8

THE FERRY TO CALAIS, France, left from Dover, just under two hours southeast of Peckham. Thankfully, the sun had set, so Echo took the passenger seat in the SUV she'd procured from her mysterious contact, and Elijah's mum and dad were in the back. The car's boot held the two small suitcases they'd packed with necessities.

Every time Elijah glanced in the rearview mirror and saw his parents' pale, strained expressions, remorse was a knife across his gut. Being what he was had completely derailed their lives. Despite them moving a lot when he was little, he'd never felt too guilty about it because he'd been a kid and he couldn't control his abilities as much. Then he'd gained control and hidden them to protect his parents.

Now it wasn't enough.

How long would his folks, the kindest humans he'd ever met, have to be on the run because of him?

Echo wasn't the most talkative vampire he'd ever known, so she didn't break the awful silence that filled the SUV as they drove toward the ferry terminal. Instead, she pulled a bag from the passenger-seat floor that he hadn't even noticed was there and rummaged through it. Out of the corner of his eye, he watched her turn on two old-fashioned-looking mobile phones and fiddle with them for a bit.

"What are you doing?"

She gave a sharp shake of her head to indicate she was busy.

Not the most personable female, was she?

The next thing that came out of the bag was a tablet computer and what looked like two passports. He wanted to ask what she was doing, but he already knew the answer. He concentrated on the road ahead as she looked at what were indeed passports and then swiped her finger over the tablet screen.

Finally, Echo turned to look at his parents and held out one of the phones. "This is a burner. Prepaid. The only contact on it is for this burner phone." She held up the other in her free hand. "This is Elijah's. You text to let him know you've arrived safely, or you use it if you're in trouble. Otherwise, don't touch it."

Elijah made a face at her bossy, cool tone. Couldn't she be a little nicer? She said she liked his parents.

His dad, however, reached forward to take the phone and replied gratefully, "Thank you, Echo."

"Sure thing." She reached back into that bag of hers and pulled out a wad of plastic-wrapped cash and handed it over, along with the passports. "Money and forged IDs."

Elijah huffed. "How the hell did you get all this in place so quickly?"

"Because I knew you were going to agree to this deal before you even knew about the deal," she replied, annoyingly smug. "All my research suggested you have a good relationship with your parents and you'd want to protect them. So I got organized."

"Thank you, Echo," Nancy said, her voice a little shaky as she took the passports. "And this is a lot of euros."

"Oh wait," Elijah scoffed. "You couldn't have possibly known I'd send my parents to France to hide."

"No," she said slowly, like she was speaking to a moron. "But the closest and safest way out of this country is mainland Europe. On the off chance we decided to send them north to Norway, there are Norwegian kroner in this bag."

"You're lying."

"Not lying." She pulled out the kroner.

Elijah exhaled. "Your organizational skills are almost as scary as you are."

"I've been dealing with psychotic assholes longer than you have."

His dad snorted from the back seat, making Elijah smile.

Any amusement died, however, when they reached Dover. Echo had already bought their tickets via the tablet by connecting to the SUV's Wi-Fi and data.

Sick to his stomach, Elijah tried to keep his senses open to danger as they escorted his parents toward the ticket office. He was trying not to think about the women he'd killed in his parents' house or the way his abilities allowed him to cremate ten people. Echo had assumed control over after that, told him to take a breath while she swept up the ashes and emptied them outside where they blew away in the wind.

The only thing that got him through it was remembering the sheer helplessness he'd experienced as he watched his parents clutch their hearts, dying before his very eyes. Even now, they looked older than they had hours before. What had that bloody coven done to them?

"I'd leave you alone to say goodbye, but I don't think that's wise. I'm sorry." Echo even looked apologetic. But Elijah understood. And his parents' safety mattered most.

As people boarded the ferry for the night crossing, Elijah memorized his parents' faces, terrified it might be the last time he saw them. As if reading his mind, his dad stepped forward and pulled him into a tight hug. "We'll see each other again, son. Don't you think otherwise." He reluctantly pulled away to let his wife hold their boy.

His mum, tears rolling down her soft cheeks, buried her face against Elijah's chest and held on like she never wanted to let go. He pressed his cheek to the top of her head and whispered he was sorry, that he never meant for any of this to happen.

"Don't you ever apologize." His mum pulled out of his hold to say fiercely. "We raised an extraordinary son who we are very proud of." She reached up to cup his face in her hands. "I wouldn't have wished for this kind of responsibility on your shoulders, my darling boy, but I have no doubt in my mind that you can protect us all from what's coming."

Emotion clogged his throat, but he gave her a tight nod.

"Look after yourself, son." Bill Webb squeezed Elijah's shoulder. "I know the choices you've had to make tonight will weigh on you ... but tough choices must always be made in war. You didn't want this war, Elijah, but they've brought it to your door, and you must do what it takes. That coven tonight was full of selfish, wicked intention that I think we all could sense. Grieve for what you had to do, but don't let it consume you."

"Compartmentalize," he murmured.

His father nodded. "And when it's over, we'll be here to get you through the aftermath."

Fuck, he loved his parents. He told them so.

"We love you too." They hugged him tight again.

And then he watched them turn to Echo. Her face slackened with bafflement as she was drawn into their embraces and showered with their gratitude and affection.

Elijah studied the awkward way she hugged them back and wondered if she wasn't used to such kindness. What was it like for her, being raised by a vampire whose sole intention was to destroy a race of beings?

Finally, they watched his parents ascend the ramp for the ferry and disappear on board.

"We need to leave, Elijah."

"I want to make sure the ferry leaves."

"We can't stick around. We can't let anyone know this is where we brought them."

Frustrated but realizing she was right, Elijah bit out a curse and turned on his heel to march away. Echo fell easily into step with him, despite his longer strides. As the scent of her perfume blew past him on the wind, he turned to look down at her. She glanced around as they walked, ever watchful, on guard. An image of her blurring through the coven, killing them with supernatural efficiency, filled his mind. She'd done that to save his parents. Almost got cooked by the sun to do it.

And he realized that the act of saving his mum and dad, of putting herself in danger to protect them, made him trust her in a way he hadn't before. Echo was as good as her word. Or at least she had been so far.

"I can feel you watching me." She sounded slightly irritated.

He smirked. "Other than the fact that you're rather nice to look at, I was thinking about what you did back at my parents' house. I've seen vamps move at speed before ... but I've never seen one move like you."

Echo shrugged as they got into the SUV, and Elijah thought she wasn't going to respond. But as she settled into the passenger seat, she said, "The general rule is that a vampire grows stronger and faster with age. However, there are some who are more powerful than others because of their lineage. By that, I mean, how closely related they are to an original vampire. William was extremely powerful and fast from the moment of his turning because he was turned by Eirik."

"Ah." Understanding dawned on Elijah. "And William turned you."

"Exactly. And my adoptive father is very particular about who he turns because of the power he's transferring to them. He's only turned a handful of vamps in his entire five-hundred-year existence. I'm the only one left in The Garm, which is probably why he wants me to be his second-in-command. Next to him, I'm the fastest, strongest vamp he's got."

"Impressive. Aren't I glad you're on my side."

To his delight, Echo hinted at a smile. He wished she'd do it more often. He wished he could hear her laugh. As if she sensed his desire, Echo stiffened and her smile melted. To his annoyance, he felt the chill in her emotions as she leaned toward the SUV's computer screen and tapped directions into the GPS.

"Where to now?"

"Gatwick Airport. According to your GPS, it's about an hour and twenty minutes from here."

He frowned. "I thought you said all the London airports will be under surveillance?"

"They will be. We're not boarding the plane to Canada the usual way."

"What do you mean?"

"There are bulk holds within the cargo space of a plane. It's where they put pets, and it's air-conditioned at the same temperature as the plane's passenger compartment. When we get to the airport, I'll find out which gate the plane is leaving from, and you and I will sneak into the cargo hold."

Elijah guffawed. "The fucking cargo hold? With the pets?"

"I've done it before. It's not comfortable, but it'll do."

"Fuck," he huffed. "Are you sure this is the best idea you can come up with? Can't we just sneak onto the actual plane from outside the gate?"

"Even if we did, what if the plane runs late? What if we arrive in New Brunswick before dawn, but for whatever reason, there's no gate available and the plane has to sit on the runway for hours until dawn?" She raised an eyebrow at him. "Do you want crispy-fried vampire for breakfast?"

He grimaced. "You have such a charming way with words. But I get your point. Cargo hold it is."

9

Keeping her expression neutral, Echo glanced quickly around once more and nodded at Elijah. She lunged with vampire otherworldliness up into the cargo hold. She walked through a narrow path between the containers that held the luggage, her eyes adjusting to the dark as she felt Elijah land behind her.

Sweeping the space, eyes dancing over luggage containers and freight pallets, Echo found a path toward the rear. "Follow me."

The bulk hold was at the back of the plane. Pushing open the heavy door, Echo eased inside the lit space and relaxed to find there was only one dog in his crate. Sometimes if she was in the vicinity of too many animals, they went a little crazy. As it was, the border terrier lifted his head with big, round, dark eyes and bared his teeth.

"Before I was a vampire, animals loved me," she commented as Elijah moved in behind her. With a small smile for the dog, Echo approached the crate cautiously as Elijah closed the door behind them. "Hey, buddy. You're on your own down here. You must be scared, sweet boy."

"How do you know it's a boy?"

Echo smirked. "I pay attention."

"Oh. Right."

The dog trembled, making her heart squeeze.

"It's okay. You're not alone now." She stepped closer to the crate and put her fingertips through as she crooned to him. "We're going to keep you company. I hope you don't mind. Are you nervous for your trip to Canada? Don't be, sweet boy. You're going to love it."

The dog tentatively sniffed her fingertips and then licked them.

She grinned triumphantly. "Who's a sweet, handsome boy? Yes, you are."

His tail wagged frantically.

"Let's get you out of this crate." She reached for the lock.

"Uh, I don't think that's a good idea." Elijah covered her hand.

The feel of his calloused fingertips on her skin made her shiver, and suddenly she was caught in those green-gold eyes. "Why not?"

Before he could answer, she tensed at the sound of two voices out in the cargo hold. She heard the words *final checks*.

"I hear them." Elijah grabbed her wrist and led her to the back of the room. The terrier barked at her departure. Pushing her into the darkest corner, Elijah covered her, his hands flat to the wall above her head. "Pull whatever shadows you can."

Somewhat surprised at his take-charge attitude, Echo shook herself out of her stupor and focused on the shadows in the cargo hold, drawing them under the bulk cargo door and toward her and Elijah. Between the two of them, they created what looked like one big shadow. It wasn't in a space that was particularly shadowy, so there was still a chance whoever was coming in would find something odd about it.

"I've never seen you like that," Elijah whispered.

Her heart raced at his nearness. "Like what?"

"Soft. Affectionate. Sweet. The way you were with the dog."

"I like dogs."

She felt his grin. "So I gathered. You, Echo Payne, are a complicated lady."

Something in his tone suggested he liked that about her. A flutter in her belly flustered her, and she snapped, "Will you shut up for a second?"

He chuckled and then silenced.

The door to the bulk hold opened, and though she couldn't see past Elijah's body, she could sense the person in the room.

"Hey, Milo. Did you hear us out there? That what's got you barking?" a man said behind them.

"Everything okay in here?" a female voice asked.

"Yeah, yeah, dog just heard us out there. Poor little fella is in here alone. I don't know ..." He strolled out, the door shutting behind him. "Don't think I could take my dog on a flight, man. Leaving him down here ..." His voice trailed off, and Echo relaxed.

Until she realized Elijah still covered her, and his head was now bent toward her, his nose at her neck.

She swallowed hard as her pulse throbbed. "You can get off me now."

"Really?" he murmured. "Pity."

He pushed away from the wall, and Echo could breathe properly again. Avoiding his intense gaze, she scooted past him and back to the dog.

"Your name is Milo, huh?" She unlocked the crate.

"You're really letting him out?"

"He can't stay in a crate for five hours." She let the dog sniff her hand again and petted his coat, getting him used to her. When he licked her all over, Echo asked him if she could lift him and slowly touched his sides so he would know what she intended. Milo allowed her to lift him out of the crate and into her arms, and he snuggled happily into her chest. He swiped with his tongue, catching her chin, and she laughed. "You are such a flirt, aren't you, handsome boy?"

She turned to Elijah with Milo in her arms and found the fae grinning at her. Raising an eyebrow, she asked, "What?"

He shook his head, grinning harder. "Nothing. You're just a big softie, that's all."

"I like dogs," she huffed, striding to an empty space of wall and settling down with her back against it. Milo happily burrowed into her for scratches and cuddles. "After I became a vampire, they seemed to hate me instinctively. I have to coax them out of their fear of me now."

Elijah settled on the wall, knees bent, his feet almost touching hers. His hands dangled between his knees. Leather cuffs covered his wrists where she'd burned him with the iron handcuffs. A chunky silver ring of Celtic design sat on the middle finger of his right hand.

"Tell me your story. Tell me why we're doing this," he said solemnly.

The urge to hide herself, to protect her secrets, was real. "It doesn't matter."

"It does matter. And we've got hours to kill. I need to know what I'm dealing with here with William, who Odette is to you, what the plan is. I can't go into this blind, Echo. If I have the facts, I can react accordingly to whatever situations might arise. Do you understand?"

She did. Unfortunately. Glancing down, she saw Milo had started to fall asleep. She kissed the dog's soft little head.

"You must have a way with animals. That dog doesn't even know you, and yet you'd think you were his owner." Elijah gave the dog an affectionate look.

"They realize once they get past the predatory thing that I'd never hurt them. They sense these things."

"I'm a bit like an animal in that regard," he replied. "I sense things. I sense danger."

"How does that work?"

"It's like precognition. My heart races suddenly, the hairs on the back of my neck go up, and I feel ... dread. Yes, dread is the right word for it."

Fascinated, Echo asked, "And this is always before something happens that might endanger you?"

"Or others near me, yes. Except ..." He narrowed his eyes and raised his arms to gesture with his wrists. "With you. I didn't sense this coming."

Remorse flooded her. It would have been so easy to lower her eyes in guilt. Instead, she forced herself to meet his gaze. "I am sorry. I didn't ... I didn't fully understand what I was doing with those cuffs."

"Well"—he heaved a heavy sigh as he lowered his hands—"you saved my parents' lives tonight, so you're forgiven."

She nodded, still uneasy, and she didn't know why. Echo just knew she didn't like it.

The plane glided forward, and Milo's heart beat faster beneath her palm. Soothing him, Echo held him tighter as they began to move. However, not long later, as the plane took off and began to ascend, Milo panicked with fright. Nothing Echo did calmed him, and her chest ached with sympathy for the poor dog. She grew angry at its owner. The terrier was small enough to fly with the passengers. He shouldn't have been left down in the bulk hold if he was terrified of flying.

A tingle of energy calmed Echo, an accidental overspill of Elijah's magic as he reached over to pet the frantic creature. Immediately, Milo calmed, his heart slowing, his body relaxing. Soon, his eyes closed and he slept deeply. Amazed, Echo watched Elijah ease back against the wall.

"Thank you," she said. The plane was loud, but with their supernatural hearing, they could still hold a conversation.

He nodded. "No problem."

"What else can you do?"

Elijah shook his head with a smirk. "No. I asked my questions first."

With another slow exhalation, ignoring the nervous flutters in her belly, Echo drew on the cool calmness William had taught her. *"Never let them see how you really feel,"* he'd always said to her when she was growing up.

"William raised me," Echo said matter-of-factly. "I don't remember anything different. As a child, he told me I was the daughter of two human friends killed in a car accident. So he raised me as his own. I grew up in the supernatural world but was taught to keep it a secret. Most of my life was spent at boarding schools in Canada. During the summers, William brought me to Europe, to his home in Munich. Sometimes we traveled to The Garm headquarters before they were in Munich, and that's how I knew of Eirik. He was like a strange, slightly terrifying uncle. I was brought up with the stories of Faerie and the prophecy ... about you."

Elijah's expression hardened. "And obviously you were taught I was the enemy. What changed?"

A bitter darkness threatened to swallow her whole as the memory of that night just over a month ago flooded back. She clutched Milo closer, taking comfort from his warm little body. "The fae I'm going to connect you with ... her name is Niamh Farren. We believe she's mated to a werewolf of unknown and mysterious origins. A werewolf who seems to be ... immortal."

"An immortal werewolf?" Elijah gaped. "What else is out there? Never mind, don't answer that ... just keep going. This Niamh woman—she's like me?"

"One of the fae children, yes. But she has psychic abilities. For a while, The Garm was tracking her because she kept turning up in places where disasters happened, and she averted them with her gifts."

"Like a superhero?"

"Yeah." Echo narrowed her eyes at how intrigued Elijah looked with the idea. "And don't even think about it. It almost got her caught by her enemies. She went off the radar again and we lost her trail. But then she showed up, alone, at my apartment in April."

"Why the hell would she take a chance like that?"

Echo paused a minute to regain mastery over her neutral expression. "Because she'd discovered the truth about my parents and about William. She left me with files she'd gathered on my family, and I spent a few weeks verifying them. Everything she shared with me was true."

"Which was?"

An image of her mother filled Echo's mind. "My mother is alive. Her name is Margaret Lancaster. She lives and works in London and is under constant surveillance by William. She's very beautiful, even now ... even with everything having been stolen from her."

"I don't like the sound of that."

She gave him a dark smirk. "Yeah, it's not a pretty story. William must have been besotted with her, but she left him for my father. A human man. And William waited until I came along to take his revenge. He butchered my father."

"Jesus fuck." Elijah blanched.

"I saw the crime scene photos." Her voice sounded dull and flat. "Multiple stab wounds all over his body. Throat ripped out. An ugly, violent, horrific way to die."

Her companion's voice was hoarse as he said, "I'm so sorry, Echo."

She barely heard him. "He stole me. Margaret, my mother, was investigated for months for my father's death and for my disappearance. She was finally cleared of all charges, but she was broken. Niamh included notes from Margaret's therapy sessions in the files she gave me. Although she's careful not to divulge William's true nature as a vampire ... she talks about him. The vile things he did to her. Killing my father, her love. And she knows he took me. She thinks I'm dead. It haunts her."

Hearing the emotion thicken her voice, Echo straightened her shoulders and cleared her throat. She sounded much more composed as she continued. "I was never given a choice in whether I could remain a human or become a vampire. The choice was made for me, and I let myself believe it was a gift. That William didn't want to lose me, to watch me grow old and die. But the truth is, it was all part of his revenge to make me into the thing Margaret, my mother, fears the most. Do you know he named me Echo deliberately? I am the embodiment of what unrequited love did to William.

"My entire existence is a lie. He stole everything from me. Including my humanity." The cool reserve she'd worked so hard to maintain cracked under Elijah's soulful, compassionate gaze. "I miss the sun, Elijah. Sometimes I ache with it. To be denied it, to be in constant darkness, knowing that the shadow world stretches before me in an awful eternity ... I haven't been happy in six years. Each day, I go through the motions, wondering if anything could ever make me feel the anticipation of living again."

"I am so damn sorry, Echo," Elijah said sincerely. "You deserve so much more."

She shrugged. "It's not all bad. I have Odette. She's my reason to keep going. And our purpose right now."

"Did William do the same thing to her?"

Rage churned in her gut. "He did. This time it wasn't personal. Her mother and father are still alive. I tracked them down via the lies that William told me about Odette when he first brought her into our lives. I was fourteen at the time, and he told me she was another orphan. In truth, her parents are Swedish. And her mother bears an uncanny resemblance to my mother. Odette and I ... people in The Garm have remarked that we could be true sisters."

"So we're going to Canada to collect Odette and keep her safe from William?"

"Exactly. We'll leave Odette with your parents. Once we've dealt with William, I'll take you to Niamh. And Odette back to her family."

"It sounds like *you're* her family."

"And I always will be. But Odette has romantic notions about what it means to be a vampire. She doesn't understand what she'd be losing. I won't let it happen to her. She'll grow up human with her human family."

"No matter what it costs you," he whispered, but she heard him.

Echo watched as he studied her, like she was the most fascinating being on the planet. "While I'm sure you think I'm not capable of it, I know what real love is. And sometimes it means sacrificing your own happiness to do what's best for the people you love."

To her shock, the fae smiled. A boyish, handsome smile that caused a flutter in her belly. "You might fool others, Echo, but you don't fool me. Of course I think you're capable of love." He gestured to the dog in her lap. "And tenderness and affection and compassion. You're also ruthless, focused, bitter, vengeful, and cold when you need to be. I see you, woman. I see you for exactly what you are."

"Bitter?" She raised an eyebrow, trying to break the sudden extreme tension between them.

"You're a little bitter." He held his forefinger and thumb close together. "A smidgen."

"Well, I have a reason." She shrugged.

"You do. And I can't say I wouldn't feel the same. I'm a little bitter about being fae because of what it's doing to my parents. That's nothing compared to what William has done to yours. And to you."

Echo nodded. "Now you know the truth. We're heading to New Brunswick to save the girl I consider a sister, and then we're taking on the leader of one of the most well-organized and well-funded supernatural crime organizations in the world."

Elijah considered this and rested his head back on the wall of the bulk hold. "Right. Well … sounds easy enough."

To both of their surprises, Echo gave a bark of laughter, jolting Milo in his sleep and causing Elijah to look at her in such a heated way, her cheeks turned hot for the first time since she'd become a vampire.

10

The nights she spent with Odette were the easiest to bear. No one had told Echo how difficult the transition would be. Three months had passed since the ritual in which she turned vampire, and an emotion akin to grief still weighed heavily on her.

She missed the daylight.

With such ferocity it shocked and appalled her.

Echo could only hope the melancholy, the longing, would dissipate with time.

For now, however, the evenings when sun set and she got to enjoy her little sister's company were the best.

Odette was a precocious six-year-old who made her laugh when no one else could.

"What are we watching tonight?" Echo asked Odette as they snuggled down on the sofa with a bowl of popcorn between them.

Her little sister considered this. "Frozen."

"Again?" Echo teased.

"Well, do you have a better idea?" Odette shrugged, her tone that of a beleaguered forty-year-old.

Laughing, Echo nodded and picked up the remote. "I'm introducing you to a Disney classic." When Echo had been a child, their father, William, had been around for her in the evenings. During the day, she had a werewolf nanny who was obsessed with Disney movies. Now that Echo was twenty, William seemed to have passed parenting Odette on to her. Not that she minded. At all. "Mulan." The movie opening credits started and Echo glanced down at her sister. "It's about an ordinary girl who becomes a warrior to protect those she loves."

"Okay, cool."

A few hours later, they'd watched Mulan (Odette was a fan) and had started Frozen when Odette's eyelids started to flutter. Echo pulled her sister into her arms, comforted by her warmth.

"Echo?" Her sister's quiet, sleepy questioning tone drew her gaze from the screen.

"Yeah?"

"There was a new girl at school today. Lucy told her our family is weird. Are we weird?"

For now, Odette was too young to know the truth about supernaturals. She imagined their father would explain the way of things to her at the same age he'd chosen to reveal it to Echo. Eight years old. She'd learned William adopted her after the death of her parents. That if she ever told the truth about who he was or any of the supernaturals in The Garm, she could cause their deaths too. Her innocence had been stripped from her and a dark responsibility placed upon her shoulders. It hadn't bothered her before. But the thought of the same being done to Odette filled Echo with fear and sorrow.

"We're not weird," she reassured her sister.

"I'm the only one at school who has a guard."

It was true. Echo had endured the same embarrassment of having a bodyguard throughout the entirety of her schooling.

"It's just to keep you safe. You know that."

"There's a new guard."

There was. Their father had assigned a hulking werewolf to Odette's daylight guard. "Gideon?"

"Weird name." Odette wrinkled her nose. "I don't like him."

Echo tensed. "Why?"

She shrugged. "Dunno. Just don't."

"Has he done something?"

Instead of answering the question, Odette asked, "How come I only ever see you at night now?"

Her six-year-old sister was a little too smart, though. "Because I have a new job that keeps me away."

"Like it keeps Daddy away?"

Echo hid her scowl. Perhaps it was time to have a discussion with their father about how rare his visits with Odette had become. "He's just ... busy. Making lots of money so we have a nice life."

"Oh."

"I'll never leave you, Odette. I might not be around all hours of the day, but I'm always here for you."

"Promise?"

"I promise."

"Love you." Odette burrowed sleepily into her side.

A lump caught in Echo's throat. "I love you more than you'll ever know."

Unfortunately, her duty to The Garm and to her father meant leaving Odette as soon as she was asleep to work. The next evening, however, her father had called at the last minute to tell her she had the night off. She didn't question it. Instead, she waited until Odette slept, then left the apartment to the one she kept for herself, where she had a fridge filled with blood. After slaking her thirst, Echo had gone for a walk around the city and returned to the apartment via the underground entrance.

Later, she would realize it was that unintended sneakiness that had made the wolf bold.

Echo woke abruptly.

Her eyes flew open and her body was stiff with tension beneath the covers. Her whole being seemed to hum with alertness.

She willed the blood to slow in her veins so she could hear, sitting up slowly and zoning in on her newly heightened senses.

The preternatural connection to the world meant she knew the sun was about to rise so she shouldn't be awake.

Something was wrong.

That's when she heard it.

Odette's muffled whimper.

One minute she was in bed, the next she was down the hall and throwing open the door to Odette's bedroom.

A large figure sat on her sister's bed, looming over her, his big paw covering Odette's mouth while his other pressed to her sister's stomach. His gaze flew to Echo's in shock.

Gideon. The new werewolf guard.

She could smell the perverse lust pouring off him.

Rage unlike anything Echo had ever experienced threatened to control her. The only thing that stopped her was her desire to protect Odette from everything. Even herself.

"Get up," she seethed.

The wolf swallowed hard. He was twice the size of her but he knew he was going to die for this. "It's not what you think." He stood slowly. "She was having a nightmare."

Odette burst into noisy tears. "No, no, I w-wasn't."

Fury and grief ripped through Echo. "Has he touched you before?"

Odette shook her head, sobbing hard.

She was so little. She didn't understand what had nearly happened to her. She just knew it was scary and bad.

"Stay here, little darling. I'll be right back. But stay here. Don't come out."

Odette just cried harder.

Gideon scowled, lumbering toward her, fists clenched at his sides. "Nothing happened."

Echo braced, sensing the change.

He charged at her.

She sidestepped him and he fell against the wall in the hallway from the force of his propulsion forward. Slamming Odette's bedroom door shut so she wouldn't see, Echo grabbed the wolf and vamp-sped them into the living room.

He tried to fight.

But her fury made her stronger than ever.

She snapped his neck.

Echo wanted to tear out his throat. Was tempted. But a dark, vengeful part of her wanted him to suffer. She called her father.

His fury was palpable.

Members of The Garm arrived to collect the repulsive werewolf. They'd hold him until William could be there to make his end slow and agonizing.

Despite the dawning sunrise, Echo stayed with Odette until she was calm enough to fall asleep. She ordered her nanny, Rosa, a strong but affectionate werewolf, to stay with her every second. They called the school to inform them Odette was sick with flu.

Only the weariness of the daytime allowed Echo to sleep.

When she woke, she checked on Odette who was quieter than usual but comforted by her sister's presence. She took a long time to sleep. Finally, when she drifted off, Echo made Rosa sleep in the room with her sister before she departed.

Beneath the many floors of The Garm's headquarters, in a basement Echo had never visited before, she found her father. And Gideon. He was chained up and had clearly been tortured for hours.

"This is the darker side of what we do," her father explained grimly. "But only to creatures like him." He studied her carefully. "I know how much you love Odette. I'm surprised you didn't kill him right there and then."

"Not in front of her." Echo's gaze moved to the werewolf whose body was covered in silver-inflicted wounds. Slashes and gashes, bruises and contusions. His face was a swollen pulp. Worryingly, Echo felt nothing but satisfaction. "And he deserved a slow death. Not a kind one."

"I was concerned your love for Odette was a weakness." Her father cupped her face in his palm, his expression soft with pride. "But you have so much control. Control ... yet a savage sense of righteousness. I'm proud to call you daughter."

He hadn't asked if Odette was all right.

Her father released her but held up a silver stake. "The kill should be yours."

Remembering Odette's sobbing terror. Her quietness this evening. Her fear of falling asleep ... Echo gave a short swipe of her head. "Inject him with silver. It'll be a long, slow, painful death. And I want to watch."

Her father raised an eyebrow but then nodded, a smug smirk curling his lips.

The next night, Echo watched as the werewolf was injected with the silver. She watched as he writhed in agony for hours before his heart gave out, and she felt the humanity bleed from her.

Odette was the last remnants of Echo's humanness. Of her soul.

That realization filled her with a yawning grief that could never be assuaged, and she knew that somehow, someday, she would have to protect Odette from losing everything Echo had lost.

11

It was much more difficult to disembark the bulk hold than it had been to board, and in the end, Elijah had to use his gifts to make the runway staff's eyes glaze over them as they walked through. Thankfully, despite her dark, memory-filled dreams, Echo had gotten some sleep during the flight—a much-needed energy boost.

Even better, the plane had arrived on time, so it wasn't light out.

And now Elijah was sulking because Echo had just stolen a car to get them to the boarding school, which was over an hour's drive south from the airport.

"I'm not sulking," Elijah said gruffly as Echo drove. "I don't sulk."

"You do a good impression of it."

"I just don't see why we couldn't rent a vehicle. You have plenty of cash in that rucksack. And I'm a millionaire, for Christ's sake. It feels wrong."

"That you're a millionaire? I agree."

"Don't bait me," he growled. "I am so far from the mood to be baited, I cannot tell you."

"That plane ride made you grumpy."

"It made you downright annoying."

Echo tried not to smirk. Needling Elijah was so much more fun than it should be. Glancing at him, she saw he was scowling ferociously out the passenger window. Sighing, as something like guilt flickered through her, Echo said, "If it makes you feel any better, I'll use the license plate to track down the owner and compensate them for stealing their car."

There was silence.

And then ... "Really?"

An ache flared in Echo's chest, and she scowled. "You're too honorable, too nice for this life, Elijah. If you're going to get through it, you're going to have to toughen up."

"If by toughen up, you mean turn into a cold, immoral arsehole, then you can fuck off."

There was more than a slight bite to his words, and she tried not to flinch at his caustic tone. "Don't pretend that you haven't been using your powers before now. Manipulating human minds ... how is that any better than stealing a car?"

"It's not the same. It was harmless."

"Messing with people's minds is never harmless."

"I didn't do anything that put anyone in danger. And anyway, you're one to talk. I know vampires have powers of compulsion."

"Only very strong vampires, and only when there's a blood connection."

"What the hell does that mean?"

She flicked a look at the pulse throbbing in his neck. Ignoring the answering dryness in her throat, Echo glared ahead at the road. "A blood connection is just a phrase we use when a vampire has taken blood from the same human several times. It creates a connection between them. Powerful vampires can sometimes use that connection to compel a person to do whatever they ask. A trait obviously gifted by the fae."

Elijah seemed to consider this. "Have you ever ...?"

"No," she replied abruptly. "I've never taken from the same human twice. I rarely ... I rarely drink straight from the source. My regular blood intake comes from blood bags. William buys them in bulk on the black market."

"So, what you did with Lincoln ...?"

"Not my usual method. But I was hungry, and he needed to die. Repulsed yet?"

"No. But I do want to know if his death bothered you."

"Why? Why does that matter to you?"

Elijah exhaled heavily. "Honestly, Echo, I don't know. I just know that it matters."

A shiver cascaded down her spine. She could feel him staring intensely at her. She answered honestly. "It bothered me. Death always bothers me. But I've learned to compartmentalize it. And I'm only bothered that I have one more death on my hands. I feel little remorse for unburdening the world of more Blackwoods. They're criminals. We tracked a plane crash in the Baltic Sea to them. A portion of their coven's bodies were recovered from that plane. Their favorite tactic is to do what they did at your concert—draw the energy from a mass of people, enough to kill them, to power up. We believe Niamh Farren was on that plane. Our guess, they killed everyone on board for the power to take her down, just as they killed over a hundred people at your gig to take you down. So yes, I'm bothered, and no, I'm really not."

After a moment's silence, Elijah observed, "He made you cold ... but it's not who you are. Who you really are shines through. I saw it with my parents, I saw it with Milo on the plane, and I see it when you talk of Odette. You're constantly fighting with who you really are."

A flicker of hot annoyance flamed to life in her gut. "No, I'm not. I'm not fighting it. I wear armor, Elijah, because it protects me. And like I said, if you were smart, you'd don some armor of your own."

"You don't fucking know me," he said tonelessly. "No, I don't like stealing. But stealing from the innocent isn't the same as taking down enemies who want to hurt the people I love. Believe me, Echo, I have no problem doing that. I think I've proven it. Being tough, having the ability to compartmentalize, doesn't mean you forgo all values and principles, that there is no line in the sand. There has to be a line, Echo. There has to be a line that you don't cross because if you do, you're no longer just someone protecting your family ... you're a fucking criminal."

"A survivor," she snapped back, glaring. "A survivor, not a criminal."

"Thief."

"Oh my God!" She threw a hand in the air. "I said I will pay for the fucking car!"

"Thanks. I appreciate it."

"You are so infuriating."

"And you are incredibly sexy when you're angry."

Echo experienced an unwelcome throb between her thighs in response. "Don't flirt with me."

She didn't have to look at him to know he was grinning. "Why? You like it. I can sense it."

Furious now, Echo scowled at him in warning. "Stay out of my emotions."

The bastard just kept grinning. "Afraid I can't. Your emotions are so much more honest than the words that come out of your mouth."

She tightened her grip on the wheel. "You are the most contrary pain in the ass I've ever met. One minute, you're Mr. Sulky Grumpy. Now ... this ... whatever this is."

"I had rather a terrible sleep on the plane, and I was a little put out about this whole car theft, but ... you have a strange effect on me. And I find that I much prefer flirting with you to being annoyed at you."

"I prefer the latter."

"No, you don't." He leaned his head back and closed his eyes. "But I'll let you pretend otherwise for now. Wake me when we get there, will you?"

A feeling akin to panic began to build in Echo as she stood in her sister's dorm room, staring down at her empty bed. It was still made. Her things were gone from her bedside table. Her clothes, except for her uniform, gone from her closet. The lingering trace of her scent suggested Odette hadn't been gone long.

So lost in her mounting anxiety, Echo flinched at the touch on her shoulder and swiped at it. Elijah held up his hands defensively and stepped back. Remorse filled her.

"Sorry," she whispered. "I didn't ... He ... he ..."

Tentatively, Elijah placed his big hands on her shoulders and gave her a comforting squeeze. "What is it?" he whispered too so they wouldn't wake Odette's roommate. "Where is she?"

Echo stared into his eyes, hoping everything she knew about the fae was true. Because she was going to need his powers. "William must know that I know. He's taken Odette. He got to her first."

Elijah's face hardened. "Where would he take her?"

Think, Echo, think.

"He must have sent werewolves, and they left during the day. They could be heading to Munich as we speak ..."

"We don't know that for certain, though. Wouldn't he entrust this to his best people, knowing how strong you are?"

He was right. William wouldn't leave this up to chance. He

might not have sent werewolves knowing they were no match for Echo. In a pack, they were, though.

Her eyes darted around the room and came to rest on Adelah, Odette's roommate and friend. If she witnessed Odette's departure, she might be able to tell them who had her sister.

"You want to interrogate the roommate?" Elijah guessed, as if reading her mind.

"After I'm done ... I need you to do the mind thing so she forgets."

He raised an eyebrow and said smugly, "And after your lecture in the car too."

"Just do it. Please."

Elijah grimaced. "Fine. You better wake her."

To say Adelah was frightened at first was an understatement.

"Shh, Adelah, it's me, Echo."

The young girl blinked rapidly, sleepily. "Echo? Echo ... what are you doing here?"

"I'm here for Odette."

"But she left." Adelah suddenly spotted Elijah and her jaw dropped comically. "But you're ... you're ..." She swallowed hard and then rubbed frantically at her eyes. When she saw Elijah still standing before her, she looked ready to burst with excitement. "You're Elijah Webb. From the Strix. Oh my God."

Echo rolled her eyes. Odette listened to nothing but music by gorgeous young pop stars that all sounded the same. But Adelah would have to have decent taste in music for a twelve-year-old. Damn Elijah's fame.

Obviously sensing Echo's growing impatience, Elijah shook his head. "Nah, I just look like him."

"No, you're his spitting image. You—"

Echo snapped her fingers in Adelah's face, bringing the girl's attention back to her. "This is important, Adelah. Where is Odette?"

The girl blinked owlishly. "But I thought you knew ... she said the people who came for her were family."

"When did they come?"

"I don't know ... about an hour ago."

Oh my God. Hope rose within Echo. "What did they look like? Do you remember names?"

"Is Odette okay? She said they were family. I promise." She looked ready to cry.

"She's fine. I just ... I need to find her, it's urgent. Who did she leave with?"

"A bunch of burly guys like the usual bodyguards your dad puts on her."

"How many?"

"Five. But the person in charge was a woman. Odette said she was your aunt Orla."

Holy shit.

Echo looked up at Elijah. "You were right. He sent his best."

His face hardened. "Someone who doesn't like getting a tan, perhaps?"

Jubilation filled Echo. "Exactly."

William had obviously worked out the truth (how, she didn't know) and was only an hour ahead of Echo. With Orla in their midst, they couldn't leave Canada until tonight. And they had to be near because the sun would rise soon.

"Thank you, Adelah." Echo squeezed the girl's shoulder and stood. "Your turn," she said to Elijah.

She watched the rock star lower to his haunches before the tween. Adelah's eyes were huge with girlish astonishment. And then as Elijah told her in soothing tones that she would forget this entire encounter and fall back into a peaceful, dreamless sleep, Adelah did just that. Elijah tucked the duvet around the girl and stood to face Echo. He looked unhappy at what he'd had to do.

That irritating flutter in her belly made itself known again as they shared a long look.

Elijah Webb was a good male.

Having been raised among a lot of males who fed right into that whole toxic masculinity thing, Echo couldn't help but feel attracted to a man who was the opposite of all that.

Sure, he had the sexy rock star persona thing down pat.

But that's all it was.

A persona.

It wasn't who he really was.

And who he really was ... well, she found it annoyingly appealing.

He raised an eyebrow, something like surprise in his gaze. "Echo?"

She wrenched her eyes from his and whispered, "I know where they are. They couldn't have gone far with Orla ... and if Orla is with them, there's probably at least one other vampire among the five men Adelah mentioned. We own a safe house in the woods at Hunter's Cove. It's private land, a couple of miles from any other property. It's where we stay when we visit Odette. It's deep in the woods—and sunlight proof."

"Isn't that an obvious place?"

"Yes, but I don't think William imagined we'd be this close behind. And he'd be guessing I wouldn't endanger Odette by attacking the cottage."

"And will you?"

"She's already in danger."

"That's a yes, then."

"My sister doesn't get hurt. But we *are* attacking that cottage." Echo picked up Adelah's cell on her bedside table. "One hour to sunrise. The safe house is twenty minutes from here. That gives us forty minutes to get inside."

Elijah nodded, impressing her with his lack of nervousness. "What's the plan?"

"To make one up in the twenty minutes it takes to get there."

"Oh. Wonderful plan. Really. Awards should be won."

Usually his sarcasm amused her, but Echo was way too anxious. "Sarcasm is the lowest form of wit." She pushed him toward the window. "Let's go, rock star, before I decide to leave you behind."

"Somehow I don't think you will. Got an awful feeling I'm going to be a big part of your plan."

"So you're not just a pretty face after all?" she sniped as he climbed out the window.

He ducked his head back in to grin at her. "You think I'm pretty? I bloody knew it."

Before she could snap back a retort, he let go, falling effortlessly out of sight.

"Smug British bastard," she muttered as she climbed out after him.

"Oi, I heard that," he whispered from far below.

12

It would seem Echo understood William well. The cottage at Hunter's Cove lit up in the dark. Guards patrolled outside, automatic weapons in hand. Wooden stakes were strapped to their hips. A precaution.

Or William truly didn't believe Echo would attack the cottage.

Elijah studied his companion as they hid in the dark forest. He could hear the water of the gulf hitting against the shore a mile away. The cottage sat in a clearing less than a hundred yards ahead of them. Together they'd pulled the shadows around them to keep cloaked from view and had a sound barrier up. At Echo's suggestion on the way there, he'd discovered the ability to smother their scents too. It allowed them to get very close.

Echo's beautiful face was pinched with worry as she took in the sight of the cottage, her love for her sister palpable. It made Elijah see the woman beneath the vampire. The combination of that closely guarded softness in her heart and the fierce warrior was intoxicating. It was making him feel things for the vamp. Dangerous things.

"You were right," he murmured. "They're here."

She looked at him. "There are two high-ranking vampires in that cottage. I know their scents. Odette's there ... she's ... I can smell her fear." Anguish gleamed in her eyes. "Why would she be afraid of them?"

Reaching out, Elijah placed a calming hand on her shoulder. He tried to soothe her with his magic, but nothing happened.

At his frown, Echo sighed. "You can't use your mind warp or anything like that on other supernaturals. We're immune."

That was new information. Good to know. "Who else is in there?"

"That's it. Orla and Roark. Plus the four wolves on guard outside. Two out front, two out back. Can't you hear their heartbeats?"

Elijah closed his eyes and tried to focus past the sweet scent of Echo, of the thrumming of her heartbeat, to those beyond. Finally, he heard them. Four different pulses outside. Three inside.

"Six." He opened his eyes and met Echo's enigmatic gaze. "What's the plan?"

"Vamp hearing is excellent. If you can cast this sound barrier over me and the wolves, I can take the wolves out before they realize what's happening. First the ones out front, then the ones out back."

"And from there?"

"Steal the stakes off the werewolves. We burst into the cottage. You take Orla. I'll take Roark."

The thought of killing the vampire filled him with dread, but he'd do it if it meant protecting a child and saving his family. "Sounds easy enough."

"You ready? Keep up with me and hold the barrier in place. No one can hear me breaking the wolves' necks."

He nodded grimly. "Got it."

A foreign sensation of determination and tightly leashed fury mingled with his own and he realized, once again, that he was feeling Echo. He didn't know how that was possible, especially considering she'd just told him his mind manipulations couldn't work on her. But it meant he was totally in tune with her and knew to move when she moved.

Keeping the sound barrier up around her, Elijah followed her at high speed as she broke the first guard's neck and then the second before the other even knew what was happening. The sound of their heavy bodies hitting the ground was heard only by them. Echo pointed to the stake strapped to the first's hip. "Take one."

Elijah did just that.

Echo gave him a nod as if to say *Ready?*

He nodded back, buoyed by how easy it had been. And all because of his gifts.

They were the wind as they flew around to the back of the house and Echo removed the other two guards from the playing field.

Echo paused, closing her eyes. She stretched herself, pushing her hearing past the sound of Elijah's soft breathing and his heartbeat that ticked a little faster than normal. His scent made her muscles tighten with awareness, but she shoved it aside and searched for Odette's scent again.

She smelled her fear.

She tried to focus past that and listen for the three distinct heartbeats.

Orla's was naturally a little faster than Odette's and Roark's.

Echo tuned into her senses, attempting to visualize their positions in relation to how far their heartbeats were from her.

Her eyes flew open, and she turned to Elijah, who watched her intently. He nodded at her to let her know the sound barrier was still up around them.

"Odette is in the middle of the room. Most likely the couch. Orla is closest—in the kitchen. Roark is by the front door. I'll go back around the front of the cabin and enter that way while you enter here." Uneasiness moved through her as she asked, "You can sense me, right?"

He nodded.

"So you'll sense when I'm ready to burst in on them?"

"Absolutely. I'll go when you go."

"Straight in the heart." Echo pointed the stake near her chest. "No messing around. If you think in the two seconds it takes you to assess the situation that you won't make the heart, twist her head clean off. Orla is old and fast. Don't give her time to react."

A hardness settled on Elijah's features. "I can do this."

With a nod, Echo hurried away, all the while hoping like hell she wasn't leading this male to his death or endangering her sister's life. She had to trust in Elijah's abilities. But more than that, she had to trust that he could embrace the darkness. If only temporarily.

Blood rushing in her ears, Echo braced herself at the front door and then vamp-sped her way through it, the door bursting off its hinges as she flew at Roark.

But he was fast.

Too fast.

Suddenly, Odette was in his arms, his hand around her throat, stretching her neck upward alarmingly far. Fresh tears fell down her sister's face.

A scream rent the air and Echo's eyes flew from her sister to where Orla burst into a cloud of ash. Elijah coughed, lurching backward as the ash covered him. "Fuck. Fucking gross."

Roark growled, pulling on Odette's hair. "Your father is going to make you pay for that. Orla was two hundred years old!"

"Well, no wonder she copped it easily," Elijah drawled, patting the ash off his clothes as he slowly ventured into the room. When Roark pulled on Odette's neck, making her whimper, Elijah stopped moving. "She was well past her prime."

Roark sneered at him. "You're the fae."

"Echo," Odette whimpered. "W-what's h-happening?"

Before Echo could speak, Roark grinned. "What's happening is that Echo sees William for what he is. Finally, the blinders have come off. Dearest Daddy is a monster, and Big Sis wants to save you from him."

Echo bared her teeth. "What's your agenda in all of this?"

His gaze raked over her. "I want to offer you a deal."

"What kind of deal?"

"You work with me to kill William so I can take over The Garm ... and I'll back off the fae hunt." He jerked his chin at Elijah. "I'm not interested in the fairy. I am interested in the power and the money and the businesses."

That Echo could believe. "You want me to sign it all over to you after William's dead?"

"That ... and you'll be my mate."

Revulsion roiled through her. "Never."

He pulled Odette's hair and she cried out.

"Stop that, you son of a bitch."

Roark narrowed his eyes. "We're good together, Echo. You can't deny how good the sex was."

Anger mingled with possessiveness hit Echo like a wave, and it took her a second to realize those emotions were not hers. Attention flying to Elijah, her cheeks flushed with humiliation that Roark had outed her shame in front of him and Odette.

Elijah's fist tightened around the stake in his hand. He looked murderous.

"Keep your filthy mouth shut," Echo snapped at Roark.

"I want you to be my mate. That's the deal. Or I kill little

Odette here, blame it on you, and help Dearest Daddy hunt you to extinction."

There was a sudden blur of movement. So fast Echo could have blinked and almost missed it. One second Roark had Odette in his grasp, the next second his head was falling to the floor and thudding with gruesome dullness before bursting into ash. His headless body exploded at the same time.

Elijah stood behind Odette, his face a mask of cold fury.

He'd moved with a speed Echo couldn't compute. It had been the same with Niamh Farren.

Echo was superfast.

But *they* moved liked they were jumping dimensions.

Odette let out a wail and rushed into her big sister's arms.

Echo wrapped her up tight, tears in her eyes as Odette sobbed. Her gaze locked with Elijah's. "Thank you," she whispered hoarsely.

He just gave her a grim nod and wiped a hand over his body. The air crackled with energy and the ash that had peppered his face and hair disappeared.

13

Hours in a cargo hold was different this time. Only slightly. Instead of Echo soothing a scared dog, she held Odette against her. In Elijah's mind, he'd understood that Odette was only twelve, but seeing her brought home to him that Echo's sister was a child. An innocent child pulled into this dark, violent world.

If it was hard for him to process as an adult, how much harder was it for her?

She seemed to believe Echo's explanation on the way to the airport, though the girl remained tearful and pale. She'd reluctantly agreed to stay with Elijah's parents until Echo could make her safe.

After sobbing for a while, the girl eventually wore herself out and fell asleep nestled against Echo.

The cargo hold was loud, but like last time Elijah could hear with his fae senses, as could Echo with her supernatural hearing.

He tried to stop himself from asking but ... remembering Roark's taunt about how good sex between the vampire and Echo had been made him want to reverse time so he could rip off the predator's head once more.

It was jealousy.

Unlike Elijah had ever experienced before.

Almost brutal in the possessiveness.

He wasn't entirely comfortable with the strength of the feeling for two reasons. He shouldn't feel anything like that for Echo. And even if she were to return the feelings, she was her own being. She belonged only to herself. Not an object for him to feel possessive over.

It was some kind of latent caveman quality that was an uncomfortable fit with who he thought he was.

"So, Roark?" Fuck. The question was out before he could stop himself.

Echo glanced down at Odette as if to make sure she was asleep. When she held his gaze again, he saw self-loathing there. "A moment of weakness after I found out the truth about William. Believe me, it's one of my biggest regrets."

"I have to say I'm glad he wasn't a serious love interest. He was kind of a giant elephant turd."

Her lush lips twitched, making his dick respond in kind. "He was more than kind of—he was *definitely* a giant elephant turd."

He laughed as she grinned.

But her smile faltered. "I hate that I gave him that."

"I hate it too," he found himself admitting.

Echo's breath hitched, her gaze questioning.

"But we've all made those kinds of mistakes." Elijah shrugged. "I once woke up next to my roommate's mother."

Echo gaped. "You're lying."

"Nope." He scrubbed a hand over his nape, laughing softly in long-forgotten embarrassment. "It was the end of first year at uni. My roommate came from money. Invited me along to their holiday home in Spain. A villa. Very nice. Had a room all to myself. One night I wake up because his very attractive and unhappily married mother is getting into bed with me."

Echo glanced down at Odette again.

"Is she sleeping?"

"Yeah. I can tell by her heartbeat. You were saying?" She didn't look at him.

Was she jealous too?

"I was an idiot and for a second let my di—body do the thinking. She knew what she was doing, if you get my drift."

"I get it."

"Yeah, well, I would feel bad about it, but his father was sleeping with his assistant, and my roommate had shagged a girl I really liked the previous semester."

"So, it was revenge?"

"Nah. Nothing so calculated as that. It just made me more amenable to being seduced by her. But I regretted it afterward."

"I think mine is worse. Roommate's mom doesn't really come close to psychopathic vampire."

At the very thought of the bastard touching her, Elijah's hands clenched into fists. "Right. Very true, love."

"I thought I felt ..."

At her sudden silence, Elijah pushed. "You thought you felt ...?"

"When Roark brought it up ... I thought I felt something from you."

The blood rushed in his ears. "What something?"

"Jealousy?"

Elijah had never seen the point in lying. Even if it complicated things. "Yeah, that's about right."

Echo's lips parted in surprise as if she hadn't expected him to answer honestly. "I ..."

He waited, wishing like hell the little sister wasn't sitting between them.

Finally, Echo shook her head as if shaking loose a thought.

Elijah found that maddening. He wanted to understand her in a way that would probably be detrimental to his health.

"So ... is that who you were in high school and college? The guy all the MILFs wanted to get their hands on?"

He snorted at the mere thought. "Not at all. Definitely not when I was a kid."

"What were you like? What was your childhood like?"

"Why?"

"I guess I'm curious."

"Well, it was a bit of woe-is-I tale. I was bullied."

"You?" She raised an eyebrow. "With all your gifts?"

"My parents did a very good job of convincing me it was dangerous to use my gifts. I didn't use them against the kids who bullied me."

"Bullied you how?" She scowled like the thought made her angry.

"Humans sense there's something off with me. Kids sensed it. They didn't want me around. They called me names. Beat me up. There was this group of lads in particular who were relentless in primary school. Mum and Dad were always at the school to ask them to sort it out, but there's really not much the school can do. Or at least that's what they said. My payback was sneaky, and I did things that couldn't lead back to me. Like tying their shoelaces together with my mind so when they stood up, they fell, but I was seated way across the classroom, so how could it be me?"

"Very devious."

"I changed their answers on tests. I even made the ringleader of this group think he was being haunted at home."

She laughed softly. "Good. I'm glad."

Elijah grinned. "Yeah, it was fun. It made me feel like I had a bit of control, even though I hated going to school. It gave me a pit in my stomach every day walking into that building."

"I'm sorry. I never would have guessed that about you."

He shrugged. "It is what it is. I think in a way it made me more empathetic. Which is a good thing when you have power like mine."

"Agreed. Is the bullying the reason you turned to music?"

Elijah grimaced. "I wish I could say it was something as worthy as that. But the truth is I had a crush on this girl when I was fifteen. Like, thought I was in love with her. However, she rejected me in front of this older boy *she* had a crush on. He was in a band. They started dating. My reaction to that was to pick up a guitar and learn to play."

"You're kidding?"

"Nope. Wish I was." He laughed, abashed. "But hey, it turns out I loved it. I love playing. I love writing music. I found some like-minded geeks at school, and we started a band. I still didn't get very far with the girls until I learned to accept that I was different. My parents had always told me it made me special, but I was angry about it for a long time. When I finally embraced it, that's when the ladies came flocking." He winked.

Echo rolled her eyes.

"Nah, in all seriousness, it changed everything for me. It freed me."

"Your parents weren't worried about you becoming famous?"

"Of course they were. I started the Strix at uni. We got signed at twenty-one. Everything was a whirlwind after that, and my parents were constantly worried I'd get found out. Then I learned about the world of the supernatural. With my gifts, it was easy to accept the truth when I met my first vampire. Then I heard about werewolves and witches and warlocks. In fact, I thought it was great. Warlocks explained everything about me, or so I thought. Until now. Never would have guessed fairy." He smirked, even though his insides were in turmoil at the thought of what his very existence meant for the world.

"You're going to be okay, Elijah. I won't let anything happen to you."

An ache spread across his chest. "Hey, that's my line."

14

"You know, if you turned me into a vampire, you wouldn't be freaking out so much right now because I'd be strong enough to take care of myself," Odette spoke up from the back seat of the stolen vehicle.

Echo had half expected Elijah to put up a fuss again about the theft, but he seemed to have let go of his scruples in the face of their dire situation. Odette's words distracted her from her thoughts on their conversation in the cargo hold. Not just about him not being whom she prejudged him to be, but about his jealousy. And what that meant.

How that made her feel.

How it complicated things when complication was the last thing they needed.

Echo turned around to look in the back seat at her little sister. Odette had been in a state of numb shock when she roused her to sneak off the plane. They'd landed at the Montpellier International Airport just after sunset and then stole an SUV from the long-term parking lot. Elijah had fried the security cameras before the theft. His powers truly did come in extremely handy.

Odette had remained quiet as Elijah drove them around the outskirts of the city and onto a freeway.

They were all silent and tired, the only sound in the car the rushing of the road beneath it, the traffic outside, and the French GPS that Elijah turned to English with a wave of his hand and a crackle of energy. He'd explained to them that his doomsday property was deep in the heart of Lozère, a rural region of the country. They'd drive two and a half hours north and then they'd have to walk half an hour through thick forest to get to the cabin.

Echo, despite her tiredness, couldn't sleep at night for obvious reasons.

"I'm not turning you into a vampire. Ever. Certainly not when you're only twelve."

Odette stuck out her chin stubbornly. "I'll find someone else to, then."

"Really?" Impatience crackled in her voice. "So you're going to live all of eternity in a twelve-year-old's body? When your mind and heart mature and you want adult things, you won't be able to have them because you're in a child's body. You'll go insane. Remind me to let you watch *Interview with the Vampire*."

Her sister, despite her youth and immaturity, was smart. She processed Echo's wise words quickly and agreed. "Fine. You're right about that. But Daddy promised he'd turn me when I was eighteen."

"He isn't your father." Emotion clogged her throat. "Odette ... you don't know what he's done."

"Then tell me. I'm not a little kid. Orla was being super nasty to me, and Roark was all kinds of creepy. I can't believe Daddy would let them treat me like that."

"He did. He had them take you to get to me."

"And you killed them. Why? Why did Daddy make them take me?"

Sighing, Echo turned back around, her fingernails biting into her palms. How did she explain this to her kid sister who was so much more of a little girl than Echo had ever been?

"Tell her," Elijah prompted. "She deserves to know the truth. Even if it hurts."

"Yeah, tell me. Tell me why the lead singer of the Strix is driving us to a safe house in France."

The corner of her lip curled at her sister's dry tone, but the smile fell away as reality set in. With a pit in her stomach, Echo unclipped her seat belt and started to clamber between the seats to get into the back.

"What are you doing?" Elijah asked, reaching for her.

"I need to be next to her when I tell her." Echo grunted, trying to squeeze through the narrow space.

Then she stiffened when she felt a strong hand on her ass.

Elijah cleared his throat. "I was trying to help you."

"Or copping a feel," she replied sarcastically.

"Can't it be both?" he teased.

Echo held back an unexpected snort of amusement. The fae had a natural way of easing the tension. She wasn't exactly Little Miss Sunshine, so it was a big thing that he could make her smile.

Odette glanced between her sister and Elijah as Echo settled into the back seat beside her. "Is he your boyfriend?"

"No," they answered in unison, and Echo cut him a dark look for his too-fast response.

Elijah seemed to sense it and chuckled.

When Echo turned to her little sister, Odette didn't find anything amusing. She looked indignant and scared out of her mind.

After a long, slow exhale, Echo launched into her story about Niamh Farren and the truth about William "the Bloody" Payne. When she was done, silent tears fell down Odette's cheeks.

"You—you're saying my real parents are alive?"

Echo nodded grimly. "They are."

"And your mom ... she's alive too?"

She nodded again, a twisting, agonizing pain knifing through her heart at the thought. "He stole us from them."

"And he did all this because your mom left him for your dad? And he killed your dad?"

"Yes."

Odette wiped at her nose, looking so much like a little girl. "But why my mom and dad?"

"Because your mom looks like my mom."

Her eyes washed over Echo. "That's it? He ruined us all because my birth mother looks like a woman he was creepy obsessed with?"

"I'm afraid so."

"And that's why we look like real sisters?"

"Yeah."

"This is true? You know this for a fact?"

"I did my own research, little darling. It's all true."

"And the fae aren't bad?" Her gaze flicked warily to Elijah.

Echo could have sworn she felt a glimmer of fury, and it wasn't coming from her. It was coming from the fae in the driver's seat.

"No. That was a lie too."

That fury simmered way down and melted into gratitude.

Complicated. That ... sensing his emotions. Echo was afraid to look too much further into the connection between them.

"I hate him," Odette hissed. "I hate William."

"I know." Echo pulled her into her arms and let her cry it out. "I'm going to keep you safe. And when it's all over, I can take you back to your parents."

Odette's head flew up, a different kind of fear there. "But what about you? I'm not leaving you. I want to be sisters forever."

Heart aching so badly, it felt like it might be cracking, Echo smoothed her thumbs over her sister's cheeks, wiping away the wet from her tears. "I won't damn you to this existence, little darling. I know you have it in your head that this life is romantic and amazing, but it's not. I miss ... I miss the sun on my face every minute of every day. I miss walking in the daytime with you. I miss the fragility of a human existence. You see ... not knowing when your life will end is what makes you *live* every day. I'm just *existing*, Odette. Existing in this hellish place of eternal darkness and blood and violence. And I would give up the power and the speed forever if I could just feel the daylight on my face one more time."

Fresh tears spilled down Odette's cheeks as she reached up to wipe away the tears Echo didn't even realize were slipping down her own.

"Okay," her little sister finally whispered. "But I don't want to leave you. You're the only family I have."

"I will never leave you. But I want you to think about your real parents. Really think about it. And if you decide you want to go home to them, it doesn't mean I'll go away. You'll always have me."

Odette nodded, her face crumpling again as she tucked it against Echo's throat and cried quietly.

Not quite two hours into the drive, Elijah followed the GPS off the freeway. From there it was around half an hour of driving through the French countryside. They passed through tiny, rural villages until eventually, they came to a single-track road shrouded by woodland.

Odette had fallen asleep again. Echo reckoned it was with grief as much as it was the travel and jet lag. Her strange but familiar world had been shattered.

Elijah pulled the vehicle over as the road came to an end. He turned to look at her, sympathy in his eyes as he glanced at Odette in her arms. "We walk from here."

Nodding, she gently urged Odette awake. She grumbled but

got out of the car and gripped Echo's hand like a much younger child. Echo held on tight as they followed a quiet Elijah through the dark woods. While she and Elijah had great night vision, it was proving difficult for Odette, and Echo had to point out objects in their way as they walked.

"Your parents are nice?" Odette whispered. She sounded so young. So frightened.

"They're wonderful," Elijah assured her. "They'll take good care of you."

Echo felt her sister's gaze on her face. "They really are wonderful people. I wouldn't leave you with them otherwise."

"And you're sure I can't come with you?"

"No, little darling. I need to know you're safe so I can focus on helping Elijah. I gave him my promise."

"Okay." She was quiet again for a little while and then she whispered to Echo, "He's really cute."

Elijah chuckled softly under his breath.

Echo smirked. "And he can hear you."

"So? I think the lead singer of the Strix knows he's cute."

At that, Echo laughed. Mostly from relief because Odette sounded a little more like herself.

She proceeded to ask Elijah a bunch of questions about fame and being in a band, if he had a girlfriend or a boyfriend. Eventually her chatter faded, however, and Echo heard her heartbeat increase as they walked into a clearing. Elijah's lodge sat in the middle of the woods, lit up. Odette's heart sped up even faster.

"You're going to be okay," Echo insisted. "I promise."

Odette nodded, but her face was pale with fear.

They approached the porch steps and walked up to them, not masking the sound to give Elijah's parents some warning. He knocked loudly on the door. "Mum, Dad! It's me!"

A few seconds later, the door flew open, and Bill and Nancy Webb stood there, peering out into the dark. Relief flooded their wary expressions, and Echo watched with something akin to envy as they pulled their son into a tight hug. All three of them held one another and murmured words of affection.

Echo looked down at her sister. Odette studied them, a little of her fear dissipating. Her heart slowed.

"Mum, Dad ..." Elijah stepped back from his parents. "This is Echo's sister, Odette."

"Oh, sweetheart." Nancy made the first move, stepping forward to cup Odette's face. "I'm Nancy, Elijah's mum. You must be exhausted and hungry. Come on in and let's get you fed."

Echo gave her a grateful smile as Odette relaxed into Nancy's embrace and let the older woman lead her inside.

"This is my husband, Bill. Bill, help me get some food together for Odette."

Feeling Elijah's gaze, Echo wrenched her own from her sister to him. Gratitude swelled within her.

"She'll be all right here." He gestured for her to follow him inside.

The cabin wasn't some rustic building in the middle of nowhere. It had a large open-plan living room/kitchen with a log-burning fire in the center. The kitchen was modern and well appointed. Throws and cushions decorated the large leather sectional, the room warmed by area rugs and paintings on the walls. It was as if someone had truly made a home here.

"You set up this place well, son. How did you manage it?" Bill asked as Nancy fussed over Odette. Elijah's father looked at Echo. "There's a basement filled to the brim with long-life food and a ton of dry wood already cut for the burner."

Elijah shrugged. "I paid someone to have it ready in case I needed an escape from the world."

"We've been very comfortable here. There's even Wi-Fi via satellite dish and smart TVs in every room." Bill's smile fell. "We saw on the news the boys are distraught about your disappearance."

Elijah closed his eyes briefly. "I feel terrible for putting them through this."

"You're keeping them safe," Echo reminded him. They hadn't had time to look at the news in the mad dash to save Odette. "Is it a big news story?"

"Oh, yes." Bill nodded. "Apparently, everyone is talking about it on social media. There are a ton of conspiracy theories. Especially because *we've* gone off the radar too."

"Shit." Echo scrubbed a hand over her face. "That will only fuel the Blackwoods and William. We'll stay until tomorrow's sunset, but then we have to leave."

"So soon?" Nancy spoke up.

"I'm afraid so."

Odette's lower lip trembled, and guilt clenched Echo's stomach.

"I will get back to you as soon as I can."

"And we'll take the best care of you until then," Nancy promised, smoothing Odette's hair back from her face.

The child nodded but appeared to be seconds from bursting into tears.

"Let's eat." Elijah clapped his hands, trying to defuse the tension. "I'm starving."

15

Odette fell asleep on the couch not long after Nancy and Bill fed them a dinner of tinned spaghetti on toast. They then updated Elijah's parents on what had happened in Canada, about Odette's parents, and what their plans were next. Then Elijah offered to help Echo daylight-proof the guest room she would share with Odette. Bill had found them masking tape so they could secure the curtain edges to ensure Echo could sleep safely during the day.

Elijah suddenly spoke, soft and low, "What you said in the car to Odette ... is that true?"

Echo couldn't linger too long on those thoughts, those feelings. It was a survival thing. "About hating being a vampire? About missing the daylight? Yes."

Her abrupt tone didn't put him off. "I ... I know it is. I feel ... I feel your grief. I just ... I just don't understand *why* I can feel it, and so I wanted to confirm it with you."

Unable to answer the underlying question because it was something else she couldn't think about, Echo remained quiet.

"I hate that for you," he whispered gruffly. "I wish there was something I could do to help."

"No one can help me, Elijah. I'm a lost cause." She met his gaze. "And I can't dwell on it too long, or I won't be able to do what needs to be done next." Taping down the last corner of the curtain, Echo moved to stride past him to exit the room.

But Elijah grasped her wrist, stopping her. "And what happens once you've taken your revenge and we've stopped The Garm? Once Odette is safe with her parents? What happens to you?"

His questions nudged at a thought she'd kept buried. "I won't go anywhere while Odette needs me."

His grip tightened. "And when she's gone?"

"I ... I can't live like this forever. I'd rather die."

Something like panic flashed across his face. "So, when Odette dies, hopefully after a long, natural life ... you ...?"

Echo tugged her hand from his hold, ignoring the awareness that tingled through her. "I die."

He flinched. "Echo—"

"I'm going to put Odette to bed. She needs a good night's rest." She walked out before he could take the conversation any further.

By the time Elijah woke the next day, it was past lunchtime. When he'd laid his head down in the second of three bedrooms at the back of the cabin, he'd thought he'd drift right off, having had such little sleep these past few days.

However, he couldn't get the look of despair on Echo's face out of his mind. He couldn't stop feeling that sharp, hollow pain that was her grief. And it disturbed him beyond belief that Echo had tied her existence to Odette's. That she planned to leave this world once her sister died because she couldn't bear her life as a vampire.

He wanted to fix it all for her.

He wanted her happy and safe, and he couldn't understand why he felt so much for her when they'd known each other for such a short time. Not to mention the way they'd met. He literally had scars from their encounter.

Eventually, Elijah must have drifted off. By the time he wandered into the kitchen, his mum was the only one there to tell him his dad had taken Odette for a walk to calm the poor girl down. Apparently, she was fretting about Echo leaving that evening.

"Has anyone checked on Echo?"

"I did," his mum replied quietly as she made him a coffee. "She's safe. The room is pitch black."

"Good." He slid onto a stool at the breakfast bar.

"You seem to have grown to care for her. Echo, I mean."

Elijah smirked at his mother's questioning tone. "I don't know what I feel."

"But you feel something?"

Only to her could he admit, "I do. And it's probably bloody stupid of me."

"Or not." His mum's attention drifted over his shoulder toward the hall that led to the bedrooms. "She needs someone like you to remind her there's good in the world. That there is light." She met his gaze. "She grew up in a violent world and has only known darkness for much of it. But she was meant for more than that, Elijah."

"How do you know?"

"The way she loves that little girl. The way she looks at you when you're not looking." She gave him a soft smile.

His breath caught. "How does she look at me?"

"Like you're the sun she misses."

Emotion stung his eyes. "You see more than most people, don't you, Mum?"

She shrugged, pushing the mug of coffee toward him. "I see the way you look at her too."

Elijah stared into the drink before him. "Isn't it too soon ... to ... I don't know."

"I fell in love with your father in a day," she reminded him. "With some people ... you just know. Whether it's a friend or a lover. They're our soulmates. Time doesn't get to dictate our feelings on the matter."

"I don't think she wants to be loved," he replied hoarsely.

"No, I imagine it terrifies her. But she needs it. She needs to be loved. We all do."

"Sometimes, when I get a chance to breathe, I can't believe how messed up our lives are right now. All of us."

"It'll sort itself out." His mum reached over to caress his cheek. "I never would have wanted this kind of responsibility on your shoulders. But deep down I knew you were born to do something incredibly important. And I know, in my heart, that you'll keep us all safe. That *good* will win in the end."

His chest ached. "I love you, Mum. I'm so grateful for you."

"I love you too, sweetheart. We're all going to be okay. I know it."

16

THANKS TO HER VAMPIRIC INSTINCTS, Echo knew she'd awoken a little before sunset. Lying in the safe darkness of the guest room, her supernatural hearing focused on the lives beyond the bedroom door.

She could hear Elijah packing for their long drive, explaining to his parents and Odette the plan she'd laid out to him on the plane ride here. They were driving to Scotland. To the Highlands, where the ex-fae turned werewolf and mate of Alpha MacLennan lived. Thea Quinn MacLennan. She was once fae-borne, but William had it under excellent authority that Thea's mate Conall, a powerful werewolf and Alpha of the last pack in Scotland, had turned her with his werewolf bite to save her from dying. She'd been stabbed through the heart with a pure iron blade. He'd bitten her.

It was proof that Eirik's stories were true. A werewolf mate could turn a fae into a mortal-but-long-lived werewolf. William had been furious and had considered killing Thea just to punish her for slipping through his grasp. In the end, he'd decided Conall was too powerful and respected within the supernatural world to risk war with. Thea had been left alone.

However, she was their only lead to Niamh Farren. Echo had to believe that Thea could lead Elijah to Niamh. That they could all help her bring down William and The Garm.

"Is it safe to drive there? Will Echo be safe?" She heard Nancy ask with genuine concern.

She couldn't remember the last time anyone had ever showed any kind of real parental concern for her. Perhaps William did when she was a child, but those memories were shadowed now by his lies.

"We'll make it to Calais just before sunrise. We'll find somewhere there to hunker down until the sun sets again. With the long days, we'll only make it to Yorkshire before we need to stop. Then we'll drive through the next night and stop in Stirling. The days get longer the farther north we drive. It'll take us at least three nights to get there. If it were winter, we'd get there faster."

That was the plan. Of course, if she hadn't allowed her psycho adoptive father to turn her into a vampire six years ago, they could have made it there in less than twenty-four hours.

"You'll keep her safe, won't you?" She heard Odette ask quietly. "She's the only family I have left."

Echo squeezed her eyes closed. Because that wasn't true. And there was a real possibility that if Odette decided to return to her parents, Echo might never see her again. It would be for Odette's safety. To give her a normal existence.

"I promise I will guard her with my life," Elijah vowed.

A different kind of ache warmed her chest just as the tingling all over her body told her the sun had set.

It was time to go.

They'd both remained silent as they'd trudged through the dark woods back to the SUV. Odette's quiet sobs still rang in Echo's mind and heart. She had a feeling Elijah knew she needed time to process leaving her little sister behind and that's why he didn't speak until they reached the vehicle.

"They're all safe here. No one knows about this place. I bought it under a pseudonym with cash. Even the guy who got all the supplies together doesn't know my real name."

Echo nodded. "I know. I just wish I knew for certain I'd be back for her."

"Don't talk like that again."

Again referred to the fact that she'd brought up her possible death to the Webbs while Odette was in the bathroom. Echo had done it so she could give them the name and address of Odette's real parents in case she didn't come back from this fight to deliver Odette to them herself. Bill had paled at the request, his gaze flickering worriedly to his son. Echo wished she could promise them Elijah would make it out of this fight alive too. But all she could promise was that she'd die protecting him, just as he'd promised the same to her little sister.

What a funny team they'd turned out to be.

Nancy had vowed to take Odette to her parents if it came to it.

"But it won't," she'd insisted sternly. "And you have to believe that too."

"I'm just being realistic," Echo said now.

"You're just getting on my nerves with the fatalistic bullshit, that's what you're doing," Elijah grumbled as he climbed into the SUV.

Echo smirked and followed him inside.

To keep him awake on their long drive north, Echo asked him questions about his life in the band, about their music. The conversation flowed as they chatted about music they both liked, movies, travel ... Echo even told him more about her life with William.

"There was always a wall up between us. He professed to love me, but it was from a distance."

"And you loved him."

Echo wasn't sure it was a question. "It's funny how quickly love can turn to hate when the person you love betrays you."

"Do you hate him? Really?"

"Why would you ask that?"

"Because if it comes to it, could you kill the man you thought of as a father?"

"Elijah ... I *need* to kill him. Don't you see that? Odette will never be safe while he's alive. You will never be safe while he's alive." Rage simmered quietly in her gut. "He deserves to die for the untold pain he's caused over the centuries, not just for the pain he's caused me and Odette."

"I'm sorry I asked."

"Don't be. You need to know you can count on me. And you can."

"You can count on me too."

"I already know that. You're one of the few beings on the planet I trust."

He shot her a warm look before his gaze returned to the road.

After a few hours they fell into comfortable silence, only talking now and then.

They stopped at a couple of service stations, once at the halfway point of their journey to grab something to eat at a twenty-four-hour café.

"How is the blood situation?" Elijah whispered to her across the rickety old bistro table.

"I'll need some by the time we hit the Highlands. Perhaps MacLennan will let me go hunting." At Elijah's raised brow, she chuckled dryly. "For deer."

"Poor deer."

"I won't kill it. Just take a little." Echo wrinkled her nose at the thought. Animal blood wasn't her favorite. For multiple reasons. She hated frightening them for a start.

Echo began to feel slightly antsy when they were a few hours out from sunrise. Thankfully, they arrived in Calais with plenty of time to spare.

They found a cheap hotel not far from the Eurotunnel.

"I brought tape." Elijah pulled it out of his backpack as they strode into the small room with twin beds.

Together they taped the curtains closed over the window.

A slight awkwardness fell between them as they readied for sleep. As they stood side by side at the bathroom sink brushing their teeth, Echo almost smiled at the weird, domesticated scenario. A fae-borne and a vampire brushing their teeth together before bed sounded like the start of a joke.

Elijah seemed to sense her amusement and grinned before he spat. He watched her as he wiped his mouth.

When she was done, she asked, "What?"

"Nothing." He shrugged. "I just like looking at you."

A shiver rippled down her spine.

It would be so easy to ignore all the warning signs and just give in to the attraction that had sparked between them from the first moment they met.

Yet Echo wasn't sure she could handle any more complications right now.

"We should sleep." She brushed past him and hurried into the twin bed.

Elijah followed her out after a few seconds and got into the adjacent bed. "Good night. Or good morning, really."

"Good night, Elijah."

Her senses told her he was still awake a few minutes later, but the pull of sunrise dragged Echo under, and she slipped into the dreamworld.

17

The need for blood was a mix between hunger and thirst. Unfortunately, Echo woke up with it when the sun set the next day. Her skin felt dry and sensitive as she readied in the small bathroom, her throat drier than the Atacama Desert, and her stomach clenched dully. Elijah seemed to sense a change in her mood and kept looking at her as if trying to work out what was wrong.

Echo didn't want to tell him. She didn't want to remind him that beneath her human facade lay a caged monster.

Just hold on, she told herself. They had another two days to get through and then she'd ask MacLennan if she could hunt.

That's if he didn't kill her and Elijah on sight for stepping on pack lands.

The need didn't make her irritable per se, but she did feel on edge. In a desire to curb it, she ordered extra sides at the restaurant they dined in before crossing the English Channel in the Eurotunnel.

"Are you sure there's nothing wrong?" Elijah asked as he paid for their meal. He was expounding a lot of extra energy to glamour himself and Echo whenever they were in public. Him being recognized would be the end of all their plans.

"I'm fine," she insisted quietly. "Just eager to get to Scotland."

"We'll have to stop twice again, remember. I'm thinking we stop outside Darlington in the morning and then Stirling the next morning. Just to be safe."

Echo merely nodded.

At customs for the tunnel, Elijah made the customs officer see passports when they had none. He muttered under his breath about "hating doing that," but Echo didn't bother reminding him their lives depended on it.

As Elijah drove onto the train carriage to park on the shuttle, Echo was distracted from her need for blood and the fact that she was slowly beginning to starve.

Because it suddenly occurred to her, they were about to travel under water.

A tightness banded around her chest.

"Are you sure you're all right?"

She told herself revealing her past was just a way to forget about the hunger gnawing at her gut. It had nothing to do with wanting Elijah to be reminded that she was once human. That she wasn't just a monster who starved without blood.

"When I was fourteen, I was at boarding school in Canada. It was an all-girls' school, but our neighbor was an all-boys' school. On the weekends, we'd get together with the boys. A group of us went swimming in a nearby lake. There was a girl, she was a year older. She hated me because the boy she liked, liked me instead. I didn't know it at the time. I thought she was trying to befriend me. She and three of her friends invited me farther out into the lake to hang out with them. When we were out of sight of everyone else, they grabbed me and held me under the water."

"Jesus fuck," Elijah cursed. "Evil little witches."

"Just human, unfortunately. The boy she liked was suspicious about her taking me away. He and his friends had come after us. By the time they pulled me up, I was unconscious. He gave me CPR and saved my life. His name was Hayden." She remembered him fondly, though Echo usually tried not to think about Hayden. He was part of the life she'd lost and could never get back. But it didn't hurt so much to think of him now. Echo wouldn't wonder at why.

"What happened to the girls who tried to drown you?"

"Slap on the wrist from the school," she replied dryly. "Their families donated too much money to the school for expulsion or pressing charges. I got my revenge in the end. I dated Hayden for two years until my ... until William found out and made me break it off."

"It ... it sounds like you cared about him."

"I did. He was my first everything. But it had to end because I knew it couldn't go anywhere. We had no future when William was planning to turn me at twenty."

"I'm sorry."

Echo turned to him. "I used to hate thinking about him because it reminded me of everything I gave up. But it doesn't hurt anymore. Not everyone gets to have a childhood sweetheart. I'm grateful now that I had him for as long as I did."

"You loved him?" Elijah's voice was hoarse.

"Yes. But it was teen love. It wouldn't have lasted." The words slipped out.

"Why?"

Their gazes locked as the shuttle moved and Echo was distracted from her fear of being underwater. Distracted by the intensity of Elijah's expression and the questions she could see in his eyes. Questions about them. Their connection.

Unwilling to answer any of them, Echo tore her gaze away. "I found out when I was turned that William had a hand in destroying the lives of the parents of those girls who tried to drown me."

A few seconds later, "How?"

"Financial ruin. He told me he'd wanted to kill them, but it would be too easy to trace back to us. Instead, he made sure their parents' careers were destroyed, that investments went south. He couldn't let it go." Bitterness rang in her words. "I thought it was just his way of loving me. It wasn't. He can't stand anyone to get away with crossing him. And he has patience. He'll wait until the optimum moment to punish them for any perceived insult or offense, no matter how long. *That's* the male who raised me."

Elijah let out a slow exhalation. "Why does it feel like you're warning me off?"

"I'm not." Or was she? Echo was so confused. One minute she didn't want him to believe her to be a monster, the next she was trying to talk him into it. "But you were raised by kind, brave parents. I was raised by one of the oldest psychopaths in the world."

"Which is what makes you so bloody extraordinary. You can pretend to be cold and ruthless all you want, Echo Payne. But I see through you. I see the woman who gave up everything to save her sister, to save me, to save the bloody world. I see a woman who can't bear to watch a dog cry in a crate by itself. A woman who saved my parents lives' and mine. I see *you*."

"I also tied you to a bed with iron and gave you permanent scars!"

"And you were sick to your stomach after it because you didn't know what you were doing."

"I've killed."

"So have I."

"I'm not ... good."

"No one is just *good*. We all have good in us, but we all have bad. We have light and dark. You've lived in the dark for so long, you think there's no light in you. But I see it. I see it all, and I think every part of you is beautiful. The dark and the light. Nothing you say will change that."

Fear and hope coalesced inside her. Trembling a little, she turned from the warm heat in Elijah's eyes and closed hers against it.

At least she was now more preoccupied by this thing between them than the fact that they were on a train in a tunnel in the middle of the English Channel.

18

The drive northward through the UK wasn't filled with easy conversation this time. The motorway grew quiet once they hit eleven in the evening, and Echo and Elijah fell into a tense silence. Awareness surged between them, and all Echo could hear was his heartbeat. All she could smell was that fae scent of earthiness mixed with heady, hot caramel. She could still remember what he tasted like. What an exceptional kisser he was. How his strong hands felt on her waist. Elijah wasn't like the alpha douchebags she'd grown up around. He was a modern man who respected her opinions and often let her take the lead.

But when he kissed, he dominated.

And she couldn't help but admit to herself she liked the dichotomy. She was always in charge. Always had the weight of the world resting on her shoulders.

What would it be like to let someone else take the lead in bed only? Someone she trusted.

Echo couldn't help the traitorous musings that flooded her mind. If Elijah was as dominant in bed as he was with his kisses... What could he do with that immortal body of his? Worse, in her hunger, she wondered what he'd taste like. If he'd come if she bit him while he thrust between her legs.

Not wanting him to scent her arousal, she'd quickly shoved the thoughts from her mind, clenching her hands into fists.

She wasn't going to make it to the Highlands, she realized, as her stomach clenched painfully.

Somehow she got through one more day, sleeping off the hunger, though it made for a fitful rest. She was even more taciturn on the drive from Yorkshire to Scotland, and she could sense Elijah's impatience and confusion. By the time they reached the medieval city of Stirling, one of the tiniest cities Echo had visited, she was hanging on by a thread. While she had phenomenal control for a vampire, this was the longest she'd gone without blood.

She hoped Elijah thought her strange mood was about whatever was pulsing between them. In fact, she counted on it.

They found a national chain inn in the middle of the city that allowed twenty-four-hour check-in. Using his magic to make them unrecognizable, Elijah secured them a room.

As soon as the hotel door closed behind them, Echo announced, "I'm going for a walk."

They'd left Yorkshire at ten o'clock in the evening because the sun didn't set until then in Stirling. It was one thirty in the morning when they arrived in the Scottish city. Sunrise was at four thirty, so Echo only had a few hours before she needed to be back at the hotel.

Hopefully, it was enough time to get what she needed.

"Shouldn't we stay together?" Elijah asked. "Grab a meal?"

Echo couldn't look at him. "You grab something. I just need ... some alone time. Sorry. But we've kind of been in each other's pockets for days."

She winced at the hurt and confusion she sensed in him but walked out of the room before he could make her feel guiltier.

Echo followed her senses as she left the hotel. Within five minutes of walking toward the city center, she heard the dull pounding of dance music with her hypersensitive ears. It led her to a nondescript building that didn't look like much. But there were young men and women coming in and out of the door where a burly bouncer checked IDs. The girls were dressed for nightclubbing, and the music thrumming from beyond the door told Echo she'd found what she was looking for.

More guilt rode her shoulders but her need was too great.

Echo knotted her T-shirt so it revealed the taut skin of her stomach and easily tore the neckline to reveal her cleavage. Pushing the waist of her jeans down and shoving up the sleeves of her cropped leather jacket, she put an extra swing in her hips as she strode toward the club.

She approached the bouncer and released the hold she had on her own supernatural energy. While she couldn't mind-fuck anyone unless they were hooked on her bite (something she'd never done and never would do), she could give into her otherworldly energy. And amp up the sexy.

Eyes hooded, she dared him to stop her from entering the club with a sexy smirk.

The bouncer stared at her hungrily. "Enjoy."

She didn't respond, just confidently strutted by him and inside.

Like the predator she was, she prowled through the sweaty bodies of the club goers. The scent of arousal, perfume, cologne, sweat, and alcohol was a cloying mix and one of the reasons she avoided places like this when she could.

Beams of colored light bounced across the walls and faces of the dancers. The music was overly loud in her ears, but she had an internal switch that could filter it out. So much so she could hear the shouted conversations at booths and tables, and the murmured sexy talk between lovers on the dance floor.

She searched the club as she moved through it, unused to this kind of hunting.

Then she saw him.

Tall, blond hair tied in a knot on top of his head. Scruffy beard. He sipped on a beer as he stood with friends, looking out of place among the dancing clubbers in his motorcycle boots and tattoos.

He wasn't Elijah.

Didn't exude Elijah's confidence and sex appeal.

But he'd do.

As she grew closer, she realized he was young. Perhaps only twenty, twenty-one. The beard made him look older.

His brown (not green) eyes widened ever so slightly as she stopped before him and his friend.

"Buy me a drink?" she asked bluntly.

His eyebrows rose as his gaze dipped down her body and back up. "Uh, aye. Sure. Aye, of course." He pressed a hand to the small of her back, his fingers grazing bare skin as they turned toward the bar.

She smelled his sudden arousal and glanced over her shoulder to see him looking at her ass with hunger.

So, he was an ass man.

Echo could work with that.

"What are you drinking?" the blond asked loudly in her ear.

Too loud for her senses.

She masked her flinch. "Whatever you're drinking."

"Is that an American accent?"

"It is." She smiled invitingly.

She waited until he'd ordered two more drinks and handed one to her. "Is there a quiet corner in here?"

"Uh ... no' really, but this way will do!" He reached for her hand.

Echo noted the look he exchanged with his friend as they passed. The *I'm the man* look and the responding nod of *Go get yourself some.*

She tried not to let her guilt stop her from doing what she needed to do.

It wasn't like she was going to hurt the guy.

Just ... take a little bit of blood to tide her over.

"I'm Johnny!" he told her after pulling her into the darkest corner of the club.

"Anne!" she lied, eyeing an exit door at his back.

For what felt like forever, she endured mind-numbing small talk (shouting) with the Scot. He rambled about the club not being to his musical tastes but he came here with friends (to get laid, though he didn't add that) and how this wasn't really his thing. He really wanted her to know that. Like his death metal T-shirt wasn't a big enough giveaway.

Echo cut him off. "Hey, come with me." She grabbed his hand and pulled him toward the back exit.

His eyes lit up, his cheeks flushed, and she could smell the musky deepening of his arousal.

Echo pushed open the door and hauled him outside with her.

19

THE THING about being able to sense Echo's emotions was that she couldn't lie to him. After the initial hurt Elijah felt at her insinuating he was getting on her nerves, he realized that her actual emotions declared the opposite.

He sensed her guilt as she walked out of the hotel room. However, he'd also sensed a desperate determination. And something darker. Something she tried to hide from him. Elijah had his suspicions.

Maybe that was why he followed her.

He shadowed himself and masked his scent and sound, even though he tracked her at such a distance he couldn't see her. Elijah followed their connection.

That damn bond between them.

The one that was driving him mad with need.

His suspicion grew as he strode into the nightclub, and along with it, jealousy and anger. And, yes, he could admit it: hurt.

Dancers made way for him as he pushed through the sweaty masses zeroing in on the female he hunted.

There.

Elijah found her just as she disappeared through an exit door with a tall, blond male, who shared remarkably similar coloring to him.

Possessiveness roared through him. It was unlike anything he'd ever experienced. Glancing behind him to make sure no one was watching, he did a quick scan of the club and then yanked open the exit door.

His stomach clenched with envy and indignation.

Echo's head whipped toward him, her eyes silver, her incisors descended, readying to bite the male she had pinned against the wall of the dank, malodorous alleyway. Her eyes widened, and Elijah scented her fear.

He jerked his head in shock.

Why was she afraid of him?

"What the fuck?" the blond bloke yelled, shoving against Echo to no avail.

Elijah sped at him, and it took every ounce of his control not to punch the arsehole. It wasn't his fault. Echo stumbled back as Elijah gripped the young man's face and stared into his eyes. "You came out here alone because you needed some air. If anyone asks, the blond you were with left the club."

"I came out here alone," the lad repeated quietly, dazed and disoriented.

Elijah shoved him a little harder than he needed to toward the rear exit, and like he was in a trance, the bloke returned inside, the door slamming behind him.

Elijah turned to Echo. She wouldn't look at him as she stared down the alley in the opposite direction. "I ... the hunger ... I couldn't hold off until we reach the pack."

That's when he realized why he'd scented her fear.

Elijah sensed her shame.

He charged her. Her startled, breathy cry as he pinned her against the wall fed the arousal that swirled in a thick heat in his lower stomach and groin. "Why the bloody hell didn't you tell me?"

She glowered up at him, those stunning jade eyes flashing silver in the moonlight. "So you can remember you've allied yourself with a monster?"

Jesus fuck. She couldn't possibly believe that. Elijah gripped her chin, tilting her face, her lips up toward his. "If you're a monster, I'm a monster."

She scoffed. "You don't need blood to survive."

"No, I don't. But you bloody well do. And instead of asking me, you go hunting elsewhere," he hissed angrily. "Do you think I didn't notice your prey looked like the poor man's version of me?"

"You're an arrogant asshole, you know that?"

"For once, just let that bloody guard down," he growled against her lips. "Ask me for what you need."

"No."

"Why?" Elijah pressed his body to hers, letting her feel how hard she made him. "I know you want me just as much as I want you. I can sense it. I can damn well smell it."

Her breath stuttered, puffing against his mouth. "Elijah ..."

At the uncharacteristic, pleading tone, he softened his hold on her. "Let me in. You can trust me."

"If ... I'm afraid if I drink from you ... I won't stop."

"Why?" he pushed.

"Because I want you so badly!" She shoved at him. "Get off!"

Triumph flooded Elijah's blood and he crushed his mouth over hers. God, how he'd longed to taste her again. His kiss wasn't sweet or tender. It was hungry and claiming. Elijah kissed her like he wanted to fuck her. What felt like years of pent-up longing poured itself into his kiss. Echo moaned into his mouth, her hips undulating against his as her vanilla and spice scent turned fragrant with sex. He could smell how much she wanted him, and it drove him mad.

Then a sting on his lips had him groaning as Echo bit him and sucked.

Remembering her other needs, he reluctantly yanked his head back. "Bite me. Take what you need."

Her incisors sprang down at his words, her eyes silvering completely. She panted with want, her body throbbing with two different desires.

"Echo. I want you to." He did. Elijah didn't even care if her bite hurt. He wanted to give this female *everything* she needed. He didn't entirely understand the depth of his feelings for her, but Elijah wasn't going to hide from them anymore.

"What if I can't stop?"

"Has that ever been a problem?"

"No. But ..." She tipped her chin defiantly, as if daring him to reject her. "I've never felt this way about anyone before. I don't know how it'll affect my hunger."

Euphoria buzzed through him, his erection becoming painful with want at her declaration. "Trust me," he said, his words husky with lust. "I'm strong enough to stop you if you lose control."

That's when he saw the last of her defenses crumble. She bit her lip and her fangs hung over the lush bottom one in a strangely adorable fashion. Finally, she whispered, "Not here. It reeks in this alley. I'm not doing that here with you."

Because it was different with him.

She wasn't just slaking her hunger on an unwitting stranger. A practical transaction.

This was more than that.

Before she could say another word, Elijah took her hand and fae-sped them from the back of the alley all the way to the hotel room.

Echo gasped as they blasted into the room, and she stumbled from his hold. "Whoa. The room is spinning."

Elijah steadied her. "Sorry about that. I'm a little impatient to have you."

As the room filled with the mingled scent of their arousal, *Elijah* was the one to lose control. As he kissed her, stroking his tongue along hers, wanting to taste every inch of her, he yanked at her leather jacket, then broke the kiss to whip off her T-shirt.

Her incisors sliced down again as he tore off his own shirt.

"Christ, you're stunning," he whispered hoarsely, his eyes dragging over her pale but taut skin. She wore a sheer red bra that revealed her nipples. Nipples he couldn't wait to suck and lick while she rode him. "Echo ..." He'd never wanted anyone this much. Echo was the one afraid of losing control, but Elijah felt like a starving man in a restaurant, desperate to try every part of her all at once.

But her needs came first.

He sat down on the edge of the bed and tilted his head, giving her his neck. "Take what you need."

Her tongue flashed as she caressed the tip of it over her fangs. "You're sure?"

"Never been surer of anything."

She approached him almost tentatively, so opposite from her usual assertive confidence. Elijah held himself still but couldn't help the groan that escaped his throat as she reached up to trail her fingertips down his shoulders and over his pecs and nipples. Then she surprised him by straddling him. It put her cleavage right in his face, and he couldn't help but press his mouth to her soft, cool skin.

Elijah grunted, his palms coursing down her slender back as she settled firmly on him. His balls tightened as she undulated on him. "Echo ... fuck." He panted against her mouth. "Are you trying to kill me?"

"Maybe a little," she whispered hoarsely. "Ready?"

He nodded, arching his neck again.

Her eyes bled silver, and he sensed her hunger like a throbbing wild thing between them.

Then her mouth was on his neck, tongue hot and wet, licking at a pulsing vein.

Her fangs scraped at his skin and there was a momentary sharp pain as they sank into him.

But only momentary.

At the pulling sensation of her sucking his blood, her tongue licking at the drops, Elijah groaned loudly. It was as if she was sucking on his cock instead, the sensation was so arousing.

His hands slid down her back, gripping her bottom as Echo's hips moved with a mind of their own, grinding down on him until he was mindless with desire. "Yes, fuck, yes," he moaned, his hands slipping down under her jeans to grip her bare arse.

Suddenly, Echo yanked her head up, his blood dripping down her chin. Her features tightened and then released as she cried out, her lower body shaking and trembling with her obvious orgasm.

Elijah was about to come in his fucking jeans.

Echo's eyes flew open, shock glittering in them. They were jade again. "Wow."

"Yeah?"

She nodded, searching his face like she'd never seen him before. "That was ... I've never ... wow."

Understanding dawned and with it, smug possessiveness. "You've never come before when drinking from someone?"

She shook her head, still panting. "Never." Her gaze dropped to the wound on his neck. "And I stopped myself."

"Excellent control, love." He squeezed her arse.

Echo smirked and reached out to lick the wound.

He felt it closing over. "That's a neat trick."

She lifted her head to whisper against his lips. "You taste as amazing as you smell."

"Oh really?" He flipped her, pinning her to the bed. "I have a feeling you taste just as delicious. Lie still, love. I'm hungry too."

Within seconds he had her naked and sprawled across the bedspread.

Elijah devoured the sight of her as he stripped. His cock had never looked more painful or needy and he wrapped a hand around himself, stroking as his eyes feasted on this extraordinary woman.

Her nipples puckered into tight little buds at the sight of him pleasuring himself.

The urge to thrust into her, to fuck her until they both saw stars, was strong. But the need to be the greatest lover Echo Payne had ever had ruled him.

Gripping her thighs, he spread her open.

"Put your arms above your head," he commanded.

Her breathing hitched as she followed orders, the action causing her breasts to rise invitingly. Her pussy glistened, her scent growing muskier by the second.

Elijah cocked his head, deciding to test something. "Don't move. I'm in control."

That beautiful scent flooded the room.

Satisfaction slammed through him.

Echo liked to give up control in the bedroom.

Good to know.

Without further ado, Elijah slid between her spread legs, lifting them over his shoulders, and tilting her tight perfect arse up. Then he feasted. He licked at her pussy, testing what she liked, enjoying her soft little moans as he played with her. Done playing, he suckled her clit between his teeth and pulled.

Echo's cry filled him with feral triumph as he switched between fucking her with his tongue and sucking at the bundle of nerves at her apex.

When she shattered on his tongue, Elijah could take no more. He'd learn every inch of her beautiful body later.

For now, he needed inside her.

Crawling over her, he took pleasure in watching the silver swirl in her eyes. They silvered when she was sexually aroused too. Interesting.

"Put your legs around me," he demanded gruffly as he pinned her wrists to the bed.

Her cheeks flushed as she obeyed.

"I'm going to fuck you," he huffed against her lips as his cock nudged at her hot, wet entrance. "I'm going to fuck you and then I'm going to taste every inch of you."

She pushed against his hold on her wrists as if testing him. Elijah held her down harder, and she actually moaned.

"Fuck ..." He grunted against her lips. "When I can think a little clearer, you and I are going to explore this need to be dominated."

The silver that had been bleeding back to jade turned mercury.

Elijah pushed inside her, his grip on her wrists tightening with his desire. Echo clasped snugly around his cock in hot perfection as he pumped between her toned pale thighs.

In her need, she pushed against his hold on her wrists and when he pressed her down harder, he felt her inner muscles clamp around him. She loved it.

Suddenly, she gasped. "Elijah ... your eyes are gold."

Fuck. It was something he'd learned to control over the years. His eyes bled gold when he was feeling emotions strongly. His parents had taught him how to contain it. But with Echo, he hadn't thought to hide it.

"They're beautiful," she whispered huskily. "You're beautiful."

"Bite me," Elijah demanded, wanting to feel that heightened arousal while he was inside her.

Echo pulsed around him in answer seconds before she lifted her head and sank her fangs into his neck. Elijah halted the thrust of his hips because the pulling sensation was so overwhelming. "Yes," he groaned. "Take what you need, love."

His cock throbbed inside her as she licked and sucked at his neck. Finally, she gave one more swipe to heal the wound, her head falling back on the pillow. His blood dripped from the corner of her lush mouth, and the sight was strangely erotic.

As if she sensed his feelings, her features turned taut as her inner muscles tightened around his cock.

Elijah began to pump into her again. Hard, savage thrusts as she arched her back, lips parted on cries growing in need and decibel before her inner muscles clenched around him so tightly, his own orgasm took him by surprise.

"My God!" he groaned as he emptied in spectacularly hard jerks inside her.

He was aware of Echo's arms around his waist, her palms caressing his back in soothing strokes. Realizing he had all his weight on her, he gently pulled out and rolled onto his back.

They both lay there, catching their breaths, taking in the magnitude of their sexual chemistry and the line they'd just crossed.

20

ECHO HAD NEVER BEEN MORE certain that control was her gift as a supernatural. If anyone should have tipped her over the edge, it was this fae male. His scent, his blood ... it made her incisors tingle with the urge to lengthen even though she'd slaked her hunger. She'd never tasted anything like his blood. The rumors were true that fae blood made human blood seem like cheap wine compared to a bottle of Cristal.

It wasn't just Elijah's taste ... it was what it felt like to drink him. As though they were connected deeper than any male and female had ever been. Then when he'd asked her to drink from him while he thrust inside her ... Echo had been lost to the pleasure.

No one had ever excited her more.

While she'd given up her control to Elijah, she hadn't lost it. She hadn't taken too much from him like she feared she might.

It had been ... bliss.

The bite and sex with Elijah were bliss.

In her short but painful life, Echo finally believed there was a place for that word. That it wasn't a word for a feeling that didn't actually exist.

"One of us should speak," Elijah's voice rumbled into the room.

She turned her head to look at him sprawled out on the bed, his expression relaxed and sated. The wound on his neck had already healed over, though a few drops of blood lingered on his golden skin.

Echo didn't know what to say.

She was still ... stunned.

It felt as though a thread existed between them now. A golden thread attached to each of their sternums, and when she shifted, it seemed to pull. Then, as reality returned, she felt a flood of foreign emotion.

Satisfaction, but a rising desire. Confusion. A slight panic. Overruling all, though, was need.

When she met Elijah's gaze, she knew she was sensing his emotions again.

Fuck.

She should tell him what she suspected. But ... it terrified her.

His nostrils flared as if he'd scented or sensed her fear. "Echo—"

"We should sleep. It'll be sunrise soon. We should sleep." Rolling off the bed, Echo strode into the bathroom to clean the blood from her mouth and brush her teeth. Still naked, she sauntered out and across the room to her backpack to find something to wear to bed. That hunger she'd felt from Elijah intensified.

"I'm not done with you, woman," he warned huskily.

She glanced over her shoulder before pulling on a long T-shirt to sleep in. "For now you are."

He sat up, as uncaring of his nudity as she was. She attempted to ignore his male beauty as she walked back to the bed, for fear she'd initiate sex again. "Does this mean you want this to be a onetime thing?"

Echo almost growled possessively at the thought. She bit back the animalistic urge.

Before she could reply, Elijah confessed, "*I don't want it to be. I want to fuck you until you're hoarse from screaming with pleasure. I want to bury my head between your thighs and devour you for an entire night.*"

The very thought of his head between her legs, his beard scratching her inner thighs as he licked at her, made her breath catch. She almost stumbled into the bed.

"I know you feel it too."

"I do." There was no point in lying. "But I ... it's a lot. We have enough to deal with. Let's just sleep on this."

He scowled but nodded and got up to pull on some boxers.

When he returned to her bed, she stopped him. "What are you doing?"

"Getting into bed."

She pointed to the other queen. "That's yours."

"Are you kidding me?"

"Nope. Good night, Elijah." Echo turned, giving him her back.

To her irritation, she felt the bed move as his determination flooded her emotions. His arm was around her, pulling her against his chest.

"What the hell—"

"Be quiet, love," he murmured in her ear. "We'll sleep on this, but if I get to fuck you, I get to cuddle you too."

"I—"

"Go to sleep." He gave her a slight squeeze and then she felt his body relax.

Echo was stiff in his hold for a minute or so until she sensed his breathing deepen. When she stopped fighting him, she realized she liked him spooning her in sleep. The heat and weight of him at her back, while comforting, was also foreign. Discombobulating. No one had ever held her in sleep before. She thought she'd hate it. Find it suffocating.

But she liked it.

Too much.

To Echo's shock, tears stung her nose and blurred her vision.

She'd been alone for so long. Longer even than she'd let herself admit. All of her life, in fact.

If she was right about that thread between her and Elijah, she wasn't destined to be alone. But what if he didn't want that kind of permanency? Or what if he didn't reject her, but Echo couldn't be what he needed? Her plan was never to live out her immortality. But Elijah was immortal.

Echo squeezed her eyes closed, stuffing down her rising panic.

These were all hypotheticals.

For now, they had an enemy to take down. If they were successful, she'd worry about the future then.

21

It was as if her preternatural senses felt the danger coming before it even arrived.

Echo's eyes flew open and she sat up, like she'd been yanked out of consciousness.

However, the hotel room was empty.

"Elijah?"

No answer.

Her body told her the sun had not yet set. Elijah was likely out getting some food and gas for their journey north.

So what woke her?

The door to the hotel room suddenly blasted open and there was a blur of color as someone sped toward her at a speed she'd only seen twice before—in Elijah and Niamh.

But the figure that materialized out of high speed wasn't familiar.

A beautiful redhead stood over Echo, her expression hard with dispassion.

Echo vamp-sped out of the bed, putting it between them. "Who the hell are you?"

The redhead had unusual amber-gold eyes, a tip-turned nose, full mouth, and golden freckles across her cheeks. Elven. Beautiful. Not unlike Niamh, actually.

Echo inhaled and froze.

The woman smelled like Niamh and Elijah.

"You're fae," she whispered.

The redhead nodded and spoke in accented English. "Sorry about this. It's not personal. You're just in my way."

"What—"

The fae moved. At a speed Echo couldn't compete with. One minute she was in the hotel room and the next she felt the air battering against her skin. There was a grip on her arm so tight it was like a vise. Echo tried to yank herself free as her body tingled with the awareness of nearing sunlight.

No.

No!

Suddenly, she was stumbling free of the fae, her bare feet biting into gravel and dirt as she was thrown outside into the hotel's drop-off and pickup zone. It was the first time in six years Echo had seen daylight, the sky a denim blue above her, barely there clouds, and the sun inescapable.

The hem of the long T-shirt tickled her upper thighs as a breeze blew over her.

This is how it would end.

Elijah wouldn't know what happened to her.

Odette would mourn her.

Despair filled Echo even as she gaped in horror at the redheaded fae who had delivered her to her death.

A tingling scored up Echo's spine and then along her limbs. A foreign sensation. Not unlike the feel of the sun's heat on her skin. Except this came from inside her.

And she wasn't bursting into ash.

Echo turned her hand, raising it to the sky, ignoring the

shocked and bemused looks of guests strolling into the hotel at the sight of the half-naked blond.

"What the fuck?" the redhead bit out.

Yes. What the fuck?

"It looks like that plan didn't work out the way you thought, huh?" A strangely familiar Irish accented voice sounded from behind Echo.

She glanced over her shoulder and her mouth parted at the sight of Niamh Farren stepping out of a black SUV parked in the pickup zone. A gorgeous male Echo recognized from surveillance as Kiyonari Fujiwara appeared at her side. Niamh Farren's (possibly immortal) werewolf mate.

The shocks kept coming as a huge male rounded the SUV.

Fionn Mór. Once an ancient Celtic king, now fae, made by the queen of the fae herself. He wore a three-piece suit that strained and stretched against the enormity of his muscled shoulders.

At his side was his mate. A tallish (though she looked tiny next to Fionn), lean brunette with striking light blue eyes.

Fae-borne Rose Kelly.

There was a whoosh of movement and suddenly, Elijah was between her and the two couples, his back to her chest, his arms wide, guarding her. "Stay back," he warned in a menacing growl she'd never heard from him before.

"How?" Echo asked, wondering where he'd come from and how he'd known she was in danger.

"I felt your fear." He glanced back at her. "How are you—"

"This was foolish," the redhead cut him off.

Elijah seemed to realize there was another threat and moved Echo backward away from the lot of them.

The redhead, however, smirked at Niamh. "I thought the last time we met, sister, you realized how important it was not to have all four of us in the same place at the same time."

The Irish fae cocked her head, studying the redhead. "Until I got a vision. As long as we're not among any standing stones at the gate to Faerie, we're good. In fact, I kind of needed you to fuck up like you just did. You might be stronger than us individually, Astra. But you're no match against four fae, my mate, and Echo Payne. I've seen it."

Astra.

She was the fae-borne William thought dead.

She looked from Echo to Elijah to Niamh to Kiyonari to Rose and then to Fionn.

As if Niamh anticipated her sister's next move, she was suddenly a blur of movement. She now stood between Elijah, Echo, and Astra. Kiyonari was abruptly at her side. Then Fionn and Rose. A supernatural blockade between Astra and them. They were protecting them, Echo realized, shocked.

"Make a move," Niamh purred in a dare. "I'm dying to avenge my brother."

Astra narrowed her eyes. "Not today. Not ever. We'll see each other soon, sister. And our brother, Elijah. I'll see him soon too. You can't protect the vampire forever."

Then poof.

She vanished into thin air.

"What the actual hell?" Elijah bit out.

"I think it's time we moved this inside." Fionn gestured to the hotel and the group of humans who were staring wide-eyed at them all, camera phones clicking.

Niamh flicked a hand in their direction and there was sudden cries of astonishment and dismay. She turned to her companions with a smirk. "Broke all their devices. Nosy bastards."

Rose snorted.

Echo wasn't in the mood for amusement. She was too stunned. "I'd quite like to put on some pants and then figure out why I'm not a big pile of ash right now." She looked at Elijah, confused ... hopeful. Hopeful in a way that scared her to death.

"I can explain that one," Niamh approached. "But let's get inside first."

22

Once they were safely inside the hotel room, Niamh, Fionn, and Rose put up wards around it. Defensive ones as well as a sound barrier so no one could get into the room or hear what was going on. Something primal shifted through Elijah as they'd stepped inside; it smelled of sex, of him and Echo.

He'd been out grabbing something to eat, trying to figure out how to convince Echo to give this thing between them a chance, when he'd sensed her fear and confusion. It was the worst thing he'd ever experienced, made ever worse to see her standing outside half naked in the daylight. It had taken him a discombobulated second to realize she was still alive.

Now his eyes tracked her as she rounded the bed to pull on her jeans.

"What happened?" he bit out.

"That bitch appeared out of nowhere and dragged me outside. I couldn't stop her." Echo's hands flexed in and out of fists, her fury evident. But also her vulnerability. "Why didn't I burst into flames?"

"I think I can explain that. There's a *lot* to explain." The tall, willowy, Irish-accented female who'd protected them looked suddenly drained. She was clearly fae, like Elijah. The male at her side smelled distinctly of werewolf. He slid an arm around her and pressed a tender kiss to her temple. At Elijah's curious stare, she gave him a tight smile. "The redhead is a fae-borne called Astra. She orchestrated my brother's death."

Sympathy flooded him, knowing he'd be devastated if what he was led to the death of his parents. "I'm truly sorry."

"I'm Niamh."

"Farren?" His eyes flew to Echo, who nodded. He turned back to the fae female. "You told Echo the truth about William."

"I did."

"And who are you?" Elijah gestured to the large male and slender female at his side. They'd both moved like him. "Are you fae?"

"Fionn Mór." The hulking male bowed his head slightly. He had a strange accent. Slightly Irish but not quite. "The Queen of Faerie turned me into fae centuries ago. This is my mate, Rose Kelly."

"Hi." Rose nodded and then spoke in a North American accent. "I'm one of the fae-borne too."

"Kiyo." The wolf stared blankly at him. "Niamh's mate."

"We were on our way to Conall MacLennan to find you," Echo said to Niamh. "You found us first."

"I know." Niamh smiled slightly at Elijah's confused look. "I have visions. Psychic visions."

"I've told him what I could about fae history and about the fae-borne," Echo said.

"Good. That's good."

"But maybe you can explain to me how a fae-borne The Garm thought was dead, killed by Eirik himself, is still very much alive." Echo crossed her arms over her chest and then spoke to Elijah.

"We knew about Astra. Eirik told us he'd stabbed her in the heart with iron a few years ago."

"It was an illusion." Niamh sighed. "She tricked him. Astra ... she doesn't appear to have a conscience. I've had visions of you all." She gestured to Elijah and Rose. "Since as far back as I can remember. I knew when The Garm killed the others. Astra was the only other fae-borne born with the same knowledge of our history as I was. We're the key to opening the gates to Faerie."

"Echo told me that already."

"What she might not know is that if we're all unwilling, our enemies only need one of us to open that gate. They don't even need to kill us. Just spill our unwilling blood at the standing stones. But if at least *one* of us is willing to open that gate, then that fae must spill *all* of our blood on the gates to open it. It's a test of their strength and what they're willing to do to enter Faerie."

"Astra knew this?" Echo asked.

"Yes. And it's her plan to take me, Rose, and Elijah to the gate with her."

"So why did she try to kill me? And how did she not succeed?"

Elijah shuddered at how close Echo had come to death. Her gaze flew to him like she'd sensed his feelings.

Niamh cleared her throat. "Well, I received visions of how our odds of survival, of all mankind's survival, depended on the fae-borne finding their true mates. When we have people we love who we want to protect, when we have something worth fighting for, we fight harder. So I nudged things along a bit. I don't know the exact outcome of things, but I can see what path might lead to the right result. I told Thea to trust Conall because I could see in one of her paths was a future of losing her immortality to werewolfdom with her mate. That's what happened. It eliminated her as a threat to the gate.

"Then I discovered Fionn, here, was planning to use the fae-borne to open the gates to take revenge on the Faerie queen." Her tone was dry with amusement for some bizarre reason.

Elijah stared suspiciously at the large male and he felt Echo's guard rise too.

"Oh, no need for that," Niamh said as if she sensed their thoughts. "I saw that Rose was his mate and that not only would he not hurt her but that she'd take him off the path of revenge. So, I nudged them together.

"Kiyo and I ..." She smoothed a hand over her mate's chest, her expression tender. "I didn't see him coming. Fate did all the work there. Thank goodness."

Her mate's expression softened ever so slightly as he pulled her a little deeper into his side.

"And you." Niamh's head whipped to Elijah, and he stiffened. "The most emotionally stable of us all."

Elijah pointed to himself as Rose chuckled. "Me?"

"Yes, you. Born with parents who loved and protected you. You already had something worth fighting for, but it wasn't enough. To defeat Astra, we needed something else." Her gaze moved to Echo. "We needed to take our other enemies down too. Like The Garm. So, imagine my surprise when I get a vision showing me that your mate was the vampire daughter of William Payne."

Echo's gaze flew to Elijah's as Niamh's words flowed through him.

He was surprised but not nearly as much as he should have been.

It made sense.

This deep connection, need, for Echo. He felt like he was tethered to her.

What did surprise him was there was no surprise on Echo's face. "You knew."

"I suspected," she whispered.

And she didn't plan on telling him?

The room and its occupants were tense with awkward silence. Finally, Niamh broke it. "That's why you didn't burst into ash, Echo. You've fed from Elijah, haven't you?"

Not particularly pleased at discussing their intimacies in front of strangers, Elijah let out an uncharacteristic growl.

"No offense meant," Niamh assured him. "I'm going somewhere with this."

"Yes, I fed on him." Echo lifted her chin as if daring the others to judge what she was.

"Well, a vampire with a fae mate gets a nice little gift from the mating. A fae mate's blood protects you from daylight. It turns that vampire into a Daywalker. It was one of the reasons Queen Aine of the Fae decided to chuck all the supernaturals out of Faerie. She considered there would be many a vampire desperate enough to attack the fae over the lure of becoming a Daywalker. To try to experiment with their blood and see if there was a way around the mate loophole part of the deal."

Elijah's heart raced in his chest at the news.

All Echo had ever wanted was to walk in the sun again. To live as she once had. His blood could do that for her?

She looked at him and as if she couldn't hold her guard up anymore, tears blurred her beautiful eyes. "Elijah?"

He crossed the room, a blur of movement, to be at her side. His arms moved around her as she swayed into him, trembling. It was so unlike her. Echo was usually so tough. But this ... this changed everything for her.

"How often?" he demanded of Niamh. "To maintain being a Daywalker. How often does she need to feed from me?"

Echo gasped at his question, staring up at him in wonder and awe.

It made him feel about fifty feet tall.

"Just that once. Even if you were ... even if something were to happen to you, Elijah, Echo will remain a Daywalker for the rest of her immortality."

When he met his mate's (his mate!) gaze again, he saw the many things she wanted to say but couldn't in front of their new companions. He nodded, telling her silently he understood. They'd talk later.

Turning back to Niamh and the others, he demanded, "So what now? How do we end this threat?"

"We need backup," the Irish fae told them grimly. "I've seen a final battle. And we can't do it alone. We're going to need Conall and Thea MacLennan."

"So, we're still traveling to the Highlands?" Elijah asked.

"We are. All of us. We stick together from now on."

There was silence as they all sized up one another.

Finally, Elijah dared, "Do we win?"

Niamh gave him a sad smile. "I see many paths. At the end of one, we win."

"But at the end of others, we lose?"

Fionn glowered at him. "I don't know how to lose."

It was a promise.

And a little reassuring, but not entirely.

"We've got this." Rose nodded at him. "We can take them all down. I know. Because Niamh's right. *We* have something worth fighting for."

23

THE ROADS WERE WINDING, sometimes dark from the canopy of silver birch and fir trees. The firs were lush and green while the birch trees sparser but no less beautiful. At once, the road changed, the trees disappearing from the rugged hills, opening to views of a loch glistening down in a valley of the morning sun.

The morning sun.

Echo couldn't quite believe it.

To be in the sun, to see the world in light again for the first day in years. And for it to be here, in this majestic, tranquil place.

"Lucky wolves," she murmured under her breath as Elijah trailed the large SUV in front of them. She leaned her forehead against the passenger window, feeling the gentle heat of the sun through the glass. Tears trembled on her lashes.

"I feel you," Elijah said hoarsely. "I never realized until now how much pain you were in … now that I feel you when you're … happy. But … I also feel fear? For what's to come?"

It had been a four-hour drive from Stirling to Torridon on the west coast of Scotland. A beautiful journey. So much so, the discussion about their mating had been put on hold. It was as if

Elijah sensed that Echo needed time to process her new reality. For so long, she'd resigned herself to a life without light until the day came when it was time to depart this world.

Now with the possibility of eternal love and the reality of her new life as a Daywalker ... Echo was spinning. Elijah had stayed quiet as she took in the world around her, the gorgeous Scottish scenery as they traveled north. And processed.

"I'm scared this is a cosmic joke. That any second now my skin will start to burn and soon I'll be ash."

The single-track road wound down and down toward the loch and suddenly Echo sensed it.

The buzz of werewolf power on a level she'd never felt before. It felt like ... dread.

"What is that?" Elijah asked.

"*That* is pack power." She looked over at Elijah as he concentrated on the winding road. "And the power of an alpha to beat all alphas."

Elijah's fists clenched around the wheel. "I hope Fionn knows what he's doing."

The large fae had called Conall to let him know they were coming.

"*You don't venture onto MacLennan land without giving them a heads-up, or you might just lose your fucking head*," he'd warned before they left Stirling.

"Remind me again that we trust these people."

Echo smirked. "At this point, we have no choice."

He nodded. Then ... "When will we talk about our ..."

"Mating?" Echo supplied quietly.

Elijah glanced at her. "Yes."

She could sense Elijah's turmoil. The mess of emotions rolling off him not only mirrored her own, but it made it hard for her to figure out how he really felt about their bond.

"I ... think ... we should concentrate on saving the world first," she eventually said as Elijah guided their stolen vehicle to a stop beside the SUV.

Elijah scowled but nodded. "All right. If that's what you want to do."

Reluctantly yanking her gaze from his handsome face, her eyes caught on the tranquil loch ahead and then swung wide to the building they'd parked outside of. There were many vehicles in the lot. Signage on the building announced it as Torridon Coach House.

"What do you know about this alpha?"

Echo turned to her ma—to Elijah. "Conall MacLennan is not only the alpha of the last werewolf pack in Scotland, but he's also chief of Clan MacLennan. They might be small, but their wolves are powerful and they're wealthy, thanks to GlenTorr Whisky—"

"They own GlenTorr Whisky?"

She nodded. "They also come from old oil money. And his Delta Mhairi Ferguson manages their very successful fishing company. Pack wealth is shared. This Alpha doesn't keep it for himself. Rare."

"You know a lot about him. About them."

"William did his research when it was clear Thea and Conall were involved."

"Sounds like they have an interesting backstory."

"Yeah, they do. I'll tell you about it later." Echo opened the passenger door at the sight of their group getting out of the SUV.

Elijah followed her out of the car, and they gathered with Rose, Fionn, Niamh, and Kiyo. They all stared at the coach house. Echo fought against raising her face to the sun, but her gaze dropped to her hand as she turned it in the light. She was so pale. Almost like marble. How could anyone possibly think she was human? Then again ... they'd never seen her in the daylight.

Painful hope tugged in her chest.

"How did MacLennan sound on the phone?" Elijah asked Fionn.

"Ready. He and Thea always suspected this day would come."

"I hate that it's come to this. I wanted to keep them out of it, but I know we need them. And anyway, Thea would never turn us away," Niamh supplied. "She might be wolf now, but she was once hunted for being one of us." The fae suddenly turned to Echo. "It's real and it won't go away. I promise you. I swear it."

Echo gaped at her, stunned the fae understood her fears about being a Daywalker.

She felt Elijah's attention as she stared at Niamh in gratitude. "It's just going to take some time to get used to."

"Of course."

Rose grinned at her. "Daylight suits you. Anyone ever tell you, you're kind of a total hottie?"

She chuckled at the inappropriately timed comment as Rose's mate rolled his eyes and Elijah sidled closer to her.

Rose huffed. "Cool it, Elijah. It was just a compliment." She muttered now, "Mated males and their posturing possessiveness."

Sure enough, a quick look at Elijah revealed his jaw was clenched, as were his fists.

Not quite sure what to do with the delight she felt at his obvious jealousy over a simple compliment, Echo stepped closer to him.

"You're just as bad," Fionn offered dryly. "Or was that my other mate who practically clawed the face off the blond in the bar two nights ago, *mo chroí*?"

"She put her hand on your thigh when I was sitting right there." Rose scowled up at him. "I'd like to see you restrain yourself if a male did that to me."

"Then I'd disappoint you because he'd be dead before his hand even touched you," Fionn said it so blandly, Echo snorted. Rose grinned smugly.

The door to the Coach House opened, drawing everyone's attention, and Echo raised an eyebrow at the couple walking toward them.

She'd seen photos of Thea and Conall, of course, but it was different seeing them in real life with all that power crackling between the couple. Thea MacLennan gave off enough alpha vibes to confuse a supernatural into thinking she was Alpha of the pack. She was pretty in her photos, but the tall brunette was even more beautiful in real life. Her mate was six and a half feet of pure muscle at her side. Megawatt alpha energy to match Thea crackled in the surrounding air. A wicked scar slashed Conall MacLennan's cheek, and he had strikingly pale gray eyes. Altogether he might have been one of the most intimidating males Echo had ever encountered ... if it weren't for the way he cradled the tiny baby in his arms.

Echo sucked in a breath as Thea kept close to her mate's side.

Her mate ... and her child?

Rose's head whipped around to glower at Niamh.

The Irish fae shrugged. "Did I forget to mention Thea gave birth to their first child two weeks ago?"

"Yes, you did." Rose huffed, throwing her hands up. Her sleeves slid down with the movement, and Echo saw the twin scars around her wrists. They matched Elijah's, which meant, at some point, Rose had been held captive in iron too. Renewed guilt rushed through Echo at the reminder of what she'd done to her mate. "We can't pull them into this now!"

"We're already in it," Thea called as they approached. She gave them a weary smile. "The only thing our daughter changes is how much harder we're going to fight to keep this world safe for her."

Conall nodded as he cuddled his daughter closer to his chest. "What Thea said."

Fionn approached the couple. Echo noted the pained expression on his face as he asked quietly, "May I?"

Thea gave him an understanding smile. "Of course."

"Her name?"

The wolf looked at Niamh. "Niamh Caledonia MacLennan."

The Irish fae's eyes misted, her lips parting in surprise.

Thea shrugged. "She wouldn't exist without you or Callie." Echo knew Caledonia was Conall's sister.

Adult Naimh blinked rapidly, her werewolf mate reaching out to take hold of her hand as she battled her emotions.

Fionn now cradled Baby Niamh in his arms and Echo was suddenly reminded of all she knew about Fionn Mór's history. When he was human, he'd been a great Celtic warrior king. And a father.

He'd lost his children because of the Faerie Queen.

Rose settled her hand comfortably on Fionn's back as he held the babe close against his broad chest.

"Hullo, wee Niamh," he murmured, brushing a gentle fingertip over her cheek. "Aren't you a beauty."

"She really is." Rose beamed at the parents. "Congratulations."

Wrapping his arm around Thea's waist, Conall nodded his thanks. Then his gaze instantly moved to Echo and Elijah. "These are the newcomers?" Recognition lit both his and Thea's faces. "I always thought there was something about you," Conall murmured at Elijah. "I like your music."

Elijah smirked. "Thanks. It's been a strange few weeks."

Thea laughed. "I'll bet."

"Are you two sure you want to get involved in this?" Fionn asked, reluctantly looking up from the child in his arms. "Now that little Niamh is here." His expression turned grave. "There's no pain like it ... being separated from your child for all eternity."

Fear flashed over the female wolf's face, but determination quickly followed it. "There will be no world for her to grow up in if we don't take the risk. You need us. And we need to win ... for our daughter's sake. We're in."

"And that's the last we'll discuss of it." Conall took Baby Niamh from Fionn. "My sister will look after Nee so we can talk." His eyes flicked to Echo. "I'm particularly interested to hear how a vampire is standing in broad daylight in front of us."

Elijah stepped in front of Echo, a low growl emitting from deep in his throat that sounded so animalistic, it shocked her. She gaped at the back of his head.

Conall flashed his teeth in a feral smile. "Dinnae. No need for that." His nostrils flared slightly as understanding dawned. "I wish your mate no harm." He grinned at Thea's look of surprise. "It seems we have much to discuss."

24

"So, we're the key. Mated pairs." Conall sat back in his chair, exchanging a knowing look with Thea. "Unsurprising."

Elijah surveyed the group that had gathered in the coach house pub. There was no one else, though his developing senses told him there were many wolves nearby.

"Astra thinks we're the key, and that's what matters," Niamh said.

She'd just finished updating everyone on the situation with the redheaded fae who'd tried to kill Echo. Apparently, Astra had tried to kill Niamh's mate Kiyo in Japan a few months ago because she believed her fae-borne "brothers" and "sisters" were more likely to turn to the dark side if their mates were taken from them permanently.

"But you believe some greater fate is at work?" Elijah asked. "Through your visions ... leading the fae-borne to their mated pair?"

"Aye." Niamh nodded solemnly. "We're stronger with our mates. While we all have dark in us ... our mates keep us closer to the light."

"But what about Thea and Conall?" Echo gestured to the wolf couple. "How are they still part of the equation if Thea's no longer fae?"

"Because we might be able to defeat Astra without them. But we can't defeat Astra, The Garm, and the Blackwoods without backup. And we all know the councils are spineless, corrupt arseholes too afraid to upset their own agenda by doing what they're supposed to and police dark magic users like the Blackwoods. The East Asian Council didn't even follow up with their investigation into Astra's devastating attack on Tokyo."

"Councils?" Elijah asked, confused. "Tokyo attack?"

Echo turned to him and patiently replied, "There are continental governing councils among the witches and warlocks. They're supposed to monitor the use of dark magic and punish those who commit crimes using magic. The Blackwoods are on the North American High Council, so they've turned a blind eye. And because they're so closely allied, they also have the European High Council. The others ... none of them have stepped up to stop the Blackwoods for multiple reasons, primarily money and power. Niamh's right. They once protected humans from the darker side of their magic ... but now they've all been corrupted by power and wealth and politics. They won't help.

"As for Tokyo"—Echo turned to Niamh—"William assumed it was infighting within Pack Iryoku that led to the explosions on Shinjuku."

"Wait ... the Tokyo terrorist attack was supernatural?" Elijah raised an eyebrow. Months ago multiple building explosions in the Shinjuku district of Tokyo had made global news.

Niamh nodded gravely. "It was Astra. The pack alpha"—she flicked a grim look at her mate—"knew I was fae. Astra killed her but decided to take out the entire pack in case she'd told anyone else. The East Asian Council investigated but declared it as infighting within the pack, just so they could wash their hands of it. So, Echo's right. The councils are of no use."

Fuck. Elijah ran a hand through his hair. "Are you saying we have to stop all three of them?"

Echo turned to the others. "Elijah and I took out two of William's highest-ranking officers. Something one of them said ... it got me thinking."

Fionn nodded at her to continue.

"He tried to bargain with me. In exchange for becoming his mate—"

Elijah fought hard against the instinct to snarl in outrage. Ever since he and Echo had slept together, his possessiveness over the female had grown out of control. It was alarming and unsettling, and he hoped like hell its fierceness would soften over time.

He realized Echo had stopped talking and gave her a brittle nod to continue.

Surprisingly, it was the taciturn Kiyo who offered him a knowing, sympathetic smirk.

"Roark said he wasn't interested in William's vendetta against the fae. He wanted The Garm for its power and money and businesses. He suggested if we killed William, he'd drop the fae agenda."

Conall leaned forward, gaze sharp. "And you think if we kill William, The Garm willnae retaliate? You think they'd rather claim his power for their own means?"

"I think William had three people in his inner circle. Two of them are dead and the other is me. The rest were just paid lackies. Some bought into William's crap about Faerie, but most of those supernaturals work for him because of the money *and* because of the protection that comes with being in a criminal organization like The Garm. It's not what it was. Most of the true believers are dead. I think if we take out William, the rest of The Garm will be so busy fighting among themselves for leadership, it'll give us space to take out Astra and the coven."

Elijah stared at the woman at his side, pride now mingling with the territorialism. Christ, she was fierce and beautiful and—

Her head whipped toward him like she'd sensed everything he was feeling. Her expression softened, and Elijah had to admit, he liked that he was one of the few people who provoked her tender side.

"We take out William first, then," Kiyo said. "It's a solid plan."

"Do you think we should linger here while we plan an assault against William?" Thea covered Conall's hand with hers and squeezed. "In case our presence draws the Blackwood Coven to the pack before we're ready for them."

Fionn gestured with a wave of his hand. "According to my sources, the Blackwoods are regrouping now that both Lincoln and Layton are dead. Bran has been trying to keep tabs on William. He's on the move. Took a flight to Frankfurt and is holed up there in an airport hotel while it's daylight. We should be more concerned about Astra tracking us here, but we'll know if she does." He looked to Niamh.

Niamh's expression turned fierce. "I can sense Astra. During our confrontations, it was clear Astra had a particular connection with me. After my mating bond to Kiyo snapped into place, I realized I—"

"Sorry for interrupting again," Elijah apologized. "What do you mean the bond snapped into place?" He forced himself not to look at Echo as he asked.

Niamh's fierceness softened. "A true-mate bond exists from the moment your mate enters this world. But it isn't complete until the connection is solidified. Usually through sex. Then your scents become one."

He and Echo turned to each other. They both knew their scents were as one.

Their bond *had* snapped into place when they had sex.

Elijah knew Echo didn't want to discuss it, but his territorialism and need to claim this female as his rode him. He shifted in his seat in agitation.

"You were saying, Niamh?" Thea gently pulled the conversation back. "You can sense Astra now?"

"Yes. A new development, but a handy one. That's how I knew how to find Elijah and Echo. I followed Astra. It does mean I'll sense her coming. So we're safe here for a day or so while we come up with a plan. William first. But I want to state something now and hope you'll allow me this."

Conall nodded. "Go on."

"Astra won't stop. Ever." Sorrow crossed Niamh's face. "Which means there is no other option but to kill her. And ... she confessed to forcing an Irish coven to kill my brother, Ronan."

Sympathy charged through Elijah as he remembered the Blackwoods had almost killed his parents.

"If Astra has to die ... I want to be the one to do it. For Ronan."

"The kill is yours," Fionn agreed gruffly.

Rose nodded. "Absolutely."

Thea and Conall exchanged a look, and Elijah realized the couple did this often, their bond so deep they didn't even need words to communicate. Thea turned to Niamh. "It should be you, Niamh. But we'll be there with you every step of the way."

Kiyo reached beneath the table to smooth a hand over his mate's leg. Elijah noted the gentle but possessive squeeze and envy burned through him.

All the couples were secure in their bond.

Close as any two people could be.

He wanted that, he realized.

He wanted Echo to be his, but even more, he wanted her to want it too.

His mate clearly wasn't thinking the same, however, because

she leaned forward, all business. "William. You said he was on the move ... and I wished I'd thought of it sooner, but I'm pretty sure I know where's he's flying to. Now that Elijah and I killed his two strongest officers and hid Odette from him ..." Her beautiful features tightened. "He'll know what I know. He'll go after my human mother first. He's flying to London. We need to get there before him and set a trap."

The others seemed to take this news on the chin. Niamh and Kiyo, of course, already knew about Echo's mum.

"Margaret," Niamh murmured sympathetically.

Sick of the strangeness between them, Elijah gave into his instincts and placed a comforting hand on Echo's thigh. She reached under the table, and for a horrible second, Elijah thought she'd reject him. Instead, she entwined her fingers through his and held tight as she asked Fionn, "Did Bran say who was with him?"

"He's alone." Fionn grinned ferally.

"He always was an arrogant ass." Echo nodded. "This is good. We know what kind of security William has on her. We can disable The Garm security easily enough. They're not the strongest of William's supernaturals. But the digital security is a different story. He has her work and apartment bugged and under surveillance."

"Bran can take care of that," Fionn said confidently.

"This Bran sounds interesting." Echo tightened her grip on Elijah. "If we take out the security, perhaps loop the feed to my moth—Margaret's—apartment, then we can get her to a safe house while we lie in wait at her place. Can you mask this many scents from William?"

Niamh nodded. "All the fae sitting at this table are capable of masking all of us."

"Can you mask my wolf scent?" Thea asked.

"Sure."

"Then I'll pretend to be Margaret. Mask my scent but nothing else. William needs to think there's a human woman in that apartment with a heartbeat and all."

Rose shrugged casually. "Sounds like a plan. I know he's pretty old, but between us all, we should be able to take him down."

"I want the kill," Echo echoed Niamh's words from earlier. "He took everything from me."

It was Elijah's turn to tighten his grip on her. "Not everything, love," he reminded her gently.

She didn't look at him as she whispered, "Maybe not everything. But he took enough."

"Works for me." Kiyo leaned back in his chair.

All the supernaturals at the table agreed, and Echo relaxed slightly.

"Does anyone have a laptop?" she queried.

Conall nodded. "Of course."

Echo answered the question in his tone. "I can hack William's personal computer system. Track his travel itinerary so we know exactly when he'll be arriving in London."

The alpha stood abruptly. "I'll be right back with the computer."

25.

It turned out they had more time to prepare than Echo thought.

According to William's itinerary, he was traveling to Barcelona first before flying on to London. Having to avoid daylight meant they had several days to plan and get to the English capital.

They were leaving for England the next afternoon.

Unfortunately, Echo knew only one reason William would stop in Barcelona first.

"The coven there owes him a debt," Echo had informed her companions.

Fionn had squeezed the bridge of his nose. "Please tell me you're not referring to the Catalan Abella Coven."

"Hate to disappoint, but the very one."

Catalonia's most powerful coven also happened to be one of the *world's* most powerful covens. They made the Blackwoods look like children playing with spells. Thankfully, they usually kept to themselves. Not thankfully, many years ago William had done some kindness for them that had incurred a great debt. He wouldn't tell Echo the details, but she knew her adoptive father had held on to the debt, saying he'd cash it in when he needed it most. Curious, Echo had done some research into what kind of magic might tempt a vampire.

"They can make him faster, stronger, and damn near impossible to kill."

"He knows." Kiyo bit out a curse. "He's aware we've assembled. He's also aware you know about Margaret. And he knows you know that's who he'd target. William is *relying* on us attacking him. We should change the plan."

"No." Fionn disagreed. "They'll cast the spell whenever he needs it most, so it doesn't matter when we do this. The spell might make him stronger, but it can't win against a fae ... when she or he unleashes pure daylight."

Echo sensed Elijah's confusion. She couldn't help this time because she was pretty baffled by that sentence too.

Thea gave Fionn a rueful look before turning to Echo and Elijah. "When I thought Eirik was killing Conall, this power, these rays of pure sunlight, burst out of me and killed Eirik. All of the vamps."

Echo gaped in wonder. "That's how you did it? William thought the fight must have gone on so long they were caught off guard and killed by the rising sun."

"Nope. Me. And ..." Her gaze darted to Niamh.

The Irish fae nodded. "I did it too when Kiyo was in trouble."

Fionn looked at Elijah. "If you were motivated enough, I think you're the best bet for taking William out. Now that Echo is a Daywalker, it's no longer a risk to do it in her presence."

Elijah had stared stonily back at the large fae male. Echo sensed his concern, his fear. He didn't know if he could do it. He'd spent so long keeping his powers secret that he wasn't sure what he was capable of. His gaze flicked to hers. She knew he wanted to protect her no matter what. Her chest ached.

"So, this whole plan rests on me?"

"No," Niamh assured him. "Rose and I will do our best to tap into that well of power too."

Once they'd tightened up the plan's details, Thea and Conall directed them all to their rooms. For safety, they thought it best that they all didn't stay under one roof.

The werewolves guided them to a small collection of cabins that sat on the loch not far from Conall and Thea's home.

As soon as she and Elijah were alone, Echo tore off her sweater without preamble.

Elijah's eyes turned that arousing preternatural gold as he sensed her need. "You ... don't want to sleep?"

"We'll sleep when we're *dead* dead." Echo unbuttoned her jeans. "Tomorrow we leave and we might not come back. I don't want to talk about our plan or about our mating. I just want to feel alive while I can. That all right with you?"

Fierce desire tautened his features. "Tonight we'll fuck, love. But know there is a serious conversation waiting in our future."

"I know," she whispered, heart hammering as she unclipped her bra. "But I need this from you first."

A mere blink of her eyes later, Echo found herself flat on her back on the bed, limbs splayed, and Elijah naked between her thighs.

She gaped down at him as he stared at her sex with raw hunger. "You're so fast, I don't even see you move."

He smirked at her, his golden eyes making her inner muscles squeeze with need. "Now I'm going to take my precious time, love."

As he stared into Echo's eyes, eyes she knew were silver to his gold, his thumbs met in the middle over the lace of her underwear. She gasped as he pressed down. Her hips arched off the bed as he rubbed the fabric against her throbbing clit. The act itself matched with the way Elijah stared at her ... No male had ever looked at Echo like that. Like she was the only female in the world and he was desperate for her. She experienced a squeeze of arousal deep in her lower belly, and her stomach shook with it.

Elijah's eyes dropped, catching the movement. "I smell how much you want me." His voice was gravelly. "It's driving me mad. I want to touch and lick and suck every inch of you." He closed his eyes, his teeth gritted. "It's taking everything within me to remain patient."

Echo understood, even if it still terrified her. "Then take me."

His eyes flew open again, impossibly brighter than before. He'd never looked more like a fae. Echo could suddenly picture him as a fae prince, ethereal and powerful and ... untouchable. But he wasn't untouchable. He was here and warm and hard ... and he wanted to belong to her. "Elijah."

Whatever he read in her expression calmed him somewhat. His fingers brushed her lower belly, curling into her underwear. He peeled them down her legs, and Echo whimpered with excitement at the erotic slowness of the action.

Elijah smirked devilishly at her seconds before he spread her thighs and bent his head. His beard tickled her inner thighs, the sensation unbelievably arousing. Then his mouth was on her, his tongue at her apex.

Heat slammed through Echo, and she pushed her hips into his mouth. Elijah gripped them, pressing them back to the mattress, and then he *devoured* her.

Elijah studied her reactions, sensed her emotions, and tortured her with pleasure, suckling her clit and then releasing it to lave and lick languorously every time she was on the precipice of coming.

"Elijah," Echo pleaded, reaching for him. Her fingers slid through his thick hair and tightened. Elijah growled at the slight pull and began fucking her with his tongue. She shuddered, but it still wasn't enough. Sensing her needs, he licked back up to her clit and sucked as he pumped two fingers gently into her.

"Yes!" Echo felt the climax tighten, tighten, tighten toward an upward release. "Don't stop. Don't stop!"

He pumped harder, rougher.

"Elijah!" she cried out as the orgasm flooded through her entire body, her hips shuddering and shaking against his mouth as he continued to lick up every drop of her release.

Her body melted into the mattress and Echo eventually returned to it. Disbelief and wonder awed her. "Oh my ... I've never ... wow."

Suddenly, she felt the heat of Elijah's body, the hair on his legs tickling hers, his stomach brushing across her belly as he moved upward. His harsh need made the pulsing inside Echo quicken again as he wrapped his hands around her wrists to pin her arms above her head. Echo pushed against his hold, but his grip was too strong. Elijah held her captive, his features harsh with lust.

Unbelievable desire heated her body, and that need deep inside her reawakened. His gaze dropped to her breasts, to the tight pebbled nipples begging for his mouth.

Elijah took her right nipple between his lips and sucked.

"Ahh!" Echo strained against his hold and rocked her hips between his thighs, his hard cock prodding her open.

He looked up at her and he licked and laved at her while he held her stare. Echo had always closed her eyes during sex, hating the vulnerability of holding a lover's gaze while they were intimate. Now she couldn't believe how much of a turn-on it was.

As if he'd read her thoughts, Elijah released her breast to move over her, pressing harder down on her wrists as he captured her mouth with his. His lips brushed hers, softly, sweetly, surprising her considering how hungry he seemed, and then he released one wrist to reach between them.

Echo felt him guide his cock into place and then he took hold of her wrist again. Leaning all of his weight to hold her down, he pushed into Echo.

She gasped his name at the thick hardness that overwhelmed her with its fullness.

Their eyes held, her breath scattered as he moved inside her, the feel of him so perfect it electrified Echo's lower spine.

And Elijah began to thrust.

Hard.

His golden eyes burnished with dark desire, his features taut, as he rocked into her over and over, the sensation pushing her toward climax again. After only a few drives inside her, Elijah released Echo's wrists, slipped out, and got on his knees. He reached for the back of her thighs, gripping them in his hold so her hips and arse came up off the bed.

And then he powered into her.

"Elijah!"

Her mate grunted in satisfaction as he fucked her.

Echo couldn't reach him, couldn't touch him. All she could do was take his primal thrusts. It was magnificent. So arousing. Everything she never knew she needed from a male.

Watching him, watching him watch her as he drove into her with focused determination to make her come, was about all Echo could take. Her nails curled into the sheets, shredding them, as he pounded into her, hitting her G-spot with every powerful drive. A human male would have come by now, but Elijah was determined.

Echo's cries of pleasure filled the cabin, growing higher and needier. Sweat glistened on their bodies, her heart raced, and blood rushed in her ears, wet leaking from her eyes as the sensations inside her threatened ruination.

"Come for me, love," Elijah hissed. "Let me feel you come around my cock."

She exploded, her voice hoarse with the scream she couldn't

hold back. Echo shuddered and shook against his thrusts, over and over, her inner muscles throbbing powerfully.

"Fuck!" Elijah gritted his teeth, thrusting back in against the sensation of Echo's clenching pussy. As he did, it was like her hot, tight heat clamped harder around him, drawing him back in.

It sent lightning heat straight to his balls.

"Bite me," he demanded through gritted teeth.

Echo was so out of it, he had to pull her up so she could sink into his neck. "Bite me, Echo."

She moaned, licking his throat, her inner muscles still fluttering around him. Then she pierced his skin with practiced ease and pulled his blood into her.

Lust fogged his mind as he finally released himself inside her. His own climax was long and glorious and not enough.

Elijah came back to himself to feel his mate's tongue swiping across the wound. He lifted his head to find her licking her lips. Blood stained her lips and chin, and he kissed it from her, groaning with renewed need.

He'd just come, and his cock was already hardening inside her.

They parted, gaping at each other in stunned surprise.

"Already?" Echo asked in disbelief.

Elijah grinned. "I knew you'd be the death of me, woman. Can you take more?"

In answer, Echo ran her hands down his muscled back, her nails scraping lightly over his skin, which only increased his craving. She grabbed at his arse, and he grunted as it pushed him deeper inside her.

"Is that your answer, love?"

Her eyes flashed silver again. "I told you ... I want to feel nothing but this for a while."

Elijah wanted to give her everything she needed. But he also wanted to stamp his claim all over her like some caveman. He didn't care anymore. If he had to, he'd convince her with his tongue, mouth, hands, and cock that he was the only male she'd ever need for the rest of their immortal lives.

A kind of savage desire had him sitting up and manhandling Echo onto her hands and knees in front of him. She let out a huff of surprise and then shot him a sexy, narrow-eyed look of challenge over her shoulder. Elijah took in the sight of her, all sleek curves and silken pale skin, her blond hair falling across her slender back.

Her tight arse the most perfect thing he'd ever seen.

"One day." He pressed his thumb between her cheeks, and her back bowed with surprise. "You'll take me here too."

She looked over her shoulder, her thighs trembling against his. "I ... I haven't ... before."

Possessiveness roared through him. "Then that will be just for us. But for now ..." Elijah smoothed a hand up her spine and under her hair to grip Echo's nape in a domineering way he knew she'd get off on. She shuddered, letting out a little moan that drove him crazy. He caressed her in reassurance and then guided his cock between her thighs.

Once he was inside, he gripped her hips and thrust into her tight, swollen heat. Echo's back arched at his invasion, and as he pulled out to drive back in, she whimpered and undulated into his strokes. Elijah released one hip to coast a hand up her trembling belly to grasp a pert tit. He squeezed it possessively, and Echo moaned, hanging her head in submission.

The sight of her taking him, her back arching, the way she pushed into his thrusts with mindless want sent Elijah too close to the edge too soon. He always wanted her to come first. So he wrapped her hair around his fist and gave it a tug.

"Oh!" Echo groaned as her pussy rippled around him, arching into the next drive of his cock.

Elijah tugged a little harder as he fucked her.

Echo cried out again as her pussy clamped around his driving dick, convulsing around Elijah in tight squeezes. He released her hair to take hold of her hips, pumping harder, faster into her climax. Elijah watched his cock drive into her body, wet with her come, and he lost himself in his release.

26

Sometime during the night, Echo awoke, craving him again. She wondered if this need for her mate would ever abate.

Her mate.

She couldn't deny it, could she?

The connection between them was too extraordinary.

Never mind the fact that when the sun came up, she could step out at his side and walk in its light.

All because of their mating bond.

She still wasn't sure how to discuss it. Or how to hope for a true family. How to tell Elijah that in the deepest parts of her heart, she had longed to belong to someone and have them belong to her. For no reason other than that they loved each other. In the dark, violent, vengeful world she'd been raised, she had never dared to admit such a dangerous dream.

Could she now?

With him at her side?

The words trembled on her lips as she awoke to find Elijah sleeping naked beside her. The male had wrung more pleasure from her body than she knew was possible. Echo was pretty sure a human would have had a heart attack.

Smiling at the thought, she moved down his body. His beautiful, hard, sculpted body.

It belonged to her as much as his soul did now.

She might not be able to say it out loud, but she could express her feelings in other ways. Echo wrapped her lips around his cock and slid him into her mouth. It only took a few pulls and licks for him to harden and throb.

For his eyes to flutter open and bleed into gold at the sight of her staring up at him with his cock between her lips.

"Bloody hell, woman," he groaned hoarsely, his abs rippling as she sucked harder. He hissed and arched into her. "You undo me," he whispered.

That's exactly what she wanted. His strong thighs tensed under her fingertips as her tongue trailed along a vein on the underside of his cock. Elijah's breathing stuttered before seeming to stop entirely as Echo sucked with sudden determination, bobbing her head so her mouth slid with tight suction up and down his length.

"Echo," he groaned, lifting his hips off the bed to push deeper. "Love, yes, yes, fuck!"

She smiled around him and took him deeper.

"I want to come inside you. Stop, love." As she kept sucking, his voice deepened as he commanded harshly, "I want your pussy, not your mouth, so get over here and ride me."

The part of her that hated taking orders from anyone, no less a male, prickled, but her inner muscles squeezed.

She really did enjoy when he bossed her around in bed.

But only in bed, her expression warned as she released him from her mouth.

Elijah laughed softly. "I know."

Echo kissed the sexy cut of definition at his right hip, her lips tracing a path along his torso as she moved upward. Knees on either side of his hips, she hummed with want as she felt his cock brush against her inner thigh. Taking his nipple in her mouth, tongue flicking, her moan muffled against his body as she felt his rough hands cup her breasts. Echo rubbed into him, eager for his touch. When his thumbs brushed them, she shuddered, panting against his chest.

Elijah made a pleased sound as he pinched her nipples between his fingers and thumbs. She barely had time to recover from the streaks of white-hot lightning that shot between her thighs before his right hand coasted down her stomach.

As two fingers slid into Echo's slick heat, her back arched.

"You are soaked. I think your pussy needs my cock, no?"

"All the time," Echo admitted, lost in her desire. "Will it always feel like this?" she asked as she guided him between her legs.

"Fuck, I hope so," he snarled as he slammed upward into her, fucking her from the bottom.

Echo arched backward, braced her hands on the bed beside his thighs, so he thrust into her at the most delicious angle. She moved slowly, riding him with the same tempo he'd first licked her earlier that evening. Torturous.

Echo watched him beneath her lashes as his gaze roamed over her. That burnished gold darkened his eyes as he stared hungrily at her breasts that trembled while she rode him. His hands gripped her hips, his fingernails digging in, keeping her moving at a languid pace. His features tightened as the heat between them increased and a light sheen of sweat covered their skin.

"You're my mate," Elijah declared suddenly. "I want you to be my mate, Echo Payne."

Her inner muscles squeezed with want. "I know," she admitted, tears blurring her vision. "I don't know ... how."

"There is no *how*. It just *is*." He sat up with ease, shifting their angle so he hit her deep in that exquisite spot. Echo gasped and shivered around him. He slid his hand between them, feeling where he moved inside her. "I'm inside you in more ways than one. But you're inside me too. You belong to me. And I belong to you."

She nodded frantically, the tears spilling freely down her cheeks. "I know."

Elijah grabbed her by the nape, holding her to him as he poured everything he felt into his kiss. Echo moved over him, faster, harder, their mouths meeting and parting, meeting and parting.

"Mine," he grunted between each kiss. "Echo Payne, you are mine."

"And you are mine," she growled right back.

"Yes." Elijah's eyes flared bright. "I am yours. Always."

Lights exploded behind Echo's lids as her orgasm shook through her entire body. Her muscles clenched around Elijah, wave after wave of pulsing pleasure.

Suddenly, she found herself flipped to her back. Her eyes flew open as Elijah pressed her into the mattress, her hands imprisoned above her head. His features were strained with uncontrolled need and something like love, and as he crushed his mouth against hers, he began to stroke deep inside her, his movements rough and hard.

When his lips left hers, she stared up in awe, their harsh gasps seeming to echo all around them as Echo pushed up against his thrusts. He let go of one of her arms, his hand disappearing between their joined bodies, and as soon as his thumb pressed down on Echo's clit, she flew apart, her cries filling the room.

Satisfaction hardened Elijah's expression seconds before his lips parted on a shout of release. His hips juddered as he came, his shout turning into a long groan as he ground himself into Echo and growled, "Mine."

27

The glaring sunlight of a new day disoriented Echo in more ways than one. She attempted perhaps unsuccessfully not to let the others see how she couldn't help but be distracted by the heat and light on her face.

But it brought more than the continual shock of her new Daywalker existence.

The phenomenal, supernaturally intense sex she'd had with Elijah had overwhelmed her in the moment. In his arms, it was easy to forget reality.

She was the vampire daughter of an obsessed megalomaniac while Elijah was raised by two of the best humans Echo had ever met.

She'd permanently scarred his wrists with iron cuffs when she'd held him against his will.

She'd endangered his entire family to get what she wanted.

If that wasn't enough to question seriously if Echo deserved him ... there was the fact that neither of them might survive what was coming.

Echo more than anyone.

William would kill her for her betrayal.

And she'd die rather than let him take any more from her birth mother or the people she found herself among now.

She would die before she'd let William hurt Elijah and his family.

Hating herself for it, she couldn't help but rebuild her protective emotional walls as the morning hours passed and they readied to leave for London. She could sense Elijah watching her. His confusion. His frustration.

His hurt.

The others strode toward the private jet on the single airstrip. The tiny airport was situated twenty-five minutes east of Torridon, and Conall had commandeered it so Fionn's pilot could land his private plane.

She knew the once Celtic king was rolling in it, but she hadn't quite realized it was private jet levels of rolling in it.

Everyone seemed vigilant, hypertense, and aware of their surroundings as they climbed the steps into the vehicle. But Elijah grabbed Echo's elbow before she could ascend.

"Really?" He glared at her in disappointment. "After this morning ... we're back here again?"

Emotion thickened in her throat and she knew he could hear her suddenly racing heart, could sense all of her emotions. Her gaze dropped to the leather cuffs he'd worn once as a fashion accessory, and now as a means to hide the scarred bands around his wrists.

"You can shut me out all you want ... but I will never stop fighting for you, woman."

Maybe that's how he felt now. But eventually, the reality of who and what she was would come crashing down, and one day he might wish they'd never met. "You ... deserve better." Echo gently released her elbow from his hold. "Trust me when I tell you I'm doing you a favor."

Before he could reply, she hurried up the steps of the plane. Elijah's feelings threatened to buckle her knees as a wave of desperate powerlessness flooded out of him and into her.

A few minutes later, she was seated at one end of the plane, as far from her fated mate as she could get. Niamh and Kiyo sat across from her. Kiyo had already closed his eyes, resting his head against the back of the white leather seat for a nap.

Niamh studied Echo until it started to irritate her.

As if she knew, the Irish fae's lips twitched with amusement.

"What?" Echo asked, keeping the bite out of her tone.

"It's just ... well ... after the noises coming from your cabin last night, I didn't expect you and Elijah to be so distant today."

Kiyo proved he wasn't asleep by murmuring his mate's name in warning without even opening his eyes.

"What?" Niamh chuckled. "They were very loud."

Echo stared stonily at her. "If you think I'm even remotely the kind of female who gets embarrassed about that stuff, you don't know me."

"Oh, I'm not trying to embarrass you. Sex between mates is ..." Her cheeks flushed. "It's off-the-charts intense."

Kiyo grunted in agreement, his hand moving to Niamh's thigh as if of its own accord. She gave her napping mate a look so full of love, it made Echo's attention darted past them to the male who consumed her.

Elijah stared back, gaze narrowed and contemplating.

"Let's change the subject."

"You can trust him, you know," Niamh assured her.

"Subject. Change."

"I just—"

"*Komorebi.*" Kiyo squeezed her thigh, his eyes opening.

Niamh sighed but thankfully said nothing further.

The jet's cabin was quiet but tense. Everyone was preparing themselves for the fight ahead. Echo noted Thea and Conall sharing strained looks, their hands clasped, and Echo felt another pang of guilt. They'd had to leave their daughter behind for this.

Determination suddenly filled her.

There was no way she was letting another child grow up without their parents.

If it took everything she had, she'd make sure the MacLennans returned to their little girl.

For the rest of the journey, Echo stared out the small window, watching the world pass below them in the light. It had been seven years since she'd sat on a plane during daylight. She'd flown in William's private jet but only on short jaunts when they were guaranteed darkness. Otherwise, it had been the bulk hold for her. It was still so surreal. She kept waiting for this miracle to be taken away from her like everything else.

Echo's eyes stung a little.

Because that's what Elijah was too.

A miracle.

And he would be taken from her.

Monsters like her didn't deserve miracles.

As the skyline of London came into view, Fionn got up and stood in the middle of the aisle. "We're ten minutes from the private airfield." He glanced from Thea to Conall to all of them. "My contact tells me William arrived in London just before sunrise. That gives us about ten hours to get into position before William is able to leave his hotel. Plan is we stop at my safe house, we fuel up. We arm ourselves. Then we find Margaret and secure her." His gaze landed on Echo.

Echo bit her lip. She wanted to find Margaret first, but she'd been outvoted. Everyone agreed they should be ready to fight. Giving Fionn a reluctant nod, she turned to stare out the window. Echo wondered if it would be the first and last time in her vampire existence she'd ever see the sunlight spilling across the world.

Fionn's safe house was an end-of-terrace townhouse in a fancy gated community on the Wharf of the Thames. It had six bedrooms and south-facing views of the river. Echo guessed the place would sell for a cool five million dollars. Seriously, the fae warrior was loaded.

It wasn't quite enough to distract Echo from the fact that she was about to meet her real mother for the first time. A mother who might not want anything to do with her once she realized Echo was a vampire—the same as the villain who had destroyed her true love.

For the first time in as long as she could remember, her stomach churned with very human butterflies. Fionn had a housekeeper who'd left a ton of food for them, but Echo could only pick at it. Eventually, feeling like she might scream if she didn't get some alone time, she disappeared from the massive kitchen and hurried upstairs to a guest bedroom. She closed the door behind her, pressing her palms to the wood, trying to get a hold of herself.

It was all too much.

Elijah.

Margaret.

Echo marched across the luxurious bedroom to the large window that looked out toward the river. Her birth mother was on the other side of it. She had no idea her life was about to change. Once again.

What if she hates me on sight?

Echo squeezed her eyes closed, feeling tears burn behind her lids.

Tears were so unlike her, and yet she'd cried more in the last few days ...

It was because of him.

And as if she'd conjured him, the door clicked open behind her. His scent hit her, as well as the whisper of his feelings.

Concern. Determination.

Tenderness.

Emotion stung her nose, but Echo didn't turn to him.

When his heat hit her and he pressed his strong, hard chest against her back, sliding his arms around her waist to rest his chin against her temple ... she didn't shrug Elijah off. But it took everything within her not to melt into his embrace.

"You barely ate anything," he murmured quietly.

Echo didn't respond. She wasn't sure she could.

"I sense how nervous you are. How sad. How afraid." His lips brushed her temple as his voice grew gruff with feeling. "I wish I could take all of it away. I hate that you feel so alone when I'm standing right here."

"It's just the mating, Elijah," she replied tonelessly. "If you took a minute to really consider me ... you'd recognize this—*me*—is not what you want."

His body tensed and she felt a swell of his anger push against her senses. "How very fucking patronizing of you, love."

"Elijah—"

"I have lived on this planet as long as you. I might not have been raised by a psycho, but I've met my fair share of dark beings across my travels. I'm not some naive human. And I'm not perfect." He sighed heavily. "I've used people. I ... I started the band with another bloke. Mac was talented, but he had a drug problem, so I cut him off just before the band got signed. We left him behind. He's an addict living in social housing, probably cursing the day I was born. And why shouldn't he? I left Mac behind for my own ambitions, not wanting to get dragged down by his problems. Not very honorable."

She heard the pain in his voice. His guilt.

See?

Good.

"Don't you understand? I'm like your friend. I will only drag you down. You should cut me loose."

Instead, his grip tightened, and his lips brushed her ear. "You are not a monster."

She sucked in a breath. How did he ...

"You are not just a vampire. You are a woman. *My* woman. I think I claimed you from the moment we locked eyes in that bar. And I think you claimed me right back."

"It's just physical—"

"No, it's bloody not," he growled, making her shiver with want and emotions too deep to ponder. "You are strong and the fiercest family Odette could ask for. You found out the man you thought of as a father betrayed you, was a *real* monster, and you did not make excuses for him. Despite his power, despite the very real danger to your life, despite the love you once held for him, you defied him to save your sister. And you could have walked away after that. Taken Odette and fled. But you're still here ... fighting to protect the world from him. You can lie and say it's just for Odette, and to pay your debt to me ... but I know the truth. You're here because you don't want anyone else to suffer at William's hands. The way you've suffered."

Tears slipped down her cheeks and this time, Echo didn't bother to stop them.

"I am in awe of you. I *want* you. Not because of some fucking mating bond the fates devised ... but because I've never met a woman like you. You make me want to be a better man."

Shocked, Echo turned in his arms.

Elijah stared down at her, eyes gold with emotion and sincerity. "I can't make you stop seeing yourself as a monster, and it scares the hell out of me. Because I'm afraid of what you'll do for this redemption you think you must seek. And I'm afraid that meeting your mother could go badly ... and that it'll take you away from me. I'm terrified ... because I know no matter what I say, it is up to you to realize that you're not a monster. That you are a good woman who bad things happened to."

"I believed him." She voiced the pain buried deep inside her. "I believed in his righteousness and was complicit in his evil because of it."

Elijah cupped her face tenderly, his thumbs swiping at her free-falling tears. "It is only human to love our parents. And he was a father to you for a long time, Echo. It takes courage beyond imagination to walk away from a bond like that. My brave, brave love. I wish ..." He rested his forehead against hers. "I wish you could see you the way I see you. I wish ... I wish that bastard hadn't made you afraid to believe in people again."

There it was.

He'd cut through to her truth.

"I do believe in you."

"Perhaps." He pulled away to smooth her hair back from her face, expression tender. "But that doesn't mean it doesn't terrify you."

Echo didn't know what to say.

Her issues were just one more reason this extraordinary, loving male should move on.

As if he read her thoughts again, he pressed a quick, hard, determined kiss to her mouth. "I'm not going anywhere, Echo Payne. I am going to stay by your side, even if it takes you centuries to stop being afraid of what's between us."

28

"Margaret Lancaster?"

The human female whirled, reaching for her handbag.

Echo wondered briefly if there was pepper spray in it. Or a weapon of some kind.

But Margaret, her mother, paused when her gaze locked with Echo's.

They stood in the underground parking garage of the commercial building on Lombard Street. Margaret was an executive assistant in an investment firm there. Conall had made a fake call to Margaret's work phone pretending to be the fire department informing her of a fire in her apartment building. He'd requested she come immediately.

Really, it was just so they could get her alone in the parking garage.

Niamh, Rose, and Fionn were using their fae gifts to deter anyone from interrupting their interaction.

Echo's birth mother was an attractive blond in her late forties. Still poised and beautiful, immaculately put together in her suit and high heels.

"What do you want? I'm in a hurry." Margaret took a step back as if she sensed what Echo was.

Maybe she did.

After all, she knew vampires existed.

Shaking off the nervous riot of butterflies in her belly, Echo stopped before her, cataloguing their likeness. It was uncanny how similar they were.

Margaret's eyes widened, seeing it for herself. Tears of disbelief filled her eyes. "Ella?"

Echo sucked in her breath. The name that was on her birth certificate. "It's Echo now," she replied softly.

Margaret's knees buckled and Echo reached for her as she fell to the ground, tears spilling freely as she sobbed, "No, no, I thought you were ... you're dead! You were dead!"

She tried to soothe her, quiet her, but her birth mother started to scream, "You're dead!" over and over again. Echo stared helplessly into the shadows where her companions waited.

Fionn stepped out of the darkness and pressed a hand to the top of Margaret's head. Her eyes rolled, and she slumped into Echo's arms, unconscious.

They had only a few hours before they needed to be at Margaret's apartment. The sun would set soon. With no other choice, they'd brought an unconscious Margaret back to Fionn's townhouse, and Echo waited nervously with Elijah at her side for the woman to wake up.

"She's so fragile," Echo whispered hoarsely. "Emotionally. Mentally. She shattered right before me and I haven't even told her the worst part."

"Maybe you don't," Elijah offered. "Not right now. Not when

you need to be in a good headspace for what we're about to face. Maybe you just tell her that you're protecting her from William."

Echo contemplated this and wondered if he was right. Maybe the whole ugly truth could wait until after she'd dealt with William.

Margaret groaned from the bed, and Echo sucked in a breath as her mother's eyes fluttered open. Elijah threaded his fingers through hers and squeezed.

"What?" Margaret sat up too quickly and moaned, her hand going to her head. "What happened?" Her gaze locked on Echo and realization dawned. Her lips trembled. "It wasn't a dream?"

"No." Echo released Elijah's hand and stepped forward to sit tentatively on the edge of the bed. "My name is Echo, and you're my birth mother."

"Ella." Margaret looked seconds from breaking down like last time. "How? How!"

"William stole me from you. Raised me as his daughter. I only found out you existed a few months ago. I know what he did now."

Margaret shook her head, her fear so big it seemed to expand into the entire room. "You ... is he ... you know what he is, then?"

"I know what he is. And because I know what he did to you ... to you, to my father ... I've done something to betray him. In revenge, he's coming for you."

Her terror was so strong, it reeked from her. Echo's guilt was unbearable.

"I won't let him," Echo assured her. "That's why you're here in my friend's safe house. We're going to your apartment and we'll take care of William. Once and for all."

"Safe house. My flat ... I don't understand." Margaret's gaze moved to Elijah and she tensed, squinting. "I kn-know you. You're ..." She looked at Echo. "He's Elijah Webb. What is going on?"

Echo hadn't even thought to ask Elijah to mask his face with illusion. "He's a friend. He's going to help me take down William."

"You're alive." Margaret suddenly reached out to her but pulled her hand back nervously. "I thought you were dead. I thought he'd killed you both."

"No. I'm ... alive."

"You can't go." Margaret grabbed at her hand now, her grip surprisingly strong for a human. "You can't face him. He's too strong. He'll kill you."

"I'm stronger than I look," Echo promised her.

"No!" Margaret screamed, her fear so thick now, it was pungent in Echo's nostrils. She grabbed at Echo's arms, her nails scoring down them as she tried to grip onto her. "I won't let you! I won't let you die too!"

"Margaret." Echo struggled to restrain her without hurting her. Throat burning with unshed tears, she pinned her birth mother to the bed, baring her teeth, feeling her incisors shift down.

Dawning realization filled Margaret's expression as she suddenly slumped beneath Echo. "No," she whispered.

Echo released her and stood back. "I'm sorry, but yes."

It hadn't been the plan, but she needed Margaret to know she wasn't powerless.

"When?" She sat up slowly, taking it far better than she had the news of Echo's existence.

"He made me turn when I was twenty."

"Do you ... do you feed from humans?"

"I don't kill," she promised her. "I don't hurt humans."

Margaret licked her lips nervously. "There was a vampire in William's coven. Augustine. He was old. Not as old as William, but old."

Echo nodded. She'd heard of Augustine. He had been in Eirik's close circle like William. Until Eirik discovered Augustine was working to find the fae-borne children ... to protect them and to stop the gate from opening.

"He showed me kindness ... William came for me after he

killed ... your father and ... well, I thought you ... William came to finish the job. But Augustine stopped him. He threatened him. It worked. Augustine ..." Margaret's gaze darted over Echo's face. "He was proof that the vampire does not make the monster ... the man does. William was a monster before he was ever turned into a vampire. If you're here protecting me ..." Tears fell down her face as she said, "Then I know William didn't win. I'm not afraid of you."

Echo wanted to fall to her knees and bawl like a baby. Instead, she whispered words good enough to convey the measure of her gratitude, "Thank you."

Elijah's fingers laced through hers.

She squeezed them.

"You're safe here," she assured Margaret. "I'll be back when it's over."

"And ... we'll have a chance to talk?" Margaret asked quietly, eyes still glazed with shell shock.

"We'll talk," Echo promised.

"Good. Maybe you can explain why you're holding the hand of one of the most famous rock stars on the planet."

Elijah chuckled as he gripped Echo's hand tighter. "We'll explain everything later, we promise."

Miraculously, Echo wondered if perhaps she could get past her guilt so that she and Elijah could embrace the "we" part in that sentence.

29

There's barely any room to fight, Elijah thought as he stayed hidden in the shadows of the bathroom. The flat in Central London was typical of residences in this part of the city. Fucking tiny.

Margaret's home, while stylish and cared for, only consisted of an open-plan living and kitchen area, a bathroom, and a bedroom off a narrow hall.

Trying to hide all but one of the eight supernaturals in the flat was a far greater task when the hiding spots were few. Fionn's hulking form was hidden by preternatural shadows in the back corner of the kitchen.

Niamh, Kiyo, and Conall were hidden in the bedroom closet while Thea sat on the bed.

Elijah, Echo, and Rose were in the tight bathroom.

The only sound that permeated the flat was Thea's heartbeat. Elijah was helping to mask the sound of his and Echo's while Rose masked her own.

Niamh silenced hers, Kiyo's, and Conall's while Fionn hid his own and cast a spell out to muffle any sound their coming confrontation would cause.

Echo had warned that William might know right away they were there, that he had a nose for magic. Elijah could feel her tension at his back. Still, something had lightened in her since Margaret's reaction to learning Echo was a vampire.

He was much relieved, though he knew it wasn't a miracle cure to Echo's self-flagellation.

Perhaps wiping William off the face of the planet would help.

Elijah knew when everyone else picked up what his sensitive hearing already had. Footsteps climbing the stairwell and coming to a stop outside the door. They all heard the knob turn and the door squeak open on its hinges. And Elijah felt him. He felt the power of the vampire sweep over him. He heard Echo's intake of breath and turned to her.

Her face was tight with anxiety. "He's juiced up on power," she whispered, even though William wouldn't be able to hear her beneath Fionn's spell.

But we knew that, he reminded her silently. They knew William was spelled by the Catalan Abella Coven.

"You might as well all come out to play." An accented, deep male voice seemed to permeate the entire flat like he was speaking through a public address system. "I can feel every single one of you."

A shudder rippled over Elijah at the voice and at the way Echo suddenly paled.

It was one thing to think about killing the male who raised her as a father and quite another to actually do it.

"Fionn Mór," William said calmly. "Rose Kelly. Niamh Farren. Kiyo Fujiwara. Conall and Thea MacLennan. Elijah Webb. And my darling daughter. Echo Payne, come out now and face your father. If you do, no harm will come to your friends."

Rose nodded, lips pinched together.

Elijah watched as Echo straightened her shoulders, her expression easing into bland neutrality as she opened the bedroom door. Elijah wanted to throw himself in front of her. Instead, he followed her out.

He wasn't sure what he'd expected, but a handsome man who looked no older than forty with dark hair and ice-blue eyes was not it. Echo's adoptive father, like most real monsters, didn't look like one. William "the Bloody" Payne stood in the middle of the flat as Fionn stepped out of the shadows behind him and Niamh, Kiyo, Rose, Conall, and Thea made a circle around the vampire, closed by Echo and Elijah.

He seemed completely unfazed that he was outnumbered by beings more powerful than him.

William only had eyes for Echo. "What did you hope to accomplish here?"

Echo didn't betray her feelings, though Elijah sensed the roiling mass of loathing, pain, fear, and shame she felt looking upon the ancient vampire. "What did you hope to accomplish coming here alone? It seems you knew what you were walking into."

"I didn't. I didn't sense you until I stepped inside, and by then, I was curious enough to face you."

"How did you sense us?" Fionn asked calmly.

William glanced over his shoulder at the huge fae. "Fionn Mór. You're somewhat of a legend among The Garm. And I sensed you because I'm packing a little heat of my own." He bared his teeth in a snarling grin.

"The Catalan Abella Coven."

His eyes flashed to Echo. "You pay attention. You've always paid attention. The perfect soldier—strong and intelligent and always following orders. Until now, of course. Not so perfect now. Despite your treachery, I am proud of you. The female you've become."

"Flattery won't change what's going to happen today."

"You really think you can kill your own father, Echo?"

Rage blasted into Elijah through their mating bond, but not an ounce of it flickered on Echo's face. Pride thrummed through him at her self-control. "You're not my father. You killed my father."

"I am your father in every way that counts."

"Why did you come alone? Is it because you suspect disloyalty among The Garm now that Roark and Orla are dead? I hate to break it to you, but Roark was planning on stabbing you in the back before Elijah killed him."

That information didn't even faze William. He shrugged. "I came alone because I don't need backup. You think you know the limits of my power, but I have never truly let you *see* my power."

"Is that why you're juiced up on witch magic?" Conall scoffed.

William ignored the alpha male. He kept his gaze on Echo. "We'll walk out of here together, and your friends will live to fight another day. I promise to leave Margaret untouched too."

Echo stepped forward. "You are going to leave my friends, my birth mother, and Odette alone."

His lip curled ever so slightly. "Odette is my daughter, and I will find her."

Elijah hadn't sensed it.

She'd masked it from him.

But beneath the flare of rage at William's words, he felt her intentions too late. Before any of them had a chance to move, Echo vamp-sped toward William with all her power and force, and they were a blur across the flat. The sound of exploding glass filled his ears, and his heart leapt into his throat as he watched Echo plummet out the window she'd just thrown herself and William through.

30

The air whipped through Echo's hair and into her skin like needles as she propelled them toward the ground.

Suddenly, William's deep, mocking chuckle filled her ears, and they were slowing despite her shoving every ounce of energy into splattering them onto the concrete below.

She knew it wouldn't kill them, but it would injure them both long enough for the others to take out William. The flat had been too small. Too many of her friends might get hurt or die in the tight scuffle. This gave them time.

Or it would have, if she'd known William had the ability to defy gravity!

His power pushed against the air as he flipped upright and braced his legs, his nails digging into Echo as she tried to pull away.

They slowed, slowed until William did a gentle hop onto the sidewalk that would have been comical if Echo weren't so furious. She stumbled to a halt and tried to pull out of his tight grip.

People gasped around them, darting out of their way, confused by what they'd seen.

Echo knew they'd explain it away to themselves.

She reached into her back pocket for the wooden stake and whipped it out, but William caught her wrist, squeezing so hard, agony seared through her and her fingers could do nothing but release the weapon.

Then he grabbed her by the hair, dragging her down the narrow lane between two apartment buildings.

Echo thrashed, pain ricocheting across her scalp as she clawed at his arm, trying to break free.

"You couldn't stop me even if I didn't have magic running through my veins." William slammed her into the side of Margaret's building once they were far enough from the street. It was a move that would have killed a human.

As it was, it knocked Echo to her knees, the blinding agony in her skull disorienting.

"I wanted you to be with me forever. As a family. But here you are fighting me because of some petty need for revenge. This is bigger than you or me!"

She blinked rapidly, her blurred vision clearing as she slowly rose from her knees to face William.

Spittle flew from his lips, his eyes filled with the madness Echo had lied to herself and called passion over the years.

"I'm trying to save the world from those *beings* you call friends! And you think me the villain? They would end this world!"

"No." Echo felt the back of her head, her fingers touching the knotted bloody lump that was already healing. "You don't care about humanity. You care about power. You care that if those damn gates open, you go right to the bottom of the fucking food chain."

"You should care about that too."

"I care about *them*." She threw her arm out toward the street. "I care about protecting them from monsters like you."

William shook his head sadly. "As if humans don't harbor their own monsters. Monsters worse than you or I. At least we have control over our baser instincts. Those faeries have ruined you. But I won't let them ruin Odette. And wherever she is, whoever has her, I am going to tear them apart bit by bit to get my daughter back."

Desperate wrath filled her. He was going to make this easy for her.

She blasted toward him, shoving into him with all her might. William flew into the opposite wall with such force, the surrounding brick crumbled. He juddered, falling to one knee to catch his balance, discombobulated for merely a second. His incisors slid down as he bared his teeth at her, and then he stood and backhanded her with a casualness that pissed Echo off, considering it spun her onto her back.

She ignored the injuries, the crushing sensation on her chest, and immediately flipped up onto two legs. It was just in time to block a punch.

William had trained her in hand-to-hand combat even as a human. His training had only grown more brutal when he turned her into a vampire. Before, when he wasn't hopped up on witchy power, Echo had never beaten him, but she'd lasted against him longer than most.

A flicker of sensation told her Elijah and the others were near. They'd be here soon to help her take this bastard down. She just needed to buy them time.

So she and the man who had raised her fought like two warriors. Block, punch, block, punch, until she found herself forced farther down the alley toward the busy London street. Echo was aware of a feminine gasp and running footsteps heading out of the lane. A witness to their otherworldly battle.

When William's first punch got through, snapping her neck so hard she swore it cracked, Echo was done.

Her gift against William wasn't combat.

It was speed.

Echo had always been faster than even the fastest vampire.

She used that gift now, ducking his next blow. She was a blur between space as she found the fallen stake in the street and darted back into the alley. Echo flew at William, trying to daze and disorient him as she nicked at him here and there with the wooden weapon. A dance of attack and retreat as he snarled in outrage, unable to catch her.

Echo hadn't known he was toying with her.

"Enough!" He snatched her out of mid vamp-speed as if she were a fly he'd gotten tired of missing with his swatter.

Suddenly, the stake wasn't in her hand.

It was in his, and it was pressed to her chest.

"No!" Echo heard Elijah yell from the entrance to the alley.

William pierced her flesh, and Echo was shocked to see his eyes glisten.

"Tears for me, William?" She gasped, hoping her fight was not for nothing. That she'd bought Elijah and her friends the time they needed to kill her adoptive father.

William's eyes shone ever more brightly against his silver irises. "Whatever you might think of me, you are my daughter and I love you."

"Funny"—Echo winced as the stake moved deeper into her chest—"way of sh-showing it."

Just as she prepared to become dust on the wind, Elijah and Odette her last thoughts, a sudden blinding golden light forced her to slam her eyes closed in death.

Was this how it ended?

So, it was true.

When you died ... there was only light.

31

Elijah was blinded by golden white light.

A light that blasted out of every inch of him as he roared in desperate grief at the sight of William pushing the wooden stake into Echo's chest.

When Echo and William had fallen from the window, the rest of them had attempted to follow suit, only to realize William had somehow trapped them inside it with a spell. Fionn was taking too long to counterspell it, so Niamh and Rose had taken them all one by one by using the gift to *travel*. Elijah had never deliberately attempted *traveling* before. The first and only time he'd done it, he hadn't realized he'd done it. Frustrated with his own inability to break the spell, Fionn had finally gripped a hold of Elijah and *traveled* for them both.

Only to appear at the end of the alley with the others to witness the worst thing Elijah had ever seen in his life.

His mate about to die.

Elijah had become nothing but energy and rage, grasping for something within himself to end William before he killed Echo.

The light blasted out of him in answer.

His eyes wet with tears, every inch of Elijah shook as the light faded and the world returned to him again.

Before him, Echo stood gaping down at the pile of ash at her feet.

William.

Dead.

She turned to Elijah who was vaguely aware of his companions lowering their arms from their faces against the blare of sunlight he'd unleashed. But his mate had all of his attention.

Alive, he thought, sucking in a ragged breath.

A breath that caught when his wide-eyed Echo flinched and looked down at her chest.

The stake protruded from it, and she brought her hands up hesitantly.

"Don't!" Fionn called out from his side, marching toward Echo. "That stake is most likely centimeters from piercing your heart."

Elijah hurried after the large fae, pulse throbbing in his ears. Terror gripped him, but he tried to hide it for Echo's sake. "What do we do?"

"Magic has more accuracy than we ever could." Fionn held Echo's frightened gaze. "I need you to stay supernaturally still while I use magic to remove the stake."

"Okay," she whispered, her mouth barely moving.

Elijah felt fingers intertwine with his and glanced up in surprise to find Niamh. She squeezed his hand in comfort. "Fionn can do this."

He gulped and nodded, his attention moving back to Echo. Everything was in her eyes. Everything she hadn't gotten the chance to admit.

Elijah hoped she sensed that he knew. He knew everything she couldn't say.

Something softened in her expression and she held her breath as Elijah felt the tingle of magic fill the air. Part of him wanted to look at the stake, to make sure Fionn was pulling the damn thing out as slowly and steadily as possible with his magic, but he held Echo's eyes instead.

I'm here.

I will always be here.

"Done." Fionn tossed the stake away and Echo immediately reached for Elijah. She cupped his face in her hands as if he was the most precious thing she'd ever seen.

Niamh let go of him, and Elijah wrapped his arms around his mate.

He knew he held her too tightly, a bruising embrace, but he was almost afraid to let go. Elijah buried his face in the crook of her neck, inhaling her familiar scent, groaning, and shaking in relief.

"You saved me," Echo whispered. "That light came from you."

"Yes." Elijah lifted his head to meet her silvered gaze. "It just ... blasted out of me. Like Niamh said it could."

"Nice timing," she teased, the silver bleeding from her irises as her passions calmed.

But he saw the darkness in the back of her beautiful eyes.

"I killed William."

She flinched. "He would have killed me. Maybe one day I'll have a breakdown about that, but today is not that day." Echo turned in his arms. She kept her hold on him even as she faced the others, eyes on Fionn. "Thank you."

He nodded. "You're welcome. But we're drawing attention, and Elijah just unleashed a level of power that will bring all kinds of curious supernaturals our way. I think it's time we leave."

"What about ..." Echo nodded solemnly to the pile of ash.

"Ashes can be used in spells, so I think it's best we dispose of these completely." There was a question in his voice.

Echo lifted her chin. "That monster tried to kill me. Do whatever the hell you want with what's left of him."

One day, Elijah was afraid Echo would remember that William raised her ... and what happened here today would torture her.

As if she sensed his concerns, she turned to him. "I'm okay," she promised.

Elijah could only nod and trust that she knew herself better than he did.

With a casual flick of Fionn's hand, the ashes disappeared.

"We need to go." Conall spoke up at the sound of sirens blaring in the background.

Before anyone could respond, however, Niamh let out a soft cry. Elijah and Echo turned to witness her slam backward as if hit by an invisible force. Kiyo bridged the short distance between them to catch her as she began to seize in his arms.

"Vision," Kiyo gritted out, protectively cradling her against his chest.

Elijah watched on in concern as Niamh shook with incredible force in her mate's arms. It was strange, but he'd only known the Irish fae a few days, and yet he felt a kinship toward her he couldn't explain. The same with Rose and even Thea. It *hurt* him to see Niamh in distress.

"Can't we do something?" he bit out between gritted teeth.

Kiyo scowled. "Don't you think I would if I could? She just has to go through it."

Finally, Niamh stopped shaking and her eyes fluttered open. Kiyo caressed her hair back from her face, the werewolf showing a tenderness Elijah hadn't thought him capable of.

"You're all right, *Komorebi*," Kiyo murmured hoarsely. "I have you. I'm here."

Niamh looked at him with so much love, her elegant fingers tracing her mate's jawline, Elijah almost felt like an intruder. "I know, my darling. Thank you."

"I hate to be rude," Fionn interrupted gruffly, "but I can feel others coming. We need to go now. Ask questions later."

"I'm too weak to *travel*," Niamh said apologetically, wincing as Kiyo helped her to her feet.

"I'll take you, Kiyo, and Thea first. Rose can take Echo. I'll come back for Conall and Elijah. Okay?" Fionn looked to all of them.

They murmured their agreement.

Seconds later, Elijah reluctantly let go of Echo, and Fionn and Rose were gone with their companions.

He glanced up at the Scot who had about three or four inches of height on him and was broader and more muscular. The scar on his cheek looked particularly severe now that they were alone.

Conall smirked. "Wary of me, fae?"

"No."

"I can smell it."

Elijah raised an eyebrow. "You just ... I ... I'm still trying to wrap my head around everything. I know I can trust you, but ... you're a scary motherfucker, do you know that?"

Conall grinned, his scar stretching as he flashed his teeth like a snarl rather than a smile. That was his answer.

No words needed.

Yes, Conall MacLennan knew he was a scary motherfucker.

Fionn appeared before Elijah could say anything else and then there was that disorienting, unbalanced sensation again of moving through space and time.

He stumbled into a room, the world blurring to a stop.

The kitchen of Fionn's London townhouse.

"I hate to alarm anyone," Niamh said from her spot at the kitchen table where Kiyo was forcing her to drink a glass of water. "But Margaret is gone." She wiped droplets from her lips with the back of her hand as her attention moved from Echo to Elijah. "And so is Odette. And the Webbs."

Horror filled him. "My parents? What do you mean by gone?"

"Not dead," Niamh hurried to assure him. "Astra has them. She has supernaturals working for her. They're in some kind of compound. Not far ..." Now she looked at Fionn. "She has them in Galway, not far from your castle."

"She knows where our castle is?" Rose asked, shocked. "No one knows that."

Kiyo scoffed. "Clearly she does. Why else would she have her compound there?"

Elijah was trying not to panic when all he wanted to do was fly into a rage, and suddenly, he realized it wasn't just his panic he was feeling. It was Echo's too. He grabbed her hand and squeezed, and thankfully she held on tight and didn't let go.

"Not to be a prick"—Fionn eyed Niamh—"but Astra has misled you with false visions before."

"It's not that." Niamh glowered at him. "She can't get past my guard now. This was real."

"We have to go to them," Elijah interrupted their irritating argument. If Niamh said his parents, Odette, and Margaret were in danger, he trusted her. "Now. We need to go now."

"We can't go barreling in without a plan." Fionn cut him a dark look. "Astra wants you, Rose, and Niamh. This is a trap to lure you to her. Who knows what she has in place to keep you there. We need to entrap her, not the other way around."

"My parents are in that psychopath's hands!" Elijah argued. "If Echo hadn't taken my blood, that bitch would have killed my mate!"

"That's the kind of irrational bulldozing we don't need right now." Kiyo crossed his arms over his chest. "Fionn's right. We'd be playing into her hands."

"Well, we're not just going to stand here and do nothing." Echo glared at them one by one. They stared back, unflinching. She huffed. "Interesting how no one's hurrying to do any saving because it's not your people who have been taken."

"We don't need to be here, full stop," Conall murmured dangerously. "Dinnae you forget that."

"No, no, no." Niamh stepped into the middle of the room, turning slowly to look at them all. "We will not fight among ourselves. Elijah and Echo are right. If it were Kiyo or Rose or Conall, we wouldn't even blink before going in to save them."

"Agreed." Rose nodded, stepping up beside Niamh. "So, what do you suggest?"

"I saw something she doesn't want me to see. There's a large house on the other side of the estate where the compound is. She'll be expecting us to attack the compound. But she's at the house, and there are only two guards at either entrance. I say we go to the house and we take her out." Niamh eyed Elijah and Echo. "Then we can save your family."

Elijah nodded. "Sounds like a plan to me."

"I need more details." Fionn waved off Elijah's coming objection. "I'm not leading us into an ambush. I want details of the house, where it is, who is guarding the entrances, and then we make a proper plan. Or we don't do it at all."

"I'm with Fionn," Conall agreed. "We have a daughter we need to get back to. Thea and I are'nae throwing ourselves recklessly into anything. We go in with a plan, or we dinnae go."

Echo squeezed Elijah's hand again, sensing his fear-driven impatience. "That sounds fair."

Her words soothed him somewhat. But Elijah would not feel settled until he knew his parents and Odette were safe.

32

SHE KNEW Elijah wanted to rip the world apart to get his parents back, and it wasn't that she didn't feel a similar antsy anxiety over Odette and Margaret. However, Echo agreed with the others. Astra had almost killed her. She'd been too fast and too strong for Echo to stop, and if she hadn't had Elijah's blood in her system, she'd be dead.

They couldn't take that risk with their family.

Emotionally and physically drained, she'd excused herself after a few hours of planning and bickering. She let herself into one of the guest rooms, and in its adjoining bathroom, she stared in the mirror at her bruises and cut lip. Usually, she didn't bruise in a fight unless a supernatural had swung a punch. And usually the bruise didn't last very long.

No one hit quite as hard as William.

He'd almost killed her.

He'd shoved a stake in her chest.

A crack drew her eyes down to the sink, and she realized she'd gripped the edges so tightly she'd pulled it away from the wall.

"Shit," she murmured.

She looked into the mirror again to see Elijah entering the room and closing the door. His concern was palpable as he came up behind her and wound his arms around her waist.

Naturally, more naturally than Echo could ever have imagined, she leaned back into his embrace.

His gaze dropped to her cut lip. "Why aren't you healing?"

"I am. It's just a little slower. The fight with William took a lot out of me."

"Here." He raised his wrist to her mouth. "Drink."

Her heart jumped at the offer, thirst and hunger roaring through her in instant response. Echo's eyes silvered before she could control it. "Are you sure?"

At his silence, she found his eyes in the mirror and inhaled sharply. Elijah's irises were glowing gold.

Like they did when he was turned on.

That was all the answer she needed. Echo cradled his wrist in both hands and brought it to her lips. She licked him first, feeling the throb of the large vein there against her tongue. Her incisors slid down, a burning ache forcing through her gums. Then they sliced through Elijah's skin. His warm blood filled her mouth, and the pulling sensation caused a deep, low squeeze in her womb.

Elijah groaned and pressed his arousal into her ass, his grip on her hip bruising. "Fuck," he muttered, his head lolling back and exposing his perfect, masculine throat. Echo moaned around his wrist as she imagined sinking her fangs into his neck.

The scent of need filled her nose, his and hers, and she knew the moment Elijah scented it. His head snapped up like an animal's, his golden eyes piercing hers in the mirror. Upper lip curling with lust, with his free hand, he roughly unzipped her jeans and shoved them down to her knees.

Need, want, desire had her pulling deeper on his wrist as Elijah unzipped his own jeans and pushed them and his boxers down just enough to free his cock.

"Spread," he grunted in her ear.

She did.

And suddenly, the hard heat of him was nudging at her entrance and then thrusting inside her, eased by her wetness.

He groaned as she pulled tighter on his wrist, drinking his blood as he fucked her against the bathroom sink.

It was primal and brutal.

There was no romance or sweetness.

It was pure animalistic passion and a reminder that they were alive.

In this moment, they were utterly alive.

Sated, Echo released his wrist from her fangs, his blood a smear across her lips as silver eyes held his golden ones and his cock thrust in and out of her body. So thick, so full, hitting all of her sensual nerves to build exquisite tension.

"Look at you," he growled, his hips snapping faster against her ass. "Bend over."

She did, and the angle change set off a streak of pleasured lightning between her thighs. Echo muffled her cry, reaching out to brace against the mirror as her mate drove deeper inside her.

Their harsh breathing filled the bathroom along with the sound of flesh meeting flesh.

It didn't take long before the tension inside her shattered and Elijah covered her mouth to muffle her cry of release. He groaned deeply as her inner muscles throbbed around his cock, and he buried his face in her shoulder to dampen the sounds of his own climax.

Echo clenched greedily around him as he came, bliss erasing everything but them.

It was what she needed.

That they both needed.

When Elijah gently pulled out and turned her in his arms, he cupped her face in his hands. "I don't want you to run from this."

Remembering that moment before she almost died, Echo finally felt the last barrier between them fall. "I ... can't give you children. Being what I am, I can't ... I'm unable ..."

His grip on her tightened. "Is that what's holding you back? Fuck ... Echo ... all I need is you."

"You might change your mind. Later on. Eternity is a long time."

"I don't even know if I can have children either. And who is to say what the future will bring in that regard? Look at Odette. Who knows, right? What I do know is that I won't let you go over that. Never. Please believe me."

At the sincerity in his eyes, Echo nodded. "I'm done running," she promised. "I don't want to lose you."

Elijah squeezed his eyes closed and rested his forehead against hers. "I cannot explain the depth of my relief to hear that," he whispered hoarsely. "But just so you know, I would have followed you anywhere. I *will* follow you anywhere."

Echo slid her arms around his waist and breathed in his scent. "Good. Because we have family to rescue, and I can't do it without you."

33

FIONN SNAPPED HIS PHONE SHUT. "That was Bran. The Blackwood Coven were alerted to our fight with William. They're on their way to London."

"Good thing we're on our way to Ireland, then," Rose replied wryly, gesturing to their surroundings.

Fionn's plush private jet.

Elijah was antsy to get to his parents. To Odette and Margaret.

The plan was for Fionn, Niamh, and Rose to ambush Astra and her guards at her home, while the rest of them took out the guards at the compound. Bran had retasked an infrared satellite over the compound. From their heat signatures, he'd deduced there were five werewolves and four vampires guarding Elijah's parents, Odette, and Margaret.

No witches or warlocks, which was a relief.

And if they arrived before sunset, the vamps wouldn't be a problem.

"We'll get them back," Niamh assured him, as if sensing his growing agitation. "This will all be over so—" Her words cut off as her eyes rolled into the back of her head and she began to shudder and jerk in her seat.

Kiyo was seated next to her and immediately pulled her against him to absorb the jolt of her body as the vision claimed her.

"Another one?" Fionn unclipped his seat belt to kneel before Niamh. His concern was palpable as he met Kiyo's gaze. "So soon?"

Niamh gasped loudly as she abruptly stopped shaking.

Elijah scented a change in the air.

"Fear," Echo whispered beside him. "You can smell her fear."

"Crash," Niamh gasped, sitting up, frantic. "The plane is going to—"

Once more, she was cut off, but this time by the sudden tilt of the aircraft.

Fionn, no longer seated, was yanked by gravity, soaring down the aisle while the rest of them found their legs flying up into the air as it tried to pull them from their seats.

"Fionn!" Rose screamed over the roar of the engine.

Kiyo held Niamh in a tight grip as the force of the dropping plane tried to jerk her toward Fionn and wherever he'd disappeared to.

"We need to *travel*!" Niamh cried.

Fionn suddenly appeared behind Rose, having done just that. He braced against the back of her seat as Rose's seat belt unsnapped, the cabin air tinged with the scent of magic. Using all his strength, he then reached out an arm to Thea and Conall. "Grab on!" He looked to Niamh. "Can you manage the others?!"

Niamh's frightened gaze jerked to Elijah. "I can't reach you! You'll have to *travel*!"

Fuck!

It was either that or die.

He turned to Echo.

"I trust you!" she yelled.

"I'll come back for the pilot!" Fionn roared seconds before he disappeared into thin air along with three of their companions.

"Go!" Niamh yelled at Echo and Elijah as Kiyo unclipped his belt.

Seconds later, the mated couple were gone.

Fuck, fuck, fuck!

"You can do this!" Echo yelled. "It's in your nature! Just think of where you want us to be!"

Shaking, Elijah nodded as he took one of her hands in his. "Unclip in three!"

She jerked her chin in agreement.

"One, two, three!" They unclipped their belts at the same time, and Elijah slammed his eyes closed.

Take us to the nearest shore. Take us to the nearest shore.

Freezing cold enveloped him, and his eyes flew open to a watery darkness.

Instinct had him surging upward, pulling Echo, whom he still held, along with him.

They broke the surface of the water, gasping, wide-eyed as they took in their surroundings.

A mere hundred meters or so from them, their companions waved at them from the shore. Elijah and Echo began to swim, but as the dreadful sound of an engine grew louder, he turned to watch as the plane they'd been in exploded a few seconds before it fell into the water a few miles off the coast.

Hoping Fionn had managed to get to the pilot in time, Elijah turned and began to swim with Echo toward shore.

Everyone was there, including the pilot, who lay unconscious on the rocky beach.

"The pilot is dead," Fionn relayed with grim bluntness as he helped Elijah from the water. Niamh helped Echo. "Someone killed him. With magic."

"Astra," Niamh seethed. "It was Astra. I saw too late. I'm sorry."

"It's not your fault." Kiyo wrapped his arm around her.

"She knows we're here." Fionn cursed and stared out to sea. "She always seems to be one step ahead of us."

"She has visions too." Niamh rested her head against Kiyo's. "We're matched."

"No, you're not." Thea stepped toward the Irish fae. "You have something she doesn't have. You have us. Take it from someone who had to fight alone for a long time ... you're stronger when you have someone at your back fighting with you, fighting for you." The brunette looked them all in the eye. "Astra might know we're coming, but I'd bet my life she thinks that means we'll back off and regroup after this. She can't take us all on. I say change of plan. I say we all head to the house and take this bitch down together."

"What if she's given the guards on the compound orders to kill my parents, to kill Odette and Margaret, if we attack?" Elijah asked, his fear scenting the group. Not fear for himself, but for his mother and father.

"I think it's a risk we might have to take." Conall stepped up beside his mate.

Elijah opened his mouth to argue, but Niamh cut him off. "They're right. As much as I wish I were strong enough to deal with Astra alone, I need you."

Echo slipped her hand into Elijah's. "Then together, we fight."

He squeezed her hand and nodded reluctantly. "Together, we fight."

With his magic, Elijah dried himself and Echo off.

"You *traveled*," she murmured to him, pride gleaming in her eyes.

"I dumped us in the sea."

"You saved us."

He caressed her cheek, grateful to have her by his side.

Fionn, frustrated rage vibrating from him, put the pilot's body back in the water to be found by the rescue services that were surely already on their way to the plane wreckage.

The lack of bodies and passenger manifest Bran was already working to delete from existence, along with Fionn's ownership of the jet, would be another mystery for the humans to ponder. They'd probably make a documentary about it.

Every unexplained disappearance and incident in history could be laid at the feet of supernaturals.

They trudged through the woodland together, Fionn leading the way. It was hard to imagine that thousands of years ago, he'd been a Celtic king. A ruler over where they now walked.

Elijah had been to Ireland, of course. He and the Strix had played at venues in Dublin, and in Belfast in Northern Ireland.

It was the first time in a hot second that he'd had a moment to contemplate his bandmates. The guilt of putting them through his disappearance would never go away, even if he knew it was for the best. Elijah could never return to them now, and the band would have to go on without him. Not many bands at that level survived the replacement of their lead singer.

"I feel your guilt." Echo brushed her arm against his. "What's that about?"

"Just thinking about the band. I've ruined their lives."

"No—"

"I know I've kept them safe."

"Well, yeah, but I was about to say if you want to go back to being Elijah Webb, lead singer of the Strix, once this is all over ... you can."

He frowned. "I doubt very much the guys will forgive me if I just show up out of the blue."

"You tell them you were struggling mentally. You went off to get help. You handled it badly. They'll forgive you."

"Would it be safe?"

"Once we deal with all these assholes ... I hope so. And if it is, you should keep doing the thing you love."

His chest warmed with a rush of tenderness toward her. "And would you support me? You'd be the mate of a rock star."

"Girlfriend." She cut him a weary but affectionate smirk. "You can't go calling me your mate in front of the normies."

He chuckled and for a second, he forgot they were talking about something that could be a pipe dream. If they didn't defeat Astra and the Blackwood Coven. If The Garm didn't regroup and come for revenge.

So many enemies.

So much on the line.

The thought of his parents, and how they were probably hiding their fear to protect Odette as Astra kept them locked up like animals, fueled Elijah's determination.

34

As if by magic, two vehicles awaited them when they emerged from the woods and stepped onto the road that would lead them to Astra.

The plan was to only get so close with the SUVs before heading to Astra's on foot. Echo could use her shadow gift, while Elijah, Fionn, Rose, and Niamh were using their magic to cloak everyone else on their approach.

According to Bran's satellite images, the house was situated on the southern edge of a twelve-acre property that abutted Fionn's. The compound she'd created from farm buildings was in the northwest near where Fionn's magical boundary was in place.

It was no coincidence.

The fae female was practically shouting "Nah nah nah nah nah" at Fionn. She knew all about them. More than they'd ever known about her. She also thought she owned Niamh, Rose, Thea, and Elijah. Echo almost snarled at the thought. Elijah belonged to no one and if he did, he belonged to her and her alone.

Bran confirmed there were only three heat signatures at the house.

Astra and two wolves.

Each supernatural apparently emitted a different heat signature. Fae, witches, and warlocks were closer to humans, only a few degrees warmer. Wolves ran hotter. Much hotter. Vamps, unsurprisingly, ran a little cooler than the average human.

The plan was to surround the house.

Fionn and Rose at the back entrance.

Thea and Conall on the left.

Echo and Elijah on the right.

Niamh and Kiyo at the front.

There would be no escaping them.

Echo approached the side of the house with Elijah. They were faced with a side door entrance. It blasted open when they were about five feet from the property.

A mammoth guy, as tall as Conall but even broader, burst from the entrance. His canines were down and his eyes gleamed with malice as he scented them with a deep inhale.

Echo looked at her mate and sensed his plans. She nodded. And then in a blink of her eyes, he disappeared using his nifty new *traveling* skills.

Elijah reappeared behind the wolf and punched his fist right through the male's chest.

The huge wolf bellowed in outrage and whirled out of Elijah's grip with a grunt before her mate could rip his heart from his chest.

He made the mistake, however, of thinking Elijah was the threat.

With her vamp speed, Echo bridged the distance between them and jumped onto the wolf's large back. She placed his head between her palms and held on with supernatural grip as he tried to shake her off. When she rolled over him toward the ground, she twisted his head in her grasp with all her strength, breaking his neck before she tumbled into a perfect somersault.

Popping up to her feet, she caught Elijah's admiring look a second before he pressed a foot to the wolf's broken neck and severed his head from his body.

He winced and turned to her with a sickened grimace. "Well, that was bloody disgusting."

Echo's lips twitched, but her smile halted as their supernatural hearing picked up Astra's voice.

"We've been breached. Take out the humans!"

Elijah's eyes flew to hers in horror as Astra's screech of outrage hit their ears.

"She's warned the guards!" Niamh shouted from the other side of the house. "Echo, Elijah, Conall, Thea ... Go! We've got this!"

Echo didn't wait around to argue with anyone. She and Elijah were a streak of supernatural speed. She could hear Thea and Conall changing into their wolf forms in the distance, but she concentrated on the obstacles in her paths. The trees. The bracken. Rocks. A stream. She wound her way through them as if Odette's life depended on it. Because it did.

They lunged over a low stone wall that brought them into a field with several barn-like buildings, and Echo strained to hear ahead of them. Instead, all she heard were Conall's and Thea's racing heartbeats as they caught up to them as wolves. They skidded to a halt as a door in the long, white stone building before them was thrown open. Echo shot a look at her wolf companions.

Thea was smaller than Conall, though still larger than a normal wolf. Her fur was beautiful—dark brown with flecks of caramel. Her eyes gleamed gold as the light began to fade across the land. Conall MacLennan was twice the size of an ordinary wolf, his fur so black it almost shimmered blue in the setting sun. In fact, the sun was low enough behind the trees for the vampire to step out of that building before them.

With an automatic weapon in each hand.

Their preternatural senses detected the release of the bullets from their chambers just in time for all four of them to swerve to avoid the assault. Disgust fueled Echo as they weaved around the spray of bullets. There was a time for weapons, and there was a time to fight with honor.

With a scream of rage, Echo launched herself feetfirst toward the vampire, a bullet winging through her arm with a sting seconds before she slammed into him. He soared at speed into the stone building, the crack of his head a sickening noise through the field. Echo had landed on her ass but quickly got up from the weak position.

"You're okay?" Elijah asked, grabbing her arm.

She nodded. "Already healing."

Her mate nodded and then waved a hand at the guns. They melted into the ground as the vampire groaned, coming to. A stake suddenly appeared in Elijah's hand, his magic tingling the air. He held it out to her just as a wolf came bounding around the corner of the building. Conall and Thea intercepted the enemy wolf as Echo quickly took the stake and drove it through the vampire's chest. He burst into ash, and Elijah tugged her up, leading her past the fighting wolves and into what was an old farmyard.

All three of the utilitarian buildings faced onto it.

Echo focused, trying to drown out the sound of the fight between wolves behind the stone building. "I hear eight heartbeats other than ours."

"I smell two wolves and two vamps." Elijah pointed toward the wooden building that looked like stables. "The two vamps are in there with our family."

The vamps were going to kill them.

Echo buried her fear and raced toward the barn. Just as suddenly, she was hit with a ton of weight at her back and found the ground racing toward her. She smacked into packed dirt just as burning, tearing, excruciating pain exploded from her shoulder down her back. She screamed as the wolf's scent mingled with her blood.

An unworldly roar reverberated around them, and suddenly the weight was gone. Fighting against the agonizing pain, Echo scrambled to her feet in time to see Elijah hold the huge gray wolf in a crippling bear hug. The wolf whined, his eyes widening in shock as Elijah crushed his ribs seconds before he snapped his neck. With that, he dropped the wolf, panting with outrage, his eyes a gold so bright they were almost blinding.

"Are you all right?" His voice was deep and echoing ... not of this world.

It was his roar she'd heard.

Echo had never heard anything like it.

Magic vibrated from him ... and her mate had never looked more fae. More beautiful.

More deadly.

Echo attempted to ignore the scalding pain when she realized it was her injury that had awakened the extremes of his supernatural ability. The air snapped and crackled around him as he moved toward her. He was exactly what they needed him to be right now, and having a chunk of her shoulder ripped out wasn't going to stop them. "We'll heal me later. Let's go!"

Thea soared past them in wolf form, blocking their path. She crashed at their feet with a whimper of pain. An infuriated howl ripped through the air seconds before another wolf whine was abruptly silenced.

Conall in wolf form raced around the building as Thea got to her feet, limping. He nuzzled her face, and she bussed into him in reassurance.

"Thea, you good?" Echo asked.

The wolves turned to look at them and Echo saw their eyes widen with human reaction to the sight of Elijah. Even his hair was pulling free of its elastic band like he was surrounded in static electricity. His skin glowed with the golden hum of light.

"What?" he asked in confusion.

"You look like you're about to go nuclear," she explained. "You're literally glowing right now."

"Really?" He cocked his head in a decidedly unhuman manner. "Then I guess we better find those two vamps so I can treat them to my William method."

Echo grinned viciously, even as the blood trickled down her arm, dripping from her fingertips. His cockiness was hot. "Go blow them to hell."

Elijah was a streak of color he moved so fast. Conall and Thea sped after him, and Echo sucked in a breath as the world tilted on its axis. "No," she gritted between her teeth. "You pass out later once Odette is safe."

Echo raced after her mate and their companions and as she blasted into the barn, she felt a force slick over her skin like oil. With it, the strength leached out of her.

Had the wolf poisoned her with his bite somehow?

"Echo."

She looked up as she stumbled farther into the long barn.

Elijah.

His light had dimmed, his eyes bleeding back to their human color as he stared at her in panic. "Something ... is wrong," he gasped.

Thea and Conall were collapsed at his feet, rolled over onto their sides, panting violently.

Echo's knees began to buckle as her heart raced. "W-what's h-happening?"

A clanging followed by a creak drew their gazes to the end of the barn where a dividing wall with a metal gate sectioned it off from what had looked like stables from the outside.

A beautiful redhead strolled out, locking the gate behind her.

Astra.

She beamed, her magic crackling as she strode toward Elijah. "Hullo, brother."

"I'm not your brother," he snarled.

"Where ... where are our people?" Echo spat.

Astra cut her a haughty look. "I have no use for your people other than to lure you here. So foolish." She tutted. "Even when you know your plan is foolish, bordering on moronic, you charge in to save those you love."

"What is this?" Elijah tried to lift an arm and failed.

"A little spell I concocted. Using pure iron. Of course, to be able to concoct and withstand it took me years and years of building my immunity. I had to ingest a tiny bit of pure iron every day for decades. Oh, it was agony. But so worth it." She giggled like a little girl. "When Eirik stabbed me with his iron blade, I wove an illusion to make it seem like I'd died. Oh, it hurt, and I had to heal ... but iron is no longer fatal to me. So, all of Niamh's threats to stab me in the heart with iron ... useless. Iron cannot wield me, but I can wield it." She gestured around the barn. "Right now, you're held within an iron cage of my making, and it's draining you." Her eyes dropped to the wolves at Elijah's feet. "The wolves are affected by the silver dust mingled with all the dirt."

"I won't come with you willingly," Elijah growled weakly. "Neither will the others."

"Yes, I know." Astra sighed heavily. "Fate is challenging me, it seems. However, I'm smarter than that bitch. I'm smarter than all the bitches." Her lips spread into a wicked smile. "I didn't lure *you* here, little brother." Her gaze swung to Echo. "Hullo, brother's mate."

Suddenly, Astra blinked out of existence and appeared right in front of Echo. She didn't have time to react before the world tunneled all around her.

35

Whistling moans and whining nudged Echo from unconsciousness. She frowned at the noise and then at the following chill that blasted over her body.

Wind.

Her eyes flew open, and the pain from her injury registered. She bit back a groan, feeling everything all at once. Not just the burning, throbbing, but the sticky blood coating her arm and shoulder, her clothes. The pounding headache deep behind her eyes.

The scent of grass and sea air in the distance, a scent no normal human could smell from here. But there it was. The North Sea.

Beyond the city of Edinburgh.

A groan brought Echo's head around and her heart raced at the sight.

Kiyo was flat on his stomach, a silver knife twisted in his back. Echo instinctually moved to help him, and a familiar voice screamed, "Echo, don't move!"

Her head whipped to the side in horror.

Odette.

Her hands and ankles were shackled, her back to Elijah's mother. His father lay motionless at her own shackled feet. Margaret sobbed quietly beside them, her limbs trapped with metal cuffs.

No!

Echo moved again.

"Echo, no!" Odette screamed, her face tear-streaked. "There's a stake in your back."

The words unlocked the realization that the pain wasn't just coming from her shoulder.

Now she felt the foreign object lodged in the middle of her back, way too close to her heart for comfort.

One wrong move, and she was dead.

She nodded. "Is ... is Bill alive?"

Nancy nodded back, face stoic as ever. "He tried to fight and she knocked him out."

"Astra?"

"Yes. We're on Arthur's Seat," Nancy said flatly. "We brought Elijah here when he was a young boy. Why can't people see us up here? Surely, someone will come. They'll see. We're on Arthur's Seat, for goodness' sake. They'll come. They'll see."

Echo ignored her ramblings, realizing Elijah's mother was probably in shock. "Where is she?"

"Coming back," Kiyo grunted from his place on the ground. "She—"

The air crackled and Astra reappeared.

She'd dressed the part in a pale aqua gown that suited her red hair perfectly. The soft muslin clung to her, layered swaths of fabric that suggested fairy princess and not the evil cow she really was.

"They're coming." She glanced between her and Kiyo. "It would have been better if I could have captured Fionn too, but he's

... Well, it doesn't matter. Rose cares enough about you all to come to your rescue. Like I said, moronic. They know I'm going to use them to open the gate, and yet still they come." She giggled to herself as she walked past them, the grass flattening beneath her bare feet and trailing in the fabric of her long hem.

"But first we can't have the humans getting involved, can we ... so a little spell, I think." Astra cut Echo a smirk. "I need blood. Well, more like a sacrifice, really." Her eyes hardened with madness. "This is for embarrassing me by not bursting into ash when you should have."

Echo's pulse raced as Astra strode toward Odette and the others. "What ... what are you doing?"

Echo's skin tingled and the dagger appeared in Astra's hand.

"No!" Echo tried to move, but the stake in her back shifted and she screamed in agony as it neared her heart.

Astra rounded a crying Margaret whose terror-struck eyes met Echo's as the fae gripped her by the neck with supernatural strength and began murmuring in Irish Gaelic.

The air charged, a humming noise growing louder and louder in their ears.

"Astra!" Echo crawled across the ground toward her birth mother.

"Echo, please!" Odette begged. Not for her to save them but for her to stop moving.

She couldn't.

She couldn't just let her ...

Furious, she twisted her arm behind her back to grab the stake. It burned, her flesh hissing and bubbling, and she released it with a cry. Her palm was blistered and red, the top layer of skin melted off.

Some kind of spell.

"Astra!"

Kiyo's grunting brought her gaze across the circle. He was

crawling toward Astra too, face contorted with pain as he tried to move with the silver blade in his back.

The fae's eyes bled gold as her murmurings turned frantic, and then before Echo could grab at the stake again, Astra slashed her dagger across Margaret's throat.

"No!" Echo's scream would have shattered the sky if it weren't for the golden dome that appeared over them and then spread until it covered the entirety of Arthur's Seat and the park below. It sizzled and disappeared.

A barrier spell.

Astra released Margaret and she collapsed on her back, the blood flowing too fast from her neck. Her eyes stared unseeingly up at the heavens.

Echo felt an invisible fissure split her chest.

Odette was sobbing. Nancy tried to soothe her. Kiyo roared in fury.

Echo ... Echo experienced something ancient and vengeful building up inside her, pushing through the crack in her heart to unleash itself. She dragged her gaze from Margaret to Astra, and Astra's smile slipped at whatever she saw in Echo.

"Now, now." She shrugged off her unease. "No need for the mercury eyes. It won't do any good."

The voice that came out of Echo sounded foreign even to her ears. "I'm going to rip you limb from limb."

"You can try."

Challenge accepted.

With a Valkyrie-like scream of outrage, Echo reached behind her, ignored her burning flesh, and yanked the stake out of her back. She stood. The pain from her injuries numbed as wrath-fueled adrenaline consumed her. She was a blur, her incisors out, and when she reached Astra, she went for the throat. Her fangs pierced her flesh, popping through the skin with ease, and Echo clamped her supernaturally strong jaw down and then tore her open.

It was enough to disorient her. To slam her body to the ground. Astra gurgled, blood spurting out of her neck and mouth.

In hindsight, Echo would have done anything for her usual control and calm.

Perhaps then she could have finished off the fae.

Instead, a bestial instinct to cause as much damage as possible took over. She pummeled Astra's face over and over until eventually, her fist smashed into the ground.

The fae had *traveled*.

She screamed, flipping onto her feet to search for her.

A rumbling halted her and the extinct volcano beneath them shook so violently, Echo stumbled to a knee, her injuries reasserting themselves with a vengeance. She gasped at the agony in her back and vaguely wondered if the stake had splintered in her body.

Then all thoughts distilled to one at the sight of the hill opening beneath them in four spots.

As the rumbling grew louder, the mountain trembling with what felt like rage, four monoliths rose out of the volcano in a circle atop Arthur's Seat.

Four standing stones.

A gate to Faerie.

"Astra, show yourself!" she roared into the sky.

No answer.

Echo's gaze dropped to her birth mother as she smeared Astra's blood and flesh from her mouth with the back of her hand. Tears burned her eyes.

So much pain. Echo had caused Margaret so much pain ... and led her to her death.

"It isn't your fault," Kiyo's voice carried to her. "This is Astra's doing. No one else."

Astra appeared in the middle of the standing stones. Her hair blazed behind her with unnatural wind, her dress fluttering against the curves of her body.

Her eyes were bright gold.

"They're coming," Astra announced with a smug smile.

The air crackled around them, the hair on the back of Echo's neck rising in response. Suspecting Astra would assume Echo would attack her again, Echo vamp-sped over to Kiyo instead and yanked the silver blade out of his back.

He shot her a dark look of thanks before he transformed into a wolf more quickly than Echo had ever seen a were invoke his beast. It was too fast. Then, of course, Kiyo was no ordinary wolf. Wolves had the gift of long life ... but not immortality. Yet, Kiyo did. Kiyo was the world's only immortal werewolf. Clearly, that came with perks.

Like Conall, he had thick black shining fur, and he was huge. He bared his teeth at Astra, but the fae female just grinned viciously at him.

"Now, now, it's a little too late for that."

Before Kiyo had time to charge at her, Conall and Thea appeared with Rose out of thin air. Rose held them, having brought them here by *traveling*. Then Fionn appeared. And then Elijah, whose gaze darted around the cliff top. Echo felt his relief as he spotted her. He followed her eyes as she gestured with her chin to Odette, Nancy, and Bill, who had come to in the last few seconds.

Elijah's expression softened with more relief—until he saw Margaret. His head whipped to Echo. His sorrow mingled with hers.

Astra scowled at the supernaturals. "Where is my sister?" she shrieked.

Niamh.

Kiyo growled low in his throat.

Then Astra's eyes widened as she looked beyond them to where the hill sloped downward.

Niamh's voice carried up toward them. "Looking for me, you psychotic fae feces?"

Echo might have laughed if she'd been capable of it.

Astra's paling features had Echo turning toward Niamh, and she drew in a breath at the sight before them.

A bitter smirk curled Echo's lips as she realized Astra was shocked. "Ah, you didn't see that coming, did you?"

36

For months, Niamh had been burdened with visions of what could be. Not just one possible outcome to the fight to save the freaking world, but many possibilities. With that burden came the realization that to achieve the ending she desired, she would have to move everyone like chess pieces. Not just Astra. But even the people she loved and cared about.

Even her mate.

It was a path she couldn't deviate from, but she knew Kiyo would forgive her for keeping the truth to herself.

Astra had to believe Niamh was confused by the visions she was being shown.

Astra had to believe that they were all too sentimental and emotional to care they were walking into a trap.

So, behind the scenes, using every ounce of her magic, Niamh had hidden her intentions from Astra and kept them hidden from those who didn't need to know until the very last minute. Coordinating. Fostering relationships. Explaining what was at stake. Conall had been pivotal in bringing it all together too.

Which was why, standing at Niamh's back, was not only the

entirety of Pack MacLennan but three large wolf packs from around the world, allies of Pack MacLennan, who had stepped up to fight.

Hundreds of werewolves.

They were all in wolf form and ready to stop Astra from opening the gate to Faerie.

Not just to stop Astra, though.

On Niamh's left flank were five of the world's most powerful witches and warlocks. Three warlocks and two witches, all members of the North American High Council, who oversaw the covens of North America and upheld their laws. For too long, the Blackwood Coven had gotten away with atrocities in the name of opening the gate to Faerie.

At last, Niamh had convinced the council members to bear witness to the Blackwoods' treachery.

Because the Blackwood Coven was on its way to make sure Astra failed, but only so *they* could succeed.

Just as she thought it, the Blackwood Coven breached Astra's barriers with their collective magic, popping onto the grass one after another in a formation of four lines—a wall of witches and warlocks between the wolves, Niamh, the council members, the standing stones, and the rest of Niamh's companions.

"Believe me now?" Niamh asked the council members.

Their answering dismay and wrath was palpable.

"Ready?"

They nodded.

"Charge!" Niamh screamed her order.

As the wolves rushed across the grass, Niamh ran with them. The sound of their pounding paws across Arthur's Seat echoed around her, but not beyond the barrier Astra had killed Margaret to create. Sorrow scored across Niamh's chest, but she pushed it aside to focus. Kiyo and the others battled Astra who popped in and out of existence, evading them within the stone circle, evading them. Niamh had to get to them. She had to fight to end the fae who could destroy them all.

Echo and Elijah attacked the Blackwoods from behind, keeping Odette and the Webbs at their back.

The air rushed, whipping in bitter stings across Niamh's cheeks, as she tried and failed to fix her attention on Astra.

The members of the high council worked to bring down the spell protecting the Blackwoods. Seconds before the wolves reached them, an electric tingle shot down Niamh's spine as their shield failed. The coven braced for impact as the wolves tore through their magic and into the witches and warlocks, who screamed in fear and outrage. Blood sprayed, flesh ripped, and limbs were torn from bodies.

Niamh's hair rose on her nape and her gaze whipped toward a coven member whose focus was on her. She used her magic to create a shield seconds before a blast of fire-wrapped water collided against her barrier. It shimmered with gold at the impact, and the witch shrieked in fury that Niamh had bested her.

With a ruthless flick of her hand, she sent the witch careening a hundred yards into the sky. She slammed against Astra's barrier and collapsed, unconscious.

As whimpers and howls lit the air, Niamh watched on helplessly as an enemy warlock used magic to break a werewolf's neck. Conall's howl of agony was joined by all of Pack MacLennan.

Niamh had a flash of a vision as their collective grief hit her.

Mhairi Ferguson. The wolf the warlock had killed was Conall's Delta and an integral member of his pack.

A huge brown wolf exploded in feral rage and ripped the murderous warlock to pieces.

Mhairi's mate, Brodie.

As much as she could, Niamh and the council members moved through the chaos of battle, trying to protect other wolves from the same fate. Try as they might, they did not succeed, and more wolves met their end. More overwhelming collective grief flooded Niamh's desperation to get to Astra.

A choking sensation tightened around her throat, and she instinctively clawed at it, eyes flying wildly through the melee of supernatural bodies to find her attacker.

A witch with dark curls. Niamh broke her hold and sent her flying into another witch so hard, their heads whacked together, knocking them out.

Pulling witches and warlocks off werewolves with her fae powers, dousing wolves who had been set on fire, rescuing others being crushed by rings of air and water, Niamh became the ultimate target. Magic whipped and sliced and attempted to crush her. Exhaustion pulled at that golden spirit inside her as she attempted to defend not only herself but others, all on a path to Astra.

A streak of powerful magic blasted past her shields, and Niamh felt an invisible vise wrap around her ribs, trying to crush her. She fell to her knees, gasping in agony as a witch and two warlocks clasping bloodied hands approached with madness in their eyes. There was a blur of movement and then huge jaws clamped the top of the middle warlock's head. In a gory scene Niamh would never forget, the man's head was torn from his body and tossed aside with a throw of Kiyo's jaws.

The crushing sensation eased as Niamh *traveled* behind the witch to snap her neck, and Kiyo ended the other warlock. Blood coated his dark fur and large white teeth, his eyes wild with his fear for her. Niamh smoothed a hand over her mate's head, and his ears twitched as he bussed into her.

"Thank you, my love," she whispered hoarsely before they turned to survey the scene. The grass was muddied with blood and pieces of supernaturals. Insides spilled onto the ground. Moans and whimpers and cries filled the air. All beyond the sight or hearing of the humans beyond Astra's barrier. Niamh's unshed tears burned as she took in the unseeing eyes of the dead strewn upon the battlefield.

Her gaze flew to Astra, who was fighting off Fionn and Rose. She swiped a blade over Rose's arm before disappearing. Thea and Conall had joined Elijah and Echo in battle. Echo was trying to guard Odette and Elijah's parents, but a warlock had broken past their defenses.

Niamh pulled on her magic to protect them.

But it was too late.

Bill Webb jumped in front of his wife and the child under their protection. The warlock ended his life with a swipe of his hand. A line of blood appeared across Bill's neck. Wide-eyed, he slumped to his knees, clutching his throat.

"No!" Niamh screamed as memories of her beloved brother Ronan's death at the hands of another coven slammed through her mind. A golden light blasted out of her, targeting the warlock.

He burst into a cloud of ash.

But it was too late.

Elijah's father lay upon the ground, *gone*, as his wife sobbed over his body.

Astra.

Niamh searched the battleground and found her swiping the same blade she'd taken to Rose over the back of Elijah's neck. Just a nick before she again disappeared. Niamh looked to Thea, Thea who believed she was no longer fae. Sure enough, Astra appeared in front of Thea, causing the wolf to rear back and bare her teeth. Astra dragged the blade across Thea's side. The female alpha growled and swiped a paw, catching Astra's leg before the fae disappeared.

Niamh braced.

Astra appeared right in front of her.

Magic tingled at Niamh's fingertips and the weight of the weapon filled her palm. Lethargy washed over her, but Niamh fought through it. She couldn't kill Astra like other faes. But that didn't mean she couldn't weaken her with iron. The iron blade had a thick leather handle to protect Niamh's skin.

She slashed the blade across Astra's face before Astra could nick her with her own weapon. The redheaded fae cried out in disbelief, clutching her bleeding cheek. Betrayal lit her aqua eyes. In her madness, she still somehow thought she and Niamh were meant to be. Two halves of the same coin.

"I am nothing like you," Niamh hissed and rammed the iron blade into Astra's heart. "It might not kill you, but it fucking hurts." She twisted the knife.

Astra gaped, falling to her knees with a choking sound. With one last wide-eyed look she slashed out with her dagger, catching Niamh's forearm. Then she disappeared.

Dismay thickened Niamh's throat. But she'd known this could happen.

That it most likely would happen this way.

Even as Niamh ran toward the standing stones, crying out for her fae brethren to follow her, Astra reappeared in the middle of them. With a shriek of pure fury, she held out the blood-tipped dagger and slammed it into the earth beneath her feet.

Fionn dove at her, rolling her out of the circle.

Yet Niamh knew it was too late.

A crack. Like the loudest thunder she'd ever heard.

It boomed across Arthur's Seat, shaking the rock beneath them. The fighting supernaturals cried out and all turned to watch as their dimension split open. A ball of fiery golden-red light appeared in the center of the stones.

Then like bolts of lightning, the golden-red light splintered, a streak attaching to each of the standing stones.

Slowly, the ball dissipated as their reality split apart and the gate to another world appeared before them.

Instead of sky and the city of Edinburgh, an otherworldly

forest of blues and greens the shades of which Niamh had never witnessed except within her dreams came into being.

Faerie.

Astra had opened the gate to Faerie.

That definitely had to be dealt with.

But first ...

Niamh was a blur of color as she wound through the bodies of her comrades and enemies to find Fionn holding a weakened Astra against the back of one of the standing stones with a spell.

Astra murmured under her breath, trying to break the casting with her own.

Fionn looked at Niamh and gave her a small nod before he stepped aside.

The corner of Astra's lips curled. "Have you come to kill me, sister? It's too late, you know. Even if you kill me, it's too late."

"That's where you're wrong. I know how to close the gate."

Astra narrowed her eyes.

"You're lying."

She studied her fae sibling, feeling nothing, knowing the very darkness of Astra's soul better than anyone. She was a plague upon this world. A plague upon Niamh's world.

"I guess you'll never know for sure."

Niamh ran at her, watched with satisfaction as Astra's eyes widened with shock even as she fought to free herself from Fionn's spell. She would have, eventually. But with a dagger in her heart, she was weakened.

Weak enough that with the right velocity, Niamh's palm hit the edge of the dagger's handle like a Mack Truck. The entire weapon shot through Astra's chest and heart. And just in case it wasn't enough, Niamh punched her fist into Astra's chest cavity and wrapped her hand around what was left of the heart muscle.

She tore it free.

Not in the least surprised to see her heart had blackened with evil.

The mad light died in Astra's eyes. Her body slumped to the grass.

Niamh concentrated on Astra's heart until it burst into flames. She dropped it on the earth and watched it turn to ash.

A gentle hand settled on her shoulder.

Fionn. She looked up at him. It wasn't over. "We need to close the gate," she said. "You make sure Astra can never come back."

The hulking Celtic fae nodded. He had a strong stomach. He could do what needed to be done. Split Astra into pieces and scatter those pieces to the ends of the world before turning them to ash.

Nothing else would do.

Whirling around, Niamh could see the battle was ending. Only a few Blackwoods remained now, and the high council members were dealing with them. The packs were already beginning to collect their wounded and mourn their dead.

There would be time for her and her friends to do the same later.

Sending her thoughts into Rose's, Thea's, and Elijah's minds, Niamh spoke to them: *I need you at the standing stones. Only we can close the gate before it's too late.*

37

Niamh's voice jolted through Elijah's head as he picked his way through the fallen. Echo was safe and alive.

However, he'd heard his mother's grief-stricken sobs and almost taken a magical knife to his chest with the distraction. Seeing her up on the hill, cradling his father's body in her arms as Odette sobbed at their side ... Elijah's legs almost buckled.

Niamh's voice came again.

Elijah, grieve later, brother. We have a world to save.

Her words were gentle but stern.

Grieve later.

His mind reeled and a sob of agony caught in his throat.

So he tore his gaze from his parents to Echo who'd reached them first. Their eyes met. Her sorrow was clear. But so was her strength.

If it were her, she would pull her shit together to do what needed to be done.

Elijah channeled his mate's fierceness, tightened his hands into fists at his sides, and marched in the same direction as Thea and Rose.

To meet Niamh in front of the terrifying gate that had opened to another world.

To Faerie.

As they grew closer, he knew they too must feel the pulsating energy. It was like a powerful wave, pushing at their shins, threatening to take them under.

It was as loud as a crashing wave too.

"We have to close it before the other side realizes it's open!" Niamh shouted, her hair whipping around her face with the force of the gate's energy.

"Is she dead?" Rose shouted back.

Niamh nodded, her expression mournful. "This was the only way! I saw a thousand paths, and this was the only way!"

"What do we need to do?" Thea yelled.

"She took blood from us all to open the gate!"

"Will our blood close it?" Elijah shouted, his eyes stinging against what felt like hurricane-force winds.

Niamh shook her head. "The light! The golden light we all have within us! It's stronger once united! Pure energy! Enough energy to heal the fracture between universes!"

Thea looked panicked. "I don't have it anymore!"

"You do!" Niamh seemed so sure. "I promise, you do!"

"I'm still fae?"

"You're something new!" Niamh smiled, reaching out for Thea.

Clearly shaken by the revelation, Thea accepted Niamh's hand. Elijah numbly stretched for Rose's and then took Thea's other, the four of them united.

"Call on that golden light!" Niamh cried. "Whatever it takes! Pain, grief, rage ... call on the light! We don't have much time now!"

Determined, Elijah faced the gate, staring into the world beyond, to the ethereal forest beckoning in the distance. Alien plants and flowers of a vividity his brain could hardly process. It looked beautiful.

Beautiful, but deadly.

He didn't need to look over his shoulder to see his parents in his mind's eye. His devastated mum beside his beloved father who had died to protect the people he loved. Grief tore through Elijah and he felt Echo's too. The loss of her birth mother, a woman she'd barely gotten to know. The guilt of bringing her into this mess. Of bringing Elijah's parents into it. Her pain for her mate. For him.

The death at his back.

The mourning wolves and the decimation of an entire coven.

He used it.

He used the blood-soaked ground as fuel.

He pictured his father's face.

And the light exploded out of him.

Niamh's came next, joining his.

Then Rose's collided with both.

Thea let out a shriek of frustration.

"You can do it, Thea!" Niamh shouted. "You have it in you!"

"I don't!"

"You do! Do it for Mhairi! Do it for Brodie! Do it for the three other members of your pack who lost their lives today!"

With a scream of pure grief, Thea unleashed herself. Her eyes bled gold and the light poured out of her, streaming toward the others. As it impacted the ball of energy they created, streaks of that light split from the ball and blasted into the fractured seams of their world.

It crackled like the fiercest electricity, and just like that, it sewed the world back together, the forest beyond disappearing until there was nothing but blue sky and the city of Edinburgh in the distance.

And silence.

Niamh's hair settled into place around her shoulders.

Elijah blinked, slowly letting go of his companions' hands.

"Well done, family," Niamh whispered wearily. "We just saved the bloody world."

38

As much as relief and overwhelming pride shuddered through Echo as she watched Elijah, Niamh, Rose, and Thea close the gate to Faerie, grief lingered like a suffocating shadow in the background, waiting for its chance to smother her.

After Elijah pulled the three women to him, hugging and kissing their cheeks as they wiped away tears of exhaustion, he turned to Echo. She stumbled toward him as the others reached for their respective mates. He immediately hauled her into his arms, pressing a hard kiss to her mouth before peppering frantic, weary little kisses across her jaw and then burying her against him. Echo nuzzled his throat, not out of hunger or passion.

She offered only comfort and drew the same from him.

"I love you," he whispered, his voice trembling.

"I love you too."

"My dad ..."

Her grip on him tightened. "I know."

Together they turned. Echo slipped her hand into his, bolstering him as Elijah hesitantly moved toward his father still sprawled on the ground. Nancy had calmed somewhat, but when she looked up at her son with ragged grief, Echo heard Elijah's low animalistic sound of agony she would never forget.

She released him as he moved to his mother, falling to his knees to draw her against him. Nancy let out a keening cry as Elijah rocked her into his side, his hollow gaze on his father's face.

Echo knelt beside Odette, pulling the young girl into her arms. She would forever hate William for forcing her to bring Odette into all this. Now her sister would always hold these horrific images of war and death and loss within her. Echo brushed a kiss over Odette's forehead as she clung to her, her little arms trembling with shock.

How could Echo ever make up for what she'd put her through?

The thought of Odette's birth parents flickered like a weak flame in the back of her mind. Yet it was there. And she knew she would have to do the selfless thing.

As she watched silent tears fall down Elijah's cheeks, her own welled. For years, Echo had held herself apart. Emotionless. A wall to protect her from the world of William "the Bloody" Payne. Now all those walls crumbled into dust, and everything Elijah felt, she felt.

Elijah bravely gazed upon his dead father. Looked upon him and saw him as the man who had died protecting the people he loved.

Forcing herself to look, Echo turned to see Margaret's body.

Unlike Elijah, she didn't mourn the years of memories filled with love and support nor the future of more of that.

She mourned what should have been. What could have been.

She blamed herself for ruining what was left of Margaret's life. A life she could have finally lived in freedom now that William was dead.

"I'm sorry," Echo whispered, hoping wherever her birth mother was she could hear her.

"It's not your fault," Odette soothed.

Echo looked down upon her little sister's sweet, tear-streaked face.

"Margaret knew it wasn't your fault. We spoke. Before we came here. I know who she is. She loved you, Echo. All she ever wanted was to know you were okay."

Fresh hot tears scalded her cheeks as she pulled her sister hard against her, taking comfort in not just her presence and well-being, but in the wise words of a young girl who'd seen more of the world than most adults.

"We're holding up Astra's barrier!" a voice boomed across the hill. Echo followed it to see a tall, familiar middle-aged man who rippled with power.

A warlock.

A powerful one.

"But we need to move now," he continued, directing his words to Niamh.

Niamh nodded solemnly. "Will you help us?"

"It is the least we can do after our council failed to protect this world from the Blackwood Coven." He pressed his lips together in harsh regret.

Niamh shook her head, giving him a kind smile. "You didn't fail. You came here, and you didn't fail."

The warlock nodded, and Echo suddenly understood why he was familiar. He was Dane Aldrich, one of the highest-ranking members of the North American High Council. Echo vaguely wondered what else Niamh had kept from them after turning up here with council members and hundreds of wolves. She suspected the Irish fae had long ago hatched this plan, its blueprint kept secret so it would play out exactly as they'd needed.

They had won.

Her lips trembled as Elijah met her gaze.

Echo hadn't known until that moment that sometimes winning meant losing too.

As if she'd heard Echo's thoughts, Niamh spoke to her. To them all. "We lost a lot today!" Her voice carried on the wind. "But their lives were not sacrificed in vain. We put an end to a centuries-long plan to reopen the gates to Faerie and bring unimaginable destruction upon our world. We leave here having done what was needed for the greater good. We leave here knowing we stood for something. We stood against greed and hatred and power ... And we did it because we love. We *love*, and we will continue to love. That's all grief is. They don't exist without the other."

When Niamh's gaze met Kiyo's, her eyes flared gold for a moment and then a calm settled through the bitter hollowness around them.

Gratitude wove through Echo as she held on to Odette and reached for Elijah's hand.

Because at that moment, she'd needed—they'd all needed—the reminder that ultimately only one thing had brought them here to this moment.

Love.

Love had destroyed their enemies.

Love had mended the fracture between two worlds.

For so long, Echo had lived in darkness, in a world where love was corrupted and not to be trusted.

Now as she faced her immortality ... it was no longer with dread.

It was with anticipation.

Because now her eternal future was paved before her in love.

With *him*.

"Love," Niamh continued as she took Kiyo's hand. "Love ... is true immortality."

EPILOGUE

Five years later

TORRIDON, Scotland

"That's cheating, you know," Thea's husband's voice sounded from behind her, his tone amused.

She glanced over her shoulder, lifting her hands from where they'd moments ago been pressed to the soil in their potato patch.

Conall stood with his arms crossed over his broad chest, his legs slightly splayed as he squinted against the morning sunlight. He'd just caught Thea sending a little fae magic into the soil to help her vegetables flourish.

It was now a well-guarded pack secret that Thea MacLennan was the first hybrid fae werewolf in existence. After she'd unleashed the golden light five years ago that helped her and her fae siblings close the gate to Faerie, the fae magic her werewolf side had suppressed had started to trickle out.

Thea stood, brushing soil off her hands. "Where are the kids?"

"With their cousins." Conall stepped toward her, a heated look in his eyes.

Two years after they'd had Niamh Caledonia, they had their son Brodie. Then six months ago, Thea had given birth to their second daughter, Mhairi. With their sacrifice in battle, Mhairi and Brodie Ferguson had left behind grown children of their own who were moved by Thea and Conall's decision to name their children after their late parents. The pack had also lost Kenneth Portpatrick, Fiona Scott, and Paul Macbeth. It had been a hard hit. But together they grieved, and every year they held a large dinner and ceilidh to celebrate the lives of their fallen pack members.

"I know that look." Thea rested her hands on her hips. "Every time I see that look in your eyes, I end up pregnant."

"If that were true, then we'd have thousands of pups running around at our feet." He grinned cockily, the scar that scored down the left side of his face, from the tip of his eyebrow to the corner of his mouth, lifting slightly with his smile.

Her mate didn't look a day older than when they'd first met. Back when he was hunting her and she was trying to evade him.

When her fae powers began to return, Thea feared it meant she was destined for immortality after all. The thought of living forever had always terrified her. Even more now knowing her mate, while long-lived, wasn't immortal. However, Niamh, with her extra fae abilities that truly made her the most powerful being on Earth, had assured Thea she could sense her cells aging.

Sure enough, after Mhairi was born, Thea found her first gray hair.

Immortals' hair did not gray.

Time would tell for their children Nee, Brodie, and Mhairi.

They were hybrids too. Two months ago, five-year-old Nee revived a dying bird cupped between her hands. Thea had felt the familiar energy emitting from her daughter when it happened and knew she'd inherited Thea's faeness.

Conall reached for his wife, sliding his arms around her waist to pull her against his body. Beyond him, Loch Torridon glimmered in the sunlight. Their vegetable patch was on the hill behind their large house. Thea had been so lost in her "cheating," she hadn't heard Conall drive off or drive home.

Without the kids.

He caressed her cheek as she melted into him.

"Where is my Thea today? You seem lost in your thoughts. If it's too soon, you know it doesnae bother me to wait."

She raised an eyebrow.

Conall laughed huskily. "I miss you, but believe it or not, it's not sexy if you're not into it."

Giggling, Thea pressed her forehead to his strong chest. "It's not that. I'm just ... thoughtful today." She tipped her head back to meet his striking, loving gaze. "But I miss you too." Smoothing her palms over his pecs and down his thick biceps, her voice lowered with need. "How long do Callie and James have the kids?"

Conall's sister and her mate had welcomed their own children two years ago. Twin sisters, Roisin and Isla. They had their hands full as it was. Looking after five children under five wasn't an easy task.

"They have help. So, we have three hours."

Thea bit her lip even as a rush of arousal thrummed through her. "I started taking the pill again."

"I know." Conall cocked his head to the side in confusion. "Is that a problem?"

"You know?"

"Of course I know. I notice everything about you."

Love suffused her at the gruff romantic words. "So, you're okay if we're done with kids? For now, at least."

"Of course." He tipped her chin, searching her face. "I want whatever you want. We have three beautiful bairns, and if that's all we have, I'm happy."

"I just want some time with you and our kids without adding anymore babies into the mix."

"Then that's what we'll do." Conall bent his head to brush his mouth over hers. Her lips still tingled at his touch. Her excitement for her mate had never faded. "I love you, Thea MacLennan."

"I love you too."

Without another word, Conall swept her up into his arms and strode toward the house.

She laughed. "Eager, are we?"

"We went from rabid hormonal pregnancy sex seven months ago to nothing. Did I mention I miss you?"

Thea smoothed a hand over his hair as she bounced against his body with the descent. "Poor baby werewolf."

He cut her a dark look, and she laughed.

"I'm sorry, I meant poor Alpha werewolf and his ginormous alpha cock."

Conall nodded. "That's more like it."

Thea laughed harder.

But her laughter fell away as Conall entered the house via the sliding doors off their primary suite and he threw her on the bed. Their clothes were gone in a matter of seconds and when her mate pushed inside her body, Thea's entire being lit with pleasure. Her toes curled into the mattress beneath them, her fingers biting into the solid muscle of Conall's back as he moved inside her with steady, deep thrusts.

Nothing felt better or more right as being joined like this, watching the desire tighten in each other's features. Conall's animalistic growls met Thea's moans as their first mating since Mhairi's birth overwhelmed them both.

They'd barely climaxed when Conall flipped her on her hands and knees and took her more vigorously, fucking her now as they became nothing but love and lust wrapped up in each other.

Hours later, they were glowing with satisfaction as they drove to Callie and James's home situated ten minutes along the loch from theirs. Callie stepped outside to meet them, baby Mhairi on her hip. At the sight of Thea, Mhairi started waving her chubby little arms, her babbles of joy turning to tears. Her eyes flared gold as the tears turned to screaming, and Thea rushed to take her daughter from Aunt Callie.

"She's definitely your daughter," Callie opined as she handed over the baby. "Those golden eyes."

The children's very early characteristics of their hybrid existence concerned their parents. Until they were old enough to control it, Thea feared Brodie, Nee, and Mhairi would have to stay close to the pack where they were safe.

Her daughter quieted in her arms, falling asleep against Thea's chest as they followed Callie into the house.

They found James sitting on the large corner sofa with Brodie snuggled into his side and Isla in his arms. They were all sleeping. Roisin and Niamh sat in front of the television, watching a cartoon.

Toys were strewn everywhere.

The house looked like a bomb had exploded in it.

"I thought you said they had help." Thea cut Conall an exasperated look.

"Oh, we did. Una came by." Una was the new pack Delta. "But she left twenty minutes ago." Callie raised an eyebrow. "Did you enjoy your adult time?"

"Callie," Conall warned before heading over to collect a sleeping Brodie.

Nee finally noticed her parents had arrived and jumped up to run at Thea and throw her arms around her. "Mummy, we made cookies with Aunt Callie. She said mine were the best!"

Her aunt chuckled. "I said they were the best you've made. I would never show favoritism like that." Then she mouthed at Thea, "*They were the best. Dinnae eat the others.*"

Thea bit back her laughter and nodded before looking down at her daughter. "Why don't you grab some to take home? Then say thank you to Aunt Callie and Uncle James for looking after you."

It took a little while to wrangle the tired children, but Thea did so with gratitude in her heart.

They departed knowing they'd see each other in a few hours for the pack run.

Hours later, most of the pack undressed before a full moon. There were always those who forwent the pack run to look after the pack children. As Alpha and as his mate, Conall and Thea always partook of the pack run.

As the collective magic of the wolves tingled through her, Thea exulted as they all shouted as one, "*Ceannsaichidh an Fhìrinn!*"

The MacLennan motto: Truth Conquers.

Flying through the forest in wolf form, her mate by her side, Thea gave thanks to a beautiful life. Many years ago, she thought she'd spend her long existence miserable and alone. She'd never imagined a peaceful life buried in the Scottish Highlands with a fierce, loving family, a mate who excited and challenged her, and children who looked up to her and loved her unconditionally.

It was at once a quiet but extraordinary existence.

While it wasn't easy, while they'd lost a lot and suffered great trauma and tragedy ... Niamh had been right that brutal day five years ago. Grief did not exist without love. Having experienced the worst that life could offer, Thea knew how to appreciate the best.

Family.

Love.

Quiet moments of peace.

Running wild through the forests of Scotland, free and powerful.

Yes. Theirs was a happy life.

But then ... they'd *earned* a very long, very happy life together.

Galway, Ireland

Rose didn't know if it was the mating bond or if it was her preternatural senses, but anytime Fionn left their bed in the middle of the night, she eventually awoke, sensing his absence.

Sure enough, when her eyes adjusted to the dark, her hand swept over the mattress where his large, warm body should be and she realized he was gone.

But she knew just where to find him.

A sting of concern prickled her as it had almost every night for the past nine months. Getting out of bed, Rose's feet hit the cold flagstone floors for two seconds before she tiredly conjured a pair of slippers. Their home, a castle Fionn called An Caomhnóir, wasn't the most eco-friendly home in the world. During the summer days, the flagstone floors were a saving grace, but when the temperature fell at night, it was a different story. Technically, they could keep the castle at whatever temperature they wanted, but Rose was too tired to expel that much energy.

Leaving their large bedchamber, Rose walked sleepily down the hallway. The castle had two wings, and Fionn wanted everyone in one wing, keeping them close. Quietly opening the second doorway on the right, Rose peeked into the room. Moonlight spilled through the window, falling across the beautiful face of their daughter Saoirse. She insisted they leave her curtains open at night because she loved falling asleep to the sight of the moon and stars. In a few months, she'd turn five. The years had passed so swiftly since her birth.

Rose had known she was pregnant when she'd walked into battle that day in Edinburgh. It had been the most difficult decision of her life. However, she'd also known she was pivotal in the fight. And that if they'd lost, there would be no real future for their miracle child, anyway. Fionn had told her it was possible they'd have a child, but that it happened rarely for the fae, often taking decades, sometimes centuries. It was a miracle they'd fallen pregnant so soon.

Fionn had to abide by her wishes, though he'd been angry and terrified of losing another child.

Thankfully, it had all turned out right in the end. Six months after the battle, Saoirse was born. However, for the first year of her life, Fionn had woken in the middle of the night while their daughter slept to watch over her. He feared being away from her side. It had taken a lot of reassuring and talking for him to relax into parenthood alongside Rose.

But now they were back here again.

Rose blew a kiss into their daughter's room and used her magic to shut the door without making a noise. She padded down the hallway to the next door on the left. It was already open.

Stopping in the doorway, Rose felt an ache of compassion score across her chest as she took in the sight of her mate and husband.

Fionn Mór was every inch the hulking warrior, his broad shoulders almost impossible. Right now, he used his strength to gently cradle their baby son.

Their son who had come quickly after Saoirse. A miracle upon a miracle.

Ardal, at only nine months old, was proving to be a sleeper. While Saoirse had woken them all through the night with her cries for at least the first year, Ardal slept like a dream. Rose hoped long would it continue. Right now, he was safe and content in his father's big arms.

Fionn looked up at her, and her heart crashed against her ribs. So much pain and worry in his beautiful green eyes. He was terrified of losing their children. Centuries before when he'd been a Celtic king, the Faerie Queen had stolen Fionn into Faerie to punish him for killing a fae prince. In doing so, she took him from his children and his then wife. His wife ultimately betrayed him when he returned as fae. He never saw his son and daughter again.

"They're not going anywhere," Rose whispered, giving him a sympathetic smile of reassurance.

An Caomhnóir was wrapped in powerful spells that hid their estate from the human and supernatural world. There was nowhere safer for their family. Having grown up human, Rose worried for the kids' socialization, but as two of the rarest beings in the world, it wasn't safe for them to attend a human school.

Their kids were pure fae.

While five years ago they'd eliminated the greatest threats against them and the world, it didn't mean there weren't supernaturals and humans alike who wouldn't kill to have fae powers at their disposal.

It meant keeping them close until they were grown and strong enough to protect themselves.

Fionn was the most well-read being Rose had ever known, and together they were homeschooling Saoirse. To socialize her, they took regular trips to Scotland to spend time with Thea and Conall and their hybrid fae children. It was a relief to know Saoirse and

Ardal would have a community of other fae to turn to. Visits with their friends' kids were enough for now.

Fionn glanced down at their son. "He's so small."

"He is. But it's temporary. One day he'll be as tall and powerful as his father." Rose couldn't quite imagine that day yet, but she knew it would come far too quickly.

Her words seemed to upset her mate more. "True. They won't need us soon. Eighteen years is nothing when you're immortal. The years are pulled out from under you like quicksand."

Crossing the room, Rose slid a comforting hand over Fionn's broad shoulder as she trailed a gentle fingertip down her son's chubby cheek. His lashes flickered in his sleep. She lowered her voice so as not to wake him. "They will always need us. Perhaps not like they need us now, but they will always need us. And we won't make the mistake that some parents do of thinking our grown children don't have need of us. We're gifted eternity with them, Fionn. We'll always be their family because the likelihood of them finding a fae mate is slim." She squeezed his shoulder. "Whatever choices they make to foster a happy eternity, we'll be right by their side, reminding them that they are never alone."

Fionn glanced up at her, something like awe and pride in his expression. "You always say the right thing, *mo chroí*."

She smiled softly. "That's because I'm always right." Rose leaned down, whispering her lips across his ear. "Let me put our son back in his cot so you can take your wife to bed."

His breath hitched, and Rose pulled back to find that heated look in his eyes she adored. Body already thrumming with anticipation, Rose eased Ardal from his father's arms. She grinned fondly at the way his nose scrunched up in his sleep, and yet he didn't wake. Lowering him into his cot, she pulled his blanket over him and brushed her fingers down his soft baby cheek.

"We should have named you *Suanach*," Rose murmured with amusement.

"Your Old Irish is coming along." Fionn stood at her back, his hand resting on her hip. Suanach meant sleepy or dormant. "But I think we named him just right."

Ardal meant high king.

Like his father.

"Me too." Rose turned and held out her hand to Fionn.

With one last look at his son, he took her invitation and led her out of the room and back to their bedchamber.

Rose expected an immediate and thorough ravishing, but before Fionn did just that, he clasped her face between his large palms and bent low to hold her gaze. Her breath caught at the roiling emotions in his.

"Never think because of this fear I hold that I am not beyond grateful and elated with my existence. Rose Mór, you have given me more than I could ever have wished for myself."

She curled her hands around his wrists, eyes bright with joyful tears. "I know. And I wouldn't change a single step of our journey. Not when it brought us right here."

"*Mo chroí ...*" He growled the endearment as he rested his forehead to hers. "I once told you nothing should last forever. What a fool I was. Because I need you and our children to last until the final star falls out of the sky."

Rose pulled him closer at his beautiful words. "Then that's what's going to happen," she vowed.

With a groan of need, Fionn crushed his mouth to hers and they stumbled toward the bed, falling upon it with a passion that had never faded. Rose knew it never would.

Not even when the final star fell from the sky.

Kamala Rainforest, Phuket, Thailand

. . .

Niamh ogled her mate as he lazed in the precariously positioned pool that dangled over the rainforest. It was situated within the wraparound deck of the luxury treehouse Fionn had gifted to them. Because, after all, Niamh had saved the world. They had made fond memories in this treehouse, and while Kiyo had been unsure of returning to it, over the years he'd grown to love what they called their vacation home.

His strong torso glistened with water from the pool as he tipped his head back to let the sun warm his face through the trees. Niamh felt more than a prickle of arousal as she leaned against the doorframe, gaze sweeping over his taut, smooth fawn skin. Kiyo would always be the most beautiful male she'd ever seen. Sometimes it still knocked the breath out of her that he was hers.

"*Komorebi*, either quit staring or get in," he murmured, opening his dark eyes.

"Was that a request or a command?"

His eyes smoldered.

Without another word, Niamh pulled off her kaftan and threw it behind her. Naked, she sauntered out onto the deck, shivering at the low growl Kiyo emitted as he watched her approach.

Her breasts bounced, her nipples pebbling even in the warm air as she took the steps down into the shallow pool. Kiyo's chest rose and fell a little faster with excitement.

And Niamh didn't leave him waiting.

She straddled him beneath the water and he yanked her roughly over him, taking her right nipple in his mouth. Niamh's cries filled the trees as her back bowed, pleasure rushing between her legs as he suckled on her.

Reaching between them, Niamh gripped his naked cock in hand and guided him inside her beneath the water. He released her breast to groan with desire as Niamh began to ride him.

"Kiyo-Chan," she chanted over and over as her body built toward orgasm.

Her mate suddenly rose, holding her to him, his expression tight with raw need as he lifted them out of the pool. She knew his intention was to get to the bed but her little whimper of want always set him on fire. Suddenly, she found herself with her back to the floor as Kiyo fucked her with fiery need.

He gripped her thighs, lifting her arse so he could thrust into her at just the right angle.

Her eyes must have turned liquid gold because Kiyo released a wolfish growl of satisfaction as he picked up his pace.

Niamh's orgasm exploded through her, her sobs of pleasure and tightening inner muscles causing Kiyo to yell out hoarsely as he released inside her.

He delighted in looking at where they joined as he pulled out, his jaw clenching with renewed desire as he witnessed his cum spill from her.

Niamh felt an ache of melancholic longing score across her chest. One that she quickly stifled for fear her mate suspected she was discontent.

"I better clean up." She pushed off the floor, stopping to kiss him tenderly, before she strode into the bathroom to do just that.

Niamh stared at her reflection in the mirror, her cheeks flushed and dewy with sweat from their mating. It *wasn't* that she was unhappy with their life. They led a meaningful, high-octane existence, and these past few days had been a well-deserved break.

Her visions were a part of her and Niamh wanted to use them for good. Kiyo would follow her anywhere, so they used her visions to stop bad things from happening to good people.

To have money to live, they also continued to do Kiyo's old work as a mercenary. They took on jobs where they were compensated for finding people who'd committed crimes against others.

But only people Niamh knew deserved justice meted out against them.

It was a busy, dangerous world they lived in. Kiyo would have quite happily hidden Niamh away somewhere she would always be protected. But they'd both go mad with boredom.

Especially when ...

Niamh threw the thought from her mind.

She didn't want Kiyo to sense her feelings.

When she stepped out of the bathroom, Kiyo stood in her path, his arms crossed over his broad, naked chest. He'd donned lightweight pants, but his feet were still bare. Niamh loved it when he wore his thick, silky hair down, but she also loved the way the beautiful angles of his face were highlighted when he wore it in a man bun like now.

"Talk to me, *Komorebi*."

Unease shifted through her, and she gave him a mock confused smile. "You're very serious."

"Don't." The muscle in his jaw flexed, and she sensed his growing agitation.

And hurt.

"Kiyo-Chan—"

"You need to tell me why the last few times we've had sex, you've been ... sad." Pain blazed in his gaze.

Niamh hurried toward him, cupping his face in her palm. "It's not what you think."

"Then what is it?"

"I know it seems silly, but I guess we've just been so busy, I didn't realize ..."

Kiyo frowned. "Realize what?"

"Not until we visited Fionn and Rose." She shrugged sadly. Fionn had always suspected Niamh was his descendant. Thus, he treated her like an older brother might and they'd become family for real. So, when they could, they visited Fionn and Rose in

Ireland. When Saoirse was born, Niamh felt nothing but delight for Fionn and Rose, knowing his history. But their last visit to meet baby Ardal for the first time had brought something crashing home to Niamh. Then Thea and Conall to see little Brodie, Mhairi ... and Nee.

"We'll never have our own children." She tried to hide her sadness and failing. It wasn't in their destiny. As fae and werewolf, they were unable to procreate.

Kiyo's expression tightened with understanding and his hands fell to her hips. He squeezed them, his voice hoarse. "I'm sorry, *Komorebi*."

"We have a beautiful life," she hurried to reassure him. "I know that. We have a meaningful, stunning life, and I never fail to feel lucky that you are mine and I am yours."

"I know." He pulled her close, pressing a kiss to her temple. "I know that."

"I just didn't realize ... and I ..."

"You're allowed to grieve it, Niamh. We both are."

"Do you?" She pulled back to study his face. "Do you grieve it?"

He nodded. "After I was turned, I didn't imagine ever wanting children. But since you, yeah, I've imagined what it would be like to have kids with you. And I hate that I can't give you that."

"It's not your fault. It's no one's fault." She smiled softly. "In a way, knowing you feel the same actually makes me feel better."

"You know you can tell me anything."

"I know. I'm sorry." Niamh kissed his beautiful mouth. "I love you."

Kiyo held her close and whispered hoarsely, "Love isn't a strong enough word."

. . .

A few days later, as they prepared to leave their little paradise to follow a vision Niamh had of a werewolf female trapped in an abusive relationship with an Alpha in Alaska, Kiyo surprised Niamh as they got into the buggy that would take them out of the rainforest.

"When we're ready, we could foster."

Her breath caught. "What?"

Kiyo shrugged as if he hadn't offered the most wonderful idea in the world. "I'm sure we can find supernatural kids who need a good home. When we're ready, we could do that. Provide a safe haven to kids who are different and who've been left on their own. Like you and Ronan." He referred to Niamh's brother. For a long time, she and Ronan had lived on the run.

Tears of gratitude burned her eyes as she stared at this male whom she realized she grew to love more with each passing day. "You would do that with me?"

"Of course. We both know what it's like to be alone in this. If we can save others from that, I'd like to."

She reached for his hand and squeezed it. A tremendous weight lifted from her shoulders. "When we're ready."

"When we're ready." He nodded.

They traveled in silence for a little while and then Niamh repeated words Kiyo had said to her many years ago, "Now that I love you, Kiyo-Chan, forever will never be enough."

He cut her a blazing, impassioned look of adoration. "Forever will never be enough," he agreed gruffly.

Niamh rested her head against his shoulder as he drove, a renewed excitement for their future binding them together as they made their way into their next adventure.

North Vancouver, British Columbia, Canada

. . .

As the driver pulled into the driveway of the last house on the cul-de-sac, Echo had to squash the urge to jump out. The large family home backed onto the Baden Powell Trail. It was a quiet street with congenial neighbors and it wasn't so isolated that Nancy and Odette didn't have a community around them.

A hand curled around hers, and she turned to look at Elijah. He gave her a sexy smile. "You can run on in with excitement if you want," he teased.

Echo quirked an eyebrow. "When have I ever run with excitement?"

Her mate chuckled at her dry tone just as the driver opened the back passenger door for them. "Mr. Webb, Mrs. Webb."

Echo got out, nodding her thanks before stepping away from the vehicle to stare up the long driveway. The afternoon sun was warm on her face, a sensation she'd finally gotten used to again. In fact, the last five years of being able to walk around in daylight had healed her just as much as Elijah had.

A few years ago, Elijah had asked her to marry him. Obviously marrying her mate because she loved him was the number one reason she said yes. But being able to shed William's surname was a nice little bonus.

Odette had adopted the Webb name too.

But only because Nancy had adopted Odette.

It hadn't been an easy decision.

After the battle five years ago, Echo, despite the grief it would cause her, was determined to return Odette to her birth parents. Odette had turned thirteen a few days after the battle. She didn't want to return to her birth parents. She wanted to stay with Echo, Nancy, and Elijah. Nancy, in her grief over losing Bill, seemed just as desperate to hold on to Odette.

Eventually, she got Odette to agree to at least find out more about her birth parents. So they looked into them. Even surveilled them. They had two kids. Odette had a brother and sister. They seemed like good people.

However, ultimately Odette wished to stay with Nancy, and Echo couldn't bear to put her sister through any more trauma. If, when she was older, she wanted to reach out to her birth parents, she would.

So, they fudged a lot of legal stuff to allow Nancy to become Odette's guardian and for them to move to this quiet suburb of North Vancouver.

Now Odette was a student at University of British Columbia and was home for the summer.

Just like Echo and Elijah.

They'd finished the last leg of a long two-year tour with the Strix.

As Echo had hoped all those years ago when she'd tried to reassure Elijah, his bandmates bought his story about disappearing because Bill was terminally ill and then had passed away. It was a story mixed with some truth. Phil and Jamal welcomed him back with open arms, sorry for their friend's loss. Adam, who had been terrified of losing the band when Elijah disappeared, had been a little less welcoming and a lot caustic. Echo didn't like the selfish prick then, and she didn't like him now.

Of course, many stories were spread online and in the news about Elijah. The one most people believed was that he'd gone to rehab for alcohol and drug addiction. Ultimately, Elijah chose to let people believe what they wanted to, as long as he still got to play in the band—and bring Echo along with him. The guys also bought that Elijah had met Echo and she'd helped him through his family's loss.

So, for five years, Elijah continued to play music and do what he loved. Echo enjoyed the touring life. She was never bored, she loved their music, and because she was a natural boss, she kind of accidentally took over their management, and the band hit a new level of fame. After that, Adam came around. But Echo still didn't like the whiny asshole.

And now she wouldn't have to deal with him ever again.

This past year, the band had started cracking jokes about how Elijah hadn't aged a day. How Echo hadn't either. They'd almost been caught a couple of times on tour when Echo drank from her mate to satiate her vampiric hunger.

It was time. All too quickly, it was time to leave the band and disappear until they faded from human memory. Maybe then they could start over as something new.

Of course, the band hadn't been happy, but Echo found them a new lead singer who was amazing, if not quite as amazing as her mate, and she found them a new manager she thought was a solid, capable guy. The saddest part was having to cut ties with Phil and Jamal and their families. They didn't know it yet, but they'd never see Echo and Elijah again. It was too risky.

Elijah stepped up beside her after helping Darrell with their luggage.

In her excitement to see Odette and Nancy, Echo had stopped worrying about her mate. But those few minutes were over, and concern washed through her as she studied him.

"I could feel you," Elijah murmured as their driver left. He stared up at the house and Echo sensed a pang of grief.

He missed his dad.

She reached out and took his hand. "I can feel you too."

Elijah looked down at her, love and adoration on his face. He never hid his feelings. He was far more open than Echo ever could be. One of the reasons she loved their mating bond was because he could sense her feelings without her ever having to explain them. Something she'd never really been good at, anyway. "Stop worrying about me."

"I need you to be happy," she answered huskily.

Not want. Need.

His happiness was Echo's happiness.

"I'm home. You're by my side. After we spend a few months here, we're planning to travel the world so I can actually see all the places I've only ever seen from tour bus windows. I'm not sad, Echo. I promise." He turned to look at the house, his brow wrinkling. "Not about that, anyway."

It was true that after a summer in North Vancouver, they planned to travel for a year. Elijah would have to use his fae abilities so people wouldn't recognize him, but that wouldn't stop them. Echo was excited for the trip. For the unexpected. Their lives these past five years had been dictated by constant touring with the band. By keeping Elijah's secret a secret. There had been a few rumors about what he was, and they'd squashed them over the years.

It would be nice to enjoy some time together. Now that The Garm was no longer a threat, they could do that.

As Echo had suspected, the remaining members of The Garm were not interested in William's agenda. They fought among themselves to control his criminal empire and within a year, The Garm imploded from infighting.

It no longer existed.

Good fucking riddance.

"Are you ready?" Echo squeezed Elijah's hand.

One of the things she thought her mate needed now was to grieve properly. He'd rejoined the band mere months after Bill's death, and Echo didn't think he gave himself time to go through that process. She suspected the next year would be just as much about healing as it was about traveling.

Echo saw the front door open and a tall, willowy blond step out. She hopped down the deck steps two at a time and yelled, "Are you just going to stand there or get in here and say hello to your favorite sister!"

Echo grinned as Elijah chuckled. Together they grabbed the

luggage and hauled it up the driveway toward Odette. Nancy stepped out of the house after her but waited on the deck.

Odette suddenly flew into action, and Echo dropped her luggage just in time as her sister dove into her arms. She was taller than her now, which was so weird. Echo huffed at the impact.

"Oh, please." Odette squeezed her hard. "You're a vampire, you can take it."

Shaking with laughter, she embraced her sister. "I missed you, little darling."

"Missed you too." Odette kissed her cheek and pulled back before turning her gorgeous, beaming smile on Elijah.

"E!" She threw her arms around him and Elijah hugged her hard.

"O. Missed you."

"Mom baked banana bread!" Odette had taken to calling Nancy *Mom* a few months after the battle, and it seemed to heal something in Nancy.

Elijah's expression brightened. "Why are we still out here, then?" With a quick glance around to make sure they were alone, Elijah flicked his wrist, and the luggage disappeared, presumably now in their guest room.

"Ugh, do you know how much easier my life would be if I could do that?" Odette looped her arm through Elijah's and took Echo's hand, pulling them toward the house.

Not for the first time, as Odette chattered away, Echo viewed her sister as a miracle. She'd been brought into a world of darkness as a child, but she hadn't let it take away her light. And right now, that light was warm on Echo and her mate as they walked up the steps to greet Nancy.

Her mother-in-law took her by the biceps, expression affectionate, and kissed both her cheeks in welcome. Then she opened her arms to her son who went into her embrace as easily as he had as a child. Elijah hugged his mom and squeezed his eyes closed, features tight with something more than homecoming.

Finally, when they were settled in and seated around the dining table enjoying Nancy's amazing banana bread, Echo sensed Elijah's sharp sadness soften.

Was it the future they'd hoped for when this all started? No.

Bill should've been there with them.

However, the tragic reality was that he was gone.

Nancy had forged a new chapter because she'd had to, and she was busy and content.

Odette was studying to become a microbiologist with the goal of finding new and better ways to treat infections. She had a boyfriend, Max, whom Echo had thoroughly investigated, and she begrudgingly agreed adored her sister. Odette was safe, happy, and productive.

Elijah had spent five years doing what he loved and genuinely seemed excited for the future if sad to be here without his father.

Their family was doing well, despite the past.

And this was home.

For the first time in her life, Echo had a real home.

The eternity she'd been so afraid of no longer terrified her.

Because Niamh Farren had been right all those years ago.

Elijah suddenly turned to look at her, as if he'd actually heard the thought. He reached across the table, covering her hand with his. While Nancy and Odette discussed which restaurant to eat at for their homecoming, Elijah's gaze roamed Echo's face. "It is," her mate whispered, and she knew now for a fact he'd known her thoughts. "You're not afraid anymore."

Echo slipped her hand over his and gave him a wry but meaningful look. "If I was afraid, and I'm not saying I was—"

Elijah snorted because he knew she was full of shit.

"Then yeah ... I'm not afraid anymore."

"Good." His gaze smoldered. "Because I've got plans for our eternity together, Echo Webb. Beautiful plans."

At that, Echo's smile was slow and sincere.

It had taken years at Elijah's side for Echo to finally feel free of her past. Of her fears. But now she sat comfortably in her freedom. Blessed that Elijah had emotionally and quite literally brought her into the light with his love and with his very blood.

Now she couldn't wait.

She couldn't wait for their forever to start today.

Niamh Farren was right.

Love really was true immortality.

ABOUT THE AUTHOR

S. Young is the pen name for Samantha Young, a *New York Times*, *USA Today* and *Wall Street Journal* bestselling author from Stirlingshire, Scotland. She's been nominated for the Goodreads Choice Award for Best Author and Best Romance for her international bestseller *On Dublin Street*. *On Dublin Street* was Samantha's first adult contemporary romance series and has sold in thirty-one countries.

Visit Samantha Young online at
www.authorsamanthayoung.com

FEAR OF FIRE AND SHADOW

Read the first few chapters of *Fear of Fire and Shadow*. A standalone enemies-to-lovers, bodyguard, fantasy romance from *New York Times* bestselling author Samantha Young writing as S. Young.

As one of the few remaining mage in the world, Rogan was stolen as a child and placed within the palace as handmaiden to Haydyn, the last of the royal family. Now, as adults, the two young women are as close as sisters and when Haydyn falls victim to a sleeping disease only Rogan can save her. Haydyn's magic keeps peace across their land and if she dies, their whole world will fall to the darkness of human nature.

Setting off on a journey to retrieve the plant that will cure her friend, Rogan is stuck in close quarters with a protector she distrusts above all others: Wolfe Stovia. The son of the man who kidnapped Rogan and destroyed her family. At a constant battle of wills with Wolfe, Rogan knows their expedition will be fraught with tension. However, she never imagined that the quest would be so dangerous, that her beliefs would be so shaken, or that she'd find herself falling for her greatest enemy.

Fear of Fire and Shadow was previously released under the title *Slumber* in 2011.

Prologue

When I was a child, the world smelled of summer.

The heady perfume of dancing wildflowers hugged my senses as the breeze took them on a journey to soothe my cheeks from the heat of the afternoon sun. The scent of damp soil when the sun had pushed the sky too far and it wept rain for days before wearily turning the world back over to its golden companion. The refreshing aroma of lemons in the thick air of the house mingled with my mother's baking as she prepared our afternoon repast of bitter lemonade and thick warm bread, slathered with creamy butter made cold from the sheltering shade of the larder.

And my father's pipe.

The sweet odor of tobacco tickling my nose as Father held me close and whispered the stories of our Salvation and the mighty kral who lived in the grandest palace in all the land with his beautiful daughter, the princezna, how kind and gentle they were—and the reason my private world was one of innocence and endless summer.

My memories of that life never leave me. I can still hear my brother's laughter carrying back to my young, happy ears as we chased through the fields of purple and gold, racing over the farm to the brook that ran behind our land. I remember the gentle trickle of that stream and how it drew us each day, my brother sprinting for the rope swing he had looped around the strongest tree, the one with the trunk that seemed to bend toward the water as if thirsty for a taste of its pure relief. I was drawn to its coolness on my skin, its moisture in my dry mouth, its familiar smell ... like damp metal and wet grass.

Sometimes I hear my mother calling our names in my dreams.

There was no warning to summer's end. It began like any other day. I stretched alongside my brother beneath the shadow of an oak by the brook's edge, my young voice barely heard above the babbling water as I recounted the story my father had told me over and over. I could hear Father's rich voice in my head, had memorized every word, and as I recited it, I remembered to speak in the hushed, awed tones he used to make a story sound as magical as this one really was.

"Eons and eons ago, our people were the most blessed of mankind. Powerful and beautiful, we could tap into Mother Nature and draw from her powers. Magical beings, spiritual and wondrous to behold. But mankind grew envious of us, and wise as we were, we knew mankind, with so many wars already brewing among its people, could not withstand a war with us. Our wisest leaders persuaded us it was time to fade from mankind's Earth, to fade as one into a world of our own.

"We withdrew and imagined a paradise. Mankind melted around us as we fell deep, deep into the fade. When our people awakened, we found ourselves here, in a newborn land—a sky, a moon, a sun, trees, plants, water, and familiar animals awaiting them, waiting to begin the new world in peace.

"Fearful of our emotions betraying us as they had mankind, it was decided that the Dyzvati, a clan of magical evokers with the ability to lull the people and the land with peace, would reign as the royal family. The Dyzvati named our land Phaedra, splitting it into six provinces, giving a province to the clans with the most powerful magic. Sabithia, in the south, was taken by the Dyzvati, and they built a beautiful palace in the capital city of Silvera where the shores of the Silver Sea edge its coast with its vibrant silver surf.

"Clan Glava, the largest and most powerful of the mage with their many psychic abilities, whether it be reading the past, present, or future, or moving objects and summoning elements with their minds, was given Javinia to the east of Sabithia and also Daeronia in the northeast." I turned my head to smile at my brother who stared at me, enraptured. "And our own slice of haven, Vasterya, was given to the Clan Azyl, mage with the ability to seek whatever their hearts desired. Eventually, the Azyl became servants of the Dyzvati, using their abilities to seek whatever the royal family wished, helping the upkeep of the peace in Phaedra.

"Many centuries onward and the Azyl's magic evolved with their position, no longer able to seek that which they wished for themselves, only what others wanted."

My brother frowned. "That's a little unfair."

I nodded in agreement before continuing, "The province of Daeronia, beyond the northern borders of Sabithia, was given to Clan Dravilec, the healers, to keep them close to the Dyzvati." I thought on how much of a fairy tale this sounded now, a millennium on from the beginning of Phaedra. "Now there are so few mages left. Papa says there are none left in Vasterya at all. And now only the kral and Princezna Haydyn remain of the Dyzvati."

"What about Alvernia?" my brother asked in a hushed voice.

I shuddered at the thought of Alvernia; the stories I'd heard of the rough, uncivilized northern mountain people, terrifying tales of their macabre misdeeds and ignoble existence, all because the power of the Dyzvati waned toward the middle of their province.

"Alvernia was given to those of middling magical abilities. Several of the Glava went with them, as there were so many, and set themselves up in the southernmost point in the city of Arrana."

"Where the vojvoda lives?"

"Yes, where the vojvoda lives."

"I wish I was a vojvoda. Or a markiza. Or a vikomt!" he cried excitedly, pushing himself into a sitting position. "I'd have horses. Lots of horses. And gold! We could play treasure hunt!"

I laughed and nudged him playfully. "All those titles and you didn't choose the best."

"What?" He pouted.

I stood, bracing my small hands against my youthful hips, legs astride, chin defiant. "Why ... kral, of course!"

"Yeah!" He jumped to his feet now, mimicking my stance. "I am Kral of Vasterya!"

"And me?"

"My servant."

I growled in outrage. "Servant indeed."

I still remember the sounds of his beautiful laughter as I chased him for his teasing.

At the grumbling of our bellies, my brother and I reluctantly ceased playing and walked home. I held his hand as we wove through the fields. I remember the gust of wind that shook the gold and purple and blew my hair back from my face, sending shivers of warning down my spine. My feet moved faster then, and I tugged on my brother's hand each time my heart beat a little quicker.

I can still see the expression on my father's face when we appeared out of the fields, his countenance pale and slack, his eyes bleak. My mother clung to his arm, her eyes as glassy as my favorite doll's. At the sound of a horse's nicker, I turned to see strangers outside our home. Four men, all dressed in livery that matched those of their horses. My eyes were drawn to the emerald-and-silver heraldic badges with the silver dove crest in the middle. Our symbol of peace.

They were from the palace.

Fear gripped me and I had no understanding of why. I trembled so hard, I thought I must be shaking the very ground beneath my feet. Instinctively, I pushed my brother behind me, out of the view of the men looming ominously over our parents.

One of them descended from his beast. I realized he did not wear the livery. He alone came toward me like a serpent slithering on the ground, his purple cloak hissing in the breeze. His eyes were the deepest black and probing, so fixated on me I quivered in violation as if he had actually touched me.

"This is the one."

"You're sure?" asked the soldier who towered over my parents.

The serpent smiled, ready to strike his killing blow. "She is the one."

"No!" my father bellowed as my mother whimpered at his side. "Run, Rogan! Run!"

But I was frozen in place by their panic, an ice sculpture who watched two soldiers hold my father as he struggled in their arms, and a third pull a dagger from his belt and plunge it into his heart. My father twitched and stiffened in their hold, a horrifying gurgling noise making its way up from his chest to spurt a thick, bloody fluid out of his mouth and down his chin.

My mother's screams played the soundtrack to this memory before the dagger-wielding soldier strolled toward her crumpled figure, his black-gloved fingers stroking over her hair. They slid like leeches down to her throat and back up to her cheeks. And then he twisted her head between his hands with a jerk that sent an echoing crack around my world.

That's when I felt the tug on my hand and remembered my brother. With a thousand screams stuck in my throat, I whirled with him and began to run, dragging him with me into the cover of the fields, my father's last shouts reverberating in my ears. I drowned out the sounds of my shallow, panicked breaths, the hiccupping cries of my brother as I hauled him with me. The hollering and thundering behind us made me race faster.

When the thundering eased, I knew I had lost them in the fields. We were small and knew the land as well as we knew each tiny scar and line upon our palms. I headed east, picking up my brother when he tripped, shushing him when I was no longer sure we were alone. At last we reached the cave my father had punished us for hiding in only a year before. Bears, he had warned. But now I feared the soldiers from the palace more than the bears, the soldiers who wanted me and why, I did not know. They had slaughtered my parents to have me. Would they murder me too? My brother? At the thought, I burrowed him against me in the dank cave and his tears soaked my dress.

"I'm sorry," he whispered.

I wanted to tell him he need not apologize for crying, for grieving, but I feared if I spoke, all my screams would burst forth with terrifying consequences.

"I didn't mean to."

At that, I pressed him back until a shaft of light filtered over his face. He looked so lost, my heart broke again. He clutched his trousers, turning from me, and it was then the smell hit my nostrils.

I began to cry.

I did not want him to be ashamed of his fear. He was so little.

"It's okay," I whispered and made to reach for him, but his shirt slipped through my hands as he was whipped out of sight. I must have yelled, I think, as I stumbled blindly after him into a day that had suddenly turned gray, a day that had once blazed in a beautiful fire of heat and life. Now it was gone.

And as my eyes found my brother, I realized even the last sparks of the embers had been snuffed out, leaving only the fire's funeral shroud of smoke.

His small body laid at the mouth of the cave. The dagger edged in blood from his throat slipped back into its place on a soldier's belt.

The serpent stepped over my brother's body and knelt before me.

"Say goodbye to your family, Rogan. A new one awaits you."

Chapter One

I ached. I had never experienced such pain before. But I had never been on a horse for so long. It did not help I was stiff from trying to keep my body as far from the man who held me on that horse in his embrace. It was impossible not to touch him—his long arms encircled me in order to hold the reins.

I didn't know where we were. It was impossibly dark. The sun had been on our left for much of the day before moving to the right and setting. It had also taken longer to set than it did back home. If my father had taught me correctly, this meant we were moving south. I twisted my neck to look at Kir, who rode trapped between the captain of the Guard and the reins of his horse, Destroyer. Such a fitting name. He had helped the despicable mage behind me, Vikomt Syracen Stovia—one of the Glava—destroy my life, as well as Kir's.

The kral was dead.

Only Haydyn Dyzvati, Princezna of Phaedra, remained of the evokers. Kir told me Stovia was collecting those left with rare magic to help protect and reinforce the sovereign until Haydyn came of age and produced more children of the Dyzvati.

Kir was one of the Glava, a telekinetic.

"The Dyzvati power has waned," Kir had whispered to me, his eyes

flickering to our guard. That had been only two nights after the murder of my family. Kir had been with the Guard for a week. The other soldiers ate and talked quietly around the campfire. "Stovia has taken advantage of it. The way he talks ... as if the violence of his crimes is justified. He's protecting the sovereign and the peace of Phaedra with blood and cruelty. With a selfish pursuit for the last of the mage."

"But I'm not a mage," I whispered in shock. We were sitting together to the side of the fire. Strangers. But the wiry boy, a few years my senior, shared the haunted look in my eyes. They had destroyed his family too.

Kir had shrugged. "You must be."

But I wasn't. Was I?

I caught Kir's gaze as we rode swiftly and quietly into the small village. His face was taut, his eyes narrowed. Something was happening.

The horses drew to a stop with not even a snort, so obedient to their masters' will. An unpleasant shock moved through me at the feel of Stovia's hand in my hair.

"Now, little one," he whispered, "time to see how well that magic of yours works."

I shifted away from him. "I have no magic."

He chuckled. "You're one of the Azyl, child."

One of the Azyl? No. He was mistaken.

"I'm not."

With a growl, Stovia dismounted and none too gently ripped me from the saddle. My feet hadn't even hit the ground before he shook me, my eyes rolling back in my head with the force of it. "Stop pretending!" he hissed, careful not to raise his voice. He released me and I stumbled as he lowered his body so his austere face was level with my own. Those wicked black eyes bore through me. "In this village is one of the Dravilec. I want you to seek out my healer. Now."

At the command, a wave of energy crashed over me and my whole body hummed with tingling vibrancy. I turned to face the village. And I sensed her. The Dravilec. Six years old. Valena of Daeronia. We were in

Daeronia. Thought so. We were growing closer to Sabithia. To Silvera. To the princezna.

Wait.

I am an Azyl.

I swayed at the thought. Every time my father had told me the stories, I'd wished desperately for a little piece of magic in our lives.

I had been a mage all along.

I wanted to cry. I wanted to be with my family.

What would Stovia do to Valena's family? Would he murder them in cold blood if they refused to hand her over? I knew, even without my help, that he would find Valena. He was a powerful Glava. Could sense magic. But that didn't mean I had to aid in the destruction of another family.

"No," I whispered.

"What?" Stovia growled.

I spun around, defiant, hatred blazing out of my eyes. I wished I were Glava with the ability to summon the elements. I'd set him on fire and watch him burn for what he had done to me. To Kir. For what he would do to Valena.

"I said ... no."

His fist connected with my face with such force, I flew to the ground. The breath whooshed out of me at the agonizing blow to my ribs as I hit the hard dirt. My eyes watered at the painful heat across the left side of my face. Blood trickled out of the corner of my mouth and I tasted copper on my tongue.

Kir cried out my name.

But Stovia wasn't done. He grabbed me by the clasp on my cloak and held me so he could slap me across the right side of my face. The world rang in my ears.

I refused to cry.

"Find me the healer, girl, or you'll wish you were dead."

"No!" *Kir yelled.*

"Shut him up," Stovia hissed.

I heard the sound of flesh hitting flesh, of Kir grunting.

No.

"No," I groaned, lolling limply in Stovia's grasp. "Stop."

"Will you find the Dravilec?"

I couldn't. "No."

"Lash the boy to the nearest tree. He's going to pay for Rogan's disobedience."

My heart lurched, and I shrugged around Stovia to watch through blurred vision as they dragged a bleeding, crying Kir to the nearest tree trunk. They tore at his shirt. One of them produced a horsewhip, and Kir whimpered in terror. Vomit rushed up my throat, but I willed the acidic show of weakness down.

"Stop," I murmured weakly. "Stop. Don't hurt him. I'll do it."

Stovia studied me, seemingly fascinated. Then he nodded at his men and they drew Kir's cloak over him before dragging him back to the horses. His right eye was already swelling shut, matching my left one.

"Tut-tut, Rogan," Stovia whispered. "You've just shown me your weakness. I imagine I could have battered you into oblivion and you would not have given in. But you won't let someone else be hurt because of you. Interesting. And useful. Now find me the Dravilec."

I was gripped with nauseating shame as I took the guards through the winding, quaint, peaceful village. By now we had made enough noise to rouse people from their homes, and they gathered on doorsteps nervously as their eyes took in the Royal Guard and the two beaten children with them. I came to a stop at the door of a shop. An apothecary.

"Here."

Stovia smiled at me, his eyes brimming with pride. I hated him. "Yes, it is. Thank you, Rogan."

He pulled the rope by the door and a brass bell rang. We heard hurried footsteps and then the door was thrust open by an older man. He was tall and imposing.

"Can I help?" he queried warily.

"I am Vikomt Syracen Stovia of the Rada. May I come in, Mr. Rosonia?"

Rosonia's eyes widened but he nodded, his oil lamp casting his profile against the shadows of the wall. Stovia turned and nodded at two guards who strode forward to follow at his back. He pushed me past the threshold and into the shop. Sadist. He wanted me to witness this.

Once inside, Rosonia stood with a stout, middle-aged woman who appeared frightened, clutching her robes tightly around her. Two girls stood behind them, one a tall, attractive girl, possibly around thirteen or fourteen years of age. Clutching her hand was Valena, small and frightened, her large, dark eyes too big for her face.

"I come bearing sad news." Stovia emanated power and intimidation. "The kral is dead."

The Rosonias gasped at the news.

"Yes. I am afraid it is true. Princezna Haydyn is now alone in the world, the weight of carrying the load of Dyzvati too great for her young shoulders. As the only mage upon the Rada, I felt it was my duty to seek whatever Her Highness needs to aid her in her mighty responsibilities."

"What can we do to help, my lord?" Valena's father asked eagerly, his eyes full of genuine sadness for the kral.

"Very little magic remains in our world. However, I've been collecting the strongest of that which does. Here." He put his deadly hand upon my shoulder and I fought not to shiver. "This is one of the Azyl, thought to be extinct. But she found you well enough."

Mrs. Rosonia gasped at my bloodied appearance. "What happened to the child?"

"One of my soldiers. He has been dealt with," Stovia lied smoothly. "But you have in your keeping someone who could help my little Rogan."

"Mama." The elder girl drew Valena closer. "Don't."

"Valena." Mr. Rosonia exhaled heavily. "She is one of the Dravilec, then?"

"You had your suspicions?" Stovia asked.

Valena's father nodded.

"She is needed. Your daughter is needed by her people."

"You want to take her?" Mrs. Rosonia's voice trembled.

Stovia smiled. "She will be well cared for at the palace. And you may visit. She will be taught by the Royal Dravilec how to use her power. She is strong. I could taste her energy from Sabithia, it was so strong."

The Rosonias stood in silence for a moment, mother and father silently communicating with one another. Finally, Valena's father turned to Stovia and nodded. "You may take her, my lord."

I gasped in outrage. My parents had died rather than see me in the hands of this snake of a man. And I wasn't the only one outraged. The elder girl shrieked and grabbed Valena to her, refusing to release her. Valena screamed and cried, terrified and confused.

Mr. Rosonia wrenched Valena free, and his wife took her upstairs to ready her for departure. She returned quickly with the little girl dressed for traveling. All the while, she cried. Her mother hugged her, quiet tears rolling down her cheeks as her daughter clung tightly. Mr. Rosonia came over and pulled Valena away, ignoring his elder daughter who sobbed from the corner of the room. Mr. Rosonia kissed Valena's cheeks and promised he would see her soon. Then he handed her into the arms of Syracen Stovia.

Sensing what only children could, she shrieked and writhed to escape. Careful to hide his disgust, Stovia thrust the squalling six-year-old into my arms. I pressed her close, ashamed for my part in this. Valena stopped struggling and instead looped her little arms around my neck, her legs around my waist, and bawled into my shoulder. A memory of my little brother doing the same not too many weeks ago when he had fallen from a tree and cut his leg flashed through my mind, and I squeezed the girl closer, as if I alone could protect her.

Stovia hurried us out of the house, and we walked a distance away to the bridge that would take us out of the village.

"Lieutenant Sandstone," Stovia called, and the soldier trotted forward on his horse. "Take Valena. I can't carry the two on my horse."

Sandstone dismounted and tried to pry Valena from me. The girl screamed, her tiny hands gripped to my cloak, my hair, refusing to budge. And even though I winced at her tight hold, I declined to hand her over.

"That's enough," Stovia grunted. He pushed Sandstone out of the way and gripped a hold of Valena, bruising her small arms as he ripped her from me. I cried out as he drew back his arm and slapped her into silence. I rushed at him in a rage, beating and pushing at him. I was pulled off by the soldier. Stovia, to spite me, hit Valena one more time. Sobbing, furious, I fought against the soldier, only to be beaten by the pummeling fists of the captain of the Guard. The next thing I knew, Kir joined the fray, hitting and punching those who tried to hurt us. I no longer felt pain. I was too angry, too immersed in my fury to feel anything else.

Eventually I was pinned to the ground by the captain and as he stared down at me, I noticed his eyes for the first time. They were blank. Empty.

"Captain ... after we leave the village, I want you to take two of your men and burn the apothecary to the ground. With the Rosonias inside," Stovia demanded from somewhere to my left.

The captain nodded robotically, and it was then I knew. With the evocation of the Dyzvati weakened by Princezna Haydyn's grief and age, Stovia's magic was able to penetrate it. He was compelling the soldiers to do his awful deeds.

As the captain hauled me to my feet, I was weighed down by my despairing heart.

Stovia appeared before me, holding Valena close, her little cheeks red from his slaps. "You attempt to disobey me, Rogan, and I will make you pay. For this disobedience, the Rosonias will pay. You now must live with the fact you killed Valena's family."

Stovia laughed gleefully at my horrified expression.

"Don't listen to him, Rogan." Kir struggled against a soldier, his face mottled with anger. "He was going to kill them anyway. Don't let him make you think you did it."

Stovia curled his lip in disgust. "I've had enough of you. Sandstone!"

The whip appeared in the soldier's hand and Kir was thrust into the dirt.

"NO!" I screamed, my heart lodged somewhere in my throat.

"NO!"

"NO!" I bolted upright in bed. The sheets twisted around my body, my skin clammy, my hair stuck to my neck. Almost immediately, I sensed I wasn't alone. Glancing left, I saw her sitting in an armchair by my bed.

"You were having a nightmare again." Her soft, gentle eyes were sad. "More memories?"

I nodded, my throat constricted with the nightmare that still held me in its talons. "More memories."

Haydyn sighed and slowly drew to her feet. I watched her float across my large bedroom suite and pull the heavy brocade curtains back from my windows. I winced as the sunlight streamed in, too bright, too adamant, willing my bad memories away whilst I steadfastly anchored myself to them.

"I told you I'd speak to Raj to see if he had a tonic to help you sleep without the dreams."

Raj was the Royal Healer; Valena was his apprentice. I shook my head. "I told you no."

"You're the only one who ever says no to me." Haydyn sauntered back to sit on my bed. Her pale hair gleamed almost silver in the sunlight, her countenance serene except for the teasing in her lovely eyes. "I wonder why I let you."

"Because you love me," I stated matter-of-factly as I pushed back the covers. I needed to ready myself for the day.

"Yes, I do."

The statement was so melancholy, I spun to face her. It was then I saw it. The gloom in the back of her eyes, in the dark purpling beneath them. Those exhaustion bruises had been appearing more and more over the last few weeks, and I didn't like it. "Something's the matter."

Haydyn shook her head. "Just tired is all."

"Perhaps we should speak to Raj about a tonic for *you*."

She wasn't amenable but as always, to appease me, she nodded. "Perhaps."

I grimaced when I realized she was fully dressed. Most times when Haydyn came into my suite, it was still so early she was in her nightclothes. "I overslept?"

Haydyn grinned. "Haven forbid, but you did."

I rolled my eyes at her teasing. "You know I hate oversleeping. It muddles up my entire day."

"I know. That's why I let you sleep." She grinned unrepentantly. Sometimes she really was like an annoying younger sister. "You need to loosen the reins on your life now and then, Rogan."

Making a face at her suggestion, I pulled on the servants' bell to let them know I was ready for my morning bath. They would come to me as quickly as they would to Haydyn. After all, I was her best friend, her family. I had been ever since I had been brought to the palace nine years ago by Syracen Stovia. I was only twelve years old at the time. Haydyn was ten. Upon our arrival, Valena was taken from me and given to Raj. Kir lived with Syracen and his family. And I lived at the palace with Haydyn.

Both grieving for the families we'd lost, it hadn't taken long for us to find solace in one another.

Haydyn's mother had died in childbirth, leaving Haydyn alone with her father. The Rada had pushed and pushed him to take another wife, to have more children, but he had loved Haydyn's mother too dearly. He couldn't bear the thought of making someone else his kralovna. That left only the kral and his baby daughter.

Two peas in a pod they were, Haydyn told me. Inseparable. She had depended on her father for everything. Love, comfort, affection, friendship, advice, security. With him gone, she was adrift. And I happened to be the float she grasped on to in his passing. She demanded I be given the suite next to hers where I had roomed ever since. I was also granted the run of the palace as if I were royalty. In return, she looked to me for love, comfort, affection, friendship, advice, and security.

I feared my presence was hindering Haydyn to become the truly independent leader Phaedra needed, but I gave her my strength because she was the only family I had left. And because, after a number of years of begging me to tell her why I screamed in my sleep, I told her what Syracen Stovia had done to my family, to Kir's and Valena's families as well. There was only my word against his. By then I had been at the palace for four years.

Kir had escaped only a year after our arrival, and Haydyn had grown strong enough that Stovia didn't chase him for fear of disrupting the peace. And Valena couldn't remember anything before being brought here.

But Haydyn believed me. And she demanded the Rada listen. She ordered that all twelve members of the Rada Council travel to Silvera to judge Vikomt Syracen Stovia for his crimes. Even if the captain of the Guard had not come forward and confessed what he remembered doing under the compulsion of Stovia, I knew Haydyn would not have stopped until the vikomt was punished.

She was only fourteen years old then. But I was her family. And he had wronged me.

I pledged my everlasting loyalty to Haydyn that day.

The Rada *were* disgusted by Stovia's methods and ordered him imprisoned in Silvera Jail—the lone prisoner. He didn't take the news well. I remember the sweat beading on his forehead and the nosebleed he sustained as he fought to break through Haydyn's evocation. Powerful as he was, he was strong enough to reach for Haydyn to use her as a shield in order to escape. The captain of the Guard did his duty, however, and killed the threat to the princezna's life.

Syracen Stovia's death didn't ease my grief. But I felt freer than I had since the death of my family.

***

The servants arrived and Haydyn took her leave while I helped the girls fill the bath with the hot water. Like every morning, they swatted at me to stop.

"The Handmaiden of Phaedra shouldn't be doing servants' work."

I grunted at the nickname I had been given many years ago. It made me sound like something I wasn't.

After they were gone, I soaked in the tub and grew irritated at having lost productive hours in the day by oversleeping. I hurried out of the bath, toweling my long hair dry before braiding it. It hung heavy and damp down my back, the ends brushing the bottom of my spine. Quickly, I stepped into a dark rose dress of the finest velvet. All my clothing was chosen by Haydyn, and she loved clothes and jewelry. None of these things interested me but for Haydyn's sake, I wore everything she bestowed upon me.

"Ah good, you're dressed." Haydyn barged into my room without knocking. Lord Matai, second lieutenant of the Guard and a young vikomt of a good family, was Haydyn's newest bodyguard. He hovered protectively, even when she was alone with me.

I smiled indulgently at her before noting the slight strain in her features. "What's happened?"

"Nothing. I think." She shrugged elegantly. "Jarvis and Ava have requested me in the Chambers of the Rada."

I hid my concern. His Grace, Vojvoda Jarvis Rada, was the highest-ranking member of the nobility of Sabithia and the Chairman of the Rada, as well as the Keeper of the Archives. Grofka Ava Rada was a widow and the only other member of the Rada who lived in Sabithia. They were both good people, and they loved Haydyn dearly. But Haydyn relied too heavily upon their opinions, and oftentimes they forgot that Haydyn even had a voice. Particularly Jarvis, whose responsibilities and position—especially that of Keeper of the Archives, the very exclusive control over mage history (meaning no one but he was allowed entrance into the archives until his demise, and then only his appointed successor would have the privilege)—had given him an inflated sense of self.

It nettled me. But it wasn't my place to speak for her. Like a frustrated parent, I wanted her to find her voice and independence by herself.

"Well then." I threw both Haydyn and Matai a blasé smile. "We best go and see what they want."

Chapter Two

"Ah, Princezna." Vojvoda Jarvis rose to his feet, Lady Ava at his side. He bowed deeply whilst Ava dipped as low as she could into a curtsy. "Looking beautiful as always." Jarvis smiled at Haydyn like a doting grandfather. His eyes flicked to me and he gave me an expressionless nod. Jarvis and Ava were uncomfortable around me. They were ashamed of what Stovia did to my family.

"Your Grace." Haydyn gave a shallow curtsy. "My lady. I trust you are both well."

"As well as can be, Princezna. We do not bring good tidings."

Haydyn and I shared a worried look, and I followed her as she took her seat at the head of the long chambers table. I sat on her left, facing Ava. Jarvis took the seat next to the grofka.

"What's wrong?" Haydyn asked. That gloom crept into her eyes again, and I could have sworn she swayed in her chair. I was just about to reach for her when she seemed to shake herself awake. I withdrew my hand.

Jarvis cleared his throat, his expression grave. "I must ask, first of all, Princezna, whether you are feeling well? Are you in good health?"

I was surprised by his question. Unnerved, even.

"Of course," she answered, but it sounded hesitant to my ears.

"Why?" I asked, even though it wasn't my place to.

Ava's eyes were wide with anxiety. "Because it seems as if the evocation is weakened somehow."

Haydyn gasped. "Weakened? It can't be. I'm projecting the evocation at full, as always."

"We've received reports these last few weeks from the rest of the Rada, the most anxious of them being Vojvoda Andrei Rada, Keeper of Alvernia. The province is worsening; the uncivilized, loutish behavior of the mountain people grows steadily closer to his city in the south. He fears the people of Arrana may become contaminated by the aggression of the northerners and grows agitated by Silvera's 'negligence,' as he calls it."

Haydyn threw me a concerned look. "I had no idea things were so bad."

"There is more," Ava added.

"Yes," Jarvis continued. "I've had word from the city of Pharya. A rookery has sprung up on the border of Vasterya in the towns near the glass works. Gangs of thieves and smugglers are disrupting import and exportation."

Dear havens, I had never heard the like. "Thieves? Gangs? A rookery? In Phaedra?" I was aghast. We all were. My questioning gaze swung to Haydyn.

She squirmed as her emerald eyes filled with fear. "Don't look at me like that, Rogan. I don't know what to tell you. I don't feel a change in my magic."

Jarvis coughed. "Lastly—"

"There's more?"

He threw me an admonishing look for the interruption. "Yes. There's more. Markiza Raven Rada's guard is dealing with nomads—"

"The Caels?" Haydyn frowned as she referred to one of the nomadic clans. "But the Caels have lived in Northern Javinia for decades. They finally made a place their home."

"Not the Caels, Princezna. The Iavii. These Alvernian nomads are not looking for peace. They've already stolen land from the Caels, and now they try to do the same with the Javinians. Tensions are high between the Javinians and the Caels, who are being held as accountable as the Iavii."

"That's not fair!" Haydyn cried. "The Caels are a peaceful clan."

"They are. *Were*. Nothing in Javinia remains peaceful. The Javinian guards are busy dealing with disputes and protecting Markiza Raven in Novia. She calls for aid."

The magnitude of the news silenced us both. How quickly our beautiful world seemed to have imploded.

"You're sure you're well, Princezna?" Ava queried again.

"Positive," Haydyn snapped, jolting out of her seat. I watched on, as wide-eyed as Jarvis and Ava. Haydyn never spoke harshly to anyone. "I will not be questioned again."

"Of course, Princezna. We meant no disrespect." Jarvis's brow furrowed deeply.

"Now, what is to be done?"

You *tell* them, *Haydyn*, I wanted to say. But I didn't. She already appeared so lost and afraid.

Jarvis sighed wearily. "Well, I think before we panic, we should discover the realities of the situation for ourselves. I say we send some of the Guard to Alvernia, Vasterya, and Javinia to report back their findings before we decide upon action."

Haydyn seemed relieved by his suggestion. She turned to Matai who stood on guard at the door. "Lord Matai, please have one of the footmen fetch Captain Stovia."

I flinched at her command and bit my lip, my heart picking up speed at the thought of Wolfe. Captain Wolfe Stovia. *Vikomt* Wolfe Stovia, now that his father Syracen was dead. A few years my senior, Wolfe had proven himself steadfast, loyal, hardworking, and a strong soldier. He was one of the youngest captains in the history of the Guard. And I didn't trust him one iota.

He wasn't long in arriving. Wolfe strode into the room as his namesake would have done. Sleek and watchful, wily and dangerous. As handsome as any man in Phaedra, the servant girls went into twittering spasms whenever he was near. It made me feel rather queasy, to be honest.

His light blue eyes drank in the room before they came to rest upon me. His expression was inscrutable. Wolfe favored his mother's side of the family in looks, for which I was grateful. It would have been awful to witness a young version of Syracen stalking the palace halls.

Wolfe bowed deeply and smiled at Haydyn, almost flirtatiously. "Princezna."

I rolled my eyes as Haydyn smiled prettily back at him. She may as well have batted her eyelashes. A person couldn't entirely blame her. If forced to, I could admit he was something to look at.

Wolfe was strikingly tall, broad-shouldered, had a thick head of silky chestnut hair, olive skin, and beautiful almond-shaped eyes. His was a strong face, masculine and powerful. I, however, disliked it greatly.

"Captain," Haydyn said. "I need you to send the Guard on an errand for me."

I watched as Wolfe listened carefully to the news, his expression tightening as he learned of our situation. "I will send nine of my best men, Your Highness, three to each province."

"Thank you, Captain." Jarvis drew to his feet and helped Ava out of hers. "We appreciate it."

As they were about to depart, I stood and cleared my throat. "May I suggest we keep this among us? And stress the importance of keeping this information confidential to your men ... *Captain.*"

Haydyn's eyes widened. "Of course, Rogan is right. We don't want to cause panic until we have all the facts."

Wolfe nodded, but he never took his eyes from me as he smiled sardonically. "Of course, Princezna."

I glowered at him until he took his leave. Jarvis and Ava followed in his wake.

A solemn air hung between Haydyn and me as we strolled to her suite, Matai close on our heels. I was afraid to mention what had just been discussed.

"I keep waiting for you to cease your unpleasant attitude toward Captain Wolfe." Haydyn threw me a reproving look.

"You'll be waiting a millennium then."

"Rogan, really." She tsked. "He's not his father, you know."

I shrugged. I knew Haydyn thought it was unfair of me to dislike Wolfe, but I couldn't help it. He was a Stovia. No matter how much he ingratiated himself to Haydyn or into the Rada's trust, he would always be my enemy. His father had taken my family, and I had destroyed his in return. I was suspicious of his loyalty to Haydyn, when any normal man would have wanted vengeance for his father's death.

Haydyn did not share the suspicion. She sighed dreamily. "I don't understand how you can be so disagreeable with him. He's so handsome and strong."

I laughed softly at Matai's choked grunt behind us, and Haydyn threw him a teasing look over her shoulder. He would take his revenge for that.

We stopped at her suite and I checked the halls in both directions. It was clear. I nodded at them and Haydyn grabbed Matai's hand, disappearing into her suite with him. I stood guard.

Protecting Haydyn as always.

Protecting her secrets.

Protecting her love for Lord Matai.

I experienced a twinge of unfamiliar longing at the sound of her and Matai's intimate laughter beyond the door. Haydyn was akin to my younger sister, and yet she knew more of that mysterious intimacy between man and woman than I did. All I ever wanted was to be a source of wisdom and support for Haydyn. How could I be when she was more worldly than I? I was twenty-one years of age and remained unkissed.

I ducked my head, feeling silly and adolescent. I did not seek love. I'd never wanted it. However, a little romance perhaps might be nice.

I shook the thought from my mind. No. I had no time for romance. I was far too busy facilitating Haydyn's.

Chapter Three

"Mmm," I moaned, the sweet chocolate and fresh cream cake

making my eyes flutter shut in rapture. "Cook, you've surpassed yourself."

Cook grinned broadly, rolling out pastry as servants bustled around us in the enormous kitchen. Valena giggled from her seat across from me, cream caught on the corner of her mouth. "I swear, Rogan, the sweetest expression you ever have on your face is when you're eating Cook's desserts."

I raised an eyebrow at her cheekiness and reached across to swipe the last of the cakes from her plate.

"Hey!" She leapt forward to grab for it but I held it out of her reach. If we had been standing face-to-face rather than sitting across a long table, she would have taken it easily. Valena was only fourteen, but she was also extremely tall, a good three inches taller than me. "Oh, don't, Rogan." Valena's eyes widened as I pretended to pop the cake into my mouth. "Cook only made a few today."

Cook shook her head at my teasing. "I swear it could be nine years ago with the way you act, Miss Rogan."

"Well, I wouldn't have to behave this way if you made more than just a few cakes." I handed the desserts over to Valena, greedily watching as she scoffed one down in seconds. "Oh, you didn't even take time to enjoy that. Sacrilege. I should have eaten it."

"But it was mine." Valena grinned through a mouthful. "You're too honorable to have taken what was mine."

"Where did she adopt such an attitude?" I asked Cook, pretending beleaguerment.

Cook snorted. "You!"

Valena burst out laughing while I faked a scowl.

"Valena!"

We spun around at the sound of Raj's frantic voice, the kitchen coming to a standstill as he stumbled into the room. We all stared at him wide-eyed. My heart thumped as Raj smoothed back his white-blond hair and straightened his waistcoat. "Valena," he said, quieter this time. "I need you."

Valena didn't ask questions. She jumped from the table and made her way toward him. Raj gestured for her to walk before him and then turned his pale eyes on me. "You, too, Rogan."

I shared a brief worried look with Cook and hurried after the healers.

"What's going on?" I asked.

"I've been called to the princezna's suite."

I forgot all ladylike manners and lifted my dress, running as fast as I could through the palace halls to Haydyn's apartments. Servants gaped at me as I blurred by them, and I wanted desperately to shout back at Raj to hurry up. But if he did that, if he ran with me, then everyone would know something was wrong with Haydyn.

I knew something was wrong!

I cursed myself for not pressing her further, but ever since Jarvis and Ava had imparted the news of the hostility in Phaedra a few weeks ago, I was afraid to burden Haydyn.

Inside her suite, I found Matai. No other servant. Only Matai, his expression frantic as he hovered over Haydyn, collapsed on the floor.

"What happened?" I rushed to them, throwing myself down beside my friend. Her skin was deathly pale and when I reached for her hand, I found it limp.

Matai met my gaze with a grim one of his own. "I don't know," he whispered to me. "We were only talking and then she ... she just fainted. I was afraid to move her. I've called for Raj. I didn't want anyone else to know ..." He trailed off as Raj and Valena came into the room. Valena shut the door behind her.

Raj shoved me out of the way.

"What's wrong with her?" I demanded.

"Give me a minute, Rogan, for haven's sake," Raj replied through gritted teeth.

Haydyn groaned, her eyelids fluttering open. As her eyes focused, they widened in panic. "What happened?" her voice was hoarse.

"You fainted," I snapped, as if it was somehow her fault.

She looked to Raj. "Why?"

Raj shook his head. "Lord Matai, help me move the princezna to the bed."

I stood back, and Valena gripped my hand to reassure me. The gesture was sweet but ineffective.

"Lord Matai, Rogan, please leave Valena and me alone with the princezna."

I objected, "No. I'm staying right here."

"Rogan." Matai grabbed my arm. "For once, do as you're told." I wasn't even given a chance to struggle. Not that I could. Matai was as big as Wolfe. He pushed me outside the suite and shut the door behind us, his large body blocking my entrance.

"I need to be in there with her."

"No. You want to be, there's a difference."

"Matai."

"Stop it, Rogan," he hissed. A flash of sharpness in his eyes revealed his deep concern. "For once ... just stop."

I slumped at his tone, my heart pounding so hard I was sick with it. "What's wrong with her, Matai? She won't tell me."

"I know." He grimaced. "She's been overtired lately. I've tried to talk to her about it but ..."

"She keeps saying nothing is the matter," I finished.

"Yes."

Our eyes locked. We both knew something was *definitely* wrong.

It seemed forever before Raj beckoned us back into the suite. It had probably only been fifteen minutes.

"What's the matter?" I rushed to Haydyn's side and grasped her hand in mine.

She was sitting up in bed now, color returning to her cheeks, and she smiled a bright smile that relieved me.

Matai stood hovering at the end of the bed. He threw Raj a belligerent look. "Well, man, what the hell is going on?"

I shot the soldier a chiding look. He and Haydyn were supposed to hide their feelings for one another, not make it obvious to even the most unobservant person.

Raj smiled indulgently, glancing from Haydyn to Valena. "Both Valena and I have examined the princezna. We sensed only the darkness of exhaustion and so we removed it from her. The princezna is feeling much better." He strode to her other side. "As for this not sleeping, I will have one of the servants bring a tonic from my stores that should help you find rest, Princezna."

"Thank you, Raj." Haydyn bestowed a grateful smile upon the healer. "I appreciate your help."

Suddenly I was exhausted by the fright she had given me. "Next time maybe you'll do as I ask and see Raj before you collapse on the floor."

The others looked a little shocked. Not Haydyn. She appeared remorseful. Because she knew me well. "I'm sorry, Rogan. I promise not to frighten you again."

"Pfft."

"Rogan?"

"If you're all better, I have things to do."

Matai and the healers glared at me, but I did not care for their opinions.

Haydyn narrowed her eyes on me. "Yes, you do have things to do." She threw back the covers and got out of bed with a surprising breeze of energy. "Tell Jarek to ready my horse and yours. We're going to the marketplace."

I clenched my jaw but strode toward the door to do her

bidding. The marketplace! She knew I hated the marketplace. She was punishing me for my inability to admit I was frightened.

"Oh, and Rogan ..."

I stiffened. I did not like that singsong tone of hers. It meant she was up to something. "Yes, Your Highness?"

"After you speak with Jarek, please find Captain Stovia. We'll need an escort."

I grimaced and marched out of the room, her sweet laughter following me. Despite the distasteful thought of being in Wolfe's presence, I smiled at the sound of her laughter and shook my head at her mischief.

***

"There you are," I called as I came upon Jarek in the Silver Stable. We had stables almost as large as the palace because half of the Royal Guard was cavalry. There were a number of stable boys, and Jarek, a young man my age with a quick wit and warm smile, had been a stable boy up until recently. The old stable master had passed away, and I had suggested Jarek for the job. Yes, he was young, but we had been friends ever since my arrival at the palace and I had never met anyone with such an affinity for horses. There had been some upset at first when Haydyn appointed him as stable master. People assumed he was too young and not responsible enough. But he had the stables in tip-top shape in no time and now everyone could plainly see he was the best man for the job.

Jarek looked up from checking a chestnut bay's hooves. He grinned at me. "Where else would I be?"

"I don't know." I shrugged, sauntering leisurely toward him.

"Any one of the other stables. Or the kitchen. Cook made cakes today."

He sucked in a breath of mock disappointment. "And I missed them?"

"Jarek, you would have missed them even if you'd been there. Valena and I devastated the plate within five seconds."

"Valena …" He threw me a teasing smirk. "She's getting to be too much like you."

"Everyone keeps saying that." I frowned. "And what's wrong with being like me?"

Jarek studied me, his smile widening to a wicked grin. "Nothing. Absolutely nothing."

Despite myself, I warmed at Jarek's attention. We had been friends for a long time, but more and more lately, our conversations had taken a decidedly flirtatious turn. And he *was* extremely good-looking. However, that was the problem. I knew too many maids, and even a few noblewomen, who had shared Jarek's bed. Despite that reckless little voice inside that was eager to uncover the mysteries of intimacy between lovers, I didn't want to be just another girl he'd tumbled.

I cleared my throat. "Haydyn wishes to go to the marketplace right away. Will you ready Midnight and Sundown?"

Jarek nodded. "Is the Guard going with you?"

I winced. "Yes."

"You don't sound too excited about it. Here's a thought." He bent his head to mine, his breath hot on my ear. Goosebumps skated down my spine. "Why don't I be your guard for the day? I'd take very good care of you, Rogan."

"And Haydyn?" I murmured, my body vibrating with awareness of him.

Jarek laughed softly. "She has Lord Matai." He drew back only a little, our noses almost touching. "You can have me."

"Well, isn't this cozy."

I closed my eyes at the voice of interruption.

Wolfe.

Ugh, how I hated him.

Jarek sighed and retreated as I turned to face Wolfe. He leaned against the stable wall, glaring at us. "Apparently, I'm escorting you to the marketplace. When were you planning on delivering that message? A week, maybe two ...?"

I glowered. "Clearly it makes no matter since the message has been delivered."

Wolfe pushed away from the wall and strode toward me. Dear haven, he was tall. He towered over me and Jarek. "You," he bit out at Jarek, "the horses. Now. Hers"—he flicked a distasteful look at me—"the princezna's, Lord Matai's, my own, and three of my guard."

Jarek crossed his arms over his chest, not in the least intimidated. "Which three?"

"Worth, Vincent, and Chaeron," Wolfe replied through clenched teeth.

Jarek nodded tightly. His expression softened when his eyes fell upon me again, and he winked. "I'll speak with you later, Rogan."

"Jarek." I watched him leave, biting my lip against indecent thoughts as he swaggered out of the stable and into the next. Feeling Wolfe's eyes on me, I turned and met his sharp look with one of my own. "What?"

"What?" He guffawed incredulously. "The princezna has been unwell and everyone is agreeing to her outing to the market, and you're in here flirting with the stable boy."

"Stable master," I corrected, poking him in the chest with the words. "And don't take that self-righteous tone with me, as if I don't care about Haydyn."

Wolfe snorted. "Do you care? You were supposed to come and

inform me so I can protect you at market, and you're in here with your legs practically wrapped around Jarek."

How dare he? I sucked in a breath at the accusation. "You're lucky I don't slap you for that insinuation. Jarek is my friend. I came here to ask him to prepare the horses, and I was just about to come and find your sorry ass to let you know Haydyn required your company. *Not* that I should have to explain myself to you."

"*Sorry ass.*" Wolfe threw me a disdainful look. "Really? That's the language of the Handmaiden of Phaedra? Very refined."

Refined? I'd give him refined. I'd been around enough stable boys to know my share of curse words. "Oh, sod off, Captain," I threw over my shoulder as I departed the stables.

***

The city of Silvera grew quiet and the crowds parted as we moved through them on the cobbled streets. Their chatter hushed and then rose again as the people gathered together at the rear of our entourage, like a wave crashing to shore behind us.

I rode beside Haydyn on Midnight, she on Sundown. Matai was on Haydyn's other side and three of the Royal Guard were at our backs. Wolfe rode in front, his eagle eyes watching the crowds as we traveled past taverns, apothecaries, inns, butchers, bakers, and candlestick makers. The marketplace was in the large Silvera Square where people from the neighboring provinces came to sell their wares. Haydyn always had a particular interest in the artists and craftsmen of Raphizya and the beautiful glasswork of Vasterya.

"I've decided to hold a ball." Haydyn waved to Silverans who bowed and curtsied as we cantered past.

I raised an eyebrow. "A ball?"

"Hmm." Haydyn grinned excitedly. She seemed so young in that moment, despite her nineteen years. "A ball. I'll invite all the Rada and all the noblemen and women of every province. A way of showing our solidarity in an unsettling time."

"A ball?" I still wasn't convinced.

"I think it's a fine idea, Princezna." Matai smiled at her.

I sighed. "No one asked you, Lord Matai."

"Rogan, be nice," Haydyn tutted. "Anyway, Lord Matai is correct. It *is* a fine idea."

My heart jumped a little at the determination in her voice and hope bloomed. Perhaps Haydyn was finally taking charge. And I might not like fancy balls, but ... it *was* a good idea. If only because it was *her* idea.

Her face fell when I didn't respond. Abruptly, she looked anxious. "Don't you think it's a good idea, Rogan?"

I cursed inwardly. Why did everyone's opinion matter so much to her? She was as smart and capable as any of us fools whose advice she solicited. I wished she'd remember she was fair and just and royal—she should not concern herself with my opinion, or anyone else's, for that matter.

Instead I gave her a soft smile. "Lord Matai's correct. It's a fine idea."

Moment of worry over, Haydyn's expression turned cheerful as we entered the marketplace. Again, all went quiet at the sight of us, but gradually, as we trotted over to the stables, the noise level rose again.

"Please, I want you to seek out the finest fabric for me, for my new ballgown, as well as the finest for yourself," Haydyn commanded politely as Matai helped her dismount. I was so shocked by the request, I dismounted without help, forgetting I wasn't supposed to do that in public. But Haydyn very rarely used my magic and never for something as frivolous as fabric shopping.

My body crackled from the inside out, drawing me toward a fabric stall deep in the crowds of the square. "Fabric?"

"Hmm." Haydyn nodded. "We want to look our best for such an important event."

"Not the key to world peace? Not the answer to shutting down a rookery or controlling nomads? *Fabric*?"

Haydyn exhaled wearily. "Must I repeat it, Rogan, when we both know you're being facetious?"

I shrugged. "Well, I just had no idea that the form of our fashion was so incredibly important to settling Phaedrian disputes."

"More facetiousness. Lovely."

"Fine. Away I go to seek and order the fabric." I glanced between her and Matai. "What are you going to do?"

Haydyn stared a little too adoringly at her bodyguard. "Lord Matai's going to escort me around the market while I choose some gifts to present to our guests at the ball."

I threw him a mock horrified look. "Lord Matai, may I say now how much I've enjoyed knowing you, for I fear it will be the last time I look upon you." I winced. "Death by boredom is such a tragic way to go."

He grinned. "I'm sure I'll survive."

"You don't have to sound so put upon." Haydyn sniffed.

I laughed, thinking about her well-known generosity. "And just where are all these gifts going? We didn't bring a cart?"

"I'll borrow one. Or buy one. I am the princezna."

I almost rolled my eyes. She asserts her authority when shopping. Wonderful.

"Don't let me keep you. Off I go. Shan't be long." I disappeared into the crowds before Haydyn demanded I take an escort.

I breathed deeply of the thick smells. It was a strange mixture of pungent sheep's wool, beets, chocolate, oil, sweet meats, bread, perfume, paint ... oh, it was a fragrance of all the variety of the market. Usually, I disliked the crowds, preferring to escape to the cliffs some miles from the palace. I loved the peace and quiet of watching the surf of the Silver Sea crash against the cliff walls. The sea's fierceness reminded me what it was to be alive.

But I was never alone. There was always a guard with me some way in the distance.

Today, as I swept past people, some who recognized me, some who didn't—merchants calling out to me to buy their wares, desperate for what they assumed was a noblewoman to purchase some expensive bauble from them—I loved the market in that moment. Because I was alone. All alone. Free.

I was quick on my feet, dodging persistent sellers and hopefully any of the Guard who may have followed me. In no time at all, I found the stall with the fabric that called to my magic. I recognized it immediately. Velvet, the color of lapis lazuli, made from the finest silk in the textile factories in Ryl. Haydyn would look wonderful in it. I reached out to stroke the beautiful fabric when a hand clamped around my wrist.

"No, no, miss." I looked up into the ruddy face of the market seller. "Not the right color for you, miss. Come see some of my silks." He tried to pull me toward the more expensive material. I tugged on his grip, but he was determined.

I grew irritated by his persistence. "Sir—"

"With a face and figure like yours, you shouldn't hide behind heavy textures. Fine silks, miss, fine silks for you."

I tugged again. Oh yes. *This* was why I hated the marketplace.

A large hand came down on top of the seller's, ripping it from my own and holding it tight. Both the seller and I looked up into the angry face of Wolfe Stovia.

"You dare to lay your hand on the princezna's handmaiden?" Wolfe growled at the man.

The seller blanched as he looked at me, recognition finally dawning. "Oh, my lady, I meant no disrespect."

Wolfe grunted and shoved the man away a little. "Lady or servant, I see you trying to coerce a woman again, and you and I will have words."

I'd never seen anyone look so green with fear. "Apologies, my lord. I was overexcited. It won't happen again. Apologies, my lady."

Oh, for haven's sake. "I'm not a lady," I snapped, furious at Wolfe for drawing attention to the situation and blowing it out of proportion. The overbearing lout. I glared at him. "You, sir, are a bully."

Wolfe frowned at me. "And you are the Handmaiden of Phaedra and as such, a *lady*. You are not to allow strange men to touch you."

"I'll allow a mountain man of Alvernia to touch me before I take advice from you, *Stovia*." Dismissing him, agitated by his presence, his ruination of my pretense at freedom, I turned to the seller. "I want one bolt of the lapis lazuli velvet and one of the emerald silk chiffon."

I relaxed a little at having completed my task for Haydyn, but then my body hummed with energy again. I turned without thinking toward a stall some quarter of the way back into the middle of the market. The fabric that would suit me most was in there somewhere. Damn Haydyn. Damn being an Azyl.

I spun back to the seller. "Have the fabric delivered to the palace and ask for Seamstress Rowan. You'll be paid well for your troubles."

He nodded, doing this obscene half-bow/curtsy thing that made me throw a growl in Wolfe's direction. Turning sharply from them both, I followed my magic across the marketplace and drew in a breath at the pleasant sandalwood scent that signaled Wolfe had fallen into step beside me.

I stopped abruptly. "What are you doing?"

Wolfe shrugged, refusing to look at me, refusing to leave. "Just one of the more unpleasant jobs of being captain of the Guard. Protecting *you*."

"We are droll, aren't we?"

"Some people think I'm charming." He grinned flirtatiously at a passing tavern girl who continued to eye him over her bare shoulder as we walked away.

"Some people don't know any better."

"Ooh, is that judgment I hear in the voice of the lady who was flirting with a mere stable boy this morning?"

I gritted my teeth. "Stable *master*."

Wolfe raised one annoying eyebrow. "As if that makes it any more palatable. You know he's bedded every woman in the palace. You're not special."

My blood boiled beneath my skin, as it did whenever I was forced to be in proximity to this man. I tried to take deep, calming breaths. I did. I really, really did. It didn't work. "Who I choose to converse with is of no consequence to you, Captain Stovia. And may I remind you to whom you are speaking?"

He threw me a mocking look. "So, there is a snob buried under all that 'I'm not a lady, I'm not a lady, I'm just like everyone else' piffle?"

"I *am* just like everyone else. *Except*," I snapped, "when it comes to you. *You* will talk to me like I'm royalty, Captain. As in ... don't speak to me at all."

Wolfe stiffened at my insults, his face taut with anger. Our dislike was definitely, *definitely* mutual. "If you want to make this about rank, Rogan—"

I flinched at his use of my given name. He'd never called me Rogan before. Not to my face, anyway. It had always been *my lady*, despite my lack of nobility.

"May I remind *you* that I'm the one with lord before *my* name? Don't speak to me like I'm dirt beneath your shoe."

Arrogant beast. I shook my head. Just like his demon father. I laughed humorlessly, a cold, brittle laugh that caused him to wince. "You don't need to remind me who *you* are, *Vikomt Stovia*." With that, I veered from him, pushing through the crowds to escape him. I glanced back to make sure he did not follow. He didn't, but he lifted his chin in someone else's direction. It was an order.

Within seconds, Lieutenant Chaeron had pushed through the crowds to be at my side, his hand on the hilt of his sword.

My first impulse was to be aggravated and suffocated by his presence, but then I recalled Jarvis's words of warning. There was a reason behind Haydyn's idea for a ball. Quite suddenly, I was glad for our trained Guard. We had never needed them before.

But then there had never been crime in civilized Phaedra before.

Available in paperback. Or read it in Kindle Unlimited.